# ELITA

# ELITA

*a novel*

KIRSTEN SUNDBERG LUNSTRUM

TriQuarterly Books / Northwestern University Press
Evanston, Illinois

TriQuarterly Books
Northwestern University Press
www.nupress.northwestern.edu

Printed in the United States of America

10  9  8  7  6  5  4  3  2  1

Library of Congress Cataloging-in-Publication Data

Names: Lunstrum, Kirsten Sundberg, 1979– author.
Title: Elita : a novel / Kirsten Sundberg Lunstrum.
Description: Evanston, Illinois : TriQuarterly Books/Northwestern University
    Press, 2025.
Identifiers: LCCN 2024032545 | ISBN 9780810147867 (paperback) |
    ISBN 9780810147874 (ebook)
Subjects: LCGFT: Detective and mystery fiction. | Novels.
Classification: LCC PS3612.U56 E45 2025 | DDC 813/.6—dc23/
    eng/20240712
LC record available at https://lccn.loc.gov/2024032545

For Britt, with love and admiration.

And for Kristen and Jean,
without whom this book would not be.

"Jane, be still; don't struggle so, like a wild frantic bird that is rending its own plumage in its desperation."

"I am no bird; and no net ensnares me; I am a free human being with an independent will, which I now exert to leave you."

—CHARLOTTE BRONTË, *JANE EYRE*

# CONTENTS

# ELITA

# PART
# 1

IT WAS TWO PRISON GUARDS WHO FOUND THE GIRL. ON their lunch breaks they liked to drive out to the north end of the island and have a smoke and forget for an hour that the prison was only a couple miles behind them. It could be damned depressing all day inside the cellblock without that lunch break to look forward to. Concrete ceiling overhead and the white glare of the incandescent lamps like a headache that never ended. Damp, starchy smell of boiled potatoes and the yeast stink of so many men's bodies. "This job, it can drain you," the guard called Lind says into the tape, and his fellow—the other guard, Starkey—makes a grunt of assent.

Bernadette listens to the men's recorded interview in the library AV lab at the university where she teaches. A student only a few years older than the found girl sets up the reel to reel for her, smiles, then leaves, closing the door to the lab as she goes. The student's perfume hangs for a moment in the stale air of the narrow room, all girlish high notes of lily and vanilla, before dissipating against the heat. The room is mostly dark, though what light there is comes from the single globe lamp and falls thick and honey-yellow across the desk. A radiator in the corner gushes heat. Outside, Bernadette knows, the first heavy rain of early October is beating against the copper roof of the library, long ropes of water purling from the greening peak and spouting out the gaping, silent mouths of the stone gargoyle downspouts that guard each corner of the building, their terror made submissive. Below, on the ground, the earth has gone mucky, soft, moss dense. And to the west, the belly of the sky hangs low and full the way it always does in the fall, the sea about to try again to reclaim the whole of the city. How could the found girl have survived these winters without shelter? Without warm food? It's this more than anything else that compels Bernadette about this case—the unbelievable resilience of a girl keeping herself alive alone in the wild, surviving.

She rewinds the tape, listens again to the interview's opening.

"Twelve thirty-two P.M. on September 13, 1951," Detective Norquist's voice bleeds from the tape. The AV lab evaporates around Bernadette. This interview took place a month ago, but it's easy for her to imagine herself there, in the police interrogation room at Elita Island Federal Penitentiary. "Tell me where you were when you first saw her that day."

The men describe a spot on the island just past the old village center and beyond the last of the vacant houses now sinking back into the landscape, where the road ends and the grass and blackberries erupt in a thicket. They say they liked to park there most weekdays. "Nothing illegal about it. Feds closed the village in '37, but there's no rule Elita staff can't drive around the place. No rule at all about travel on the island once you're cleared to be there. They even let you take a prison vehicle. Official," Lind says.

"Nothing illegal," Starkey repeats, agreeing with his colleague. "We have clearance."

"Cleared to be there?" Norquist asks. "Do boats from outside moor at that end of the island?"

"That? That is illegal." This is Starkey. "But you know that, right? You're a cop. You know that." He says it with a tone of resentment audible even to Bernadette.

"I do, but I'm asking if it happens. Ever seen a boat there? A private boat? Someone wants to do a little fishing or hunting maybe. They come out from Tacoma and anchor at the north end."

"Never seen it," Starkey says.

"No one permitted within one hundred feet of shore. It's posted. It's well posted." Lind sniffs on the tape. Bernadette pictures him tall, thin, and blond, the reedy quality of his voice mirrored in his body.

"So, you're out there often enough to know it's deserted? Not even the accidental fisherman coming in too close? Not even at night?"

"We're day shift. Always days. But I been out there in the daytime often enough to say it's bare. Deserted," Starkey says. He's his buddy's opposite in Bernadette's imagination: squat, roundheaded, balding. His voice is deeper and more relaxed.

"You ever go hunting out there then?"

"Poaching, you mean. Us?" Starkey laughs. "Those tiny black tails? That's all you'd find. Delicate little things—not worth it. Them and birds. Seagulls. Bald eagles. Nothing anybody'd want for supper."

"You're saying no, then? No poaching."

Now Lind's voice interjects: "We gave you the goddamn answer. Not much hunting where you're from, Detective, I know, but trust me. It'd not be worth it." There's acid behind Lind's words. He and Starkey know Norquist has come over to the island on the ferry, has a badge from the county sheriff's office in Tacoma. They'll defer, of course, but he's a city cop, brought in by social welfare services to protect the girl's interests—not theirs. Yet even behind the bite, Bernadette hears honesty—Lind is telling the truth. Poaching, for a prison guard, could be the end of a paycheck. Everyone in her generation remembered before the war when there was no work to be had, and not one of them takes for granted steady pay.

"Hey," Starkey cautions his buddy.

"No, this is horseshit. Look—we done nothing to that girl, and this son of a bitch is trying to set us up to show we would. We'd not do anything to a girl."

Starkey confirms this, says, "We're in good faith here."

"Right," Lind says, a bit calmer. "That's the whole of it. No more to it. We didn't do a thing to that girl."

"I'm not saying you did," Norquist tells him. "I'm just asking. My job's to ask."

"Well, I'm answering, and in good faith," Starkey says. "You take my word. It was just lunch and a cigarette any place that wasn't the break room. A few minutes' escape is all. Not our fault the girl came running at us."

"We were just eating our lunch," Lind repeats.

On the tape, there's the sound of a page turning—Norquist shifting his notes. He says, "Tell me about the items collected there, then, from the road's end."

"Items?" Lind's threaded voice.

Static clicks on the tape. It pulls Bernadette back into her own body, which is sweating in the warmth of the AV lab. She peels her sweater from her arms and hangs it on the back of the chair, then closes her eyes, willing herself again into the present of the interrogation.

7

Norquist recites a list: "Four empty beer cans, two broken pop bottles, a piece of brown fabric matching that of the prison employees' uniforms. Does any of that belong to either of you?"

"Maybe so. Maybe so, the cans and bottles," Starkey says. His voice is rubbed soft as a stone turned over and over on the beach, round and full and smooth. Not what one expects of a prison guard. Not threatening, but gentle. The calm in his tone is practiced seeming.

Norquist asks again, "Did you attempt to trap or harm the girl? Did you see her fall? Did you push her, maybe?"

A pause.

"Not to trap her," says Lind.

"Never," says Starkey.

"We didn't," says Lind. "Like we already said, it was that one came at us. She came at us like one of them mad dogs, and that's when we caught her—only then. Self-protection."

"No," Starkey says. A little chuff of embarrassment. "No, not self-protection. It was for her own safety. She seemed not right, that one. Crazy. Like an animal. Wild. We couldn't leave a child out there. A little girl. Where's her mother at? That's what I thought. Where's this kid's goddamn mother? We caught her for her own safety."

Lind adds, "Something's wrong with her."

"Anybody could see something's not right with that girl," Starkey continues.

"You caught her?" Norquist asks. "Say more about that. What do you mean 'caught her'?"

Both men sigh.

Bernadette stops the tape, gets up, walks a circle around the table, her body a coil she's trying to loose. She shakes her hands as if they've gone numb. All through her body, adrenaline. She has anticipated this. It happens to her sometimes—the spike of nerve that lights her up, makes her shaky. But still, she hates it—this current through her wiring. In her chest, her heart trips out heavy, rapid beats. *Come on*, she says to herself. *Come on*. She draws a breath, focuses.

What she wants is to hear Starkey say the word *child* again. She wants Norquist to repeat his question back to them: *Did you harm the child?* What do the men remember of that moment? The flash of a little body through the tall grass. Hair that might have been fur. White snarl of the girl's bared teeth. They must have stopped their lunchtime conversation to squint out across the tangle of the overgrown field. Must have, both of them, squinted into the pearled light of a September midday sky. There would have been the sound of the tide rushing against the shore not even five hundred feet off. Sound of breeze in the alders. Could they have heard the girl moving through the grass? Bernadette doubts it. She also doubts that the girl would have been unable to hide herself if she'd wanted to. She didn't have to be seen. So what happened in that moment that made her tear out of the field toward them? Or is that a lie the men have agreed to tell?

What the police report shows is this: one of the men did get out of the truck to chase the girl down. She fell to her knees, lacerating the skin on both kneecaps and both palms. When Starkey and Lind brought her into the prison office, her hands were tied with rope behind her back. Her ankles, too, were bound. She had a cut across her left shoulder blade, jagged—presumed to be caused by a thrown rock. Her fingertips were stained purple. She'd been gathering blackberries before the men spotted her, or—Bernadette guesses—before she spotted them. But the report does not make clear who was the first threat: the men or the girl. In one scenario, the men throw rocks into the bramble and hit the girl, who—defensive—charges them. In another scenario, the girl charges them first, animal-like and unprovoked. In the report, Starkey and Lind claim she came out of nowhere, suddenly, growling, spitting, and wild-eyed as if rabid. But why? And who is she? And how long had she been there alone on the island? There are no answers to these questions—not yet. According to the report, the girl doesn't speak.

Once she's able to still her nerves, Bernadette sits back down and rewinds, starting once more from the top. Whoosh of silence. Vibration of the strip of tape passing through its reels. She listens again to the interview.

"Did you attempt to trap or harm the girl?" Norquist repeats his question at the end of the tape.

"Never," says Starkey.

"Something's wrong with her," says Lind.

Norquist sighs. "Fine. I see we're not getting any further today. Be at the addresses you gave us in case we need more information." He ends the interview. "One thirteen P.M.," his voice says.

The tape clicks forward, wordless, and stops.

## 2

BERNADETTE BASTON IS A LECTURER IN CHILD DEVELOP-ment with a specialty in language acquisition, teaching in the Psychology Department at the state university in Seattle. As a teenager she had dreams of moving to New York City, maybe training as a literary scholar or a classicist or a linguist. She could travel, she thought, and see the places where the mythologies that had saturated her childhood imagination were set. The whole of her girlhood had been spent as an only child on a far northern lake, with just her parents and her books to keep her company. Maybe if she could get out—go to Italy, Greece, the islands where the Vikings had rowed to shore in their great ships—the world would finally dilate for her.

But before any of that could happen, her parents died—first one and then, suddenly, shockingly, the other—and Bernadette, who'd always felt alone, truly was entirely on her own. She took what they'd left her and went to school anyhow, completed her undergraduate degree, carried on as close to plan as possible. But by her graduation, the war was on. Instead of graduate school, she enrolled in Red Cross training, joined the Army Nurse Corps, and was dispatched to France in late 1944, where she was one of several nurses handed a hospital of children to oversee. She was unprepared. The children were as young as nine months, as old as nineteen. Their mothers had been civilians and political activists and artists and prostitutes. Catholics and Protestants and Jews. All of them were orphaned. Some of the children had only ever known war and nothing of what the world could be beyond it. All of them were dangerously malnourished, and the bulk of Bernadette's work was simply feeding them. This was careful, fragile work in the early days of a child's rehabilitation. Often, the children were so starved that they no longer felt hunger. Their lips were blistered with the effects of their starvation and their tongues swollen. Some of them had forgotten how to chew and swallow without choking. Their digestive systems were unable to process anything but the most basic foods at first, and most of them came to the hospital with diarrhea, with parasites, with dehydration.

Bernadette walked bed to bed in the long, airy hall of the hospital—once a factory for the manufacture of women's dress coats—spooning pablum from a tin bowl into one mouth after the next. "Open, love," she'd say, gently, and then she'd wait. The room was cold, sterile, and shadowless. White light poured in from the high bank of windows—windows originally installed so that the daylight could stream in and fully illuminate even the tiniest of stitches running through a length of fine wool coat hem. But the light felt surgical now, the way it cut into the children's faces, their mouths becoming dark holes when they obeyed her and opened for the next spoonful.

She had expected the children to come to their convalescence ravenous, wanting, but it was impossible to desire, Bernadette learned from them, if all you knew was the denial of your needs. This, she still thinks, is the Ouroboros of adaptive self-preservation. The mind and the body working together as one to devour the only human emotional states that make survival worthwhile—the drive of desire, the temporary but vivid joy of satisfaction. Why want if the desire cannot be satisfied? At some point, all unrequited desire becomes pain, and so the body shuts itself down to survive.

Many of the children in the hospital also no longer walked, cried, or spoke, and for this they became objects of medical interest. Was the erasure of such basic developmental milestones in cases of severe trauma mental or physical—or both? Doctors from Switzerland, France, England, and the United States arrived with this question, often observing the children with a detachment that made Bernadette wonder about the distance between scholarly objectivity and direct cruelty. She, too, wanted to understand, but no, she thought. *No.* She would take the messy work of spoon-feeding and sponge-bathing and diapering a child any day if it meant holding on to the child's humanity—and also her own. The children would relearn it all in their own time, she knew. Intuitively and without doubt, she knew this. She wanted to say it to every touring physician and scientist: *Let them be, and it will all come back to them. Not all learning can be taught.* But then, slowly, she witnessed it happening, and so did the observers. The children ate and put on weight. They began to smile again. Some of them resumed speech, though what they said was careful, an echo still rather than a voice.

And then the war ended. One by one, each girl and boy was claimed—religious institutions took them in, as did organizations for war orphans, or occasionally a distant aunt or cousin. They left, and for the first time since Bernadette had arrived at the hospital, no new children arrived for care in their place. The beds remained empty. In the factory building, the light changed: white to cream, pale green to the full-throated songbird yellow of summer. Bernadette went home, though she was not the same.

In the United States again, she returned to school, but this time a graduate student of psychology and child development. She found Maslow and Piaget and John Dewey, and the individual pinpoints of her experience began to assemble in her mind like the flickering outline of a constellation in the night sky. Development, she understood, could only progress in the presence of desire or curiosity. And neither of those could be created externally by a teacher but could only come from within—and only then once the body, that restless creature, was sated and safe. She had lived this reality in the hospital, seen it again and again in the children who'd come there with nothing but their own survival instincts keeping them on this side of the ground. And she had lived it herself, after her own parents died. Though she was not a child when they went, their deaths left her bereft just the same, and also suddenly alone in the world with only herself to rely on. Now she believed it was universally true. She used other scholars' case studies to write her master's thesis—she would not write about the children in France and make her own future on their suffering. She learned to make compartments within herself, to close certain pieces of her past away in order to respect them, but also to preserve her ability to keep going. She would look forward only.

This is when she fell in love, and in falling found another way to close off that past: she could make a new life, a home, a whole new family, and start over. She married a classmate, Fred Farrell, and followed him to the University of Chicago, where he would be a fellow and she would finish a doctorate. She made it through almost a year of her coursework before their baby was born. A daughter. Wilhelmina, after Fred's grandmother. They called her Willie. That was March 1947. Bernadette stopped her studies. She nursed and diapered and walked Willie in a secondhand stroller up and down the slush-mucked sidewalks of Hyde Park. The pear trees lining the old World's Fair green burst into white blossom in late April. In May, Willie rolled from her back to her belly on a quilt spread across the sand of Lake Michigan's shore, and Bernadette clapped and clapped, an audience of one. In June, Fred was offered a postgraduate fellowship in New York. And in July he left without her. One morning he was simply gone, no word to her about why, but a month's rent in an envelope on the kitchen counter.

Babies slow down the progress of the mind. Families have needs and expectations. A wife made of milk and sweat and exhausted babbling is no longer an interesting partner. All of this she understood. Early on, they had agreed on this point: there could be no development without desire. They'd agreed on it in the abstract, though, or so she'd thought—an academic agreement. But now, she realized, Fred was living the agreement, and she was left alone with their daughter.

And so she took the money and Willie and went west, where no one knew her and her shame at being left might feel smaller. They moved into a basement apartment near the university in Seattle. Bernadette let everyone assume her husband had died. She lucked into a part-time lectureship when its previous occupant got a better position midsemester. She could work for half his wage, which pleased the university.

"See?" she said aloud to Willie. "We'll weather this." What did that mean, though? Bernadette wasn't sure anymore. Motherhood, especially alone, was exhausting. There was little energy left in her each evening with which to envision a future. It was all she could do to get through the night and handle the tasks of each new day. Three mornings a week, she left Willie with the elderly widow who was her landlady and lived in the apartment upstairs—Mrs. Iversen—so she could walk to campus and teach her classes. Mrs. Iversen was kind and didn't ask too many questions, made the assumption Bernadette allowed her to make about her family situation. She was grandmotherly. She called Willie *Miss Wilhelmina*. Sometimes she baked almond cookies and arrived with a tin of them still warm to hand to Bernadette. "For after your supper," she'd say. "I see you hardly have time to catch your breath." And Bernadette was grateful for this—the cookies and the acknowledgment.

She found Seattle a difficult place to make into a home. The neighbors were standoffish. People at shops and the library and the park didn't step forward to introduce themselves or say hello; they were polite, of course, but nothing more. She often saw other women with their children at the park, sharing a thermos of coffee on a bench while the children played, or standing side by side behind the swings, but even between them there seemed to be little conversation, little open friendliness. People tugged their sweaters around themselves, spoke quietly about the weather, smiled, and looked away. And so she never met anyone, never felt free to invite another woman and her child for a walk or over to the apartment for a cup of coffee. To herself, she wondered what could've come of it if she had, anyhow? What could there be to say? She was husbandless, a professor, leaving her daughter in the care of a near stranger; these other women would hold their judgment just long enough to finish their coffee and go. Tight smile. Clipped wave. Better to say nothing than to pry. Leave folks to themselves. *Tsk*, she'd once heard Mrs. Iversen cluck in response to a newspaper article about a family who'd lost their farm during the war but had managed since then to open a grocery on Pine Street. *Why tell about the farm? Just say they'd opened the store. Don't put your garbage on the front lawn.*

Eventually she understood that this chill was cultural here—not really about her, or not exactly. But still, she was lonely. She was alone. And she was trying. To Mrs. Iversen with her almond cookies and to the women at the park and to the secretary in her university department—to all of them, she wanted to say, *You know, I am trying, and it isn't exactly easy here on my own.* But this—a personal confession about struggle—wasn't the kind of thing a person was welcome to say.

In the long run, she decided, it didn't matter. She was accustomed to her own company and to Willie's, and they were happy enough. Most afternoons, Bernadette and Willie took long walks through the neighborhood or napped on Bernadette's double bed in the dark warmth of the apartment. She remembered her undergraduate reading of Plato and thought: *We are in the cave.* Everything she saw in it—this hollow carved into the time between what was and what would be—was just a shadow of all that existed beyond reach right now, outside this existence she and her daughter were living together. How long could shadows satisfy her?

It was during that endless, sunken winter and wet spring that Willie began to speak, and Bernadette—her scholarly compulsion to understand wakened by this shift—documented it. *This?* soon became *What this?*, which soon became, *What name this?*

*Tree, cat, house, rock*, Bernadette named the world for Willie. She took to narrating their days. On a walk through the campus quad: *The grass is wet now because it rained last night. Let's look up at the sky. Will it rain again? The sky is gray and cloudy. I think it will rain before dinnertime. While we eat, we should open the curtains and watch the street get wet.* On and on she talked them through their days.

There was a nonsense to it. She was self-aware around students and passersby. She recognized that the repetition and simplicity of her sentences reduced her in their estimation. She was a nesting doll, the biggest and most complex version of herself opening up and revealing what she really was—nothing but an absurd little nut of a mother doll, nestled inside a host of false shell-selves. This, she hated. But each night, after Willie fell asleep, when she could become the researcher again, she returned to her true self, pulling out her notebook and recording the day's developments, detached from her personal bond to her subject and intellectually curious and driven and interested in the world more abstractly again.

*Acquisitions: Ball, weed, robin, sweet.*

*Two-word phrases used correctly within situational context: Willie wants. Go out? No, this.*

*Observations: Subjects encountered more than once are easily remembered and named with near one hundred percent accuracy. Example: When we saw a robin in a cherry tree on campus today, Willie pointed to the spot across the quad where we had also spotted one yesterday, suggesting image recollection. She said, "Bird," and I responded, "Robin," which she then repeated. The hard r remains a developing sound. She often substitutes a b for an r, particularly when the r falls at the start of a word.*

Pages and pages of these notes filled Bernadette's notebooks. Willie added words as the months went on, eventually lengthening her phrases toward full sentences and beginning to capture the nuances of language, like person and tense. When she erred, Bernadette repeated the phrase with the correction. *I want milk,* she said back when Willie said *Willie wants milk.* Or *I play outside?* when Willie said *Me outside too?* She watched these small differences in construction flicker in the pools of Willie's eyes like reflected light on a pond. This was teaching what could be taught, was it not? The names for each bit and bob making up the world were already determined by the rest of humankind and not up for individual discovery. Unless you were Adam. Or Linnaeus. Language was a kind of landscape, and just like land, it was always the men who got to settle their feet on a bit of sand and call it a new shore. She and Willie would have to find their discoveries internally.

The only correction Bernadette never made was to Willie's persistent conflation of *you* and *I.* This felt sacred, untouchable. It would, Bernadette knew, pass with time, but for now she held close Willie's linguistic blurring of their two bodies, their two selves. This, she would not let her scholarship dismantle and pick apart.

"I hold you," Willie still said when she climbed onto Bernadette's lap.

"And I hold you," Bernadette always responded.

Willie grinned and patted Bernadette's cheek. "You love, Mama," the girl said.

"I do. I do love."

## 3

BERNADETTE MEETS THE GIRL ON A TUESDAY IN LATE October 1951. A storm is predicted for afternoon, but she settles a still-sleeping Willie with the neighbor, Mrs. Iversen, for the day, takes the two buses the trip requires in the predawn darkness, and boards the 6:00 A.M. Elita Island ferry anyhow. On board are the prison's next shift workers—several guards wearing heavy rain slickers over their brown uniforms, a tall man in the black pants of the kitchen staff, and a group of three women sitting close together and speaking Japanese in hushed tones. The prison was used to intern Japanese American men only a handful of years ago, Bernadette knows, and she imagines the bitter necessity that would bring these women to wash laundry or mop bathroom floors at Elita now. She folds her hands in her lap and turns her face to the window.

Outside the glass, the world is a churning mass of gray sky, gray sea. Ropes of rain unroll along the window. She's glad she's brought her slicker and not the umbrella, which would be useless in this wind. She's worn wool pants, a sweater, rain boots. The report the sheriff's office gave her described an island remote enough to feel desolate, undeveloped. The road from the ferry to the prison is paved, but the prison yard will be mud this time of year. "No-man's-land," Detective Norquist had said over the phone. "Expect to get muddy."

"I'll be there," Bernadette told him. She had anticipated being less than welcomed, but it amused her that he thought a little mud would keep her away. How did he imagine most women had spent the war?

At the island dock, the workers pull up hoods, tuck brown paper lunch sacks and purses inside the flaps of their jackets, duck out of the boat and into the gusts of wind roiling up from the beach. Bernadette is last off the ramp. There's no shelter at the dock, as there would be at most ferry landings—just the pier, some wooden steps down to the beach, the high barbed-wire fence. Two guards stand as a checkpoint at the fence, and when she reaches them, she withdraws her ID from her bag, as well as her letter with Norquist's signature and the county seal pressed into the page. She's been told a car will meet her, and there is a black sedan waiting just on the other side of the fence. When she climbs inside, it smells of dust and cigarette smoke.

"I'm Professor Bernadette Baston," she announces as she offers her ID, but the driver waves her off. He's a guard, the brown uniform shirt collar visible beneath his coat. Bernadette can't see his face, but the bald back of his head is thick skinned, a fold of scalp lapping up against his neck.

"Look, honey, I don't need your name. You're only here if someone invited you. I'll drop you at the front door," he says. "You step inside for processing. You got anything on you not allowed, be prepared to leave it at the desk. And I'd hand it over rather than wait for them to find it. Because they will find it. Just my advice."

"What would I have on me?"

"Weapon of some sort, camera, contraband you might be thinking you could exchange for some insider information, that sort of thing."

Bernadette shakes her head. "I'm not a journalist."

"Just giving you my advice," he says. "Take it or leave it."

"I'll show them my camera." She has a Dictaphone too, but she'll keep it in her bag and take her chances.

The front door turns out to be another gate, with more guards. Inside the building, she smells both sterility and men. The phantom hackles at the back of her neck stand and prickle there beneath her sweater, hidden from everyone but her. *Danger*, her body is saying, and it makes sense that it's saying that in the presence of the men caged here. What does she sense? Smells of hair oil and of bleach, of sweat and kitchen work. Vegetables boiling and the brown smell of cooking meat. Something more bodily under it all too—not blood or semen, but like those odors. Bernadette thinks about the way animals can scent threat before they see it. How far removed is a human from that creature state, really? How different from a feral child is a grown and educated woman?

At the reception desk, she is documented, then ushered through another gated doorway, where one guard pats her down while a second watches. She holds her breath as his hands move along her armpits, hips, the insides of her knees. When his face is close to her own, she smells coffee on his breath, feels the bristle of his whiskers brush her cheek. He makes her turn in her camera, then opens her bag and finds the Dictaphone, though when Bernadette smiles and plays dumb, she is allowed to keep this. She's handed off to a final guard, then, who escorts her down a long, chilly corridor to a whitewashed concrete room with two chairs and a table.

Seeing the prison in person raises again in Bernadette's mind the question of the girl's confinement. Why has the girl been kept here, in the prison hospital wing? Why not the children's hospital in the city? Why not the university hospital? Is it legal to keep a female minor citizen charged with no crime here in a federal men's prison? Is it just?

This is her first question when Dr. Brodaccio enters the room. Brodaccio is short, thick-haired, dark-eyebrowed. He wears tiny gold-rimmed spectacles that he drops to his chest, where they hang from a thin cord. He does not strike Bernadette as unkind, though she finds him clinical, detached in a way that reminds her again of the hospital in France. *Where is your humanity?* she wants to ask him. *Why is a child not where children belong?*

When she does ask this, though, the doctor appears unruffled. He shakes her hand, lays a file on the table between them, and sits. "It was determined that she would fare better here, away from the city. As you must know, her case has drawn quite the following. She's been in every newspaper in the state. Out here on the island, there are no journalists or—" he pauses, and his eyes rove the room—"lookie-loos to obstruct or interfere with her recovery and development. She's become, you understand, something of a celebrity, and so she must be protected."

*A girl confined in the name of her own protection*, Bernadette thinks sarcastically. *How unlikely that is to cause harm!* She reminds herself to withhold, to restrain. She thinks about the soles of her feet feeling the concrete floor through the rubber bottoms of her boots. It's something she did during the war in moments when she felt herself lifting out of her skin with fear or rage or the unnerving swim of uncertainty. Rooting herself. Feet on the ground. To Brodaccio she says, "Are you implying that I am a 'lookie-loo'?"

"You, Mrs. Baston, have been thoroughly vetted." The doctor smiles, pushes the file toward her.

She could laugh at the number of errors he's just admitted—*Who is Mrs. Baston?* she could ask. *How thorough was that vetting?* But she nods, draws in a breath. "I just want to understand the thinking. I ask this as a scholar of psychology and child development, with an interest in the girl's mental state. This seems unnecessarily institutional for a child's recovery site. And she is the only child here, I assume? And, yes, I've seen this—" a finger on the file. "Detective Norquist sent me a mimeograph."

"Psychology is not my concern. I am a physician. The girl is in no state to be integrated into the society of other children."

"By your judgment, or someone else's? Is there a social welfare advocate?"

"Mrs. Reach sees her daily. They walk the yard here, apart from the prisoners, of course, and it seems to comfort the child to be in this landscape. It's her home. You forget that, perhaps, but this island is her home."

"That's been established, then? That the girl has been subsisting here alone for some time?"

"We believe so, yes."

Bernadette nods. Feet on the ground. Behind her eyes, she sees the white light of that other hospital, each child's face scrubbed expressionless in that awful, chiseling light. "I'm thinking of her as a little girl," she says. "She is just a girl."

"Well, we're assessing that. We think she might, in fact, be adolescent. There are physical signs that she is older than first suspected."

"She still can't tell you?"

Brodaccio shakes his head. "She remains nonverbal."

"Does she have a name? A name you're calling her? I feel we're talking around her like she is the file and not an actual person."

He smiles. "You and Mrs. Reach should meet." He opens the file and points. *Atalanta Doe*, it reads. "Mrs. Reach likes mythology."

Bernadette sits back in her chair. "Where is Mrs. Reach? Should she not be here for this meeting?"

"This was the date on which *I* had time for you."

"Right. Well, then, I'm ready to meet Atalanta whenever she is ready to meet me."

Dr. Brodaccio sends one guard to speak to another. There's the sound of heels in the hallway beyond the little examination room, then silence. Bernadette feels her body buzzing with the effort of waiting, the armored energy of the conversation she's just had. Across from her, Brodaccio sits with his arms crossed, the wide round face of his wristwatch audibly ticking out the seconds. He is a man with no problem idling, Bernadette registers. This is interesting. She herself can hardly bear this long and empty fifteen-minute pause. What a waste to do nothing for a full quarter hour. When was the last time she just sat and stared at a wall? This is the difference between Brodaccio's life and hers—the privilege of time to fritter away. *The luxury!* she thinks. And him just taking it for granted. At home, she could have dinner made and three student exams marked in fifteen minutes. She could have Willie bathed and a pot of coffee brewed and a paragraph of research edited. She stands from her chair, walks to the doorway, and peers out into the hallway.

"The girl will not be hurried," Brodaccio repeats. "You want her in a fit state to meet, don't you?"

"What happens when she's rushed?"

"Have you ever tried to catch a bird, Mrs. Baston?"

"She's been here for weeks, and she's not on a schedule?"

"You have her daily routine documented in the file Detective Norquist sent."

"What behavioral responses have you noted when she's pushed to a task she hasn't self-elected?"

"Again, I refer you to the file. I thought you'd read it."

"I read it. I'm asking you to elaborate on the psychological state you've witnessed in the child when she is forced into externally determined tasks."

"I am a medical doctor, Mrs. Baston, not a PhD. I have documented observable facts in this report. I will leave all speculations about the girl's mind to you, the student to whom Detective Norquist has inexplicably given access to this case."

"Student?"

"Is this research not intended for your unfinished dissertation?"

Bernadette's face stipples with needles of heat. "I was invited to consult with you. You vetted me."

Brodaccio nods, smiles a tight purse, lifts the hedges of his eyebrows. "I appreciate a female with ambition. I have a daughter myself. And, obviously, I did not forbid your participation in this case. But whatever you plan to do with the girl will not impede the real objective of rehabilitating her. She is my patient. That must be understood."

"Is that what this day has been about, then? This—agreement? Am I not actually here to meet the girl at all?" Bernadette slides her rain slicker from the back of her chair and begins to hoist her bag's strap over her shoulder, but, as if cued, the girl appears just then in the doorway, a nurse at her side.

The child is exactly as Bernadette has pictured her: small, wiry rather than fragile, her face made hard with exposure to the island's wind and weather. As the girl enters the room, Bernadette takes in the particulars of her movements, her carriage, her appearance. She is like a collage of a girl rather than a unified whole. She has the body of a child: a flat chest behind a pink dress someone has likely donated, ruffle at the knee. A bow hangs half-untied from the fawn-colored ponytail at the back of her head. But her hands are those of an adult—large and strong, tanned and rough. Her feet are big, yet gentle in their steps. She walks in a way that is animal rather than child: fluid and alert, doe-like. When Dr. Brodaccio stands and the nurse pulls out the chair opposite Bernadette's, the girl looks at it as if she's never seen a chair. "Sit," the nurse says, and she grasps the girl's shoulders and maneuvers her into a seated position. The girl fidgets. Her arms are ropey, the veins raised under her skin. Her hands flutter like birds across the tabletop. "In your lap," the nurse says, and, taking hold of the girl's hands, settles them in her lap.

"Hello," Bernadette says.

The girl's eyes dart swiftly around the room, and when they land on her, Bernadette watches them narrow in observation and assessment.

"Hello, Atalanta," she says.

"She doesn't respond to it yet," the nurse says. "The name. It means nothing to her."

"Atalanta," Bernadette says again, and this time she points at the girl as she says it. "I'm glad to meet you. I'm Bernadette." She points to herself. "Atalanta," as she points at the girl. "Bernadette," and she lays a palm against her own chest.

The girl does not make eye contact. She lifts her angular face as if to catch the current of Bernadette's breath, her perfume, the stink of damp on her clothes. Bernadette thinks of another feral child she read about in her research to prepare for this meeting: Victor. A twelve-year-old boy found in the woods outside Aveyron, France, at the end of the eighteenth century. He was taken in by a doctor and raised to the age of eighteen, at which point he ran, disappearing once more into the deep wood, though in the end he was caught again and forced to live as others thought he should. In the doctor's report on Victor, Bernadette read this line: "The child is closer to animal than man, a boy with hair like a pelt, manner like a wolf." She had understood the doctor's meaning immediately. The children she met during the war were also wild in this way—unpredictable, sometimes made dangerous by their fear. Once, a boy bit her hand when she reached out to feed him. He flinched as she moved toward him, lunged before she could draw back. The ward doctor had put a stitch in her finger and suggested she isolate the child in the quarantine room as punishment, but Bernadette refused; she couldn't be angry with the boy. Now, here, she sees that same wild fear on Atalanta's face. *I'm safe*, Bernadette tries to transmit across their distance. She holds out her hand, low and palm up, the way she would position herself to offer a stray dog a scrap of meat. *Safe*, she makes everything about her body say. *I'm safe.* But when she steps forward—just an inch—the girl lets out a trembling, full-throated growl, and instinctively Bernadette jumps back.

"Okay," Brodaccio says. "Okay, now, child." On his face, a self-satisfied little grin.

Bernadette puts her hand back into her pocket. "It's fine," she says to the girl. And to the doctor: "Trust is built with time." She hooks her bag over her shoulder, folds her rain slicker over her arm.

"You're leaving?" Brodaccio stands.

"I'll be back," Bernadette says.

"This was a lot of effort for five minutes of contact, Mrs. Baston."

"Indeed, it was," she says. She brisks down the corridor, unaccompanied this time, no sense in waiting for the escort when she's on her way out. She retrieves her camera, then shoves out into the rain, a gray mist fine as sea spray and smelling of the ocean. She thinks of the girl out in this, for years possibly. A girl whose body is land and whose land is an extension of her body. Girl as island. Girl as sea-foam. Atalanta, mythical girl of Greek legend, left by her father to die in the woods because she was not born a son.

Tonight, she knows, she will crawl into bed beside her own girl. Her own fatherless daughter. She will say, *Are you ready for a story?* And Willie will clap Bernadette on the cheeks and shiver with happiness the way she does every night when the story is about to begin. What could be better than a good story?

*There once was a girl*, Bernadette will begin. *Her father left her to die, but she did not die.*

*What? What, Mama?* Willie will ask, and Bernadette will shush her.

*Hush, if you want to hear*, she'll say before she continues. And then: *The girl did not die. Instead, she met a bear, and the bear became her mother.*

*A bear-mother.* Willie's breath like a sigh.

*Can you imagine?*

*Yes! Tell more!* Willie will say and snuggle into Bernadette's side.

*Oh, little pearl, little barnacle, little cub. Oh, daughter*, Bernadette thinks now, conjuring this picture of the two of them. *Did I teach you this? Did I teach you intimacy, laughter, how to listen to a story?* She wonders: how do we learn to trust another person enough to love? To love without thinking every moment about that love withdrawn, though it surely will be—for all of us—one way or another. Is there a window for those lessons, open only for a little while? Is a mother the window?

Bernadette boards the ferry, finds a bench where she settles her dripping bag, and slides her feet out of the humidity of her boots. Beyond the thick windows, the sea rocks and tosses, color of a jade stone. Bernadette again pictures Willie tucked close. Here they are in her mind: mother and daughter, like skin and bone. Mother as hearth and daughter as flame. Daughter as tide and mother as pulse. Mother as worry and daughter as wish.

The question with the found girl, however, is not about a child's making but about a child's remaking. And can a girl even be *remade*? Reconfigured after wildness has uncoiled every childish curl and crimped every gentle breath into a snarl? Bernadette thinks of the way a fern unrolls its tentacular fronds, slow and delicate. A miracle of growth in the hard, intemperate spaces of darkness. What happens when the wildness is tamed? What is lost in that erasure?

Beneath her, the boat thrums and rattles, pulls with the groan of a whale away from the dock. Bernadette is tired. She feels the cold damp of the weather under her ribs. It seems as if this whole day has evaporated, but no matter. She'll be back, just as she's said. She'll do whatever it takes to actually find this girl.

4

SHE'S STILL ASKING THESE QUESTIONS A WEEK LATER when she meets Nora Reach for lunch at a coffee shop not far from the university library. The day is dry, crisp, and windy. Outside the coffee shop's wide front windows, unraveling skeins of cloud spill west to east across the washed-out blue of the sky. Bernadette arrives first, orders a plate of fries and clams, a cup of black coffee that she caramels in a swim of cream. She reads while she eats and waits, this time another book on child development—Erikson's *Childhood and Society*. She has read and reread the section on Erikson's theorized first stage of development, in which he posits that by the age of two, a person learns either to trust or to mistrust the world, their caregivers, and other people. Is this always true? And if that narrow sliver of time closes before trust is learned, is the opportunity gone forever? This seems key to her understanding of Atalanta, and she needs to know, at what point did the girl's parents abandon her? And what was her state of care prior to that abandonment? There can be no clear path forward until these questions are answered, and as Brodaccio has made his position on anything but the objective facts of the child's current condition clear, Bernadette has turned to Nora Reach for more information.

In the file Norquist gave her, she found a letter detailing the official agreement between Elita Island Federal Penitentiary and the state to share custodial care and guardianship of the child, and designating Nora Reach as the state's child welfare case manager. Bernadette has pictured Nora like a standard copy of the few other female social workers she's met in the field—which is to say, soft around the edges, maternal. She's pictured an ankle-length skirt, hair in a braid or two, and a face clean of makeup. She's surprised, then, when the woman who must be Nora appears at the door, unknots an ivory silk scarf from around her close-cropped head and tucks it into her bag, beaming a broad grin at Bernadette. Not at all to type.

"Mrs. Baston?" She shakes Bernadette's hand and begins extricating herself from a cashmere wrap, a brown velvet blazer. She's middle-aged—maybe forty-five—and chic. She sets a neat burgundy leather clutch on the tabletop, orders a lemon water, black coffee, and half a BLT. She smells of orange rind and clove—some expensive perfume. A single garnet dewdrop hangs from each of her earlobes; they catch the light and toss spangles across the Formica tabletop each time she turns her head. *Monied*, Bernadette registers, which in her field must mean she either married into it or inherited it.

"Mrs. Reach?"

"Not *missus*, I'm sorry to say. They call me that—it's motherly, right for the job, but not accurate. You can call me Nora."

"Nora," Bernadette corrects herself. A picture of a privileged upbringing, including the luxury of college study and a chosen career in penniless public service, comes together in Bernadette's mind, puzzle pieces snapping to fit.

"I knew it was you as soon as I saw you sitting in the window," Nora says. "You have that look of attention I expected."

"Look of attention?"

"I remember it on the professors I knew in school. People who are always thinking."

"I hope most people are always thinking."

"Oh, they aren't."

The waitress interrupts, bending over to pour the coffee. Bernadette notes Nora's curt nod when her mug is full, the way she opens her paper napkin like unfolding a newspaper and settles it over her lap. She has etiquette-lesson posture, stirs cream into her coffee, and taps the spoon on the edge of the mug once before laying it face down on her saucer. *She's all right angles*, Bernadette thinks, and wonders if the woman's interest in Atalanta is more colonial than maternal—the challenge and thrill of taking on a girl who isn't just a case, but a potential to prove the merits of a "civilizing" influence. There were doctors like this in the ward, Frenchmen who were opposed to the Germans' imperial dreams but not their antisemitism. These doctors treated all their young patients the same, though less out of compassion than the very French belief that liberty, equality, and fraternity were vehicles to the erasure of difference. When those children who had been dumb with trauma began to speak, they were rewarded with praise and encouragement only if that speech was in schoolbook French.

At the table, Nora Reach carries on. "What I've learned in my years of serving the public is that most people simply don't think all that much. At least when they aren't forced into it. They aren't thinking like you and I are, anyhow, if I can jump in and make an assumption about our shared nature for a moment." Nora smiles. As she talks, the waitress returns with her order. "Thank you," Nora says. "It looks fine." But when the waitress turns, Nora sighs. To Bernadette she says, low, "They've overcooked it." She uses the tines of her fork to pull the bacon from the BLT, strip by strip, until she's stacked a tidy pile at the side of the plate.

"We should get to the files," Bernadette says.

"Yes, just let me finish this thought. You'll find it interesting. I just read something about this, actually," she continues. "About thought habits in Americans. It was a study of some several thousand people, examining typical adult mental processes." Again, her head turns, and flashes spark across the tabletop. "I'm telling you this because it's just your area, isn't it?"

"I study children."

"Yes, but thinking in children. And what was most fascinating about this study was the number of participants who said they often aren't thinking anything at all. Can you believe that? Their minds are just blank. Like a canvas without paint, or the sea without boats, or whatever comparison you want to make. Blank. And I thought, how impossible to believe. But, of course, also not impossible when you consider empirical evidence."

*God*, Bernadette thinks. The coffee shop is filling with the heat and breath of this woman's talking, like a big white balloon swelling, swelling, and she a little dew bead of humidity sitting inside it. She so wanted to like this woman, to find an ally in her. She shifts in her seat to unstick her trousers from the sweaty backs of her knees, looks at her watch. There are a mere two hours and twenty-three minutes until she needs to return to the apartment to collect Willie. Two hours and fifty-three minutes until she must walk Willie to the park so the child can run off her energy between the swings and the slide if there's any hope of her sleeping tonight. The days are short now in these last weeks of the year, and the afternoon goes thin quickly, daylight draining away in what seems like no time at all and the sky flooding with a blue-black spill that swallows the playground in dusk.

The other day she let Willie dally too long on the swings, and suddenly they were alone in the darkness. *We have to leave*, she hurried her daughter, and Willie must have heard the lace of worry in her voice because she began fussing. Willie, her sweet girl who's never known a moment of real danger, has a capacity for worry that surprises Bernadette. There are monsters in the bedroom closet at night. There are spiders beneath the bed. Outside, tucked between the branches of the bare forsythia bush, Willie sees the bony fingers of a witch. *No*, Bernadette says to her, over and over, a lullaby of reassurance. *No, no. That's just stories. Not real.* But the girl has the kind of imagination Bernadette herself had, before the war—vivid and toothed with the fangs of fairy-tale terrors. The kind of imagination only the privilege of safety grants a person. Willie's mind is never a sea blank of boats, never a white canvas. And that is true, it seems, of most children, who, if left to fill their own time, always turn to play, to invention, to imagination. Imagination—that internal music of the human mind—is like an egg, though, isn't it? Bright yolked with the possibility of a life of its own, but only if the shell that holds it can remain intact, and oh, that shell is fragile. As soon as the real wolves step out from the wood and bare their teeth, the shadows of their dream brothers dissipate like smoke. A child who is surviving can only survive. At least, this is what Bernadette has observed in the past. But what about the found girl? All that time alone on the island—did she play? She must have. Could her response to trauma be different because her trauma was different? Not abuse, but isolation? Bernadette writes in the margin of her notepad: *Observe idle behaviors. Typical or atypical self-entertainment? A's internal life?*

To Nora Reach, she says, "What have you seen in terms of the child's innate patterns of play?"

"What child?" Nora's face washes flat of expression.

"The child. Atalanta."

"I wasn't suggesting that the child has no thoughts."

"Of course not—you were talking about a study you read, but in terms of the girl, what have you seen?"

Nora shakes her head, sets her utensils crossways, an X, over the picked-apart remains of her lunch, and shoves the plate to the side. "Let me get my notes," she says.

Bernadette sees her mistake—the woman has nearly recoiled. She flushes. She's getting this all wrong. She can't worry about Willie right now or she'll lose this opportunity entirely. She sighs, says, "I didn't mean to offend you."

"I'm not offended. I simply thought we might break the ice before working, but I see that you're a woman with an agenda." Tight smile. Lift of an eyebrow.

"I'm just aware of the time," Bernadette says. She hesitates. She's always reluctant to say anything about Willie to the people she works with—it alters their way of looking at her. "I have a daughter," she says. Flare of heat at the nape of her neck. "She's at home with a sitter. I'm on a clock."

Across the table, Nora shakes her head. "A child? But I understood that you were a professor." Again, a lifted brow, a look of disappointment.

"Yes. I am. And I have a child."

"You know, I petitioned them to let you in on this. Norquist, Brodaccio. I looked you up. A woman child development specialist! How interesting, I thought. I'm giving you an opening. You may not have been made aware of my hand in things, but you should know that the men in charge weren't eager to allow you to carry on your project."

"My project?"

"Teaching the child to speak."

"You found me—not the other way around. And I think you misunderstand what I do."

Nora clucks her tongue at this. "Look, it's not simple, convincing two state bureaucracies to admit a woman with a personal interest that serves—really—no one invested in this case at an institutional level."

"I wouldn't call it a personal interest." Bernadette feels the coffee shop contract around the two of them, the heady, giddy swim of Nora Reach's earlier chatter rushing out the door and away, and the table turning into a concrete barrier between them. She wants to stay on this case, so she'll have to submit. "But you're right, I'm sure neither of us is particularly welcome. We have to be allies."

"I've been assigned to this case. This is my work. I'm not a hobbyist."

"And neither am I. Again, you sought me out for some reason. Perhaps it's best that we keep our focus on that." Bernadette flips to a clean sheet of notebook paper on her pad, lifts her pen. She sighs, meets Nora's eyes. "Here's the bottom line: if you want me to help, I need you to tell me what you know about Atalanta's history. I've spoken to Brodaccio, who sees her simply as a body. Norquist is interested in her as a victim. But you—you, I believe, see her as a human, a child. That's where we line up, you and I."

Nora nods. "That's true."

"I need to understand the child's history. Her personality. Her possibility. I believe you're the only person involved with this case who can help me. And I have just over an hour and a half to hear what you have to say."

This—flattery, in essence—turns out to be the right approach to opening Nora Reach's files. For the next hour, Bernadette simply takes notes. The waitress appears and refills their water glasses. Outside the window, the light thickens into the waxy white stillness of afternoon. "This is so helpful," Bernadette says at one point, nudging for more. There's a nearly imperceptible lift in Nora's voice as she talks, and it's clear that beneath her sheen of class and resentment, she does care about the child, does see her as a girl in need of care.

What Nora reports is this: the state agencies involved have so far been under the working assumption that the girl was dropped recently on the island's shore by boat or perhaps smuggled over by a prison employee and abandoned, but it's becoming apparent that neither of those scenarios are likely. More reasonable, based on the child's physical condition, verbal delays, and intimate knowledge of the island's landscape—is to believe that the girl was born on the island, or that she's been there—wild and surviving alone—for most of her life.

"Born there?" Bernadette repeats. She scribbles this onto her pad.

Nora smiles, leans forward on her elbows over the tabletop. "I know. It seems impossible, but I've done some digging around in the island's archives, and it's not."

When the island's civilian village was evacuated in '37, the state accounted for every passenger boarding the ferry off island, and later that manifest was checked against island records of births, deaths, and marriages. A handwritten query from a clerk has turned up in the files from that period, and in it he notes a birth—of a female child—in the year 1933 that cannot be matched to either a corresponding death or departure from the island. It could be that this child, Atalanta, is that female baby, which would put her now at age seventeen—much older than she appears.

"How could she be seventeen?" Bernadette asks. She has bolded and circled the number on her pad. It seems impossible when she recalls the girl she met—barely the size of a twelve-year-old.

"Dr. Brodaccio's physical examination noted the presence of breast buds," Nora says, her voice low. "And the dentist who looked at the child claims she has some of her adult molars. That was puzzling when we believed her to be preadolescent, but now . . ." She waves a hand through the air as if pushing aside that first assessment.

"There's a family name, then," Bernadette says. "If a birth was recorded, there's a family name."

"All we have is the query from the clerk to a prison employee who lived on the island and claimed the birth of a dependent in requesting a week's leave in 1933, but then left the island in '37 alone. The note is handwritten. *Requesting account of child, female, Marley*, it looks like it says, though the handwriting is muddled."

"Who was the employee?"

She shrugs, sighs. "A prison cook named Tor Anderson. He quit the prison job when he left the island. I found census records showing that he moved to California, where he took a position in the kitchen of a resort on the coast. Then he was killed in the Pacific. There's no resolution to the query about the child in the files." She lays one hand over the other, sits back in her chair. "So. A standstill."

"Could Marley be the mother, not the child?"

"Maybe."

Bernadette can't tell if that *maybe* carries a tone of real possibility or just polite dismissal. She shakes her head. "I was hoping for more."

"Weren't we all," Nora says, though her tone implies a strand of delight in the mystery of the girl, the shadow veil trailing every detail of her history. The girl might be traceable to a biological mother, or she might not be. She could be a child, or within months of eighteen. Nora shrugs. "If only she could tell us. But, of course, that's where you come in. The linguist."

Bernadette lets out a breath. "Not a linguist. You've misunderstood my work, I think. I study child development. I'm a scholar, not a schoolteacher."

"You teach."

"Yes, but college students. Not preliterate children."

"How different is that really, though? You can teach one person, you can teach another." Nora shifts, unclasping her clutch and withdrawing the ivory scarf, which she knots at her throat this time rather than snugging it over her head. She slides three dollars and a bright silver quarter onto the table. "I'll cover lunch."

"Have you actually insinuated to Norquist and Brodaccio that I will teach the child to speak?"

"Not insinuated. I've told them directly that the benefit of having you on board is that we might get more development out of the child. Specifically, language development. Norquist needs a testimony. Brodaccio has been on the island for years, and he's intrigued. He thought he knew everything about the place, and this girl is new. You have access so that they can get access."

Bernadette frowns, frustration fizzing under her breastbone again. "But you've misled them. I can't promise what you've offered them. That's not what I do."

Nora buttons her blazer, winds her wrap around her shoulders, and casts a hard stare at Bernadette. "We all have to be flexible and innovative here, Bernadette, and we all have our work cut out for us with this girl. I got you a job, not a ticket to a show." Her face softens then. "And what future does the child have if she never speaks a word? She has to learn something. Everyone is capable of learning something. I believe that, anyway. Don't you?" She taps her watch. "Aren't you on a timer," she says, and Bernadette's eyes follow her as she swings open the coffee shop door and gusts out into the street. The wind kicks up the tails of her wrap like the brown wings of a plain-feathered bird.

This, Bernadette remembers, is exactly how she herself had left Brodaccio—brusque, unapologetic. She has empathy for Nora Reach, despite the snobbery, despite the horrible promise Nora has shackled to her wrists. It's the impulse toward survival that they have in common as the two women on this riptide of a case—nothing else. And, it occurs to her, this is also what they share with Atalanta. It's why they're both drawn to her, why they need to understand her rather than just assess her. *This girl who has pulled it off*, Bernadette thinks, and then questions herself: *Pulled what off?* But she already knows the answer. Solitude. Silence. The abandonment of being exiled from any structure that might protect her—a system, a village, a family. And now, the inability to conform to expectations.

How long can the prison keep her? How deep is Brodaccio's curiosity, really? How long will his tolerance last for this diversion from his regular load of inmate patients? And will the strain on Norquist's pride and budget eventually lead him to dismiss Atalanta's case? There's a clock on the work, and it has been sped up by Nora's new information about Atalanta's past and her age. A little motherless child in need of a savior is a darling who commands attention. But an eighteen-year-old woman without any of the corseted assets of a socialized girlhood? Different beast entirely.

Bernadette nods to the waitress, who is hovering at the counter, waiting to clear the table. "Thanks," she says, and adds another fifty cents to the pile of money Nora left on the table. She gathers her notebook and bag and goes to her own girl.

## 5

BUT BEFORE ANY MORE CAN BE DONE, BERNADETTE IS forced into stillness. Willie is sick—some childhood virus serious enough to manifest a 101° fever, but not serious enough to merit a doctor's visit. They sink into the bog, the two of them at home, Bernadette indulgently turning up the radiator so that the apartment becomes a balmy, cozy cloister. She makes chicken soup, and they listen to the radio for hours. The university's classical station plays Stravinsky, Chopin, a long and reedy violin concerto that the announcer credits to a student composer. This is the background soundtrack to whole, swollen afternoons in the woolen cocoon the two of them have made of the apartment.

"We're monarchs," Willie says as she nestles into Bernadette's side on the third afternoon of their quarantine, her arms wrapped around herself like the wings she's imagining. Willie has never seen a monarch in life, only in books, but she loves them. Bernadette has told her that it was Linnaeus who first named them—*papilio*, which is Latin. But, of course, he couldn't have been the first to name them, to see them. So much exists below the gaze of the namers, outside the range of their vision. Willie is too young for this lesson yet, but she'll learn it in time, as all girls must.

For now, Bernadette only pulls her closer and says, "Where will we migrate when we hatch?"

"New York." The girl doesn't hesitate. In her mouth, the *r* falls away from the second word, and Bernadette hears *yolk*. It's charming. *If only*, she thinks. A new yolk, the two of them hatching, new creatures to a new horizon.

"Oh, not New York," she says. "It's too cold for us there now. Butterflies can't survive in the cold."

Willie pushes her face into Bernadette's side, piglet or puppy, the rooting instinct of babyhood not entirely grown out of her. "Mama," she says, her voice smothered soft by Bernadette's sweater. "It has to be New York. Daddy is there."

Bernadette kisses the girl's forehead where the fever is still pulsing just beneath the skin. "Maybe."

This is a new fascination—*daddy*. It's unremarkable, in the developmental sense, for a child of Willie's age to have sudden and acute awareness of the construct of a typical family structure. Father, mother, brother, sister. Her playmates all have fathers. These men appear at the park on Saturdays, the one day their wives are untethered from the children for a few hours at least. The fathers all wear woolen overcoats at this time of year, hats. They stand in a stiff row behind the swings, pushing harder than the moms, so that the children squeal and kick their legs at the height of their swing's reach, at the peak of the arc. "Higher, Daddy!" almost all of them demand. Bernadette has watched Willie watching these men. Willie knows no men up close. She says hello to the postman if he happens to be at the mailbox when she and Bernadette return from a walk. She waves to Mr. Ruskin across the street if they spot him in his yard, picking at the weeds in his vegetable plot. He grew pumpkins and acorn squash and zucchini this year, and when he called to Willie to offer her a pumpkin earlier this fall, she hid behind Bernadette rather than answer him. "I want one," she whispered up to her mother. "Tell him I want one, Mama." It was Bernadette who crossed the street to accept the pumpkin and thank him. Willie stood on the sidewalk before their own apartment with her hands clasped, her face pinked with paralyzed delight. It worried Bernadette, just as the gaze of fascination at the park worries her. What will happen to her girl who is both enamored of and silenced by the presence of men? She knows. Of course she knows.

And this is why, a few days ago, when—inexplicably—a card arrived in the mail from Fred bearing a note to her and a check with a memo line reading *For Wilhelmina*, Bernadette handed the note to Willie. "From your father," she said.

"My father?" Willie repeated.

"Yes. Your father. Fred," Bernadette told her. "In New York. He's in New York, which is why he can't be here. But he sent this for you, because he loves you. You're his daughter, and he loves you, just like I do."

Willie had beamed. Stars might have popped like glycerin bubbles from the top of her blond head, she was so evidently delighted by this news.

And if it was a mistake to open this door, it's too late to close it now. Willie is sprouting wings to fly to him. She is, in her imagination, already halfway there.

Bernadette regrets it all. How easy would it have been to erase Fred from Willie's story of herself and their family? To go on as they are without accounting for him? What will he add to Willie's life but a vacancy? Bernadette pictures a paper snowflake. When the paper is folded, the snips of one's scissors seem small, insignificant, but they bloom into holes when the paper is opened. What happens to a girl cut here and there by the disappointments, the absences, the failures of her childhood? What vacancies is she left to patch in herself as she grows?

Bernadette's thoughts turn to Atalanta—not the real girl on Elita this time, but the myth for which she has been named. A child whose father left her when she was not his wished-for son. Where was her mother? The mythology leaves her out. Her name was Clymene. That's all Bernadette knows about the woman who would let her husband leave their infant daughter in the woods. What would compel a woman to allow such abandonment? Fear or protection—those two poles of motherhood.

"We will fly south," she says to Willie. "That's where the monarchs go. Where it's warm. Where there's so much milkweed, they can land anywhere and stuff themselves."

"Milkweed," Willie repeats as if the word is a lozenge of candy she's holding on her tongue.

Bernadette relaxes, the derailment having worked, and tells her about the pink clusters of milkweed flowers like tiny stars. She talks, and Willie's eyes drowse, her lids dipping, fluttering, closed. *Are we a broken constellation? Two-thirds of a working system?* Bernadette thinks, looking at her daughter's sleeping face. But no. No. She knows they're fine. The check from Fred—unexplained and appearing out of nowhere—is a sign of something, maybe, but not of her need. And Atalanta's mother wasn't really Clymene. Her mother was the bear, the rescuer, the mother of the safe den and warm hibernation. In their bed, Bernadette tucks the blanket around them both more snuggly.

THE NEXT DAY, BERNADETTE MUST TEACH. WILLIE'S fever is lower, but she's weak and too tired to get out of the bed, flushed faced and sallow eyed. Mrs. Iversen, comes, as always, and Bernadette kisses Willie on the forehead as she goes. There's a wail on the other side of the apartment door as she closes it, and then Mrs. Iversen hushing Willie into calm again. Bernadette hesitates, but she bites back her impulse to sweep inside and scoop up Willie. *Go,* she tells herself. *Go!*

It takes a moment, but she goes. She drops her hand into her pocket, walks away. *Damn it,* she thinks. Her chest is tight under her coat. It's like slicing her own wrist to walk out on her still-sick girl. She stalks down the block, her heels striking the pavement at a clip. *Eyes to the horizon,* she thinks, to keep herself from turning back. *Pay attention.* It's a trick from the hospital days: salvation is always in the details. She lifts her head now, focuses. Breeze rioting the evergreen points of the trees. Peaty smell of smoke and leaves. Late-morning sheen of the November frost still glittering on the shingles of the rooftops. Walk, walk. The laces begin to loosen in her.

The farther she gets from home, the easier it is to keep walking. *Ha!* she thinks, remembering Fred and his check. *Isn't that true.*

When she looks up again, the sky is a high, fine white like the opal skim inside an oyster's shell. It's a perfect autumn day, and she is out in the world. Out in the world for the first time all week. The thought of this opens in her like an amaryllis. For the first time all week, she is alone. That's all it takes. Suddenly, she wants to run, just to match the movement of her limbs to the lift in her chest at the inner ring of that word—*alone*! The word comes from the Old English *all ana,* meaning *wholly* and *one.* She turns this definition over in her head like a shell, examining outside and in, convex and concave. The whole of her is here. She is wholly alone. She is whole alone. The words become the beat of her heels on the sidewalk, an internal chant. And like she's conjured it with this spell, her concentration—so wobbly and hard to harness when she's with Willie— becomes crystalline as cut glass. *There it is,* she thinks: *my mind.*

She can turn her thoughts with the slightest touch now, like driving a car, and so she steers herself toward the case she's neglected since she saw Nora Reach a week ago. Atalanta, the child who only ever has been *all ana.* What can she make of the girl's history that will help them work together? How can she approach working at all with a child who has learned to exist so fully without the company of others that she has been inverted by her solitude? Or not inverted, but reverted. Maybe. Or is that entirely the wrong way of thinking about things? Reversion suggests backwardness, a retreat or recoil to an earlier state. But it necessarily also implies a progression stopped.

Bernadette crosses the lawn that marks the edge of the campus, notices too late that the grass is soaking her feet. She speeds forward anyhow, in a hurry now to keep up with her thoughts as they unroll. What if there has been no progression? What if what one doctor sees as reversion, the child herself might understand as stasis or survival? Not time folding back on itself to return to some earlier point in development at all. What if there are no points in development—or at least not points on a line that projects in only one direction? She thinks about Willie's monarchs, who eat the lovely milkweed not because it is attractive but because, through its release of poisonous cardenolides in their bodies, they make themselves unattractive prey. What may the girl have done and chosen that might look like stunted growth but is in fact clever protection? Perhaps it is not just that Atalanta has failed to progress as typically protected human children do but also that the model built for typically protected human children cannot possibly map the constellation of knowledge an unprotected child must acquire.

Bernadette flies up the steps and into her classroom, where—already—rows of mostly young men are seated and silently waiting for whatever she is about to deliver. "I'm here!" she says as she swings herself into place behind the desk. She does not add what she's thinking: *Here to deliver your parcels of learning!* It's a dagger of a thought, but she does hate this moment before every class when they all stare up at her, expectant little vessels, waiting for her to drop off the day's bundle of information. She'd like them to be standing when she comes into the room. She'd like them at the blackboard, already writing their own questions about last week's reading. Why aren't they talking to each other when she arrives? But they never are. They're obedient participants in the system, just as she is, she supposes. Teacher as postmaster, and student as recipient.

She sighs—this time aloud—and opens her satchel on the metal desk, lays out her book, her pencil, the little paper box of chalk sticks she prefers to carry herself rather than use the cigarette butts of chalk the prof before her leaves behind. She turns her back to the students and hears them sit up in their desks, open notebooks, pick up their pens. A collective. *Oh, people*, she thinks. *You school of minnows.* She writes in loopy, heavy-pressed chalk cursive: What is knowledge?

"I'm going to tell you a story," she says, returning to face them. "Picture this scene: A child runs naked through the long grass at the edge of an island's northern point. It's summer." Bernadette looks out at the wrinkled brows, the pens paused over papers, and continues. It's warm and the sun is high, she tells them. The tide is low, and when the child breaks through the wrack line and hits the sand, her feet leave shining welts in a long line behind her. She slows, pauses, stoops to look closely at the sand, then stomps here, stomps there, testing the pocks the clams leave. Little vents. One only bubbles, but the next spouts, and like a dog she is on her knees and digging. Her face is flecked with mud-sand. Her long hair falls over her forehead. As fast as she can scoop sand from the hole she's making, water wells to fill it, but there it is! She plunges her arm down to the elbow and tugs, tugs, leans all the way back to wrestle it up from the muck, and finally comes up with it—a geoduck.

"I'm telling you the true account of a child recently discovered to have been surviving alone in the wild near here. We, who are working with her to understand her development, are calling her Atalanta. She survived on geoducks, clams, mussels, the occasional fish and seabird, berries. She was alone. For years, maybe. And so my question to you is this: What is knowledge and how does it develop in children? If a child isolated in the wild—presumably from a young age—is able to feed herself through hunting and foraging, who taught her these skills?"

The classroom is quiet. Bernadette hears the radiator click on and hum, click off. The windows have gone opaque with the humidity and warmth of everyone's breath against the outdoor chill on the other side of the glass. She waits. She wants to know what they think so that she can discern what she thinks. She doesn't have an answer. This is how she typically teaches, though she would never say as much to a colleague. It's less interesting to have all the answers than to have the floor long enough to ask good questions.

A young man in the front row raises his hand, contends that what she's described is the result of physical instinct. The body feels hunger—a physical need—and teaches itself to fulfill that need.

"But how does it learn?"

"Trial and error," the student says.

"No," another student—a boy with red hair and a splatter of freckles. "I mean, yes, trial and error." He flushes to the ears. "But also, watching the animals, right? Seagulls go for clams that same way, but with their bills."

"Interesting," Bernadette says. "Someone extend that line of thought."

One of the two women in the class—Sharon—picks it up. "There was a French boy—I can't remember his name—"

"Victor of Aveyron," Bernadette nods. "Good. Yes. Keep going."

"I read about him. Eighteenth century. A doctor took him in, I think."

"Yes, that's right."

"And he documented observing the boy hunting. The boy watched other animals first, tracked their methods, and tried to replicate them."

"Exactly," the red-headed boy says. "That's what I'm thinking just makes the most sense. Think about any child. Think about yourself. Did your mother teach you how to pick up a fork and knife and cut your steak? Or did you watch her do it first and copy?"

"It's not just language that we learn through modeling," Bernadette says. "You're right."

They go on, trying out theories, remembering their own childhoods. One recalls watching an older sister tie her shoes, memorizing the loop and pull, until he could repeat it himself. Another thinks about church— the relentlessness of every Sunday of his childhood spent in a pew, and the early confusion about when to rise, when to kneel, when to open the little red hymnal and when to close it. It was meaningless until he paid attention and mimicked the people around him. And then he understood. Knowledge is often gained via socialization, he tells the class.

The hour lapses. The students thank her, pack up, leave the classroom. Bernadette stuffs her things back into her bag, flicks off the classroom lights, glides along the waxed glow of the corridor's overhead fluorescents on the linoleum and down the wide staircase to the building's double doors. She is buzzing, lost in her head after that lesson. She has a plan now. Knows what to do and ask and whom to visit next in puzzling through the pieces of Atalanta's history. She's been coming at the case all wrong, and she understands that now. She has forgotten to think about the girl as a girl first. Forgotten about the importance of the story in the history.

At the market on the corner near her apartment, she stops and buys milk and eggs and a few treats to take Willie, for whom this afternoon has probably been impossibly long and dull. Or maybe not. How can one ever really know another person's experience, even the person to whom one is closest in the world? Still, she is the mother, protector, bearer of nurturing and also, sometimes, peppermint sticks and lemon drops for sore throats.

When she gets home, she thanks Mrs. Iversen and bustles Willie from bed into the bath and fills the tub. "Go ahead," she says, when Willie asks if she can take a peppermint stick with her into the water. Bernadette's own mother would have been appalled at this. It's unsanitary, crude, eating in the bath while you sit in your filth. Like an animal, her mother would have said. But who cares? Willie is happy. Bernadette smiles at her daughter, little frizz-headed cherub. The girl's body is still a swell of creamy baby fat at the knees and elbows. The dimple of her belly button like a divot in a mound of soft dough. She splashes and grins, the ache of her illness temporarily forgotten. Appease the body (in this case with sugar), and the mind will rest, Bernadette knows. She remembers a boy in the hospital who could not sleep unless permitted to hold a slice of bread under his pillow. The doctors protested until she convinced them that it was a small concession they could make to calm the boy. One slice of bread a night as the cost of the child's calm? What did it matter? She wants Willie not to have to wrestle with silly rules about civility that stunt a person's joy, a person's journey toward the fullness of a life lived. A woman's socialization is so much about learning to lose, learning to forgo, learning not to want. Atalanta has missed this for the lessons of the body, the landscape. Her mother has been the bear, and maybe there's something wonderful to that.

In the tub, Willie brings her palm down hard and fast, and a spray of water lashes up and splatters Bernadette's blouse. She laughs.

"How's your candy, baby?" Bernadette asks.

The girl raises an eyebrow, grins slyly. "Delicious," she says.

"Delicious? Where'd you hear that word? Was it Mrs. Iversen? I bet she says things like that all the time when I'm not here, doesn't she?" A wink. The idea of Mrs. Iversen saying such an unabashed word is ridiculous to them both.

"*Delicious* means good," Willie says.

"Yes, it does," Bernadette agrees. "It does."

6

FOR THE NEXT WEEK, BERNADETTE WORKS TO CONSTRUCT for herself a clear history of Elita Island. The coastal Indigenous people were the first to set foot on the island, and it wasn't until the mid-nineteenth century that a crew of British explorers arrived on its shores. They named it Wallace Island, for their ship's captain, but the name disappears from the records within only a handful of years in favor of Elita, the name bestowed by the French Canadian fur traders who next claimed the land. In Latin *elita* means "chosen," Bernadette reads, and this makes sense, given the island's geographical location—one in a cluster of islands not far south from a much bigger archipelago in Puget Sound. It was selected by these men for its abundance of deer and rabbit, and also for its shoreline, which is long, and for the grade of the slope into the sea, which is sudden and severe. The steep coast allowed traders' boats to anchor close to the island without running aground, and later—when the federal government took over Elita in the late 1800s—the drop-off, coupled with the frigid water, made it an ideal setting for a prison.

After the fur traders left, it was Scandinavian and German immigrant farmers who moved onto Elita in the 1860s. Bernadette finds a map of the island from the early years of its homesteading, each settled plot tracked with a dotted line and the owner's name hand-printed on the page. Olassen and Nyberg and Carlson and Wallin and Ecklund and Berg. Swedes, nearly all of them. People who liked the distance from neighbors and the sound of the seawater lapping at their farm's edge, who missed the home smells of salt and linden trees and wood

41

softened by months of damp weather, and so settled on Elita, a place that might have been on the Baltic Sea. They knew what such sandy soil was good for—strawberries and potatoes, radishes and root vegetables. They understood the coastal climate, how to spare the berries from the ground mold and keep the barn roof from leaking on the animals during the winter months of lashing sea storms. The other settlers on Elita—those who didn't arrive as farmers—came as fishermen. They built docks off the northern and southern points of the island. They caught rockfish and halibut and salmon and rowed over to nearby Adela Island, where the seafloor fell away much more gradually and was stubbled in the barnacled rocks beloved by crab. There, they set their crab pots out each day before dawn. An early island recipe booklet Bernadette finds among the archives offers directions for making a Mrs. Larsson's crab bisque and a Nils Torvaldsson's clam and potato chowder.

These men and women lived on the island alongside the prison from the start. The first prison on Elita went up in the 1870s. It housed federal criminals—gangsters and kidnappers, forgers and bootleggers and murderers. Men carried by rail across the territories to this far northwestern outpost as additional punishment for their crimes. Men who in the photographs Bernadette finds in the university library archives are all dressed in the striped cotton shirt and trousers of the convicted. They are men of all statures and appearances—short and tall, fat and lean, bald and curly haired. Many of them have unusually pristine mustaches—a fad of the prison's prime era. They meet the camera's eye with glares or vacant gazes, which is less a mark of the men's characters than of the camera's limitations. They would have had to hold still for several long seconds, waiting for the shutter to open and close. No smiling. Still, looking at the photographs, Bernadette can picture these inmates in life, and they are an intimidating bunch. Not for the first time, she wonders how the island residents felt about sharing their home with prisoners. For years, the settler-residents simply lived their lives on Elita as if it were any other place, running their farms and dairies and fish markets, sending their children out to play on the beach or in the fields, walking the dirt roads between farmsteads with baskets of eggs or potatoes or freshly dug-up clams to swap. Did they worry about their safety? About escape attempts? About waking in the night to find a man with a knife standing over the bed, or opening the back door in the morning to find a runaway tucked into a cow's stall? The letters she finds say nothing of this. They speak of the usual concerns of farming people—the heavy rains one autumn, the unexpected early freeze another winter. They talk of sick children or a newborn colt or a cake made and enjoyed on a Sunday afternoon. Everyday life, in other words, being lived on Elita just as it was everywhere else.

There are records documenting a shingle factory at one end of the island, a church, a tiny post office, a school. What a curious upbringing it must have been for the children of Elita to be raised there in the backyard of the prison, on a tiny island accessible only by private boat. It was a village, in the true sense of the word, and very likely its people were something more like a large extended family. They would have required one another for survival. They would have known each other well. And the letters she finds speak to that too—neighbors who looked in when someone came down with a fever, who invited each other over to mend a roof or deliver a lamb or share a stew. Neighbors in dispute over a property line or a pilfered crab pot or a perceived slight.

Not all of these neighbors were Elita residents, Bernadette discovers. There was a great deal of interisland traffic between Elita and her sister island, Adela, back when Elita was still residential. The islands shared a Lutheran church on Elita and a Catholic church on Adela. Their men fished together in the stretch of water separating the mounds of land, and their women united in forming a single Ladies Auxiliary that saw to the islands' Fourth of July picnic and winter sock drive. There are photographs of these, too, in the archives—one dated 1919 of women in white dresses and straw hats standing around a long table crowded with pies. Another is dated from just before the prison closed the island to residential life. It pictures two women, their arms outstretched like tree branches and draped in pairs of knitted socks like tinsel from boughs, each sock's ribbing marked with two letters. At the bottom of the photo, someone has annotated: *Mrs. R. Berg and Mrs. J. Riis show off their wares—socks initialed by their knitter in the traditional fashion.* There are Adela and Elita resident names in the recipe booklet. Adela and Elita faces intermixed in photographs of island weddings and Christmas pageants. When Elita was closed for good to residents, their dead were exhumed from the graveyard and their remains boated across the narrow channel to Adela for a second burial there. Bernadette wants to read those gravestones, wants to poke her head into Adela's grange hall and St. Eulalia's Catholic church. If Atalanta had been born to a local woman on Elita, someone on Adela knew her.

It's for this reason that a few days after Willie's fever recedes, Bernadette forgoes another morning in the library stacks and instead swaddles the girl into woolen pants and rubber boots, a rain slicker, and hat and mittens, and they take a bus to the ferry dock in Steilacoom. Like Elita was, Adela is a private residential island—no public beaches or parks—and the ferry over is private as well, just a local tug, primarily intended for Adela islanders' use. The man who captains it is sixty, if not older, grizzled by the wind and the saltwater so that his bare head and whiskered face are chapped bright pink. He grins at Willie as she and Bernadette board, takes the coins Bernadette hands him for their fare and jangles them in his big palm before picking out the shiniest penny and handing it back to Willie. "You keep that one for me. It's too pretty to put in my dirty old pocket." Willie flushes under her muffler and says nothing, but she closes her fist around the penny.

There is only one other passenger—an elderly woman pulling a metal trolley stuffed with bags of what appear to be books. She takes the only seat inside the cabin, and so Bernadette and Willie remain on the deck, Willie tucking herself into the folds of Bernadette's open wool coat, only her face peering out to see the water. It's a clear day, the Sound glassy and nearly transparent. Bernadette points out the blood-red and egg white–like blossoms of jellyfish bodies below the surface, the brown-black bulbs of a kelp garden floating like an armada of buoys on the waves, the sequin flash of a school of herring. Where the light hits it, the water blanches waxy and pale gray, but in the shadow of the boat it is deep jade green in shallow spots and midnight blue in deeper ones. The breeze kicks up the clean, briny smell of it, and Bernadette finds herself breathing full breaths, something in her head already unkinking out here away from the city.

"You have a friend on the island?" the captain hollers against the noise of the motor, and Bernadette tells him that no—they're true tourists, just out for an adventure.

He nods and turns his face back in the direction of Adela. Looking at the island, he has the gaze of a man looking at his beloved. He's lived here forever, Bernadette decides. His grandparents' graves are here. He knows what the island looks like in drought and snow and flood. She's charmed by this—the idea of knowing a place as well as you know your own body. It's so foreign to her. She believes Atalanta has this knowledge of Elita, and she wants to unbutton it and find out what the girl sees that she herself cannot. Before she can ask the captain any questions, though, the woman inside the cabin is knocking on the glass at her and gesturing at Willie. They venture inside.

The cabin is stuffy, an electric heater set up in one corner, its coiled wires humming and bright orange with heat. "Don't touch that," she says to Willie, and Willie clasps her two hands together as if to stop an impulsive swipe at the thing. There's just the one metal seat positioned against the cabin's back wall—a garden bench, wrought iron painted white. Against the other wall, a shelf of navigational charts, a thermos stowed away, a paper bag spotted with the leaching grease blots of whatever the captain is going to have for lunch in a couple hours.

The elderly woman motions Willie closer to the bench, and Bernadette nods. "It's okay." To the woman, she says, "This is Willie. I'm Bernadette. We're just visiting Adela for today." She might offer more, but she wants to see what will be useful and well received. If this woman is the resident she's hoping for, a conversation on the boat will make the rest of the day more productive. But—as she remembers one of the hospital's doctors saying—if you want someone's trust, you have to lead with an ankle before you flash the whole thigh.

"Visiting whom?" the woman asks.

*Ah*, Bernadette thinks. *There's that chilly local response I was expecting.*

The woman has a face like an apple gone soft with age, hair in a long white braid over one shoulder, a red hand-knitted hat on her head and a matching scarf around her neck. Under her coat, Bernadette spots the hem of a skirt and beneath it, the legs of denim trousers, leather work boots. Her bags, too, are more visible from this vantage than they were before, and it is indeed books she's trucking onto the island—five brown paper bags and one wooden crate, all full of books. Bernadette tips her head to read what she can of the titles—*Jane Eyre* and *Animal Farm*, a

Nancy Drew and several colorfully covered picture books. Books by Kerouac and Mitford and Chandler. Dime-store paperbacks at the top of one, westerns, judging by their titles. Books and books and books.

"You're planning on a lot of reading," Bernadette says, and the woman nods.

"For the library," she says. She pats the top sack of books.

"You're the librarian on Adela?"

"Oh, we're not big enough for a librarian. We have a volunteer, and I help her out now and then. I have a friend in Tacoma who collects all the used books she can and donates them to our shelves. I retrieve them when she has enough to fill the buggy."

"I know that," Willie says, jumping in. She points at the top picture book—*The Egg Tree*.

The woman lifts the book from the pile and opens it. A brilliant jewel-toned watercolor of a rooster blooms across the pages. "About a rooster, is it? Do roosters lay eggs?" She pulls a face at Willie, faux perplexed.

"They do not." Willie says it as if affronted, and the woman laughs.

Like a turtle drawing in its head, Willie opens the flap of Bernadette's coat again and slides back inside it.

"Oh, don't be shy," the woman says. "I was pulling your leg, but I see that you're too old to be fooled. We both know roosters don't lay eggs."

"I'm four," Willie says. "That book has paint eggs, not real eggs."

The woman flips through the pages, and in a moment looks up and says, "You are correct. And it looks like a good story, too."

It takes another few seconds, but Willie emerges from Bernadette's coat and seats herself beside the woman on the garden bench. Together, they bend their heads over the wide pages, reading, Willie's hands still clasped, fingers interlaced, and the woman's arthritic finger poked out and tracing the calligraphic lines of the red-and-yellow rooster's swoop of breast and scallop of comb.

Out on the deck, the captain's coat is billowed with the breeze of the boat's motion. Adela is no longer a black stripe on the horizon but a brown-green backbone rising out of the sea. Bernadette can see a cluster of white triangles—the roofs of the village buildings, and out along the island's long flank, other houses, just visible here and there between the trees.

She could imagine herself living in a place like this, if circumstances were different. If Fred had stayed and they'd had another child or two. There's a draw to the island paradox of living with both isolation and intimate community. She understands the pull. She pictures a wooden A-frame house—little kitchen and a lofted bedroom snug under the peak. A deck that she could stand on in the morning with a coffee mug between her hands and watch the mist lift like veils of gauze from the treetops. She imagines Willie on the beach with a bucketful of beach stones and clamshells and little cloudy bits of brown and blue and green sea glass.

Her own childhood was spent on a beach, a lakeside beach in the middle of the country. The trees were deciduous, and the water was fresh. It smelled like peat in the autumn and like grass in the spring. She had an old tire swing tied to the wide arm of an oak, and from the high point of its arc, she could let go of the rope and free her body from Earth for a brief, glorious moment. From there, she could fly out over the narrow last strip of shoreline and fall into the cold break of the lake's water. She has a clear memory—clearer than almost all her memories of childhood, in fact—of the way that plunge felt, the shock and thrill of it. The sink and rise. She liked to open her eyes underwater and look up at the sky on the other side of the surface—like looking through a warped piece of glass at a world far away. Below water, the world was sepia colored, yellowed as tea. Her body in it was as brown as iodine, and when she moved, a million tiny bubbles erupted from her skin and trilled toward the surface. She was a penny dropped into a giant glass of champagne. And then the pop—the surge of one powerful kick and she could shoot herself back up into the air, gasping, laughing. Her mother often called time from the shore, as if the whole thing had been a contest: *One minute, six seconds.* Or else she chastised: *Too long, Bernie. You had me worried I was going to have to come in after you!*

That was all a long time ago now. Another life, as people say of whatever life they lived before the war. There is, for Bernadette and everyone she knows of her generation, the time before the war, the war itself, and the time after. Life once seen as a fluid and continuous linear unrolling became something else with the war's fissure—something exploded. Now she thinks each person is like one of those glass fishing-net buoys cut free from its net—a single body floating on a wide and unpredictable sea, and what one can count on is the lack of certainty in what lies ahead, the lack of a reliable direction. The people who refuse to submit to that truth, in her experience, are either inconsolable or intolerant. Fred could be in that latter group at times, his faith in academics a kind of religion for him. It gave him a binary to hold on to—a world divided into this or that, $X$ or $Y$, true or false, backward or forward. It offered the certainty, in other words, that he craved more than anything else. Instead of embracing the exploded view of a life, as Bernadette had, he'd run from it. He could not accommodate what didn't fit within the fence he'd erected around his intellectual sanctuary—Willie's birth and the mysteries and terrors of parenting an infant being just one example. What do you do when your love for another person outpaces reason? When the fear that is the flip side of that love is irrational at times, and overwhelming? When the boundaries set so carefully around your heart and time and trajectory dissolve? Parenthood is the swing and the drop, the plunge into a world inverted. Parenthood shatters a person, fragments her, splits and bursts her into something different—something bigger than she was before, but also something less controlled. This is not a devastation so much as a reconstruction, Bernadette thinks. If Fred were here to share it with her, she would say this to him. *Isn't it a marvel watching the way Willie is like you and like me, and yet also only herself? How she's mirroring this bit of the world and that bit of the world and yet is also something no one on earth has ever seen before? Doesn't she just take your breath away?* But he's missing it. All of it, and even if he were present in their lives, he isn't the sort of man who can easily change.

She's thinking of this and not—as she should be, she reminds herself—of the case and the day's work ahead when the tug's beefy flank bumps up against the wooden dock at Adela and jostles her back into herself again. The captain idles the engine, jumping from deck to dock like a much younger man. She watches him tie the boat off with a rope he loops in a quick knot around a cleat. Stepping back into the cabin, she speaks Willie's name, and both Willie and the old woman look up as if they've been submerged in the same dream. There's a new book on the woman's lap now—*The Lion, the Witch and the Wardrobe*.

"Mama," Willie says, her face pinked with heat and delight. "This book is delicious."

THEY WALK INTO THE VILLAGE WITH THE BOOK WOMAN, whose name, Bernadette learns, is Signe Aalund. Bernadette tows the book trolley, which is no easy task on the muddy, unpaved road. Several times they all have to pause while she bends to dig its narrow tires from the mud-sand muck of the wet roadway. At her side, Signe and Willie walk like old companions, both of them talking away about the chapter they've read in the Lewis book, about the children who are sent away from their war-threatened home and taken in by a country relative. Bernadette listens without interrupting their conversation. She hasn't talked to Willie about the war at all, really, other than to say that she lived across the world before Willie was born, that she worked with children who were sick and needed help. That sometimes she felt scared. This has seemed like enough for a child as young as Willie. Why stitch into her imagination so early the reality of violence, the reality of how people harm one another? But to her surprise, Willie sounds entirely fascinated by the idea of children surviving without the protection of parents or home. Children sent out on their own to survive the wilds of the world's shadows. Willie asks Signe question after question, and Signe answers in plain, uncomplicated truths: Yes, Signe says, there was a real war. What is a war? Well, it means a fight between countries. Yes, people were hurt, and some died. Signe's own son died, she says—her only son. Bernadette feels her breath catch in her throat, but the older woman simply keeps walking, nodding patiently at Willie's questions. "He wasn't a little boy," Signe says. "He was a grown man. He was a soldier. He died on an island that I haven't seen, but he wrote me letters about it before he died, and he said it looked a lot like this island, which gives me comfort. He wasn't home, but maybe he felt more at home than he might have some-where else."

As Bernadette watches the two figures a few steps ahead of her, Willie slips her hand into Signe's, says nothing more. Their feet fall into unison.

When they reach the village at the top of the long, sandy hill, Bernadette says, "Hand Mrs. Aalund back her book. We can look for a copy in our library, at home, Wills."

"But I want to read," Willie says.

"Exactly. We'll find it, and I'll read it to you so you'll know what happens to the children."

"But I want to read, Mama." Willie's voice has the thin quality that means tears.

"Wilhelmina, that book is our friend's book." Bernadette would like to avoid a fit today, here. She'd like to make use of the few hours they have on the island and not stand in the street engaged in a struggle with her daughter for the whole village to witness.

"Oh, let her keep it," Signe says. She pats Willie's hand between her own two, releases it. "Keep the book for now," she says, this time directly to Willie. "But it's a library book, so this is a loan. Just put it in the mail when you've finished and send it back to me. Here—" she bends and tears the edge from one of the bags in her trolley, pulls a pencil out from her coat pocket, and in a moment hands Willie a curled-up bit of paper. "You have my address now, and you can just send that book my way when you're through with it. No harm done."

Willie's face is a sunbreak. She squeezes the book to her chest.

"Thank you," Bernadette says. "That's kind of you."

"Not really. As I said, it's not my book. It's no one's book. That's the reason we have a library here—to share books none of us have on our own shelves." She nods. "Now, the help I can give you is about a block away. You want to see the library too, yes? Your daughter tells me you've come to our island for information."

Bernadette passes Willie a look. She never mentioned the purpose of the trip at home, but, of course, children are always more attuned to what's happening than adults give them credit for, and Willie is perceptive. She sighs. "I have come for information," she says. Why shroud it at this point? Maybe Willie has just inadvertently sped up the day's work.

"You're a history teacher? Your daughter says you teach."

"Just how much of my life story did you two cover?" Bernadette teases Willie, and the girl shrugs.

Bernadette offers only the most basic details of her interest in the island: she's looking for more information on a family named Marley that would have been on Elita before the village there was closed to residents.

"This is your family?" Signe asks.

"Not mine, but I have reason to be invested in finding them."

"Your husband's then?"

"Not my husband's."

As they walk, the trolley trips alongside Bernadette's heels, bumping hard now and then over the uneven gaps between squares of sidewalk. On either side of the village's main street are the white shops she could see from the boat, their signs marking them as a grocer, a Chinese restaurant, a bakery, a VFW hall, and at the end of the long block, the library. It, like the other buildings, is wood sided, painted white, with wide concrete steps leading up to the double-front doors. A ceramic planter is leggy with rosemary, and on the doors hang two evergreen wreaths, each wound in red ribbon. It'll be the holidays soon, Bernadette recalls, so whatever she needs, she must gather today before the whole world slows down for a month.

"Look," she says to Signe. "I'll be honest with you. I'm here on behalf of someone else. A young woman I'm working with." She pauses. "A student. She can't locate her family herself, and so I'm helping. It's important that I find whatever I can for her."

"That's good of you," Signe says, "helping someone not even kin." She stares at Bernadette for a long minute, all the wrinkles of her face deepening with the pursing of her mouth and furrowing of her brow. An assessment is being made, Bernadette recognizes. She seems to pass, though, because Signe says, "I'll introduce you to Louise, and she can get you whatever documents are available." She tugs at the trolley. "You can lug that up and inside for me." She turns to Willie then. "Come," she says. "We'll open the doors for your mother."

It takes several minutes to heave the trolley up the front steps. Under her coat, a stipple of sweat breaks out on Bernadette's chest and back, and when she reaches the doors, she stops to unbutton the neck of her blouse and open her coat to the cold air for a moment. Inside, the library smells as old buildings often do—like must and wood varnish and stale air. The place is both more and less than the word *library* conveys. It's part town hall, part city records, part post office, part book exchange. There are high windows along the roofline, and the late morning light spilling through them is white and glittering with dust motes. Just as she's hoped, the front hallway is lined with village photographs. She pauses to take in each one: a town picnic; a city council portrait from 1922; a school photo from 1932, all of the children sitting straight backed in their rows of desks while a slim young woman—the teacher—stands with a stiff expression at the back of the room. Here's one of the main street she's just walked, though in the photo it is banked in at least three feet of snow. Here's one of the boat dock, which she knows is on the other side of the island, several work boats and sailboats tied to its cleats. At the end of the hallway, she spots a photo of what appears to be a hospital ward— white metal beds in a row, white sheets folded smooth and tight around the mattresses, a man and a woman in the white gowns of staff standing at the foreground of the image.

"Where is this?" Bernadette asks.

Signe comes close, cranes in. "The grange was converted, briefly, into a ward. During the flu year. End of the first war." She taps the photo with a finger. "That's Dr. Willis Newton and Miss Haven Wright. She was our midwife for years. Delivered my own boy, in fact, and the two others after him who, bless their little souls, didn't survive long in this world." A cloud shadows Signe's face before she continues. "Haven passed last year. Which is a shame for you. She might have been your best bet. She delivered everybody's babies for, what, fifty-odd years out here. Adela and Elita babies, both. If someone was delivering, Haven was there."

"Did she go to Elita for deliveries, or Elita women boated over to her?"

"Oh, depended. If there was time, a mother might get her husband or her father to ferry her from there to here. Haven kept a room in her house for deliveries. Mostly Elita women who used it. If you could stay in your own bed, why wouldn't you? So, most Adela deliveries, she'd just come to you. Mine were all delivered at home."

"Was I born there, Mama?" Willie asks. She has been sitting on a cushioned seat, the book open over her lap, flipping through the pages to find the illustrations.

"You were born in a hospital."

"Was I sick?"

"Hospitals aren't only for sick people."

"That's a topic of debate, I'd argue." Signe chuffs a sound of resentment. "I don't intend to be taken to one for any reason but sickness. And not even then, if I can still say to say. Better to be free than trapped."

"I was a nurse," Bernadette says. "I don't have any fear of hospitals." She steps away from the photo, making note of the name—Haven Wright. Not a name easily forgotten.

"In the war? You served where then?"

"Yes. In the war," Bernadette says. "Did Haven have children of her own?"

"She was an import to the island. Came out here turn of the century from somewhere out east with a husband who died before their first winter was through. No babies to the marriage either. Haven could've left, but she kept the house and the garden, and let the farm to renters. When she died last spring, they took it over. Mayer's the name. The son, he lives there now, in her house. You could ask Louise for more information." Signe looks at her wristwatch. "I have lunch to be making. My husband will think I fell off the ferry."

"Thank you for all your help," Bernadette says. "And for the book." She looks to Willie, nods.

"I like it," Willie says.

"Of course you do!" Signe tells her. "You write me a letter to put with the parcel when you send it back. I want to know your review after you finish reading."

They part ways at the little front desk. Louise, the volunteer librarian, is younger than Signe, but not by much. She offers to let Willie sit with her while Bernadette searches the catalog—all of it typed on index cards and kept in homemade wooden boxes—and so another hour is spent, Bernadette at the single reading table, old island record books spread before her, while Willie stays at the desk with a cup of hot chocolate that Louise has procured along with a plate of cheese sandwiches from some back kitchen. There's usually no eating in the library, she hears Louise explain to Willie, but today can be the one exception.

It is touching how these women have taken Willie in—and, Bernadette supposes, her too, by extension. This is why people come to the islands and stay, this reliability of their neighbors, this sense of built-in intimacy. It's charming. Or maybe—Bernadette reconsiders—it's confusing. How is it that Willie—a stranger's child—can step onto the Adela ferry and be immediately swept into several embraces, and yet Atalanta lived for years unattended, abandoned, untouched by the care of any person? The two islands are not that separate. It seems impossible, if the girl was born on the islands, that no one on Adela knows who she is, knows who her mother is—or was. Knows that the child was not carried across the water with the rest of the town's population when they left. There is too much interconnection in this community, too much long history never forgotten. What was it Signe had said of Haven Wright? *She was an import.* A woman who'd moved to Adela at the turn of the century still considered an import by local account even now, in 1951. The place has memory.

The first book Bernadette opens is a record of school attendance at Adela's only schoolhouse. She can track that in the year 1935 the school's registration jumped by ten students. This correlates with what she already knows about the transition period prior to Elita's closure—the government gave the town notice, and they shut the place down bit by bit rather than whole cloth, all at once. The post office on Elita shut in April of '35. The school closed in June. The following September, all Elita children of school age were ferried across the water to Adela and absorbed into the school system here. She runs her finger down the list of names and lines them up against the 1934 list, writes the names that only appear in '35, though there is no Marley. The next book is a record of births and deaths, and though she scans a full decade, from 1927 to 1937, she spots no Marley there either. Also, no Marley listed in the St. Eulalia parish records of tithes, baptisms, confirmations, marriages, and burials for those same years. Marley itself might be a wrong road. But it's all she has to go on at this point.

She closes the books, packs her things. She thanks Louise for Willie's hot chocolate and sandwiches, and asks—as if it's nothing but an afterthought—a question about the name: "Do you know of a family called Marley here on Adela? Or maybe at one point in the past on Elita?"

The woman furrows her brow. "Marley isn't ringing any bells. You could look at the graveyard, though. Or ask at the prison. They have Elita's records."

No one at the prison is going to turn records over to her, a civilian, of course, though she could ask Norquist about it. He's likely already requested whatever documentation is available. Bernadette makes a mental note to talk to him about it. "How do I find the graveyard?" she asks instead, and Louise writes out the directions for her on a little hand-drawn map of the island, which Bernadette thanks her for and tucks away.

When she and Willie leave the library, it's past noon. The sky is as thick as custard, and the line on the horizon that she knows to be the mainland is a heavy, blue smudge between that sky and the chop and curl of the water. A brisk wind has picked up. Past the edge of town, they cut west, as the map leads them, down a gravel-and-mud street of houses, most of them narrow clapboards on narrow lots. The school is at the end of this road. It's housed in the same building it has always occupied on the island—a wide, white two-story wood structure with a yard stripped to dirt by children's feet and by winter. There's a playground on the far edge of the schoolyard, and Willie begs to play in it, but Bernadette sweeps her up and carries her on a hip the last half-mile to the graveyard instead, saying, "We can't play there, sweet. It's for the schoolchildren only. And you don't go to school until next year." Willie fusses, rubs her face into Bernadette's neck—hard, at first, but then gentler. She's tired. The day has been too much already, and they aren't done. She wants to apologize to her daughter; she shouldn't have brought her out on this research trip, shouldn't expect so much of a girl only four years old. But by the time they reach the graveyard, Willie has a second wind, wrestles herself free of Bernadette's hold, and dashes away between the stones. Maybe it's disrespectful of the dead to let the child run around like this, but they're alone. And, anyway, Bernadette's own respect for the dead isn't pious or reverent enough to warrant slowing Willie down. The dead are dead, she'd say to anyone who might ask. It's another lesson of the war she can't shake off now.

While Willie gallops the graveyard's perimeter, Bernadette moves among the gravestones, bending to read their names and dates. She's brought a crayon and paper for grave rubbing if she should find anything useful, but she picks her way through the whole cemetery without spotting a Marley. Overhead, the sky shifts, darkens. It's midafternoon when she looks at her watch. A raindrop hits the watch face, then her own face. "Willie!" she calls. She turns a tight circle in place, squinting out across the span of the graveyard. Where is Willie?

There have been several moments like this one in Bernadette's life. Moments of terror. Moments that might be a precipice or a bog—one step and the whole of her will go under. But before that drop and paralysis, there is an inner unfurling, a terrible flowering of all her worst fears, every bristling, horrible possibility. Is this the moment in which she becomes not just a mother, but the mother of a missing child? Not just a mother, but the mother of a drowned child? Not a mother, but a woman who lost everything.

Bernadette stands in the center of the graveyard and yells Willie's name again. Nothing. Then she runs.

She is picturing Willie in the dark mouth of the woods at the western edge of the cemetery. She is picturing Willie in the foam mouth of the water at the bottom of the steep hill that falls away from those woods and ends at the beach. She runs. She runs. She runs. "Willie!" she calls. "Willie!"

But then the response: "Mama?" And like that, Willie is a body again, a girl, not a ghost. Willie is a figure against a thicket of snowberry bushes. She's been plucking the white bubbles from the twigs and stomping them flat on the ground, a mash at her feet. Her book is still clutched to her chest. "Mama?" the child says. She looks pleased at first, then bewildered.

"What are you doing?" Bernadette says, furious.

"Stomp berries!" Willie says and slams her foot down. The white berries pop like little gunpowder capsules.

Bernadette sweeps Willie into her arms, squeezes. Willie's fat cheek is freezing cold against the heat of Bernadette's. Her breath is sweet with the hot chocolate from the library. Her fingers on Bernadette's face are sticky.

She's crying now—not because she's hurt, but because the tone of Bernadette's voice has terrified her. "Mama," she says, a plea.

"You scared me."

"No, you scared me." Willie pats her face.

That awful net of Bernadette's potential future selves reels back into place in the dark closet of her heart. *God*, she thinks. Today is not the day she loses her girl. It doesn't matter that she's found nothing useful here. They will both board the tug home, crawl into their bed tonight, and wake up together in the morning, all just as it should be.

What is the language for this quick bloom and wither? This anticipation of a fear made real in the mind without evidence, without logic? It is the body surviving. Imagination twined to evolution. Bernadette thinks of the bear-mother who draws her cubs into the heat of the den to keep them alive through the winter. It would take a strong will or an absence of instinct—one or the other—to fight the innate maternal terror of the lost child, to resist the innate compulsion to search until the child was found.

She rolls this thought through her mind as she and Willie walk back to town, hands clasped now. The school is emptying, children whooping and shouting to one another across the yard, running with schoolbags banging against their backs down the muddy road toward home. How could a parent stand to let any one of them go missing and unfound? It isn't possible. She knows this for sure now: Atalanta was left, not lost. Possibly left barely old enough to regulate her own body temperature. Barely old enough to feed herself even in a house stocked with food. Certainly not old enough to protect herself from the weather, from the water, from predators, animal or human. No mother would leave her behind if abandonment—if the child's death—wasn't the intention. The truth of this is a stone sinking through Bernadette, a heavy frustration weighing on her chest. Has she really believed, in some hidden corner of her mind, that the child was lost? That this quest she's on is to find a bereaved mother and not a parent guilty of attempted murder? She's already seen the worst the world does to children; she has no excuse for whatever splinter of naivete has been holding on to that hope. She stops and picks Willie up again, hugs her close, feels the rise and fall of Willie's chest through the layers and layers of their sweaters and coats and scarves. *You and me*, she thinks. *You and me.*

THE TUG ARRIVES BACK AT THE DOCK AT FOUR THIRTY. This time, Bernadette and Willie are the only passengers. On board, just as this morning, the cabin is a warm box of light. From inside, Bernadette and Willie watch the water roil in a black churn around them as the engine starts and the captain maneuvers away from the dock. Bernadette holds Willie on her lap as the boat cuts through the waves. She is aware of the waste of the day—a whole damn day. But also, what is this moment with her living, breathing daughter? Not a waste. Willie smells like bread rising, like chocolate icing. She rests her head on Bernadette's chest, tired. Bernadette kisses her crown, says, "Stay awake. We want to read your book when we get home, don't we?" But it's too late, the girl is sleeping.

They cross water that might be oil, it is so thick with darkness. Light slides on its surface and the far shore seems at first a melt of colors bleeding together into slick pools, but as they draw near, the shapes of land and building divide, then the dock at Steilacoom becomes distinct. Finally, the tug shudders and jolts, pulling to a stop. Willie wakes and is fussy. Bernadette gathers their things. "Thank you," she says to the captain.

"You know, I figured someone would come looking for more about that girl. Eventually, I thought, you'd show up," he says.

It takes her a moment to understand what's happening, but then all the nerves beneath the skin at the nape of her neck tingle. "The girl at Elita? Are people talking about that?"

"I have a buddy at Elita was questioned about it, so I know. I guessed you were here for that when I saw you this morning."

"Your friend is Starkey or Lind?" she asks.

"Starkey. We hunt sometimes. He has a dog, Rand. Good little bitch."

"Hunting at Elita?" She's thinking of the rope found with the girl. Thinking of the stone thrown, the story about the girl running out of the woods. Hunting, of course. All hunted creatures run.

The captain shakes his head. "No. No hunting allowed out there."

She waits, but he doesn't offer more. At her knee, Willie begins to twist away, so Bernadette picks her up, shifts her weight foot to foot in a rocking motion. "Give me one minute, baby," she says. "One more minute." She doesn't have time to dig around for more details about hunting on Elita—that will have to wait. Willie is about to burst into a wail, and then the conversation will be entirely finished, and she will have lost it—this scrap, which is all she has. She says, "Well, you're right about my trip today. I came looking for a family named Marley, who would have lived on Adela or Elita, before the closure." She keeps her attention on the captain's face as she says the name—*Marley*—and something does move beneath his expression, but it's not fear or aggression. It's like watching a reflected cloud passing on the surface of water to see one muted thought drift away and another appear behind his eyes. She doesn't know what to make of that, exactly.

"No family named Marley's ever been on either island," he says, "not as long as I been here, and I been here my whole life."

Bernadette keeps up the rocking. At her shoulder, she can feel Willie growing sleepy again, the weight of her body somehow heavier in her fatigue. "That's what I've been finding," she says. "Nothing."

Now his face becomes still and calm; whatever weather was passing through his mind a moment before is gone. A decision's been made, maybe. Or a worry has lifted. Or maybe he scanned his memory and simply found nothing to hold on to at all. But then he says, "There was a Marlowe. On Adela. She had a boyfriend, worked at Elita. He left in '37, '38—somewhere in there—and didn't come back."

She says, "Was that her Christian name or her surname? Marlowe?"

"Oh, that was years ago. I wouldn't remember." He nods—done.

On her shoulder, Willie sighs, and Bernadette turns, ready to walk away, but another question materializes, and she calls back up to the captain where he stands on the tug's deck. "Is Starkey from Adela? Is that how you know him?"

"Starkey's folks are out at the end of Brier Road, same place they've had for years. You'll excuse me now," he says.

The engine revs, and in a moment the tug is nothing but links of light on the black surface of the water, breaking and assembling, breaking and assembling as the waves of its wake lap and dissolve.

*The effort of the camouflage*, Bernadette thinks. Starkey's and Lind's voices from the recorded interview come back to her. Neither one said anything about being from Adela, about knowing the girl. But Starkey would have, wouldn't he? He would have known her mother if she was an Adela girl. That's likely. Or more than likely, even, given the size of the place. And what about the hunting? Why is it nagging her? She lets her mind jostle the bits of that interview she's pinned to the wall of her memory, and then it comes to her: Norquist asked about poaching on Elita, and Starkey dismissed it. *Those little black tails? Delicate little things*, he'd said, hadn't he? Something like that. The word *delicate* forms in a rill of foam on the skim of Bernadette's mind. Why had he said that word? What an unusual word for a man like Starkey to use. Or maybe not. Maybe she has him all wrong. She also remembers thinking his voice on the tape was gentle. Thinking the tenor had a soap-soft rub coming through the tape to her where she sat listening in the AV room. *Delicate*, he'd said about the animals on the island, but then later—about the girl—he'd said *like a mad dog*. Atalanta wasn't delicate. Atalanta was a mad dog, charging the men that September afternoon, according to their claim. By their account, she was all snarl and threat. *All seventy-five pounds of her*, Bernadette thinks.

It's dark on the dock now, she realizes suddenly. It's dark and cold, and she is standing alone among the empty boats with her sleeping child weighing her down. The tug has entirely vanished into the darkness, and sea fog is rolling in across the water's surface in slow, lengthening fibers of mist. There's the lap and drip of the place—everything oily looking in the slur of the dock lights. There's the slap and clink of rigging from the nearby work boats—a lonely, vacant kind of sound.

"Wills," she says. "Wake up." She sets Willie to standing, and for a second, the child's legs are unsteady, wobbling under her weight. "Come on, it's cold and damp out here. Pull your muffler up. We shouldn't be standing here in the dark by ourselves now," she says, but Willie is slow, fussy. She drags behind, lolling at the end of Bernadette's handhold, clutching her book and complaining about her cold nose.

"Come," Bernadette says. "You're fine. Look, you're fine. Pick up your feet, darling."

"Mama," Willie says, finally fully awake again.

"What? Will you walk, please? I can listen to your question if you can walk with me."

Willie fusses, drags her feet. "In my book, a girl finds a lamp. In the picture, a forest with a lamp in it is there. Is that a true thing?"

"What do you mean by 'true thing'?"

"True," Willie repeats, as if the repetition alone is clarity.

"True as in a place you could really go and see in the world, or true as in really in the book?"

Willie sighs. "True," she says again.

It's not a far walk to the narrow shelter of the bus stop. A lamp outside the shelter casts a green-gold haze through the shelter's three glass sides and roof. Bernadette realizes the captain said he knew what she'd come for from the start, but he'd made her wait all day for it. Because he knew and she didn't. Because she was there on Adela to ask questions, and because she's—the word comes to her like a burst of salt on her tongue—an intercessor. But *intercessor* isn't the word she wants. It has a religious connotation, doesn't it? As if her cause is spiritual. As if she's acting on behalf of a larger belief and not just curiosity and an academic project. She means something else, she thinks, though the word she wants doesn't present itself.

"Like that lamp," Willie goes on, pointing to the one casting the queasy glaze on everything.

Bernadette would like to let this go, but she says, "What?"

"In the book. The forest lamp. It's like that."

"Well, so, that answers your question, then, about the story's lamp being true. That's what lamps truly do look like. They look the same, so they're both true. What you see is what's true."

Willie scowls. "No. You're wrong."

"Wilhelmina—" Bernadette starts, but the bus arrives in a flare of white lights and hissing brakes, and they climb on, her frustration fizzling with the change in her comfort as they enter the humidity of the bus's interior. They need to eat, she thinks, both of them. She needs to take off her shoes and her brassiere, and Willie needs a bath, and this day needs to end.

"Lap," Willie says, and Bernadette scoops her into her arms. "Read now," the girl says. "Please, Mama."

So Bernadette opens the book and starts reading, looking for the lamp.

7

IT'S SNOWING THE NEXT MORNING WHEN SHE LEAVES Willie with Mrs. Iversen and takes first one bus and then another through two cities to Norquist's office at the Sheriff's Department. Outside the fogged bus windows, the snow falls at first in a scatter of small, icy flakes, but by the time she's walking the two blocks from the bus stop to the County Building, the flakes have thickened, fattened. They hold together for an instant when Bernadette opens her palm to the sky, fragile bristles of ice on her skin, before melting into a droplet. It makes her grin to herself. She hasn't seen snow since leaving Chicago and is surprised at this delight. She imagines Willie must be thrilling at home, begging Mrs. Iversen to take her out to play. Maybe it will still be snowing when she gets back and they can go out together, she and Willie, in their rubber boots and mittens, and make a snowman.

The thought calls up the last winter she spent in the Midwest, when she was still pregnant with Willie, and it snowed from October to April. She remembers those months of life as crusted over in an armor of dirty white. The temperature might rise a little above freezing for an afternoon, only to fall again by dusk, and so the snow that fell never melted, but simply hardened on top of the existing accumulation. There were knee-high drifts at the curb of every street, clumps calcifying on the lawn of the quadrangle. Snow rimmed the sills of the apartment windows. It clung in caps on top of street signs and mailboxes and the seats of park benches. Well into the spring, crystallized rings of old snow circled the base of each scrawny little city tree in the park, and patches of it went grainy against the sand at the lakefront.

It felt oppressive to her. She could not walk easily without slipping, as heavily pregnant as she was, and so she moved slowly, afraid of her body and of the ground beneath her. She gave up her daily outdoor walks in favor of taking the bus to campus and walking the warmed hallways of the university, where she was physically safe, if entirely out of place. The male students and professors gave her a wide berth when they spilled out of the classrooms on the hour and spotted her there, maneuvering her swollen body down the corridors. She was obscene to them, she realized. She was confusing. She'd known some of them before her pregnancy— young scholars who worked beside her husband or were his mentees. One or two of them had rubbed up against her at a party when he'd had too much to drink. Another handful had openly appraised her from across seminar tables or lecture halls. They recognized her still, she was sure. And what did they think of this change in her form? As a woman, she was already primarily animal to such men, and the belly completed the transformation from human to beast. But did it make her more or less desirable? She sometimes wondered. Desire and fear are so close, really, in the human heart: the two blades of the same scissors.

In a way, she found the men's discomfort funny. There was power in being the object of their complicated anxieties. What did they think?

That she would give birth right there in front of them? That she might open her blouse and begin, like Hera, spurting milk from her breasts? *Don't worry, boys,* she wanted to say to them. *This is how galaxies are made.* But none of them would so much as make eye contact with her. She was swollen. A bear, lumbering, smelling of musk and fur. A whale on the waxed linoleum, swimming upstream. The boys always sidestepped her though, averted their gazes, and then, as the new hour arrived, they disappeared again into classrooms whose doors shut on her before the good conversations began inside, and she found herself alone in the hallway, in the silence again.

Now, she swings open the glass doors to the County Building and climbs the stairs to Norquist's office without anyone's second look following her. She's worn her one good black suit beneath her winter coat and pulled back her brown hair in a chignon. She's not the sort of woman whose face draws attention, but she's not plain either. If she makes a little effort, she knows, she's nearly pretty. And today she's made an effort—a bit of lipstick, some faint rouge. Tasteful, professional. At her neck, she's tied her only silk scarf in an attempt at replicating Nora Reach's elegant ivory knot, though unfortunately her own scarf is a sallow yellow. It isn't quite right, but it's the closest facsimile she can manage, and she's glad she went with this rather than her usual teaching uniform of worn blazer and wool skirt. It is allowing her to nearly blend in with the people she passes—clerks in their own dark suits and ties, secretaries in pencil skirts and patent-leather heels, uniformed officers whose faces all seem the same under the brims of their matching hats. The building has the look of official business. Black marble floors, strung with threads of white like cracks in old ice. Walls the color of paste. Each office door is made of imposing dark wood and windowed in bubbled privacy glass. As she passes, she reads the titles stamped on the brass plaques at each doorframe—COUNTY ASSESSOR and COUNTY CLERK, BUILDING INSPECTOR and CENTRAL PERMITTING ADMINISTRATOR. Bernadette climbs a second flight of stairs, and there is Norquist's name on his own brass marker, last door at the end of a long hallway.

She hasn't made an appointment, but when she steps in he's there behind his desk, a man who exactly fits the voice she recalls from the tape: slim and dark-haired, a few years her senior, probably forty. He looks up, then frowns and stands. This is manners, not recognition, she realizes, which is good. She's disrupted the power balance in the room, at least for a moment, and it gives her a chance to slip in without being immediately dismissed. "I'm Professor Bernadette Baston," she says, extending her hand across his desk.

His expression breaks. "You've been to Adela, I hear." He sits and gestures at the chair Bernadette has already slung her coat over.

This is a surprise, but she smiles. "My friend the tugboat captain called you?"

"Your friend? No, but if you're asking then I'm guessing he probably will soon. It was Signe Aalund."

Bernadette draws in a breath against the sting of this. She long ago learned how to lock down the armor in these moments when she'd rather crumble. "That's unexpected news, but Mrs. Aalund is entirely within her rights to notify authorities if she feels some violation has been committed, though I can't image what that violation could be, Detective." God, she hears it in her voice despite herself: that bone-brittle formality.

When she looks at Norquist, his face has softened, and she knows he's spotted the language as her tell—she's wounded. He shrugs. "There are rarely real allies in small communities. You probably already know that, but it's easy to forget."

"I haven't forgotten." She pauses. "I won't forget again."

"Again? I'm not sure why you were there in the first place." Norquist leans forward. "It should be unnecessary for me to have to remind you of this, but you have provisional permission to participate in this case, and only as a—what did Nora Reach call you?—a language acquisition consultant. She persuaded me to let you on, but at this point I don't think she'd feel any personal affront if I told her your permission had been revoked."

Bernadette sits back in her chair. She'd wondered if Nora had reported back to him after their lunch, and now she knows. "I'm not a language specialist, Detective Norquist. Not in the sense Mrs. Reach may have conveyed to you. I've made this clear to Mrs. Reach and to Dr. Brodaccio, who both seem to have different understandings of what I do. I am a professor. My interest in Atalanta is scholarly. I want to work with her to understand the effects of early exposure to language on childhood language development, or, in her case, the absence of exposure. I do not teach children to speak, but if in our time together Atalanta also grows in her own language development, that will be an interesting outcome, and I will document it. It is not, however, my primary objective here."

Flare of heat, rush of adrenaline. Under her blouse, Bernadette is sweating. Her heart trips at her collarbone. She sits forward in her chair, just as Norquist has done—a gesture she remembers reading somewhere conveys authority—and for a moment, Norquist stares. This, of course, is what he does. Bernadette reminds herself that his professional specialty is the interview bent toward intimidation. She's heard him at it on the tape and believed she was prepared by that tape to be his subject today, though in person his stare is even more unraveling than she anticipated. She feels less that he's trying to intimidate her into compliance than that he is reading her, and the longer he holds his eyes on her face, the more certain she is that he's calculating her integrity, untying the strings of the mask she put on before stepping inside this building today.

The best strategy is to do the unmasking herself. Again, she repositions herself in her seat, unknots the scarf at her neck, and lays it across her lap. "Look, I'll be transparent with you," she says. "I've just told you my reasons for my interest in this case, which—by the way—Nora Reach brought to me. I did not come looking to insinuate myself into Atalanta's life or anyone's work with her. It was your people who sought me out, and I have only ever been honest about my skills and training, and also about what I am unprepared to take on. If it doesn't suit you to give me access to this case, that's your prerogative, though I hope you'll allow me to continue. There's value in this work that is larger than one child's experience. There's a great deal to be learned through Atalanta's case about language acquisition in all children. Or that's my belief, anyhow. It's why I'm here, Detective. It's the only reason I'm here. And I'm proving myself honest about that objective again today simply by coming here to offer you what I learned during my visit to Adela—which, I'll note, is an entirely voluntary act on my part, and one from which I stand to benefit nothing."

She sits back. She hadn't realized while speaking that she'd moved so far forward that her elbows were resting on his desk. Now she folds her hands in her lap just as her mother taught her to do when she got overexcited as a child.

A pause, and then Norquist nods. "Okay," he says. "I'm listening."

She lays out the details of her conversation with the tugboat captain, careful only to offer statements and not ask questions, though she has them ready when Norquist sighs and closes his eyes.

"Detective, let me just ask you: You've read up, I'm sure, on the midwife who served the islands for years? Haven Wright?"

"I haven't."

"You have the birth records for the years Dr. Brodaccio suspects could be Atalanta's birth years?"

"I do. But, as you likely know, there's no clarity in those records."

"That's where the midwife comes in. She's deceased, according to locals, but Signe Aalund seemed to have plenty of information on the midwifery practice on the islands between 1905 and 1948, if you're interested." She smiles. "And, obviously, you've been in touch with Signe, so you'll know how to reach her if you want to."

He opens his eyes. This time the stare is a reassessment, Bernadette notes, and one in her favor. "Let me be honest with you now, Professor Baston. Mrs. Aalund is not my biggest fan."

"Oh really? She was perfectly kind to me yesterday, which is why I was caught off guard when you said she'd called to complain about me."

Norquist shrugs. "I didn't say she complained. I said she called. The rest was your own misinterpretation."

"I don't understand."

"She called to compliment the Sheriff's Department for finally—I think her words were—taking our heads out of our asses and hiring a female detective."

Bernadette laughs before she can stop herself.

"Did you impersonate an officer of the law, Professor Baston?"

"I . . ." she stumbles. "Detective, I can absolutely assure you that I was very clear about my reasons for being on the island, and I did not at any point identify myself as anything other than a scholar."

"Right. I got that from Signe. She said you told her you—hold on." He pauses, shuffles through a folder on his desk and holds up a piece of paper on which she can see his scrawled notes. "She said you told her you are a teacher and that you were there researching on behalf of a student."

He lifts his eyes to hers. "And also that your daughter told her the student was a girl raised by a bear."

Again, the heat at her chest and face, the rush of her nerve plummeting through her. "I did say Atalanta was a student. That was not entirely truthful, but I think you can agree that it was also not entirely a lie. And certainly not a legal offense."

"That's not the point of interest here, Professor. You have a child who you took to Adela to interview locals about this case on which you have no authority?" He sets the paper back into the stack, closes the file.

"I'll just say again that I never misrepresented myself, Detective. If there were holes in what I did say that Mrs. Aalund herself filled—perhaps piecing together bits of what she's heard in the news, which we both know every *Post* reader in the region has read, with little fragments of nonsense my daughter told her—well, I have nothing to account for there. I can't help Mrs. Aalund drawing her own conclusions, however incorrect they may be. She strikes me as a woman who doesn't turn down gossip, but it seems to me that knowing that about her gives you, Detective, a beneficial edge. That woman is an archive. If something happened on Adela or Elita, she knows and has squirreled it away in her mind. She is more than happy to share if you simply spend some time with her." Bernadette's face is fire now. She touches a cheek with the back of her hand. "And where I take my own child, so long as I am not endangering her, is—I believe—still my choice as her mother?"

Norquist nods again. She can't tell if she's overstepped and annoyed him, or if he's entertained by this stir on the case. It occurs to her that this, too, is a luxury of his sex and authority—this ability to remain unreadable, to sit in a conversation with a face that registers nothing. She would never get anywhere in her work with that kind of cold reserve. She requires both the armor and the will to strategically remove it, to show herself. A flat, stone-faced approach is a privilege she'll never have. It's only in flashing the angles of her cut that she gains any ground.

She sighs—audibly this time. "If you'd prefer I step back and keep my work strictly to the hours Dr. Brodaccio has granted me with Atalanta, I'll *obey* that restriction." She hates to use that word, but it is reliable traction with certain men, and she's banking on Norquist being one of them. She watches him slacken on the other side of the desk, something of the resistance dissolving from his face.

"I was actually going to ask you to do the opposite of stepping back, Professor. Signe dislikes me, as I've already said. And that boat captain? He served time between the wars for something—not a long sentence, but long enough that he has a fairly sizable chip on his shoulder about cops. You see what I'm saying. I could go on like this about the rest of the population out there. Why do you think folks choose island life? It's not for the company. They're not talkers, islanders, not usually. Old Norwegians and Swedes—stubborn people. Believe me, they can be exclusive. And a bunch of 'em on Adela are only there because they had to leave Elita in '37, and it was the government that forced them out. Who do they think I am, Professor Baston? I'm the government."

She's confused. Is he crediting her with having a way with the islanders? "I'm not sure what you're asking of me."

"You're getting information I'm not." He shrugs. "They like your kid, maybe." Slight twitch at the corner of his mouth—he's teasing her, she sees. It softens her a little. Maybe she's been too prickly, making assumptions. That armor getting in her way this time instead of protecting her.

When he opens the file again, he slides out another sheet and offers it to her. In his handwriting, there are two dates. "Come back and help me with interviews. Plan on being here the whole day each time. Interviews with witnesses can take a while, depending. And I might have myself called away at some point in each interview and let you have a go without me. Since they trust you. You're a teacher, right? You study people. So study them."

"*Them* who? Is that even legal?"

He lifts an eyebrow, taps the first date—December 28. "This one is Signe Aalund. I didn't know I wanted to talk to her until she talked to me, but now I need her in here. She doesn't know she's coming in yet, so if she contacts you, don't mention it."

"She won't contact me."

"Good."

Now he touches his finger to January 3. "The other date is Len Starkey. I'm bringing him back."

Bernadette frowns. "You're waiting that long?" The waiting will kill her, she thinks.

"Most of us break at the end of the year, Professor."

He stands. "I'll see you after the holiday. Read this before the interviews." Again, he shuffles through the stack on his desk and this time comes up with an envelope labeled LEN STARKEY (Copy). He passes it to her and shakes her hand. "And I shouldn't have to say this, but do not bring your child."

Outside again, Bernadette stuffs the envelope into her bag, buttons her coat, and reties the scarf at her neck—this time because she's cold. The snow is still falling—tiny, hard flakes that hit her face like the points of pins. She tucks her head low and moves into the wind, toward the bus stop. Her coat flaps out around her with each gust, and she must pull it close. Inside her shoes, her feet go numb with the cold, and she wishes she could have reasonably carried a bag big enough to hide a pair of wool socks, a pair of boots. She feels she is made of something soft, something unstable, something bound to crumble soon. Willie's monarchs flutter into her mind, and she thinks, *Yes, yes. A monarch.* Fragile, winged paradoxes. They withstand the battering of wind and miles of flight in migration, but they're made of nothing, really—legs like threads and wings of dust.

She shivers waiting for the bus—hard shivers that shake her whole body so that she must wrap her arms around herself to keep from visibly trembling. It's the adrenaline fade more than the cold making her shake, the slow drop of coming out of tension. Funny, but she hadn't realized just how bad it was talking to Norquist until now. She is good in a crisis and a mess afterward. Always. There's no way to skein the threads of fraying anxiety back into a tight ball once they've unwound in her, though, and so she simply lets the shaking rattle her under her coat until finally the bus appears—headlights, chains on the tires—clattering over the skim of new snow and bellowing a dieseled sigh right in front of her. The door opens. Heat in a gust. She steps up, pays, walks on her numb, dumb feet to the middle and sits.

*How?* she thinks. If this is her physical response to one conversation with Norquist, how will she pull off interviews with Signe and Starkey? This is all so different from standing in front of a classroom. The stakes are so high, and she's not trained for this at all. She's not a cop. Bernadette repeats that to herself: *I'm not a cop.* The more she thinks it, the more she feels her own fear shifting shape until it looks like something else entirely: anger. She is not a cop. She should simply have said no. She's not even actually employed on this case. They're not paying her for her time, for her questions, for her apparent ability to build a trust Norquist cannot. In her abdomen, the tremors have stopped. Now she's all fire, all indignation. She will need to convince Mrs. Iversen to take Willie for two full days, and over the holidays. And with what money will she pay for that? She has no idea. No idea. But this is Norquist's line, she sees. Decline this, and she's off the case entirely. And then what? Nothing. *Honestly*, she thinks, *nothing*. It's not as if there's a committee somewhere waiting for her work. No colleagues anticipating her findings. She's solo. If she had to guess, she'd say it's this that the islanders see in her: isolation. What was it she read about the monarchs in Willie's book? They migrate en masse. To avoid predators, and for the shared heat of their many bodies when the temperature drops. The collective nouns for them are *swarm, kaleidoscope*, and—her favorite—*rabble*. A *rabble* of butterflies. They are nothing without one another. This she also remembers now: their wings aren't actually made of dust but of scales. Little flashing plates of protein armor. But what goddamned good is the beautiful armor if the fight is waged by an army of one? She's not really Norquist's partner in this, whatever his file in her bag might suggest. She's a tool. She can't forget this. Her fear needs to calcify, to scale over as determination rather than shake her to rubble. She'll be welcome until she's not—that's a certainty, and so she has to make use of the time she's been given, or her research will never progress.

At the bus depot in Tacoma, she disembarks and stands in the cold again and waits for her transfer. Now the snow is falling fast and hard, rafts of it accumulating on the rims of the sidewalks and on the traffic islands. The second bus is overheated, crowded. A man who smells of too much cologne takes the seat next to her, and her head begins to throb beneath her brow. She's hasn't eaten since breakfast, and now it's midafternoon. The sky is the color of warm milk, a skin of fog sinking from cloud to treetop, where it freezes. She wants to be with Willie in their bed, blankets pulled up to their chins, safe and snuggled.

But then, finally, her street. The bus lets her out, and the day falls away behind her. All that weight she hadn't acknowledged she was carrying dislodges from her shoulder blades and slips off. There are a couple inches on the ground here. In the low, ivory light of these last hours of the winter day, the streetlamps have come on early and toss glitter over the snowy street and lawns. The trees are outlined in white, and the hedges all have pill-shaped caps. It's not far down the block that she spots two pairs of footprints in the snow, just filling in again—an adult and a child. *Willie*, she thinks, and she picks up her pace.

Her door is unlocked, all the lights on inside the apartment and the caramel smell of coffee hitting her in a draft of warm air as she steps in. Willie's on the couch, and beside her is Fred.

"Surprise," he says, standing, a sheepish look on his face. He closes a book—*The Lion, the Witch and the Wardrobe*. He's been reading it with Willie—the copy Signe lent her. Fred's been reading it. The bookmark falls from between the pages when he tosses it to the cushions.

Bernadette is dumbstruck for a second. "It *is* a surprise," she manages to say. She has the feeling of falling from the top of a swing's arc—breathless, as if everything inside her has been slammed into compression. "Where's Mrs. Iversen?"

"I sent her off. Told her I was your husband. She had to be convinced, but the photo of you in my wallet did it. She seemed shocked to find that I am among the living." He lifts an eyebrow but steps forward and hugs her. She resists before relaxing into him. His face is bristled and warm against her cold cheek. He smells the way he always smelled, and she hates that she remembers this about him, and that she notices it and wants to bury her face in his neck.

"I haven't said you were dead. I just haven't said you weren't dead."

"That's flattering." He laughs. "Take off this wet coat and get your feet to the radiator," he says. "You're freezing." He unbuttons her. Takes her bag from her shoulder and her coat from her arms. He brings her a cup of coffee from the kitchen. When she sips, she tastes milk and sugar. He remembers how she takes it. Why would he remember? What does it mean that he remembers? She needs to sit down.

*Is this what it feels like to dissociate?* she thinks. She's read about the sensation in textbooks but never lived it. She is a person split in two—a wood block axed straight down the middle. One-half of her is the skin—holding the warm mug of coffee, tasting the cream and the sugar. Her consciousness has slipped the skin horizon of her body, though, and is hovering above her, a breath, a vapor, a knowing that this cannot end well. She stretches her feet toward the radiator, takes the blanket Fred hands her from the couch, and wraps it around her legs without feeling anything.

"Mama," Willie says, a note of fear in her voice.

*Oh, Willie*, Bernadette thinks. She's forgotten to scoop up her daughter—to even acknowledge her daughter.

"Mama, you're sick?"

The question jolts the two halves of Bernadette together again, and she begins shivering once more. "No, baby," she says. "I'm just so cold. Come sit with me and warm me up, please. I want to hug you."

The look on Willie's face is unmistakably relief. "Are you angry?" Willie whispers when she's settled on Bernadette's lap. She smells of the winter air—tang of snow and funk of her child sweat under her sweater. Fred hasn't bathed her, hasn't changed her, for which Bernadette is glad. It occurs to her that he will likely want to be part of such things now, but no—*no!* she thinks. Is that what he wants? Is this a visit or a move? Resentment opens like a thistle blooming in her. His very presence is a violation of their intimacy—hers and Willie's. Not because he's Willie's father, but because he's a stranger to them both now. Because he left without a discussion about leaving, and he has returned without an invitation. No.

"Are you angry, Mama?" Willie asks again, on the verge of tears now.

"I'm cold, I said. Just cold."

Willie tucks her head into Bernadette's neck, blows warm breath against the crook there. "Mama," she whispers. Words like spines. "Is he my dad?" Willie kisses her cheek and her whole body relaxes in Bernadette's arms—finally safe to ask.

*Oh, my sweet girl.* The whole afternoon collapses into place in Bernadette's mind: Fred at the door, and Mrs. Iversen bewildered. Willie unable to confirm this stranger's identity. And why should she know him? She was an infant when he left. She has no memory of his face, his voice. *But what shame!* Bernadette thinks. What shame this day must have seeded in her girl. Even as young as she is, Willie knows that most children recognize their fathers. What must she have said when Mrs. Iversen turned to her with the question? What could she have said? *Yes, Bernadette imagines Willie saying. Yes, that's him.* Words can bring a wish into being. Every child knows that. And from that confirmation, it was no leap at all to actually trust him. She must have decided to trust him, to bring him her book. She was there beside him on the couch when Bernadette opened the front door, letting him read to her. Playing model daughter to Fred's delighted-dad act. *Of course*, Bernadette thinks again. Willie's been waiting for this moment all her life. The thought swallows Bernadette's whole heart like a sinkhole opening up in her. She looks at her daughter's face and sees something worse than worry—guilt. Willie loves him already, this father—the only father she's ever been offered.

*What is the collective noun for a cluster of betrayals?* Bernadette thinks. *A regret. An anguish.*

"Willie," she says. "Everything is going to be okay." It's no promise of anything but her own reliability, and that she can guarantee. She pulls her daughter close.

"It's snowing." Willie puts her hand to Bernadette's cheek.

"I know. Isn't it beautiful out there? Did you play in it? With Mrs. Iversen?"

Willie nods. "With him." She points. "That dad."

"*That dad*," Fred laughs. "Funny, kiddo."

Bernadette is crying before she can stop herself.

"Hey, now," Fred says. He's at her side. He pulls a handkerchief from his pocket. He's always had a handkerchief in that pocket, Bernadette remembers. She used to iron them flat and smooth, fold them into perfect squares, and tuck them in a stack beside her own underwear in their shared drawer of their single dresser in that tiny apartment in Hyde Park. But she takes it and wipes her eyes.

"Why are you sad, Mama?" Willie says.

"Not sad," Bernadette tells her. Sad is too small a word. She wants to walk backward out the door and backward down the street and backward up the bus steps and backward out of this day so that it can be unfolded again in a different configuration—one that does not end with her trapped.

Fred leans over her and kisses the top of her head. "Give your mom a little space, sweetheart." To Bernadette, he says, "I told her I'd take my girls for dinner, but then the snow. You have something here, I'm sure, right? Aren't we all starving?"

"Right," Bernadette says, wiping her eyes. "I'm sure I have something."

In another minute, she knows, she'll stand up on her wood-block feet and go into the kitchen and grill cheese sandwiches for the three of them, and they will sit at the little dinette table like a family and eat. And then what? Her mind cannot roll forward any further than dinner. For now, she says, "Wills, you're heating me up, you little furnace. Hop off my lap." And to Fred, "Just give me a few more minutes to sit. It's been a day."

He retrieves the book from the couch. "You want to pick up where we left off, Wilhelmina?"

Willie jumps from Bernadette's lap to Fred's and curls up like a little cat in the circle of his arms. She's content, Bernadette sees.

"Ready?" Fred smiles.

Bernadette lays her head back on a pillow and closes her eyes. In a moment, Fred's voice fills the apartment with the next chapter of the story.

# PART
# 2

## 8

THAT NIGHT, WILLIE FALLS ASLEEP AT THE DINNER table. Her face is pinked with the chap of the snow and wind, her curls tangled where her hat mussed them. First her eyes go swollen with sleep, and next thing Bernadette knows, she's out.

"Is this her routine?" Fred asks, putting down his own fork and standing.

"She's just worn from the day. It was a lot for her—the snow, and then you. She's still little."

"Right." He shakes his head. "I'm not used to children. I forget that they nap."

Bernadette lets this go and says only, "She does still nap, and she probably didn't today."

"Where does she sleep?" Fred says. "I'll tuck her in." He moves to lift Willie from her chair.

A blade of panic cuts through Bernadette. She hasn't thought about sleeping. Is he expecting the bed? Is he expecting Willie's spot? And where will Willie go? "She sleeps beside me," Bernadette says. "In the big bed. That's been easiest."

Judgment crosses his face, but he carries Willie into the other room. In his absence, Bernadette gets up and goes to the cupboard. She has nothing but bourbon, left over from when Willie was sick and Bernadette thought she'd surely catch it too and would need a toddy to sleep. Now she finds glasses—jam jars, really—and pours for herself and for Fred, carries them to the couch, and sits.

"This isn't a good habit, you know," he says when he returns, "letting her sleep in the bed with you."

"It's been best for her."

"I don't mean for her. I mean for you. There's research on this, Bern. You remember the study we read? Deep sleep is only possible without

77

frequent interruption. You need the deep sleep to dream, and you need the dream to—as Freud said, and I know you remember this bit—release the 'safety valve.' It's how a brain restores. Are you dreaming, or is she kicking you in the night and waking you out of any near deep sleep? You'll be exhausted if you don't get her into her own bed sooner than later."

*I will be exhausted?* Bernadette thinks. "I dream fine. Why are you here?"

Fred smiles, sits back. "I wondered how long it would take to get there. You haven't lost your way with the riposte."

"I couldn't ask in front of Willie."

He shrugs and grins that impish grin of his. "I've missed you."

"I don't believe you."

"It's true."

"Well then, why today? For four years you've missed me, but today you actually show up? What's different about this week than all the others before it?"

He sighs. "I regret things. I regret that I've missed so much of her growing up."

She says, "That's not an answer." To herself, she thinks, *It's not the right answer.* It still centers him, his regret, his lost time—not Willie's or hers.

Another shrug, though she does see the slope of real regret in his shoulders, and when he looks at her, there is shame on his face. "My fellowship funding ran out."

"But your research?"

"There's a university here. I can just as well get on the faculty here as anywhere else. It was time for a change." His face softens. "And Willie's here. And you're here." He reaches for her hand. "I came to my senses."

She wants to ask what he's not telling her. She wants to ask why he didn't write ahead to see if she, too, felt it was time for a change. Instead, she says only, "Have you already written to Dr. McIntosh? He's chairing the department now. I assume you looked him up."

"I'm meeting him tomorrow."

There's a burning at the pit of her gut. He managed to write ahead about the job, but he didn't send any word to her. "And, what?" she says. "You think you'll just walk right into a job?"

"That's what we'll hope for, isn't it? Otherwise, I'm bagging groceries or washing dishes somewhere." He sits forward. "Which I will happily do,

Bern, if that's what it comes to. You're here, and our daughter is here, and so I am here. I should have been here a long time ago, but I am here now."

In the other room, Willie stirs. "Keep your voice down," Bernadette says, her own voice a rush of hot air between her teeth.

They both pause, listening, and Willie babbles again, now clearly sleep sounds that are nothing but nonsense.

"She's fine," Fred says, but he gets up and closes the bedroom door.

When he sits again, she says, "What's the job? The one McIntosh is offering you."

"There's no offer, just a meeting. He's agreed to meet with me—that's all so far."

"Because I don't want to quit working. You understand that, right? I'm just making headway in that department, and I'm not quitting now."

"I know you love your work."

"Did you tell McIntosh about us? Did you write to him as my husband?"

"Not specifically. I said my wife and child were already settled in Seattle, and I was looking for a position. That's all. He won't put it together."

"And you won't tell him at the meeting?"

"I don't have to. Are you ashamed?"

That spill of lava in her belly again, but she won't be baited into an argument. "Don't tell him." She meets Fred's eyes. "Please. I like my work. I need to work." She hates that she has to frame it like this—a request of him, but she knows what will happen if the department hires him. There are only so many bodies to fill classes. There are only so many salary lines to extend. And she's already behind, last to be contracted, first to be cut whenever there's a shortage. If he knows they're married, McIntosh will look at Fred's salary and see her bills paid, her need for the work evaporated.

"You've done so well, holding it together out here on your own. But I want you to know that you won't have to work forever if you don't want to."

*Done so well on your own.* She could reach out and slap him. She says, "I want to work."

He nods, relaxed. "We have nothing but time to make these decisions, B."

A pause. The apartment has contracted around them. Her head swims, and so she drinks. The bourbon burns at the back of her throat, but this burn is welcome, numbing. "My feet are still cold," she says.

"Put 'em here." Fred pats his lap, and she lifts her feet onto his thighs. His hands are warm and firm and familiar.

When she met him, the first physical attraction she felt was to his forearms, his hands. Strange, she knows, but she liked the moon curve of his clean fingernails, the prominence of the bone at each wrist. He'd spent that summer before they met at home on his parents' farm in Nebraska, working the harvest and saving money for books, and he was tanned and gilded from the months in the sun. She wasn't looking for strength in a man—that wasn't the attraction. No, it was the effort, the drive evident in those clean nails at the end of such obviously hardworking arms. He wanted off the farm. He wanted libraries and debates and work with a pen on paper. Clean hands and agile thoughts. He'd do anything to materialize that vision for himself, and his desire radiated from him. If she'd known better as a younger woman, she would have understood what she had to learn the hard way later: that loving him would mean loving his ambition more than she loved her own. She knows that now, and yet still, here she is, relieved to be back in the light he casts. She hates the smallness of herself.

On her ankles, his hands are pale now with the long and sunless eastern winter, and the fine blond hairs on his arms are a baby's down. How long has it been since someone touched her? *Forever*, she thinks. *It's been forever*. It's a dangerous thought.

She swings her feet to the floor. "You can sleep on the couch," she says.

"Okay. For now." A wink.

"You weren't invited, remember."

"Does a husband need an invitation?"

She turns, makes herself solid. "This is my house, Fred. Mine and Willie's. I mean that."

His face shadows—not anger, but that same shade of shame she saw earlier. She looks away so that she doesn't have to look at him.

At her back, he says, "I wouldn't have married you, Bernadette, if I'd wanted a simple girl."

"Good. I'm glad we understand each other."

As she moves to leave, he stands, reaches for her, kisses her. It catches her by surprise. She hasn't been kissed since he left. Four years, nearly. She doesn't suppose the same is true for him—there have been other women, she's certain, and what's she supposed to do with that knowledge? But she doesn't have energy to care about other women. She can only care about herself, about Willie. About his absence in their lives. She pushes his shoulder, pulls away. "Stop," she says. "I'm not over being angry with you." She gets him blankets and a pillow and says good night.

Outside her own bedroom window, there is none of the usual noise of passing cars or people walking home after the last bus. The snow is a damper. She feels as if she's taken a sleeping pill. There's wool in her head, or clouds, or the thick tide of the sea sloshing first against her brow and then the back of her skull. The moment she lies on the bed, her fatigue is paralyzing. It's the bourbon. She's not used to drinking. The bourbon and the day. Some days are oceans wide. They submerge you. This was one of them. She submits to her exhaustion and lies entirely still, listening to the roll of Willie's breath and watching through slitted eyes the patches of light and shadow on the wall. The shadows shift and shift again as on the other side of the bedroom door Fred turns on the bathroom light, then turns it off. He turns on the lamp in the front room, and a few minutes later turns it off. She hears him rustling the couch cushions, and then the whole apartment is silent. She closes her eyes. She opens her eyes. She closes her eyes. Sleep is coming like water rising. She just has to wait.

Blue strips of snow light fall into the room through the split between the bedroom drapes. The blue is veined with the black shadows of bare tree limbs. It looks like the undersides of leaves, she thinks. Like the wings of lepidoptera. She might be in a wood. She might be under a canopy of blue leaves. Her mind moves her gently to Elita Island. She is there at the far western edge of the island, under the water. Under the drifting striped silhouettes of a kelp bed. Above her, jade-green water and blue sky. Above her, white eye of the moon, watching like a godly protector. *Oh, Atalanta*, Bernadette thinks. *Oh, Willie. You fatherless girls. You unwanted daughters.*

She is so tired. She follows her breath down further, like following bubbles below water. But no—bubbles buoy up. Whose dream is this?

she thinks. Hers or Willie's? Is it possible to share a dream space? It must be. *Think of Jung*, she tells herself. Think of all that collective treasure and dreck that exists between humans. All night, she and Willie breathe each other's breath. The room becomes their bonded, humid consciousness. Of course it makes sense that they—mother and daughter—could pass between one another's dreams like moving through thin membranes. It's placental, she thinks, this barrier between them. It's permeable. One of them is always nourishing the other. Tonight, she's following Willie's dream—the blue and the bubbles. It must be Willie's, and it's hypnotic. What's that state called between waking and sleeping? She remembers the page of her psychology textbook where she read that word—the word for hallucinations that the sleeper experiences before real sleep begins. *Hypnagogic*. It comes to her. Its letters take shape behind her eyes. A word made from a lace of bubbles that pop and transform—fish now, ash now, moths. They whiten and wing and rise.

Is it okay to give in just because you're so goddamned tired? She sighs. She'll follow Willie down. She'll let her daughter's dream tow her under. She will. It's what a good mother should do. This is her last thought before she surrenders fully to sleep.

9

IN THE MORNING, HE'S GONE WHEN SHE WAKES UP. THE couch is tidied, and there's coffee still hot on the stove. The meeting with McIntosh, she realizes.

Outside is a wonderland. It kept snowing through the night, and the yard is buried under at least four inches. Each shrub has become a gnome in a pointed hat, each of the evergreens a fairy-tale prop. She'll take Willie out to play in it as soon as she's up, but she won't wake her. Both of them were clearly exhausted. Bernadette hasn't slept this late in months, and it galls her a little to think that the difference was perhaps less her fatigue—which is chronic at this point—and more the deep relaxation of knowing she wasn't the only adult in the house last night. She believes she's been a good parent on her own, that she's weathered the worst of the moments with grace—or at least patience, and so it's disappointing that some part of her has been hiding her fear from herself. Or maybe it's not been fear, she reconsiders, but hyperattention. That animal instinct to be on guard always, like a dog that sleeps with its ears perked and its back against the wall. Has she been so keyed up all these years on her own that she hasn't allowed herself real rest? It's possible. She hates that it's possible.

When she first married Fred, she had trouble sleeping beside him. She'd never slept in the same bed as anyone else. As an only child, her childhood bedroom was hers alone, and beyond that, her room was the attic of the house, and so she couldn't even hear her parents moving around downstairs. When she went to bed, she was entirely alone, and it was a delicious aloneness. The attic room was often either colder or warmer than the rest of the house, but she didn't mind; the temperature shift added to the sense that she had been transported. She had books of her own in this world, a slim wooden desk that her father had painted pale pink to her specifications, a rocking horse skinned in real horsehair, a bed layered in quilts and sheets onto which her mother had hand-stitched a ruffle. For light, she was permitted a Coleman lantern that hissed when lit, and the hissing became a comforting white noise that later, when she encountered the same lanterns during the war, was like hearing a lullaby. What was best about the room, though, was simply the fullness of her own company there.

She's built this same privacy into her apartment. There's an alignment of herself and a freedom possible in this space that she has rarely achieved anywhere else—as if that same internal landscape from her childhood has materialized again, like a pop-up book she's carried with her all these years and only just now been able to open. Willie is with her, of course, but it's different sharing her space with Willie than with anyone else—Willie, who is of her and from her. When she shared an apartment with Fred, back in Chicago, she never felt this ease. That place was his maybe even more than it was hers, though she was its keeper. And when they were both there, together, she was always aware of the psychic space he required—of the way his needs were the landlord and her own just a tenant.

Sometimes she's thought that her trouble with sharing an external space is more about the teeming wildness of her interior one. She can't remember a time in her life when her own thoughts weren't alive, weren't unfurling faster than she could possibly tend to them. What she sees in Willie is also this—the saturated imagination, the way a story can be fully immersive, the urge to ask too many questions for other people's taste. And wasn't this also what Nora Reach immediately spotted in her and thought they shared? This propensity for thought where others—unbelievably—experienced every moment of solitude or quiet as more or less mental idling? But she and Willie and Nora are all loners, all inhabitants of childhoods spent primarily among adults. When she finally went to school, Bernadette was bewildered to find herself strange among the other children. She didn't know how to talk to them to elicit the kind of response she anticipated. Where an adult would laugh at her joke or show interest in her question, another child would take on a look of confusion or ridicule and often just run away to play with someone more suited to childhood than she seemed to be. And she's witnessed this same strangeness already in Willie, and also Willie's burgeoning awareness of it in herself. It stings to see. It raises for Bernadette this question: Did Willie come to the world this way—and did she herself? Or were they parented into oddity, into a preference for solitude? And what about a child like Atalanta, without any nurture? Can a psychological temperament even be applied to a child whose identity has been solidified purely around the drive for survival? What might be read as introversion in a typically raised child might just be instinctive fear in a child like Atalanta. What might be taken as the traits of extroversion in another child could simply be the desire for the safety found in a pack.

Bernadette gets her notebook to write this down, and as if she's rung a bell, Willie appears, all wag and kisses, up and ready for the day. Bernadette sighs. "Hello, love." She puts away the notebook and scoops Willie into her lap.

"I want pancakes."

"Oh ho! Pancakes? You're waking up with demands now?" Bernadette tickles Willie until the girl slides to the floor in giggles.

"Pancakes!"

Across the room, a gust of cold: Fred at the door with a pink box in his hands, his face reddened with the outside cold. "How about doughnuts?"

Willie cheers, rushes him, throws herself around his legs. How quickly her affection has turned.

Bernadette finds plates and pours Fred the last of the coffee. "This is a treat," she says by way of thanking him. He didn't deliver on his promise of dinner, but he's brought breakfast. That's something.

"Treats!" Willie grins. She eyes the box for a long moment, then selects a fat, iced doughnut confettied in colored sprinkles. "Tweets! Willie likes tweets, Dada!"

Before she can stop herself, Bernadette snaps: "What in the world was that? Wilhelmina! You don't baby-talk." Her tone is sharp. It's rare for her to chastise Willie, and when she meets Willie's eyes, she sees what is unmistakably shame.

"It's fine," Fred says. "We're celebrating, right, Willie?" He turns to Bernadette. "It went well with McIntosh. There's apparently someone taking a sabbatical in the spring."

"Jorgensen," Bernadette says. "I know. It's supposed to be an open call. I heard it would be posted in the new year."

"We'll see. Maybe not."

She feels a rush of heat to her face. "Not posted? Did he say as much?"

"Not in so many words, but why post it when a replacement has turned up? Save the work and hire me."

"Is that what's happening?"

He holds up crossed fingers, beams at her.

She turns her back to the table. Her hands shake as she refills the coffeepot. She's known about the sabbatical replacement all year. Jorgensen is ancient—a tomb rather than a man. There's a good chance he'll retire during the sabbatical, go emeritus and never return. And then the job will become permanent, and the temporary position will become a near-guaranteed permanent hire. Of course, she hasn't really thought she'll be the one to get the job—there are no women in the department, and she hasn't completed her PhD. But the work with Atalanta might have been something on her side. The work might have made a difference to her candidacy. She's thinking this and not paying attention to the rising heat of the faucet's water as she fills the coffeepot. It scalds her fingers. "Goddamn it!" she yells.

"Hey," Fred says. He takes the pot, turns the water to cold, and cups his hand around hers. The pain slowly dissolves. "Relax. You can relax now. I'm here." He says this into her ear. His breath is warm, close. It tickles the skin just under her collar.

She lets out a long breath.

He turns her toward him. This time he asks first, then kisses her neck, her cheek, her mouth.

*God*, she thinks. *What is Willie seeing?* But this is normal, isn't it? Parents showing affection. What Willie has *not* seen up until now has been abnormal. Bernadette is two selves again, one sliding sideways above the other as Fred leans her against the counter's edge. She lets herself kiss him back, and the two selves click back into unity for just an instant. For just an instant, she is in her body—a mouth and tongue, a neck and breath. She feels the familiar shimmering of desire, despite herself, like the bioluminescent flickering of fireflies suddenly rippling across the darkness of an empty June field. For one second, she does not think at all.

When she pulls away, Willie is watching, a puzzled look on her face, and Bernadette second-guesses herself. Maybe this is merely confusing for the child. Maybe she's botching everything in letting Fred simply glide back into their lives with no fight, no resistance, no punishment for his absence. *This dad*, Willie said, and what is Bernadette to make of that? What is she modeling for Willie—strength or weakness? Forgiveness or passivity? It's a mess. All of it, a mess. She sidesteps Fred and says, "I'm showering."

"Eat, Mama," Willie says. "Please." The look on her face is a plea—she wants them all together, a family.

So Bernadette dries her hands on her nightdress and sits at the place they've left for her between them. "Okay," she says, capitulating. "Let's eat."

FOR DAYS, THEN, THEY EXIST TOGETHER IN THE SLACK-tide motions of a domestic life Bernadette can neither convince herself to actively choose nor to resist, but there are luxuries to having Fred back that she cannot ignore. She goes to the grocery store with his cash and buys more than she's ever before purchased in one trip: a beef shoulder roast and a net sack of red potatoes, flour and butter and a box of the little white sugar cubes Fred prefers for his coffee, eggs and bacon and two tins of dried fruit to make the holiday bread she remembers her mother making each year. Outside, the snow melts. Every afternoon they go walking, and at the park, Willie tells anyone who will listen that Fred is her father. "My dad," she says at first, but Bernadette hears her testing out "daddy" later. She cannot help but observe her daughter as a subject at times, though as soon as Willie catches her staring, Bernadette slips back into her mother self and calls, "What is it, Wills?" In her mind, though, she is taking notes, marking the subtle shifts she sees in the child over the days since Fred appeared.

Willie's language acquisition and usage has strangely stalled, it seems. She retreats into baby talk if she wants Fred's attention, particularly if she's attempted to verbally connect with him at least once and the attempt has failed. Bernadette speculates that the slowdown in acquiring new words and using more complex sentences is likely a result of Willie's brain prioritizing development in another sphere. This can happen. Development is asynchronous in children. A leap forward in one area of growth often results in a pause in the growth of another area. Bernadette goes back to her notes to confirm this, and finds that, during the weeks surrounding Willie's first steps, for instance, her linguistic experimentation seemed to stall.

She believes the baby talk, however, is another thing entirely. She raises it with Fred one afternoon while Willie is napping. Fred has made more coffee, and he brings it to her on the couch, then pulls up a chair so that they can talk face-to-face. This is Fred's preference, she remembers—a psychologist's trick that he absorbed as part of his personal idiosyncrasies: he wants to face whomever he's speaking to in order to establish deep attention. When they first met, she found it incredibly attractive—a man who really wanted to hear what she had to say. But that isn't actually what it is, she knows now; he wants her eyes on him and only him.

"I've noticed the baby talk, sure," Fred says, "but I assumed it was typical. She's only four, Bern. She's playing a part sometimes, for attention. Children aren't my area of study, but that seems normal, right? And, beyond that, her language skills are clearly advanced." He smiles. "Have you heard some of those kids at the park? They can barely string three words together. Little window lickers."

"Don't say that—especially not around Willie. I don't want her repeating something ugly."

"Fine, but it's true. You've heard her. She's bright."

"She's advanced, yes. She's also had the advantage of being the only child in a household with an adult who lavishes her with attention and spent the first years of her life essentially narrating every moment of the day to her. Most kids don't have that."

Fred nods. "She wants to please you."

"What?" She frowns. "That's not what I said. I said she's had my attention, not that she's trying to please me."

"But she is. Trying to please you, I mean. You can't see that?"

"She's not my lapdog."

He laughs. "No, but she's a pleaser. And you reinforce it when she says something that pleases you, and you punish her when she fails to please. Have you not noticed that in yourself?"

Bernadette's chest constricts at this. "That's not how I'm raising her."

"Maybe not intentionally."

"Give me an example."

"She baby-talks, and you stop her and say, 'We don't do that,' or something along those lines, which is punishment. She points out the water level rising on one side of the locks, and says, 'That water is growing,' and you smile and hug her and reward her by repeating herself back to her."

Bernadette thinks back to this moment. They did take the bus to the boat locks in Ballard a couple of days earlier. There, the Lake Washington Ship Canal and Puget Sound meet in controlled channels that allow boats to safely pass between them. For over an hour, Willie stood at the rails of the walkway above the locks, watching the water level rise and fall between the constructed barriers, and then, when the lake and the sea became one and the barriers opened, Willie clapped and stomped at the boats smoothly sailing past her through the channel. Bernadette delighted in watching this—Willie as close observer, as mechanical thinker. Her little face so obviously displayed the wonder and curiosity going on in her mind, and when she made the comment about the water growing, Bernadette did—just as Fred has remembered—beam at her and reflect back to Willie what she'd just said. Is this not how a parent turns the soft tissue of the world into working muscle for a child, though? This recognition of the perceived and confirmation of the theorized is what makes the ground solid under a child's feet.

Bernadette says, "She constructed the knowledge herself, and I merely let her know that I was witnessing that construction."

He laughs. "How is your pride in her not a reward?"

"So, you're saying I should withhold my pride?" Now she laughs.

"I'm not saying that. I'm all for the reward. You know this. I have no issues with Pavlov. I'll do something good right now if you'll just give me a little treat." He nudges her with his feet, but she's not budging.

"Maternal encouragement is not a reward. That's theoretical nonsense. Come down from your ivory tower, Professor, and sit awhile among the real people of the world."

He laughs. His knees are against hers. She hasn't realized that she's edged forward on the couch as they've been arguing. She hasn't realized that she's missed arguing. She reaches out and holds him by the wrist, pulls him toward her for a kiss. How long since her brain has felt lit up like this—not because she's lighting it herself, but because another person is challenging her, pushing her, taking her seriously? This is what it has always come to for them: the charge of conversation is the first spark. She stands and directs him to lie on the couch, then sits, her knees around his hips.

"Wait," he says. "Wait—shouldn't we—?"

She feels her face pink. "I don't have anything here."

"In the medicine cabinet?"

"I've been alone. Always alone."

Now the color rises in his face, but he slides out from beneath her, disappears into the bathroom, and returns, fitting back onto the couch, just as before.

In the back room of her brain, she is unreeling this. She is unpacking what it means that he was prepared to be with her, or with someone. She is unpacking what it means that he stopped her. "Be quiet," she says into his neck as she unbuttons his shirt, unfastens his belt. She is saying it to herself and to him both. She puts her hand over his mouth, and when he smiles behind her fingers and licks the underside of her knuckles, she grips his jaw more tightly. "Be quiet," she says again.

What she doesn't expect in herself is the relief she feels—both in looming over him, her hand at his lips, his teeth, and in the intimacy. She should deny him—punish him for what he's done and not done—but she wants him, and it would only take a moment for her thoughts to begin churning again and her body to become lost to her, and she doesn't want to be lost to this right now. Hasn't she already been denied enough? Over the years alone, she's talked herself into believing that she can do without sex. That she is a person for whom the physicality of life is simply less important, less necessary than intellectual stimulation. *Like a nun*, she's actually thought—an idea that neither accurately represents her own desire nor has anything to do with actual nuns, a group of people about whom she knows nothing. There was pride in the lie, though. And under the pride, there was self-protection in telling herself that she was set apart. Able to need less than other people. That she could be an anchoress of the stronghold she'd built for herself and Willie, and through the little slatted hagioscope in the wall, she could see just what she wanted of the world on the other side. What arrogance—and what fear! As if it's possible to shut the gates between the two spheres of self and function fine enough. As if the body alone is capable of handling basic survival, and as if the mind alone is capable of making meaning. It was the story of herself she had to create in order to survive her intense, impossible loneliness, she sees now. But being with Fred is calling her back into her own skin—not because of his hands and mouth and hips against hers, but because she's opened the shutters to her own desire again. And from this other vantage, she finds herself relieved to be unified, brain and body one, even if only for now.

They throw the pillows off the couch and roll together onto the floor. His head hits the leg of the coffee table, and she weaves her fingers into his hair. He smells familiar. She has never known anyone else's body the way she knows his, and it comes back to her where he likes to be touched, how to fit her knee around his ribcage just so. How he fits himself to her. She bruises the knobs of her spine on that same coffee table leg at some point. She thinks about the risk of this—the emotional knots she's retying—but puts it to the side. He is her husband; she is his wife. Isn't that still true?

"We need a bed," she says, after they've pulled their clothes back on and straightened the table and are sitting side by side on the couch again, finishing the coffees they abandoned.

"We have a bed."

"Willie's in it."

"Time for her to move into her own bed, I think."

Bernadette shifts. She doesn't want to consider this yet. "I don't know. It will be disruptive for her. She's used to sleeping beside me."

"What would Freud say, I wonder?" Fred grins.

She laughs. "Oh, god. Please shut up."

"Actually, that's probably exactly what he'd say." Fred slides into a ridiculous Austrian accent: "*Shut up and have her again, man! And for zhat, you vill need a bed.*"

She bumps her shoulder against his. "You're terrible. Willie will hear you."

"Worse yet: What if Mrs. Iversen can hear me?"

The idea strikes her as hilarious, and this time she laughs loud enough that Willie does call from the other room.

The rest of the evening is tempered by their hour together on the couch, the waxiness of her interactions with Fred having been warmed away and the atmosphere in the apartment smooth and even glossy with the new-old snap they've brought back between themselves. At bedtime, Fred reads to Willie, and then, easily, as if he's rehearsed it, says, "Hey, Wills, don't you think you're big enough to sleep away from Mama?"

Willie looks to Bernadette. A tenderness crosses the girl's face.

"I think you're plenty big enough," Fred says, and Willie nods.

"I am," she says. "I am big."

He asks what she thinks of a campout, which Willie's never heard of, and the two of them spend the next half-hour building Willie a campsite in the front room out of blankets and pillows.

"You can call me, and I'll come to you," Bernadette says when she bends to kiss Willie good night.

"Mama," Willie reaches up and puts both her hands on Bernadette's face. A whisper. Her breath is like the steam rising off warming milk.

Bernadette's own breath seizes in her throat. A kiss then, and a hug. The light over the sink left on in the kitchen for Willie's sake. *Good night, good night. Have a good sleep in your camp. Have a good sleep in our bed. Good night!*

The apartment is warm and close around the three of them. Bernadette climbs beneath the sheets and waits for Fred to take his place beside her. He wraps an arm and a leg over her body. She has forgotten that he's the sort of sleeper who falls out of consciousness like stepping off a curb—one moment a kiss on the back of her neck, the next rhythmic snoring. How he manages this remains a mystery to her, an otherness in him. She lies awake under the weight of his arm still there at her rib cage and thinks, *Maybe this?* Maybe this is what she wants, after all. Maybe this is what's best for Willie, despite how well it has seemed to go so far on their own. Maybe this is the way it should be from now on.

From the other room, there's the sound of Willie shifting, moving. Bernadette thinks she should get up and go to her, check on her, but Fred's arm is a reminder to wait—let Willie come to her. How much has her perception of Willie's needs been her own needs projected? Is a child born capable, more or less, of survival without so much intervention? And at what point does the intervention become less parental love and more parental need to be loved?

*I am loved*, Bernadette thinks. She repeats it to herself. Pat on the head, treat on the tongue. Good girl. What's the harm in a reward now and then?

10

JUST BEFORE THE AUTUMN TERM ENDS IN MID-DECEMBER, the department secretary stops her with a message: Nora Reach has called to say that arrangements have been made for Bernadette to visit Atalanta. She'll need to be at the dock for the island ferry at 8:00 A.M. *Your presence is imperative*, Nora has dictated to the secretary, and the poor woman has underscored it three times to indicate what Bernadette assumes was the intimidating tone over the telephone.

*Finally*, Bernadette thinks. She's been anxious to get back, the long delay in scheduling a second visit to the girl incredibly frustrating. Each time she's inquired, though, Brodaccio has put her off, citing troubles with the girl's health, poor timing, a holdup with his paperwork. She was beginning to wonder if the case had fallen apart entirely, so it's a relief to be called in now, even if only at short notice.

The one hitch is that she still hasn't yet told Fred about Atalanta. It isn't that she's intended to withhold the information, but the case is her work, and she feels now more than ever that she must keep a boundary between her work and her personal life. Fred has been back to the department once already, this time for a second meeting with McIntosh at which other senior professors were also present, and he came home reporting that they were waiting for his documents to arrive from Chicago and New York, but he was pretty sure the job was in hand. He was jovial telling her the story of their meeting and the impromptu lunch following it. "Nice bunch, all of them," he said. "You must know them, right?"

"I do," she said, though she registered the implication in his phrasing—*You must know them*, in other words, when her colleagues spent a day describing the scholarship of their department to a prospective candidate, her work had not come up.

She wants to remain invisible as Fred's wife throughout his hiring process, but she doesn't love how it feels to find herself so completely beside the point. How can it be so easy for him to simply appear and slide into place in the department where she's labored for years now without a promotion? Each time Fred mentions the job, she feels as if he's held a lit match under a pilot light in her chest and she has to fight herself not to flare.

What she does have on her side—*all* she has on her side—is the work itself, and so it must be sacrosanct, protected from whatever interference or interruption or judgment Fred might pass if she were to tell him about it in any detail. He'll regard her work with Atalanta a misuse of her time, any outcome she might get anecdotal at best. She guesses he'll tell her there are better case studies in childhood language acquisition to be had than this unpredictable girl with an unknown history. He'll say she's let her heart rather than her scholarship lead her. That's her intuitive sense of things, anyway. But now that she'll need to make three or four trips to the island in the next month, she sees no way to hide it from him. He'll have to stay with Willie when she goes out to Elita, and he'll expect to know where's she going when she's not with them.

She decides her best route is to lay it out piece by piece rather than all at once, the way she might offer him a strange new food as an hors d'oeuvre rather than a main dish. *Have a bite of this . . . just a taste, easy to swallow.* It's manipulation as self-preservation. She's not proud of it.

"I'm going to be gone Friday," she says over dinner the night of Nora's note.

"You are?"

"It's work."

"What can they expect of an adjunct at the end of the term?"

It's irritating, the dismissive subtext of his question, but she pushes that thought to the side. She doesn't have time to be resentful right now. "This isn't university work," she says. "I'm assisting a social worker—her name is Nora. She's asked me to do some observations of a little girl."

"You're consulting?"

"Yes, I guess it's consulting. But not for money. This is just helping someone. A friend, you could say."

"You've never mentioned her—Nora."

She smiles. "It hasn't been important, but I have a few friends here." The lie is bile on her tongue. "Willie and I have been here a long time, really. I have a few women friends." She turns to Willie, who is mostly not listening, but singing to her plate of potatoes and scrambled eggs—what she will eat in place of the roasted chicken Bernadette has fixed for the actual meal. She never cooked like this for just herself and Willie, but having him at the table still feels like hosting company every night. "Willie," she says, "didn't I have lunch with Miss Nora not long ago? I told you."

Willie shrugs.

"This time she wants me to come out to the facility where the child is being cared for—it's a day's trip. I'll be gone, and you and Willie will have a whole day to do something, just the two of you." Again, she turns to Willie. "Wills, what do you and Dad want to do while I'm with Miss Nora on Friday?"

And that's the release—all it takes to send Willie flying off, planning a trip to the park and a doughnut at the bakery down the street and a walk to the neighborhood shops to look at the Christmas decorations and the window of the drugstore, and the whole dinner conversation unrolls as smoothly as if she's written the script for it, which, in a sense, she has.

Friday, she gets up early, Fred still asleep in the bed. This time, she dresses with Nora's gaze in mind—tweed trousers as a concession to the cold of the ferry, but a cream-colored silk blouse with a bow at the neck, and her long winter coat with a red scarf Fred brought from out east to wrap around her shoulders. On her feet, she wears a pair of wool socks over her nylon stockings, and a pair of boots over those, but she tucks a pair of heels into her bag to change into once she's through the prison doors. She pins up her hair in a firm knot at the nape of her neck and finds her only tube of lipstick before deciding a red lip would undo whatever good impression she wants to make. Nora will appreciate professionalism but not vanity.

She lays a kiss on Willie's forehead. One on Fred's lips, flush on his mouth, deep enough to stir him to waking.

He rolls himself toward her, tugs her nearer. "You smell good," he says.

"I'm out the door. I'll be back for dinner."

He sighs, runs a hand down her thigh as she draws away. "Stay."

"Work," she says. "I'll be back." And then she's at the door and on the front step and free, metallic tang of wind filling her nostrils and fingering in around the collar and cuffs of her coat. She could fly all the way to the bus stop.

The island ferry is late by ten minutes—because of bad chop, someone tells her—and it's only when she gets on the boat that she understands what that means: the boat rocks like a child's toy on the whitecaps of the waves. Bernadette grips her seat and keeps her eyes on the horizon. She's not seasick, but the toss of the water's spray against the windows and the keeling side to side are nerve-racking. She doesn't think the boat could pitch all the way over, but it is just a small passenger ferry.

She's paying attention to this rather than her fellow travelers when Nora sits beside her. "I always try to take the first boat when I go out," Nora says, as if she's read Bernadette's surprise. "I like an early start to the day, and Atalanta still keeps an animal's schedule." Nora clarifies: "Up at dawn, bed as soon as the sun sets, which is only late afternoon these days."

"Babies and little children keep that schedule too, not just animals." Small smile—not a correction, she means to say with her face, just an addition. She has no desire to throw off whatever kindness Nora is willing to extend her today.

Nora raises her eyebrows. "You made an impression on Norquist. I don't know what you did, but it was his suggestion that I bring you back out today. Brodaccio had to listen to him. I'm hoping you prove him right."

Interesting. She responds, "And am I here today to perform an observation of the child? That was my assumption, based on the message you left with my secretary." *My secretary* is a ridiculous phrase, but she needs the leverage of even the suggestion of authority it gives her.

"No, you're here to work with Atalanta. Not observe her—we talked about that before, did we not? You can observe all you want, of course, but do your observing while also working directly with her. That's the agreement." Nora turns away. "Norquist thinks you might be the road to a breakthrough." The tone in her voice is unmistakable: she feels undermined. Bernadette recognizes the blade of professional resentment.

"Breakthrough," Bernadette repeats. "Why are we looking for a breakthrough? Are we on a schedule now?" Her guess is that one of the men—Norquist or Brodaccio—doesn't think things are moving quickly enough. No new development in the girl means no new firsthand information about the case, no end to the interruption Atalanta poses to the prison hospital's schedule, no relief from the pressure on both men's offices to find answers and get the child (and the public) a happy ending.

"I don't want to unduly influence you by giving my thoughts now, but I'm certain you'll see the problem." Nora sighs. "But beyond what you'll see with your own eyes: a journalist has pitched Brodaccio rights to a tell-all story about the case. Brodaccio has been opposed—and I mean thoroughly opposed—to exposing Atalanta to the world until now. We both know it's not in her best interest. But I believe he's seriously considering this one." Nora touches Bernadette's sleeve, the look on her face a plea that reads as nearly maternal. "She will suffer if she becomes an object of curiosity. She will never have a chance at a life outside an institution if she becomes the nation's favorite little freak."

The term strikes Bernadette as awful, heartless—*freak*. "An article is a terrible idea," she agrees.

Nora squeezes Bernadette's arm—a moment that catches Bernadette by surprise. Her arm warms under Nora's palm. "Please say that—to Brodaccio," Nora says. "Please tell him it will get in the way of everything."

Again—just as she saw during their lunch—she recognizes Nora's honest care for the child. Whatever she might think about Bernadette's presence here, Nora really does want the best for Atalanta. They share this, the two of them. Maybe only this, but it might be enough to anchor their work together—to connect them.

"Okay." Bernadette smiles. "I have no idea if he'll take anything I say seriously, but I'm happy to give him my opinion."

"Not your opinion—your professional perspective. That's how you frame it with Brodaccio. Don't let him wiggle even the edge of a knife under your expertise." Her eyes are dead set focused on Bernadette's. "You can't give them any room for doubt, you see what I'm saying?"

Bernadette wants to say, *My expertise? But I thought I was just a mom with free time to kill on this little hobby.* She nods though. "I see what you're saying. He's not my first doctor." She grins.

"Ha!" The suddenness of Nora's laugh splits the static tension of the ferry's cabin. "Nor mine."

They both laugh, and it's good to laugh with another woman—to share this subtle joke that only another woman could understand. Bernadette feels a thread of hope that maybe they'll learn to trust one another after all, she and Nora.

When they disembark, the white plate of winter sky has cracked with a network of illumined hairline fractures. Defined honey-gold beams of morning sun column down into the black toss of the sea and scatter sequins across the surface. It smells of nothing, Bernadette notices—not of salt or seaweed or that green-brine scent she's expecting. It's too cold, and the wind is too brisk. She flips up the collar of her coat to shield her ears from its bite.

After the checkpoints, Nora sails them both through the prison's corridors. She knows this place and navigates the hallways like she owns them. Her heels on the floor type out an intimidating beat, and Bernadette remembers the second pair of shoes she's packed in her bag. She'd like to disappear into the restroom and make a quick change, smooth down her hair before facing Brodaccio, but is there even a ladies' room in a men's prison?

"You can use the private bath in the hospital wing. They've closed off the west end of it for Atalanta. No men allowed beyond the doors there."

She registers Bernadette's face and adds, "It's protected. There's a guard at the door day and night. Not to worry. I wouldn't leave the girl here if she weren't isolated. She just wouldn't be safe."

Again, it comes to Bernadette that the isolation—like everything about Atalanta's situation—is a two-faced coin.

There's a wait before they're let into the hospital wing. This is typical, Nora assures Bernadette. Atalanta has fits, resists the nurses' care, throws her food, and sometimes bites. Brodaccio considers all visitors a reward, and therefore he refuses to admit visitors when Atalanta is not in a calmed state. "Rewards reinforce, of course," Nora says.

"Not necessarily, and who's to say that visitors are a reward for Atalanta and not a threat? I would expect a child in a state of heightened fear to present as either hysterical or paralyzed. The behaviors you're describing are absolutely typical and not concerning to me."

Nora seems to consider this. "Say that to him, too. I'd like to end this nonsense about keeping me from her."

"We can't assume that what we recognize as enjoyable or comfortable or secure is what she will perceive and experience positively. She's had an entirely different childhood than any child any of us have ever worked with, and it strikes me as best practice to simply observe her before applying any prescriptions for how to treat her."

Nora nods. Again, she seems to be reassessing Bernadette. "I'm glad you're here," she says. "I told you it was Norquist who insisted, and it was, but I'm glad you're here."

When they're let into the hospital wing, it's not at all what Bernadette has expected. The long narrow room is, in general shape and color, reminiscent of a hospital wing, but someone—Nora, she gathers—has transformed it into a schoolroom. There's a blackboard on wheels along the wall across from the bank of windows. Posted behind it are the basic decorations of any kindergarten class: a strip of paper on which the numbers 1 through 10 are written out, large and neat, and paper cards on which all twenty-six letters of the alphabet are printed in red ink. There's a table in the center of the room, with wood-backed schoolroom chairs around it, and on the floor is a braided rug. There are picture books on a shelf, and baskets of toys—blocks and dolls and little metal cars, a tea set, and a stuffed bear. And at the end of the room opposite the guarded door, there's a folded screen, and beside it an oversized crib. Beside the crib, standing as if she's been told to *stay*, is Atalanta.

It's been almost two months exactly since Bernadette last saw her, and the girl has grown. She is still short in stature, but her arms and legs and face have filled out on the diet Brodaccio is feeding her. She has paled with so many days inside, out of the sea's weather, but there's a healthy flush to her cheeks and a gloss to her hair, which the nurse has combed into two long braids that hang over Atalanta's shoulders. She's wearing a full blue skirt that stops at her knees, and a blue sweater. Her anklets are trimmed in lace. These must be Nora's work—the touch of extra care obviously not from Brodaccio's hand.

"Atalanta," Nora starts in a commanding tone, but Bernadette holds up a hand and stops her. She lays down her bag and walks to the center of the room, where the table is, and pulls out a chair.

"Hello," she says, her voice low and melodic. "Could I play with your blocks?" she asks, turning her face to Atalanta. She points to the basket of wooden blocks on the floor. The child follows her finger's line but doesn't get up to retrieve the blocks or bring them to the table. "I'd like to play with the blocks," Bernadette says, and again points.

Nora moves to get the basket.

"Atalanta can get them," Bernadette says. She waits and looks at the blocks.

She isn't certain this will work, but she has an intuitive sense that it's her best bet with this child. Maybe there's an element of truth to the body being a network of chemicals and reactions, to human behavior being a neat little chain of replicable actions reinforced by rewards and redirected by consequences. She herself wears a coat when it's cold outside—because she doesn't want to feel discomfort. She eats when she's hungry—because she doesn't like the ache of an empty stomach. She returns home to Willie—and now to Fred—because to be loved and to love is one of the few securities, one of the few true pleasures of life. But to paint the human with this fat stroke is to miss every nuance and complication, every trip of the will and bend of desire or fear or sorrow. Atalanta is fed and safe now. She is warm and clothed and not in physical pain. Bernadette is convinced that what remains is her loneliness. Her desire to connect. Why else the fits of fear when visitors arrive?

They threaten something else in her—not her ability to survive. She has already proved that she can survive, both alone and also here, in the company of her medical stewards. But survival is not enough. That's what's so entirely fascinating about her! Atalanta survived without the pack, and it made that basic, evolutionary human impulse toward social inclusion redundant for her, or if not redundant then at least gratuitous. But what if the tantrums before each guest arrives are a demonstration that her drive to connect remains? That it terrifies her to be excluded—to be made other by an observer's gaze, to be outside the ring of human relationship?

Atalanta walks to the basket of blocks. She has the gait of an animal—halting, but also fluid somehow. Her every step is made with a kind of grace that is also charged with an awareness of her surroundings that humans, largely, have forgotten. She swoops down and touches the basket.

"I'd like to play with the blocks, Atalanta. Can you bring the blocks?" Bernadette says.

The child does not make eye contact, but she does begin to pick up the blocks, one by one, and hold and turn and roll them in her hands.

"Let me just help her bring them to you so you two can get to work," Nora says.

"Give her one more chance." And to Atalanta she repeats, "Can you bring the blocks here?" Bernadette points to the blocks, then lays her palm on the table.

The girl lifts the hem of her skirt so that it becomes a hammock, and into it she begins to place the blocks, one at a time, until the fabric of her skirt is bellied low against her narrow bare thighs. She fixes her eyes on Bernadette, and for an instant a current seems to pass between them. *Good job*, Bernadette thinks, as if she can transmit the thought across the room to the child. "Yes," she says. "Bring the blocks here."

At that moment, the door at the back of the room swings open. Both the guard and Brodaccio step inside, and all at once several things happen. There is a racketing clatter as Atalanta's skirt drops and all the blocks fall to the floor and scatter. She lets out a low, loud growl, yanks down the underpants beneath her skirt, and wets herself. Urine streaks down her legs and splatters the linoleum between her feet. A wide-eyed expression that might equally be fear or anger flashes across the girl's face. She lifts her skirt again, and this time begins rubbing herself and groaning.

"No!" Brodaccio says, and as he starts to step forward, Nora intercepts his path and reaches Atalanta first. She crouches to the girl's eye level and whispers something Bernadette cannot hear, gently takes the girl's hand, and holds it by the wrist.

"She will need another bath now," Nora says. She's gone strict faced, stoic.

The nurse whisks in and directs the hissing Atalanta out of the room by the shoulders. The guard follows, and the door swings shut behind them.

"God," Nora says. She is visibly shaken. "This is what I anticipated." She looks stricken—*No, shamed*, Bernadette thinks. It's curious, and she files it away to think about later. "This is what she does now when she's agitated—the touching." Nora's face winces at the word as she says it.

"She's beyond rehabilitation, I'm afraid," Brodaccio says. He takes the chair across the table from Bernadette. "What we've discovered is that what appeared at first to be environmentally caused delays are likely retardation."

"I disagree," Bernadette says.

The doctor grins, a self-satisfied look of *Of course you do*. He says, "You've seen her—what, twice, Mrs. Baston? And for less than half an hour each time? I really don't think you're in a position to challenge my diagnosis."

"I'm not challenging it. Not yet, anyhow. I'm simply saying that I don't believe the child has had the opportunity to truly allow anyone to know her." She sees splotches of anger like a rash rising from beneath Brodaccio's collar, but when she catches Nora's eye, she knows she'll have support if she continues. "She has had, so far as any of us know, little to no human contact for the majority of her life. And while it seems logical to believe that her earliest years must have been spent with a guardian of some sort, what we cannot know is what that relationship was like. Was she mistreated by that guardian? Was she physically hurt, molested, screamed at, left to sit in her own waste? We cannot know, Dr. Brodaccio, but based on her later absolute neglect, I don't think we can rule out severe mistreatment of the child from the very beginning of her life, and so it will take us time to teach her to trust us. And until she trusts us, I have little faith that we'll know anything measurable about her intellectual capacity."

Nora drops into the chair beside Bernadette's as if what she's just heard has let the air out of her. "I couldn't agree more, Professor Baston."

Bernadette registers this as gratitude. It's more important, she's realized as this morning has gone on, that she align herself with Nora Reach than with Brodaccio. He may have the unquestioned right to authority at Elita, but on a practical level, it is Nora's office that has jurisdiction over the child's care. The child is a citizen, not a criminal confined to Elita's guardianship forever. While a court might be less likely to side with a woman on most matters, in the case of a child's welfare—particularly a child like Atalanta, who is at once sympathetic in her size and history and fragility, and also clearly damaged and (if Bernadette is being brutally honest) socially repulsive in her behavioral deviations—any judge will side with two women who want to provide care. For once, she thinks, the ridiculous assumptions about women's inherent maternal gentleness that she's fought against all her life might actually serve her interests.

Brodaccio sits back in his chair, which is sized for a child. He's too big for it, his knees up around his chest and his bottom spilling over the sides of the seat. In a different context, Bernadette would laugh. He shakes his head. "I'm going to propose to the state that she be institutionalized indefinitely," he says.

Nora looks as if he's punched her.

"What's the benefit of releasing her now rather than waiting another few months?" Bernadette asks. "Is it just cost?"

"Cost is one component, yes," Brodaccio says. "And cost is no small issue when you're talking about the budget of a federal prison, Mrs. Baston. Don't think for a moment we're given any room for luxuries out here. I've closed down an entire wing of the hospital unit for this child—an entire wing for one child. And that's not even taking into consideration the cost to my own practice here."

"There are men going without care, you're saying?" Bernadette asks. "Incarcerated men are going without care they need?"

The splotches of his fury have reddened his earlobes now and the jowls beneath his sideburns. "Is the implication you're making that I'm negligent in my responsibilities? Because that is a gross misreading of what I'm telling you."

"I'm not implying anything, just asking for clarity."

"I find that to be a passive-aggressive response, Mrs. Baston."

*Passive-aggressive.* It takes Bernadette a moment to scroll her mind's archives for the term, and then she remembers reading it once, in a psychological study of soldiers during the war. She hasn't asked Brodaccio about his history—but it materializes for her now, like a landscape behind a lifting fog: he's a veteran. A military doctor. She'd put money on that. And like all the doctors she knew during the war, his medical practice was tempered by his military training. He wants efficiency, compliance, clear correlations between directives and results. No doubt he gets this in treating his incarcerated patients. The American prison system is not so different from the military, after all. In some sense, both organizations exist to rout out of man his creaturely instincts and behaviors, but in another, they rely on meeting man at his most animal self—the self easily conditioned to react to external stimuli in predictable patterns. Put a leash on a dog, and eventually the dog will learn to stop running.

"Do you need space, Dr. Brodaccio?" she asks now. "Mrs. Reach and I can surely find between us someone willing to foster the child during the course of her rehabilitation, if the issue is merely practical."

Brodaccio stands so quickly, his boy-sized chair falls behind his knees and clatters on the floor.

"Wait," Nora says. She too stands, though liquid now, not shaky. "That reporter who came to you, Phil, he will not be permitted any access to the girl once she's under private care. The welfare system will protect her identity. She won't be your patient anymore, and I assure you, you'll have no legal right to disclose information about her as a medical curiosity."

Bernadette feels her breath vanish from her throat. She looks to Nora, who offers only a tiny, nearly imperceptible nod in her direction. *Wait,* she understands Nora to be saying. *I have this under control.*

The doctor folds his arms over his chest, nods. "I haven't made any decisions about that yet."

"And you don't have to—not so long as she remains at Elita."

At the end of the room, the doors swing open again, and the nurse presents the girl, her hair now wet and plastered to her skull, though straight and combed. She's wearing a new dress—pink this time. Tiny corsages of deep aubergine flowers speckle the fabric. She looks sickly once more, which is maybe the result of the color against her skin, or maybe something more. Bernadette tries to gather her focus and pay attention to the child's movements, the little winks of her facial muscles and twitches of her hands. If the nurse is mistreating her when she's out of Brodaccio's sight—or if, worse than that, Brodaccio has condoned some type of physical punishment after events like the one Bernadette has just witnessed—she wants to spot the effects. *What is it?* she asks herself. What is it in the child's body and face that's catching that snag in Bernadette's chest now? But she can't land on anything certain.

"Atalanta," Nora croons. She walks toward the girl. The child does not snarl or flinch, Bernadette registers, as Nora approaches her and touches her hair. Nora lays her hand flat on the girl's head, cups the girl's cheek. Under her breath, she sings something. Or that's what Bernadette believes she hears—singing, though it could be the recitation of a poem or a passage or a looping single sentence. She watches the girl lean her face into Nora's hand. Her eyelids sink, open, sink, open, as if she is fighting sleep or sedation. Has she been sedated by the nurse? Does that account for this shift in her behavior? Or is it just the comfort Nora has established between the two of them?

Brodaccio sighs. To Bernadette, he hisses, "This—," as he gestures toward Nora and the girl. "This is not rehabilitation. This is nannying. Does this child need a grandmother, or does she need a physician? That's what I'm asking you."

Nora turns, slow as if her blood has become syrup in her limbs, and smiles. In the same low singsong she says, "Professor Baston, Atalanta would like to be read to now."

What happens for the next hour is as strange as any fever dream. Nora ushers the child toward the crib and lifts her inside, where the girl sits, at first cross-legged, then loose, her legs splayed in front of her and her arms lanky in her lap. She is a ragdoll, a floppy pet. Whatever drug the nurse has given her has slurred her birdy movements to ones more reminiscent of an underwater mammal. She unrolls herself to eventually lying prone. She lets her tongue unfurl from between her lips and seems to chew it. Her eyes don't fully close, but they drift, her long eyelashes dusting her cheeks every now and then before she lifts them again, still awake, but barely. Her wet head leaves a dark halo on the linen of the crib's mattress.

The book Nora chooses is *Alice's Adventures in Wonderland*. *Fitting*, Bernadette thinks. Here is the white rabbit, scurrying down the garden hole. Here is Alice, shrinking, growing. Roses and potions and slippery language that Bernadette would never choose herself for the early learner, but—of course—that's not true, she reminds herself. This is exactly the approach she's taken to Willie's developing language and literacy. *We'll read whatever you want*, she's said to Willie countless times. She wants to see Willie with a book in her hands—whatever the book. She wants to see Willie's mind swimming into the current of a story, whatever the story. That's the hook. That's the drag that will tow her toward reading, toward words, toward a voice she can claim someday as her own and never doubt and never allow to be silenced. Bernadette believes that: love of story is more important than learning individual letters or whole words. What you want to build in a child is a desire for narrative, a love of that slip from one world into another. Fred would say this is just more conditioning. And maybe—maybe—he's right. But Bernadette thinks it's more innate than that. Story is part of the social inclination inherent to all humans. How do you know who you are? who another is? where you've been and where you belong? Story is relationship. Story is meaning. For this reason, though, she isn't sure how Atalanta will take to it. Does she have within her—somewhere deep—that innate need for relationship, for connection? Or has it truly been uprooted from her? Bernadette looks up from the page every now and then to try to track Atalanta's reaction to the words she's speaking.

Around the crib, the room fills with midday winter light. The ribbons of sunlight that were splitting up the cloud-bank sky earlier have broken it into barges of cloud now that blow visible across a blue sky. The radiators in the room kick on and off. Under her blouse, Bernadette is damp with sweat, but she reads, and Atalanta doesn't interrupt her.

When they reach the end of a chapter, Nora says, "We'll leave it there for today."

Bernadette closes the book and stands.

In the crib, Atalanta's drowsy eyes follow her as she crosses the room, but when Bernadette looks back once more after turning to put the book away, the child has finally closed her eyes. Her chest underneath the pink fabric of the dress rises and falls in heavy, even breaths: sleep. Bernadette thinks of Willie. This girl is someone's Willie. Or could have been. The thought breaks her.

Nora bends over the crib rail and pulls up a white blanket, tucks it around Atalanta's shoulders, and what Bernadette observes on her face in that moment is the worrying, complicating, unmistakable gentleness of love.

It takes time to gather their things and arrange the next visit—next week, Brodaccio agrees.

They pass through the prison's checkpoints and board the ferry, which at this point in the day is nearly empty, just a few guards and laundry women leaving their shift and heading back to the mainland. The early afternoon sky has gone pewter blue with a band of rain coming in from the west, and the day's wind has churned up enough particulate that the water is a milky jade green, opaque as glacial water.

"They're drugging her," Bernadette says.

"I think it's just a barbiturate."

"*Just?* She's so slight, though."

Nora shrugs. "It won't hurt her. She needs to rest after her fits. She gets so agitated sometimes."

"Is there a pattern you've noticed? To the fits?"

"I'm not there consistently enough to see any patterns yet. That's why I need you to keep advocating for me to have more access." Nora nods. "What you did today was perfect." She pauses. "Thank you."

The boat groans with the slosh of a big wave, and Bernadette holds the edge of her seat. The rain is now a visible sheet of weather like a blue veil traveling across the water. "It's like the fit was an escape hatch," she says aloud to Nora. "And afterward, she wasn't in her body anymore."

Nora shifts, frowns. "That's poetic, but nonsensical. She'd been tranquilized. Of course she looked vacant. Haven't you ever taken Veronal? It's like stuffing your ears with plugs and jumping off the high dive. You don't come up again right away."

This is a new window into Nora. Is she anxious? She seems so controlled, so self-assured. Bernadette wants to ask more, wants to say something that will extend the connection they've made today, but she's not sure what won't seem too personal, too prying, too revealing. What she's remembering from her own past is the strange swim of the aftereffects of twilight sleep. Coming to in a hospital bed, brand-new Willie in her arms, and her mind a dark box. She couldn't recall the delivery. She couldn't recall being cleaned up or propped against the pillows or handed the bundle of her sleeping daughter. Time had clearly passed, but where had she been during the hours she couldn't call up in her memory? There was a hole in the timeline of her body. A vacancy. But Nora won't want to hear about childbirth.

"Maybe that's it," she says instead, sidestepping the personal altogether. "Maybe it's just the sedatives. Could you persuade Brodaccio to cut back on how much she's given? She needs to learn to self-regulate, anyhow. She can't do it with the drugs in her system."

Nora sighs. "She's uncontrollable in those moments, you know. You saw it. She becomes, I don't know. Rabid."

Bernadette remembers what Starkey said on the tape—*like a mad dog*. She hasn't believed him until now, but maybe he wasn't fabricating it. Why, though? In this context, rabid means aggressive, doesn't it? She remembers Atalanta's growl. Why did the girl swing into such aggression in that moment? There's no answer yet.

The boat docks, and she and Nora linger on the sidewalk for a moment. The rain hasn't hit yet, but it's right behind them. Nora withdraws a plastic rain cap from her bag and fastens it over her hair. "Listen, focus on what you're here to do—language. The rest of it isn't yours to worry about. I think you're valuable to my work here, and I don't want you stepping on Brodaccio's toes and getting yourself removed." She leaves Bernadette alone on the sidewalk just as the first fat drops begin to splatter on the pavement.

## 11

FRED IS OFFERED AND ACCEPTS THE JOB IN THE DEPARTment just before the holidays arrive, and with that his mood—and so the mood of the household as a whole—lifts like an inflated balloon. He wants a big Christmas—it's his first with Willie, and he needs to make up for what she's missed. *What you've missed*, Bernadette thinks but doesn't say, though she leaves the Christmas preparations mostly to him, not stepping in to help unless directly asked. It turns out, though, that he doesn't need her; his festivities far exceed any she and Willie have known in their holidays alone. One morning, he takes Willie out and comes back carrying a noble fir over his shoulder, which he sets up in the front room. It fills the apartment with the scent of a forest in winter. He and Willie string popcorn garlands and spend a full day cutting pictures from a stack of old *National Geographic* magazines and pasting these to cardboard backing for ornaments. Bernadette looks on from the couch.

Fred is good with Willie, it turns out, and Bernadette isn't quite sure what to make of the mess of emotion that washes over her watching them together. She doesn't want to name it—and maybe she can't, even if she allows herself to try. It's too muddy a puddle. A soup of happiness and relief, yes, but also regret and loss and self-doubt and a little envy, if she's honest, because where does their father-daughter duo leave her? Willie's allegiances have shifted, and so the foundation under Bernadette's household has shifted too—suddenly, seismically. She misses the way Willie used to race to her the moment she walked in the door after work, used to throw herself into Bernadette's arms, used to curl up in her lap after dinner each night. She misses Willie sleeping beside her in the bed, breathing curls of her sweet still-babyish breath onto Bernadette's cheek in the dark cocoon of their shared nights. Now Willie is quite happy in her tent in the front room each evening. She asks Fred to read to her, climbing into his lap for bedtime stories. Bernadette has become their third wheel, and the rejection has cracked open what feels like a crevasse through her. That's an awful, selfish thought—she knows—when Willie is clearly so delighted by Fred's attention, and the shame of not being fully happy for her husband and her daughter only complicates her own ache at being outside of their love.

*Is this one nice, Pops, Papa, Poppers?* Willie asks Fred after each completed ornament, and Fred frowns at whatever lopsided tiger or swan or basketful of fruit she's clipped out and says, *Wills, that's the best ornament I've ever seen in my life*, and then they both beam with their shared happiness in one another.

The one benefit of their infatuation and Bernadette's exclusion is the time it has bought her for work, and at just the right moment. She's been out to the island to visit Atalanta again since the last time, and she's convinced Brodaccio to give her access to the child more regularly in the new year. *Consistency and repeated exposure to concepts are the keys to learning,* she tells Brodaccio, and he can't argue with that, though he makes it clear that her visits are an inconvenience to his schedule. In a broad sense, there are still no notable changes in the girl—she hasn't spoken, and her movements remain skittish and unpredictable. But on their final afternoon together before the holiday, Bernadette manages thirty minutes on the rug beside the child, Atalanta stacking and rearranging a pile of blocks while Bernadette does the same with a different pile nearby. It's a kind of parallel play, not unlike that of young toddlers, and it is a step toward socialization. To hold the girl's attention and presence, Bernadette speaks in low tones, making her own movements slow and deliberate, and narrating her actions: *I'm going to pick up this square block and set it on top of the rectangle one.* She senses the girl listening, watching, though her eyes never meet Bernadette's. It feels like a breakthrough, nevertheless, this closeness. Atalanta's growing comfort with the company of others is remarkable to Bernadette, and there are moments when she wants to reach out and hug the child, just as she would hug Willie, but she withholds that instinct. Such a gesture would scare Atalanta, she knows, and—more than that—it would not be appropriate. Atalanta is her subject or her patient, or maybe her student, in the softest understanding of their work together. It would influence the research to become emotionally affectionate with the girl, and it would undermine the credit she's secured with Brodaccio to show maternal connection. Bernadette remembers what he said about Nora—she was a nanny, a grandmother, not a clinician. If Bernadette wants to maintain her access to Atalanta, she will need to find a way to be warm enough to hold the child's trust but not so warm that she loses Brodaccio's. And she does want to maintain that access. When she leaves the island after the final visit before the holiday, she goes with the understanding that she'll be permitted back on a regular schedule in the new year. This is progress.

Beyond the visits, Atalanta and her history remain as mysterious as ever. Bernadette pores over the file Norquist gave her, which is full of details she's read again and again, though she keeps returning to them, looking for anything she may have missed that will make Atalanta's situation clearer. One particular document has set a hook in her brain that she can't dislodge: the initial police report filed after Starkey and Lind brought the girl in that day in September. They both claim, on the record, that they were eating their lunch when a creature moved through the tall grass and caught their eye. This was followed by a bark. *We thought it was the pack*, one of the men said during the first call to Norquist's office. They couldn't have a feral dog loose around the prison grounds. They stepped into the road expecting to see a dog and instead the girl came charging out at them from the brush.

Bernadette doesn't remember anything about an actual dog coming up during the interview she listened to back in the fall. She wonders why Norquist didn't question them about this then—or if, maybe, the men's story changed in the days between the initial call and the formal interview with Norquist. Or maybe it's not a detail that matters. Still, she makes a note to ask him.

She feels a sense of disorientation and distrust of her own questions as she reads through the file. *I'm not trained for this*, she thinks. How is she to know which details are important? Which questions are valuable? She has to remind herself that this isn't a novel she's reading, in which an author has taken a polishing cloth to the surface of every word. In real life, the details do not always align, the timelines are tangled, and people's memories are porous and often simply wrong. Maybe Norquist didn't question them about a dog because a dog on the island would be impossible after so many years. She's heard stories about deer swimming between the nearby islands of the archipelagos in Puget Sound, but never dogs. And what she knows of the evacuation in '37 is that it included a full sweep of Elita's village, and that every last resident household was accounted for. Still, the way the language of the report reads—*We thought it was the pack*—is oddly offhand, as if there's common knowledge about Elita that she's missed. What else is she missing?

It's unsettling to feel so much self-doubt, both at home and at work. When did the ground beneath her feet go too soft to stand on? And how is she supposed to move forward when she barely trusts herself to take a step? She closes the file and puts it away for the duration of the Christmas holiday.

ON CHRISTMAS EVE, SHE AND FRED TAKE WILLIE DOWN-town. It's cold and drizzly, and the bus smells of the damp wool of other passengers' coats and the sweaty bodies beneath those coats. The windows fog up from so much human heat, and Willie sits on Fred's lap drawing hearts and letters onto the glass with her fingertip.

Downtown, they let Willie loll in front of shop displays and the rainbow glow of glass bulbs strung up on awnings. Fred has brought along Bernadette's camera and takes photos of Willie making a silly face in front of a decorated tree, standing beside a wooden snowman, smiling as she presses her face close to the glass of a store window. He buys them all lunch at a diner, and Willie surprises Bernadette by trying a cheeseburger and making her way through two-thirds of it.

"She usually hates meat and cheese touching," Bernadette says to Fred, and Willie scowls.

"You don't know everything about me, Mama," she says.

It cuts, somehow, even though it shouldn't, and Bernadette is still thinking about it when Fred hands her five dollars and tells her to run into the toy shop while he takes Willie to ride the Christmas carousel that's been set up in the center of the shopping plaza.

In the toy store, Bernadette wanders the narrow aisles for several minutes, totally unmoored. Is it true that she doesn't know her daughter as well as she thinks she does? She picks up a teddy bear and sets it down again. Picks up a boxed puzzle and puts it back on the shelf. In the end, she buys a doll with Fred's money, then walks three storefronts down the street into a bookshop where she selects two books for Willie with her own saved Christmas money, as well as a book for Fred and, after a moment's deliberation about the ethics of it, one for Atalanta as well.

They take the bus home in the near-dark of four o'clock, the sky deep Egyptian blue and studded with the lights of so many windows lit up. She closes her eyes and lets the motion of the bus sway her inside her coat. How is it possible to feel this lost at the very moment when so much of what she's wanted is just solidifying for her? Fred takes her hand and laces his fingers through hers as if he's read her thoughts. Bernadette looks at him. Willie has fallen asleep in his arms, her little face on his shoulder. She resembles him, Bernadette has seen clearly since he's been back. The upturn of her nose and the straight set of her chin. She makes expressions that Fred makes, even though she hasn't possibly spent enough time with him yet to have absorbed his mannerisms. So much of her is him, copied, replicated, and carrying on. She is his daughter through and through, and perhaps the thread between Fred and Willie tightening has left Bernadette's own tie to Willie feeling looser, and her own certainty unraveled. Maybe what she's experiencing as Willie pulling away from her is just Willie growing up, and if so, then that's good. Willie's knowledge of the world is widening, as it must. Fred is part of that expansion, but it's bigger than Fred. It's the child's movement toward individuation, toward self-actualization.

"Do you think Willie is ready for nursery school?" she asks Fred as the bus jostles them around the corner of one porch-lit neighborhood and into the next. Behind the shimmer of front windows, Christmas trees glow.

He looks down at Willie's sleeping face, and Bernadette registers the softening in his own expression as tenderness. He loves their girl. He knows how much he's missed.

Something in Bernadette aches, splits, wells up. She puts her head in her hands.

"Hey," Fred says. He squeezes her.

She turns her face away from him. "I don't know what's wrong with me." She's never in her life cried as much as she has in the days since he came back to them.

He leans, kisses her head. He smells of the tang of the city, the smoke of the cigarette he finished while Willie made her last round on the carousel, the soapy warmth of his neck beneath the collar of his shirt. It would be so hard now, she thinks, to let him go again.

"I think all mothers have trouble letting their babies grow up," he says.

It's wrong, of course. That's not her trouble. She's been waiting—really waiting—all these years for Willie to grow out of her babyhood. Not that Bernadette hasn't loved Willie as a baby, but it's so much easier now that she isn't quite that dependent. It's so much easier to truly delight in her now that Willie can speak, has ideas, is her own little person reading the world in her own little way. Bernadette has never been the sort of mother who is swallowed by maternal nostalgia. But mothers don't get to say they won't miss their babies without sounding like monsters themselves. She will be misunderstood. And so she nods, wipes her watering eyes.

"There's a nursery school on campus," she says. "A lab school. Like the one in Chicago, but smaller. She could go there. She could walk with us to campus in the mornings. I was actually thinking about it even before you came to stay."

"*Walk with us,*" he says, repeating her words.

"What?"

"I love that. I love the picture of the three of us walking to campus in the mornings."

It takes her a moment to respond. He's rarely sentimental. She's been watching him with Willie all week, but she hasn't quite let herself think that he'll stay, that he's really choosing them this time. "It's a good picture," she says. "I agree."

He kisses her forehead. "I still can't believe I got the job."

She lets out a quiet breath. "I knew you'd get it. They want you."

A look she both loves and hates rises to the surface of his face. She thinks, *Oh, I remember you, golden boy with the fragile ego.* He knows they want him, but he needed her to say it too, to make it real, and now she has. He grips her hand again, kisses her again.

He says, "I think Willie is going to knock their socks off in nursery school."

Bernadette laughs. "It's not Harvard. It's just playtime and the ABCs."

"She's bright. It's the truth."

Bernadette strokes Willie's warm cheek. "She is."

They ride the rest of the way without speaking, hands clasped between them. The sky goes navy, black. When they get off the bus, Willie wakes up and is refreshed by the nap, delighted to be out at night with both her parents. She laughs and chatters and convinces Fred to hoist her up on his shoulders for a piggyback ride home. The temperature has dropped, and the dampness still in the air from the earlier rain feels frizzled with crystals of ice. It leaves a fine sheen on the sidewalk and the grass and the trunks of every tree along their block. "Watch your step," Fred says, reaching for Bernadette's elbow. "It's slick. You don't want to slip." He offers her his arm, and she takes it.

## 12

THE DAYS JUST AFTER CHRISTMAS PASS WITH THE urgency of syrup. What at first felt like the luxury of vacant hours with nothing to do but lie around in the apartment, eating and reading (and then, during Willie's naps and after she went to sleep at night, making love or drinking bourbon or playing endless rounds of gin sitting cross-legged on the bed) has become a slurry hardening around Bernadette's feet. Each morning, she wakes feeling the weight of so many hours to kill ahead of her. She's bored and listless with nothing useful to do. Fred notices and says, "You really have no idea how to relax, do you?"

"No, I don't."

He laughs, but she's in real misery until the morning of the twenty-eighth, when Norquist calls her just as she is about to slide her arms into her coat and free herself into the rising gray morning. "Signe Aalund's interview for today is canceled," he says. Signe, apparently, is feeling unwell and won't be able to travel until after the New Year.

"I don't believe her," Bernadette says before she can stop herself. She's been counting on getting back to work with that interview, and the idea of sitting at home for another day makes her feel like she could put her fist through the kitchen wall.

"Neither do I," Norquist says, and there's amusement—appreciation—in his tone. "I want to know more about how you got to that conclusion though."

"Are you working today?"

"I'm prepping Starkey's interview, actually."

"I can be there in an hour," she says, and in exactly one hour she's sitting across from him, the file she's pored over open on his desk, and its contents spread out so she can pick through them with him.

It's a Friday, and the office is still running at holiday capacity, all of the day-shift officers present but only the essential secretarial staff. Norquist himself looks more relaxed than the last time she met him—no tie, and the shadow of a beard darkening his jawline. She rushed him today, she concludes. He hadn't anticipated her being ready to come in for this conversation after Signe's cancellation, and when she insisted on coming in, he'd had to hurry out the door to meet her. But then she reconsiders this; he could have put her off until Starkey's interview on the third. She wonders what kept him from telling her to stay home. Does he have something to share with her about the case, or a genuine interest in what she might have discovered and want to tell him?

She's wired, either way. Wired to have left the house. Wired to have walked an extra bus stop's length in the fog and chill after she mistakenly stepped off the route too soon. Wired to be in this room having this conversation for which she is absolutely overprepared, though entirely undercredentialed. When Norquist meets her eyes and says, "So, what're you thinking?" it's as if he's tripped a switch.

She directs him through the details of the Starkey interview that have punched up through the current of her thoughts like snags in a river. "I don't know yet why," she says, "but this bit about the dog is worth a follow-up question."

Norquist sighs and sits back in his chair. He smells of sweat, and she realizes he didn't even shower before coming in. It occurs to her that maybe he didn't call her from home, in fact, but called from here. That perhaps he spent the night in the office—or out on a case or a shift—and hasn't slept. She realizes that it wasn't his eagerness to work with her that left him looking rumpled, but exhaustion and overwork. It's a deflating thought, and she pulls back from the desk.

"Have I imposed, being here?" she asks. There's heat at her cheeks and her chest. "I'm just thinking—I mean, I'm just reassessing. You look tired."

He smiles. "I'm tired. But it's fine. I have a daughter. She has chicken pox. It was a rough night. I slept on my ex-wife's couch to be there and give her a night off."

He's never spoken about his personal life, and it reassembles him for her—a father, an ex-husband, a man willing to take a night shift with his sick kid.

"Sorry about the state of me," he says and pinches the wrinkled collar of his shirt.

"How old's your daughter? Mine's nearly five."

He smiles. "I already know that about you, of course."

"Ah, right. Signe Aalund. How could I forget?"

"Actually, no. I knew about your girl before Signe told me. It was Nora Reach, actually, who reported that first."

"Reported?"

Norquist shakes his head, sits forward again, elbows on the desktop. For a long moment, he stares at her, and though she wants to look away, she lets him hold her gaze. He sighs. "I trust you. And I'm a good judge of character."

"Your divorce might say differently."

He spouts one loud, guttural laugh. "I like you, see? My ex-wife would certainly like you. You're a straight shooter, and that's why I want you on these interviews. You say what you see, Professor." He catches her eyes, says, "Bernadette."

"Why would my daughter come up by way of Nora Reach?"

"She told me about your kid months ago. Said she considered it 'worth note' and to add it to your file."

"I have a file?"

Norquist shrugs. "Everyone has a file."

Bernadette's mind rewinds to that lunch with Nora back in the fall. What had she said about Willie that had raised Nora's hackles? She can't remember now. Maybe it was just the fact of Willie's existence, her motherhood itself the real liability. She says, "I don't understand why she cares enough about my personal life to report its details to you. What possible bearing does my daughter have on my involvement with this case?"

"None, so far as I'm concerned."

*He says that now*, she thinks, but she wonders how different he can be from the men she went to school with. From her professors. From the men in her department now—men who would choose Fred over her every day, though she has actually proven herself in the classroom time and time again and—so far as they know, anyway—he is merely a fellow man with a degree. She says, "Is the implication supposed to be that I've done poorly? Or that I will? That I'll neglect some aspect of what I've committed to because of my other obligations? Do you not, Detective Norquist, also have an obligation to your child and yet manage to honor it while still meeting your professional responsibilities? Or perhaps your wife holds sole responsibility for the care of your child?"

Again, that single, gut-born laugh. "If you don't count the paycheck, then I guess she'd agree with you."

His amusement only incenses her more. She feels the wave of adrenaline gathering in her. When it crests, she won't be able to sit still in this chair without trembling. She stands. "Can you direct me to the ladies' room, Detective?"

"Hey. Hey. It's not worth getting worked up about."

"I just need a minute. I'll be right back."

"Listen, this isn't particular to you. Nora is a bulldog about all her cases, but she's taking this one personally. She's protective of the girl. I'm sure you can understand that as a mother yourself."

*As a mother yourself.*

Norquist goes on. "She doesn't want to jeopardize Atalanta's safety. That's it. The reporters have spooked her. She's just being cautious, Bernadette."

The tone of condescension. *Bernadette.* As if she is a child to whom this must be carefully explained. As if she is hysterical.

"You've endorsed it, though, her back-channel gossip. That's what I hear you saying, Detective. You've taken Nora's notes and tucked them away in my file, and you haven't told her you're not interested in her Nancy Drew act."

He lifts an eyebrow, smiles. "I could have said something similar about you, actually. After your trip to Adela, *Miss Drew.* But I see your value, just like I see Nora Reach's. She means well. She's protecting the girl. That's it." He shifts, taps the files on the desktop. The conversation about Nora Reach is over. "The ladies' is three doors down on the left. I'll pull up the Starkey questions and we'll get back to them when you've collected yourself for work."

She moves without feeling, watches her body walk out of his office and down the corridor. In the bathroom, she finds a handkerchief in her bag and runs it under the cold-water tap, wrings it out. Inside the stall, she takes off her blouse entirely, raises her skirt, sits on the toilet, and spreads the cold cloth over her chest. She might be made of needles. She lets the cool sink under her skin. She wishes for ice. Wishes for a lake she could dive into and submerge herself. She smells of sweat.

She wonders at Nora's construction of her: the struggling mother, just trying to playact at intelligence, at relevance among the adults. What would she think if she could really see Bernadette's life? That Bernadette is failing at marriage and at professorship and at motherhood? What if she'd seen that awful few minutes on Adela when Willie disappeared? Or Fred just walking into the apartment, totally unannounced and unchecked, a stranger to Willie? Fred climbing right back into

Bernadette's bed as if he hadn't left her? As if she were nothing but his whore, there when he wanted her, forgotten when he didn't.

*Oh god. Oh god.* She bends forward, puts her head between her knees.

It occurs to her what Nora Reach's work really permits—the incredible legal weight Nora pulls if she wants to. She can have a child removed from a parent if she believes there to be neglect or abuse or immorality in a home. She can throw doubt onto a mother's abilities to care for her own daughter. What would Bernadette do without Willie? What would she do to hold on to Willie? She would run, she thinks. She would break the law, cross the border, give up everything. She would take Willie and leave. The words spill like oil onto the wave still simmering in her bloodstream.

Why would Nora doubt her like this? What risk does she pose to the case? What threat does she pose? The broken bits of understanding she's gathered about Nora Reach fit together in her mind, a cracked but clear window.

It takes her a minute to gather herself.

She puts on her blouse. At the mirror, she swishes her mouth with water, reapplies her lipstick, tosses the handkerchief into the wastebasket, and hopes she doesn't smell like a dog.

When she opens the door, Norquist's office is fugged with the odors of his sweat and cigarette smoke and coffee breath, and she realizes he isn't the kind of man who's sensitive to indelicacies. He looks up. "Good. You're back. Better?"

She sits. "What is the presumed order of positive progression in Atalanta's case?"

He sets down his paperwork, leans back. "This isn't where I thought we were going next, but explain what you mean."

"She learns to control her bodily functions, say. She learns to behave in socially acceptable ways. She maybe even learns to speak. She's taken off sedatives. She's ready to leave the island. Then what? Where does she go?"

"A foster family."

"And how is that family chosen?"

"There's a registry of families. They're vetted."

"Vetted by whom?"

Norquist pauses. "By Nora Reach, ultimately. At least in this jurisdiction. Why? What are you digging at here?"

"And what if the child is rejected by all the foster families on the list? Or if the families are found to be inadequate matches? She goes where then? An institution?"

"Yes. An institution."

Bernadette nods. "I'm just wondering if Nora Reach herself is on that list of volunteer foster homes."

"I wouldn't know that, honestly."

"But could she be? Could she vet herself, I mean?"

"I suppose she could."

Bernadette nods again. "And do you know if she's tracking other threads in Atalanta's case? Going out to Adela, maybe? Talking to Lind or Starkey off the record?"

"That, she cannot do."

"Should not or cannot?"

Again, the dry smile from Norquist. "These are good questions. I'm not saying they aren't. I'm just saying this isn't why you're here today. You're here to set up the Starkey interview, which is authorized and likely to go somewhere. Chasing down far-fetched possible overstepping on the part of the assigned social worker seems to me a fairly fruitless use of our time. I can't engage in a tit for tat between you two ladies."

"That's not what I'm suggesting."

He draws an audible breath. She's annoyed him. He says, "Fine. But I'm suggesting we get to the Starkey interview. Before you have to leave."

She says nothing for a moment, assessing how far she can push him—not far, she ultimately decides. "Okay," she concedes. She shuffles the papers on his desk, comes up with the first report, and hands it to him. "I want to ask him about the dog pack."

IT'S LATE AFTERNOON BY THE TIME SHE LEAVES THE office and boards the bus home. The sky has gone powdery gray, the clouds feathered and glaucous as the broad wing of a gull. She is spent, wholly and utterly. It's wearing to keep proving herself. It's wearing to wonder all the time if the effort will be wasted anyway. She thinks for the first time in a long time about her own mother, who studied classics in college, who read Latin and Greek and French and Italian, who wrote poetry on little scraps of paper that she kept in her pockets and then threw away. What good were they? No one else would ever read her poems. It used to upset Bernadette—this defeated discarding of a whole possible life. But now she understands that it was less defeat and more exhaustion. At some point, the work is worthless.

*Can you inherit weariness?* Is it possible that the seeds of her mother's fatigue have been sitting dormant in her own bones all these years and are just now sprouting—little seedlings of self-doubt, of resignation, fanning open in her, choking out the light she's tried to let in? She thinks: *Willie will be next,* and it's an awful thought, but just for now—just for this day—she lets the shadow in her grow.

At home, he's waiting for her. "Good day with your friend Signe?" he asks, and she just nods. She will have to tell him the truth about everything—about Nora and Atalanta, about Norquist and Brodaccio—soon, but not now. He will hear it through the department eventually, or (she thinks this darkly) Nora will simply stop him on the street—what's to keep her from that now? And either of those would be worse than simply telling him herself. But not tonight.

Willie has been bathed, and she and Fred have made pancakes and eggs for supper. Willie talks butterflies again as they eat. Fred has taken her to the library, to the room where the big encyclopedia is kept, and he's read to her all about the monarchs. She has remembered the words *cycle* and *migration,* and Bernadette thinks that in another life, not that long ago, she would have delighted in these acquisitions. She would have written them into her journal after Willie was tucked into their bed. *Multisyllabic word retention with context,* she might have noted.

After dinner, Bernadette clears while Fred puts Willie to sleep. They take drinks to the bedroom, close the door. She undresses, climbs beneath the blankets, finds his legs with hers. "I need you," she says. She wants to anchor her body to itself at least for now, at least for a few minutes, and she needs him for that. She wants to be wholly present inside her own skin.

Fred puts his mouth to her neck, to her breast, to her thigh. He smells of maple syrup. His whiskers prickle her cheek. She's been lonelier than she's let herself know, and now, like a single domino tripping a collapse, just one kiss can knock her over with need.

"What's wrong?" Fred asks, a whisper. "You're crying. Should I stop?"

"No," she says. She tucks her face into the curve of his neck and shoulder. "Don't stop."

13

ON THE THIRTIETH, A LETTER ARRIVES IN THE MAIL with Willie's name on it, a wax seal on the back as if it has sailed through at least half a century to reach her.

"What is it? What is it?" Willie bounces on her toes. The script is small, shaky. The return address reads *Aalund*. Inside, a Christmas card, and tucked into that, a little folded piece of paper addressed to Bernadette. Willie gets the card—a pen-and-ink drawing of a gnome, round bellied and mushroom nosed, his feet oversized and his hat tall and pointed as a dunce cap. Inside, Signe has scrawled out a message: *Happiest Christmas! God Jul! Come back to my island and we will trade books! ~ Your Friend the Crone, Signe*

"What is 'crone'?" Willie frowns.

"Witch," Fred says. "Is your friend a witch?"

"Not a witch," Bernadette says. "Just an old woman."

Willie laughs. "A witch! She'll teach me spells. She has Turkish delight!"

They've finished Signe's book, and Willie is enraptured by visions of loving lions and white witches and Turkish delight, though the box of actual Turkish delight Fred bought at a specialty market downtown and set under the Christmas tree for her was clearly a disappointment, as she's eaten only one of the candies.

Bernadette opens the note sent to her, and in it she finds Signe's same cursive: *Bring your girl for New Year's, and we will eat cake.*

It takes little convincing to get Fred to agree to a trip out to Adela on the holiday. They've had enough of the apartment, the three of them, and he's seen nothing of the landscape here, she tells him. Won't a day out be the perfect way to begin the new year? The buses aren't running, but Mrs. Iversen has a sedan, and if Fred is driving, she'll agree to let them borrow it for the day, provided they return it with a full tank of gas and no mess in the back seat. They load it up early on New Year's Day, packing in extra sweaters and Willie's rain boots, Bernadette's camera, a bag of books for the library, and a tin of coffee they'll give as a gift.

It feels like freedom to drive in a car of their own rather than riding the bus. They could just keep going, Fred says, smiling from behind the wheel. "All the way to California. What do you think of that, Wills? We have nothing to stop us, now that we have wheels." He honks the horn into the blue dawn. The car is a beast—a '37 Ford that looks like the carapace of a large, black beetle, but Mrs. Iversen has kept the interior pristine, and Willie beams from her perch in back. There's no one on the road, which opens up before them as they leave one city and wind the highway curves toward the other. The mountain is out, and Fred actually gawks at the size of it on the horizon—a massive island of blue and white floating in a bank of cloud above the earth.

"Do you know it was Captain Vancouver who named it Rainier?" he says. "After one of his buddies. Rear Admiral Rainier."

"That's a wrong name," Willie pipes up from the back. "A mountain is too big for a person name." Bernadette whips around to look at her. Now and then, Willie spouts something like this—some bit of wisdom or reflection that seems to have come from beyond her, through her. How else could a four-year-old hold such apt ideas about the world when she's known so little of it yet? Bernadette thinks of Jung and his collective unconscious. She says, "You know, Willie, I read that the people who first lived here called it another name that meant 'Mother of Waters.'"

"Yes. That's a better name. A mother can be like a mountain, but a man can't."

Fred laughs. "Out of the mouths of babes," he says.

In the back, Willie bursts into tears. "Don't laugh at me," she says. "It's not nice to laugh at me, Daddy."

"Oh now, Wilhelmina. I'm not laughing at you. Don't be so thin-skinned!" He shakes his head, goes on grinning, not seeing the sting, but Bernadette threads her arm over the seat and reaches for Willie in the back. Willie's hand is warm and dry and still fits entirely in her own.

They park at the boat dock, buy cups of coffee and a cocoa for Willie and drink them standing in the bright, cold fog of early morning. The tug runs even today, Signe promised in a footnote to her letter—*Island people have family coming and going for New Year's dinners and whatnot*—but she failed to state the times of the tug's arrivals and departures, and so Bernadette is relieved when the shape of the little white boat materializes out of the fog on the horizon and chugs toward the dock. Just as before, the captain keeps them waiting while he bustles around the deck, and only in his own time descends the walkway and takes their toll. "Where's that penny I lent you?" he asks Willie as she steps forward. She turns to Bernadette, her face blanched, and shakes her head just once before the man lets out a run of laughter. "The look of her!" he chokes. "Thought I was serious, didn't you, darlin'?"

In the cabin, Willie climbs into Bernadette's lap and buries her head in her mother's shoulder. "It was a joke," Bernadette whispers. "He was joking with you."

"But I didn't know, Mama. Why is everyone laughing at me? I don't know I'm funny." Her eyes well, but she doesn't cry this time, and Bernadette kisses her forehead, kisses her cheeks.

"What's wrong?" Fred, who has been at the window, marveling at the water, sits beside them. "What's wrong now, Wills?"

"The penny. She misunderstood."

He grins. "It was just a tease, Willie. He was just teasing you."

"That's not nice."

"You need to toughen up a little, honey," Fred says. To Bernadette, he adds, "We got her up too early. She's tired."

Bernadette catches his eye over the top of Willie's head, mouths the word *stop*, and he sighs and goes again to the window, taking photos of the water through the glass with his back to them. Later, she knows, he'll tell her she's coddling Willie, babying her. She has no desire for that argument now. She wraps her coat flaps around Willie's body, enclosing the two of them. *Not yet*, she thinks.

The sail out to Adela is smooth, untroubled by wake or wave or even much wind. No other boats seem to be out on this holiday morning, and the water is a bolt of black satin rippling out in all directions. Mirrored cloud bodies pass on the surface, silver-white and dissolving with the stretch of the waves' motion. Willie hopes to see a jellyfish but gets instead a little bob of seals—four sleek, earless dog heads poking up to look around before going under again and then, a few long seconds later, reappearing somewhere else.

At the island, they disembark and begin the long walk to Signe's place, and when they finally arrive, their feet wet with mud and their fingers and toes frozen from the mile of road they've just traversed, Willie dashes up the front steps and begins babbling about the seals.

"Oh, tell me! I've been wondering how my friends the seals are getting on this winter," Signe says, as if she's been waiting on news of them. She hugs Bernadette, shakes Fred's hand, and says, "Who is this handsome fellow you've brought along today?" She ushers them in, where a woodstove is burning and the smells of cake and coffee and something delicious roasting in the oven remind Bernadette so powerfully of a holiday at her own mother's house that she nearly buckles at the knees in gratitude. They sit at a round kitchen table that Bernadette notices is set for four before Signe deftly slides in a fifth setting and her husband, Martin, draws another chair from somewhere and helps Willie into it.

Signe has prepared for Willie as only a grandmother could, and she hands the girl a small breadboard and a scoop of flour, a ball of golden dough, and several cookie cutters to play with while they wait on the roast. Fred follows Martin out to the yard, where the sunlight is full now, the door of the mud porch swinging shut behind him. They'll go out later, too, Signe tells Willie. There are sheep to see in the field, and a horse named Holly in the barnyard, and six hens in the coop they simply call "the ladies." Willie laughs at this and cuts another star into her dough.

"What names do you call the sheep?" Willie asks.

"Their names are Sana and Anna and Pretty," Signe tells her. "Pretty makes the best yarn."

"Pretty! That's not a name!" Willie dissolves again into giggles, then says, "Do you know that mountain named Mother of Waters?"

"I *do* know that mountain, but I know her by another name," Signe says. She grins. "Now I have one for you: Did *you* know I have a cat whose name is Canary?"

Again, Willie bursts into laughter at the hilarity of this misnomer.

"You have your hands full with that one," Signe says to Bernadette, low enough that Willie won't hear. "Stick of dynamite, isn't she?" A wink. She hands Bernadette a paring knife. "Help me peel, won't you."

Elbow to elbow, the two of them strip skins from potatoes over the deep sink, a pile of peels accumulating like leaves. It would have been like this with her mother if she'd lived, Bernadette can't help but think. Though that's not true—it wouldn't have been so easy with her mother; nothing ever was so easy with her mother. Still, there might have been holidays in the kitchen at the lake house, the radio playing Beethoven or Debussy, the smell of strong coffee in the pot on the stove, a tray of spice cookies cooling for later on a holiday like New Year's. They'd have opened the single bottle of champagne they'd drink all year, her parents. One glass for each of them, even Bernadette, the bubbles a revelation on her tongue every year, like miniature cracks of lightning against her palate, followed by a burst of sweetness. Then a walk in the snow around the edge of the frozen lake, its water the color of a dove's wing and as matte as cool wax. Her father liked to watch the stars come out on New Year's night. He said it was a good sign for the year if you could see the stars, and so he waited, blanket around his shoulders, on the porch, Bernadette in her hat and wool coat and muffler beside him, as the stars began to open like flowers budding in the darkness—one, two, and then— always—as if someone had blown the top off a seed dandelion, a million at once. *Good year*, her father always said, and smiled at her. *Good year*, she knew to return, like a blessing between them. What would it have been to give her parents Willie? To give Willie them? What would it have been to have their pride in her own mothering? To get a wink from her father, a kiss from her mother that meant *Your girl is beautiful. Your girl is bright. You've loved her just as you should, Bernie. Just as you should. You are a good mother.*

She thinks this looking at the sparkling droplets of water hitting the sink basin and can hardly breathe for a moment.

"Oh, my dear. Are you okay?" Signe lays a hand on her arm. She has wound her long braid around her head in a crown today, and her cheeks are flushed with the work of peeling.

"I appreciate this, you know. Asking us out. It's a lovely holiday."

Signe smiles. "I thought to myself, *If she has people, she'll be with them,* but I wasn't sure you did have anyone out this way. I hoped you'd drop in."

"You're right. My people are the ones I brought with me today. That's it."

"Well, my Christmas was lovely and quiet, and I'm glad that now you and I and Martin and your girl and your very beautiful husband can have a meal together."

Bernadette laughs. "He'll love that you've called him beautiful."

"I'm an old woman, I know, but I still have eyes, and that man is beautiful."

Bernadette waits for her to ask about Fred—what he does, why she didn't say more about him the last time they met—but Signe doesn't. Instead, Bernadette says, "I'm not sure you're a reliable judge. I hear you figured me for a detective on our first meeting." She grins over the sink at Signe. "I'd have loved to be a detective when I was a little girl. Sherlock Holmes was my favorite, and then Agatha Christie's Poirot and Miss Marple when I was a little older. Such an exciting life. But I'm really just a professor."

"Well now, see, that's new information itself, isn't it? Professor!" She puffs out her cheeks and raises her eyebrows. "And you said history teacher when we met, so I wasn't entirely wrong that your story didn't line up."

"I didn't say that. I just let you say it without correction."

"That's exactly what a detective would do."

Bernadette laughs, tosses a bare potato into the big pot beside the sink. "I gather you've put together my reasons for coming out to Adela, whatever I might not have told you then."

"I'll say this to you—if ever there was a man who deserved the sharp-eyed attention of a lady detective, it would be Lenny Starkey. I heard you all interviewed him." Signe slips her last peeled potato into the pot and maneuvers the pot around Bernadette to the stovetop. She nods at Willie and lowers her voice. "He's been a little shit since that age, and I remember everything. He grew up with my Benji. Never a good influence, but how much say does a mother have over those sorts of friendships, really?" She checks the roast, slides a pan of knotted rolls out from the oven and sets them on the cooling rack, and wipes her hands on the towel tucked into her skirt waist.

This is interesting—Len Starkey and Signe's son childhood friends? Bernadette notes it, files it away to come back to later, and turns instead to her real curiosity for today. "Actually, since we're talking about island history, I'd love to know more about Haven Wright."

While Willie works away decorating her cutout stars with raisins and cinnamon, Signe pours coffee and unrolls the story Bernadette came to hear. It wasn't just a midwifery clinic that Haven ran, Signe tells her, but also—when the circumstances called for it—an adoption service. Nothing official, of course, but more like matchmaking. A family from Dog Island across the inlet, or from Headwind Bay, or over even as far as Steilacoom, might put in a word with Haven, via someone they knew at Adela or Elita, that they were looking for a child, and Haven would pay a visit to the family, see that their home was in order and ready to care for an infant, and if she got the right feeling from them, she'd line them up with a girl wanting a way out of a bad situation.

"*Got the right feeling from them?*" Bernadette repeats.

"A good family feeling. Like they were clean people, and maybe had a crib already waiting and just hadn't been lucky in that way naturally themselves. She wasn't selling babies or anything awful like that, I mean. She wasn't running a baby racket. There was no profit in it for anyone, just a service to help folk out. It was in good faith."

The phrase rings in Bernadette's head, an echo of something else. In a moment she remembers: it's what Starkey himself said on the interview tape. *I'm in good faith.* A tic of his island upbringing still in his manner. She'd missed it then, and so had Norquist, most likely.

Over the years, Signe says, there were likely fifteen or twenty babies who passed through Haven's hands from a birth mother to an adoptive family in that way. A family in need connected with a girl, and everybody went away happy in the end. Only girls from Adela and Elita, though—that was Haven's rule. Bernadette asks why only island girls. "Oh, well, I don't know," Signe says. She sighs, seems to think it through. "She saw herself as providing a necessary service for our local girls. I always thought that was where her heart was, really. She'd come from outside, you know, and never was considered one of the islanders. Not by most. I think that hurt her, after everything. I imagine it would. There was maybe something to proving herself loyal in it. Loyal to the island."

"Is it just clan thinking? That who's in and who's out?"

Signe waves a hand through the air, shrugs. "You could say that, sure. Yes. Clan is a good word for it. No one would ever be anything but nice, of course. You need a ride home from the dock or a cup of sugar or what have you, anybody out here would help you without a thought. But nice isn't the same as welcoming, is it? And, oh, will they talk about you behind your back!" Her expression suggests nastiness rather than just talking. "It's an old-fashioned mindset. It's never made sense to me, but then I'm not from here either."

"You're not?" Bernadette hasn't imagined this about Signe. She seems so fully knitted into the fabric of Adela.

"Me? No, no. I married into this place. Martin's from here, way back. It's his grandfather's farm we're on, but smaller. His father sold off part of it after a bad gambling run, and Marty sold off another good chunk in '32. We couldn't run it ourselves. And then our boy died, and we thought, well, we've no one to come take it after we go. It's just dirt once you're dead, right? So we sold a little bit more." She laughs. "We kept this last parcel, and it's just right for what we can manage."

"Where are you from then?"

"Bright Lake, by birth. Then Dog Island. Then way up north to Vashon Island when I was a little older. My dad worked the fishing boats. We went where there was work."

Bernadette maps this in her head, the map muddied with her own unfamiliarity with the place but clear enough that she knows Vashon is hardly "way up north"—not even as far north as Seattle. Distance is relative to time here, it seems. The longer a person has been on this land, the farther away anywhere else seems. Adela—like Elita in so many more ways that she first realized—is a self-contained world of its own. She says, "So you remain ever the foreigner, too? Like Haven."

Signe raises her coffee cup and clanks it against the ceramic of Bernadette's. "To the intruders," she says. "We keep the gene pool sane."

Bernadette laughs.

"What is 'gene pool,' Mama?" Willie asks, and while Bernadette hobbles through an answer simple enough to be clear to a four-year-old but complex enough to satisfy her particular four-year-old, Signe gets up to tend to the meal.

As she helps Willie transfer her cookies to a baking tray, she thinks about Haven, who isn't turning out to be far off from what Bernadette constructed of her: a woman on her own in a place that would never embrace her, working and working and working to prove her merit, to prove her place beside her neighbors, even down to saving their daughters' reputations and protecting the futures of their grandbabies. So it goes. It's a story that could be told anywhere, and it never changes. *Not for certain women*, she thinks. She considers Nora Reach. Old Mrs. Iversen in her apartment alone. Her own mother leaving her studies for the invisible, safer life at the lake. Herself. Atalanta. She stands with the cookie tray, kisses the crown of Willie's head. *And you, little solo child, my barnacle daughter, my cub, my wild pup. You, too, I think. It's destined already, your life of thinking too differently to blend in.*

"It's a constellation, Mama," Willie says. "Look." She traces her fat finger around the tray, no discernible connection rising, like Orion's belt or Cassiopeia's throne from the ghost thread her daughter traces, but still she nods, says, "Yes. Yes, it is."

THE MEAL IS SERVED JUST AS THE MEN RETURN. THEY sit at the table and eat family-style, and under the table Bernadette feels Fred's knee bumping hers so that she will meet his eye, and when she does, he's looking sated, happy, like a man seeing his own desired future.

Afterward, Fred requests a family photograph, and so they arrange themselves on Signe's couch, which is soft and old, the worn upholstery covered by a blue hand-knit blanket patterned in a sea of stars and white flecks. "Did you make this?" Bernadette asks, about to praise it, but Signe waves off the compliment before it can be issued, nudging Martin to take the photo, and then he and Fred swap spots, Fred stepping behind the camera while Martin and Signe sit on the couch with Bernadette and Willie. "I'll send you a copy," Bernadette offers, and Signe smiles, says she'd love that.

Then they walk—all five of them—around the perimeter of the farm. Signe's slow, and Bernadette matches her own stride to Signe's pace. Martin and Fred take Willie on ahead to the barn with a reminder from Signe to keep an eye on Willie. "Mind that she doesn't go near the stalls, Martin," she says, her voice sharp. And to Bernadette: "Even a calm mare will kick if frightened." She and Bernadette pick their way across the muddy field. The sunny afternoon has gone gray and soft with deep-bluish clouds that look as if they could rip open and spill a whole storm at any moment, and the air is damp with the humidity of the low sky. Bernadette can't get over the light on the islands, the way it changes as the clouds shift, as the tide rises and falls, or as the storms roll in and blow over. She's been out on the islands when the light is hard and the clouds crackle with silver threads, and also at times when the air seems washed clear and the light is as liquid pale as fresh water. But just now—with this oncoming storm drenching the sky in a velvety gray, the light is richer, thicker, more saturated than she's ever seen it anywhere in her life, and beneath it the trees are greener, the mud chocolatey, the dead yellow grass of the field a pulsing, polished gold. She takes a deep breath and sniffs the rain and the salty seawater smell of the breeze. She could live here, she thinks. Fred's face at the dinner table comes back to her and she recognizes what he felt then—that intuited sense of home. That *yes* somewhere buried in her own heart burbling up. She could be happy here.

She says, "You're lucky to be in such a beautiful place, you know? I would never have come out here if not for this case with the girl, but I'm glad I know the islands are here."

Signe looks at her and nods, curt. "That's the first time you've confirmed it for me."

"What? The girl?" Bernadette sighs. "You knew though."

"I knew. We all read the papers too. We guessed from that first story back in the autumn, those of us out here. There's been word of her before this, you know. Word of sightings."

Bernadette turns. "No. No one's ever said that to me. You can't be serious?"

"Oh, truly. Sightings for years. People out on their fishing boats at dusk come back and say they've seen a girl in the brush on the beach at Elita. Fishermen out in the early morning come back with stories for their children about the ghost girl of Elita. That's what they believed before—or what they said, anyhow: she was a ghost."

"How long? I mean, for how long have people been seeing her out there?"

Signe frowns. "I couldn't tell you. Through the war, I know that. There was a whole story sometime during the war—I couldn't pinpoint it—that the girl was diverting submarines from the islands. Going down under the water and using her abilities to ward them off."

"Abilities?"

Signe chuffs. "People are silly. They'll believe all manner of nonsense. I think it was mostly just good stories. But there were folk who believed they really did see a girl swimming near the beach at Elita. More than once I heard that." She nods as Bernadette gapes at this. "So we figured, when the first story came out in September, we figured there's our ghost, not a ghost after all."

"No. She's a real child. I've met her. Several times."

"You've met her," Signe repeats, astonished. "And she's well? I mean, I wonder that she survived out there." She clucks her tongue. "Seems a marvel."

"It is. It is a marvel. She's young, but maybe not so young as she looks. Now that you're saying she's been sighted for years, I'm wondering if even the oldest guesses at her age are off the mark."

"Everyone out here knows it was Lenny Starkey who found her, and he's your answer, I'd say. I'd bet on him, and I don't bet."

They stop, and Bernadette turns to face Signe. In the breeze and the chill, Signe's cheeks have bloomed with distinct pink blots, and the bulb of her long nose is red with cold. Around her face, her hair has frayed from its braid, and wisps of white fuzz like a halo of wires frizz out. *Crone indeed*, Bernadette thinks. She might be Elli of Norse mythology—the old woman who could beat Thor in a match of strength. The set of her face when Starkey comes up is distinct—a hardening. A memory.

"The girl's father," Bernadette says. "Starkey is her father?"

Signe's expression turns inward. She shakes her head. "What I can tell you is Haven didn't trust him. For a while, he was the connection. She didn't drive, Haven. It was the one thing she couldn't do, I think, but it was a problem. She had to get to the mothers, of course, or they had to get to her. So she employed him—Lenny. For years, she employed him. He was maybe fifteen, sixteen when he started running a kind of local taxi service. His parents out on Brier Road, they had a mechanic shop going for a while. His dad ran it, but Lenny helped. And so he learned to drive, and he had a truck someone had dumped and he'd fixed up, and he started doing a little business for himself during high school, motor-ing people place to place on the island, or even sometimes across on the barge to the mainland or wherever, and that's how he landed this side setup with Haven, shuttling her patients. She paid him, and he got her to a birth or got a delivering mother to her, and every now and then, when she had a baby to place with an adoptive couple, he acted as her stork.

And he was quiet about it. That was the agreement: he was quiet if he wanted to be paid."

"But he wasn't quiet."

"He was quiet enough until he wrecked his truck on a delivery."

"A delivery of a mother?"

"A child. A child was meant to be received by an adoptive couple on Dog Island, and a few days after Lenny's wreck, this poor man shows up at Haven's door raving mad that she's tricked him and he's going to report her to the county court for operating a sham clinic. It's a minute before everybody on the island knows that this man and his wife had made an agreement with one of Haven's mothers, and the baby never got to their door."

Bernadette's heart is a clot in her throat. She looks to the barn's yard where Martin and Fred have Willie up on the horse and are walking her around slowly inside the fence, Martin holding the reins and Fred at it again with the camera. Willie's hair is a racket of curls. Her face is flushed with delight that Bernadette can see streaming out of her, like light from a bulb. She imagines this other child without being able to stop herself—a baby, swaddled into a basket on the seat of a truck beside young Len Starkey. Where did that child end up?

"What year was that wreck?" she asks.

"My memory is '37, but someone could tell you for sure."

"Len Starkey should be able to tell me for sure."

"He should, that's true. Though, I doubt there's anywhere you'd find record of that crash outside of island talk. The truck was gone. Lenny said it went in the water."

"God," Bernadette says, and Signe nods.

"And you're sure these two things are connected? The crash and the man at Haven's door?"

"Folk believe so. That's why I'm telling you. Talk has always been that they might be connected." Signe stuffs her hands into her pockets, and again Bernadette sees that set of her jaw. "It's just hard to put away, isn't it, though? Len wrecks a truck no one ever sees again, and a week later the gentleman comes storming Haven's door about a baby never materialized?"

Bernadette repeats Signe's phrase in her head: *It's hard to put away.* She considers Signe sitting with this barb in her heel all these years, waiting, licking at it like a dog with a thistle in its paw. And then Bernadette showed up on the island, asking questions, and suddenly the wound opened again. Isn't this the way of things? Bernadette looks again at her daughter, now sliding from the horse's height into Fred's arms. *It's hard to put away.*

"What happened to the couple?"

"Oh, Haven talked the man down. Told him there'd been an error. She kept a list of desiring families, and I'm sure, though I couldn't say this for certain, that she matched them with another mother's baby later." Signe flashes Bernadette a meaningful look.

"She never reported Len."

"He wouldn't be working at Elita if he'd been reported for any of the crimes we're suggesting, now would he?"

"That's true. You're right."

"And what would've happened if Haven reported him? Word of an old woman running an uncertified clinic and adoption service? Just a skip and a jump for folk to consider what other illegal services she may or may not have been offering there, and then what? Her words against his—and his parents longtime business owners on the island?" Signe shakes her head. "Haven couldn't've said much if she didn't want to go to prison herself, now could she?"

A yelp, then, and Bernadette swings around to see Willie racing across the field toward her, Martin and Fred not far behind. The conversation with Signe is over. The sky is spitting—she feels a raindrop on her bare cheek, then one on her hand as she reaches out to catch Willie in her arms. She'll have to come back to this. For now, she sweeps Willie up and kisses her neck. "You smell like horse," she says, and Willie laughs.

"Mama-mama-mama-mama," Willie tumbles the word in her mouth like turning over a stone in her hand. "Mama, I rode a horse!"

They walk back in the onset of the rain and wait it out in the warmth of Signe's kitchen. There is almond cake and more coffee, Willie's cookies, which turn out to be flavored with cardamom and butter—not the shortbread Bernadette remembers from her own mother's oven, but something spicier, foreign to her.

By midafternoon, they're walking through silver puddles back to the dock. The tug is there, and the light, waning now, is blue like the inside of a cut-glass candy dish her mother had. Blue like the marbles she played with as a little girl. Blue like the wing of the blue morpho butterfly picture in one of Willie's library books. Bernadette remembers the picture with clarity: royal-blue wings outlined in black, opened wide across a full page, and beneath the image the name *Menelaus Blue Morpho*. Why, she wondered when she and Willie first read about it, would a butterfly share a name with Menelaus, bereaved king of Sparta? Menelaus whose beautiful wife ran off with young Paris. Menelaus whose grief began a war. A man less a butterfly and more a moth, a wasp, a brown recluse spider. A man spinning a snare made of his own regret.

They stand at the dock while the tug pulls in, and soon they're in the little cabin again, heater chugging away and the windows sweaty. This time, Bernadette leaves Willie and Fred inside and steps out onto the deck alone. The water is clearer than usual because of the cold. She could look a mile down, she thinks, if it were not going dark already, but the light is failing, draining away. First day of the year, gone.

She looks back at Adela, trail of lacy wake between her and its shore now. This shoreline is staggered, sloping, bracketed by a line of barnacled boulders and smaller rocks and then a stretch of stony sand before the water. But on the other side, she knows, the island ends in sheer earthen cliffs that fall straight down to the beach when the tide is low or to the rush of the water when the tide is high. She pictures Starkey's truck careening out into the shadowed sky and falling like a bright meteor into the water. She pictures it sunken somewhere out there. The pull of the water would tug it away from the island, but not so far that it couldn't be found, perhaps. How deep is the water beyond the island's shelf? Deep, she knows. In some places, very deep. There have been pods of whales sighted in these waters. Fishing nets have pulled up giant Pacific octopuses and the white, flaccid bodies of deep-sea squid. There are stories of boats lost to storms that never again rose to the surface. If Len Starkey's truck disappeared, it likely disappeared into the water, and for good. But why? And how could he himself survive such a wreck? The water is cold as well as deep. No man would survive a fall from the height of one of the island's cliffs and then also a swim in this frigid sea. Part of Elita's draw as a prison site was exactly this—the impossibility of escape. The water is too cold, too rippled with crosscurrents and tides, too deep. She thinks again of what Willie said of the mountain—Mother of Waters. Puget Sound and all her bays are traces of a glacier that moved across this land far in the past. She's read this. She pictures the great mountain like one of those giant Pacific octopuses—body and long tentacles of ice. The octopus pulls in her legs and leaves basins behind her. She shivers, and seas stream off her skin. A mother can be a giant. A mother can be monstrous and beautiful both. What's under this water? The shell of an empty truck. The body of a baby? Bernadette doesn't want to believe that. It's better to consider what Signe has implied: Atalanta is the baby grown. Survivor of something only Starkey knows, and he not even all of it. Maybe. And if that's true, then where is her mother? Still out there. It's possible. And if it's possible, Bernadette will find her. Helen came home to Menelaus eventually, didn't she? Grief is like a tide, too; it returns to the same shore again and again.

From inside the tug's cabin, Willie knocks on the window, waves when Bernadette turns her face toward her, like the tide turning to face the moon.

## 14

SCHOOL BEGINS FOR FRED AND WILLIE ON THE THIRD OF January—the same day as Starkey's interview at Norquist's office. Bernadette has lain awake all night thinking about how to broach this with Fred. It's time to tell him about the case, she's decided. He should know. It doesn't feel right anymore to keep misleading him by omission. And she needs him to understand that she's working—she's still working, and this case is important to her.

She wakes early, packs three peanut butter and jelly sandwiches into three separate brown paper bags and is waiting at the breakfast table with eggs and toast and coffee when Fred appears, already showered and dressed. "Morning," she says. "I was hoping we could eat together. I want to talk about something." She smiles.

"Oh, Bern," he says. "I just—" He frowns. "I'm just a little . . ." He sits. His hands are shaking. The color has drained from his face. He puts his head on the tabletop.

"Hey," she says, startled, reaching for him. She walks around to his side, rubs circles on his back the way she would for Willie in a moment of panic. "What's this about? You're going to be great today."

"Will I?" he looks up at her, anguish on his expression. "How can you be sure?"

"Fred," she says his name like a breath let go. "You're an excellent teacher. You know you are. You're a genius. Remember when your adviser said that? A genius." In truth, she's always thought that was a little embarrassing—the way the word *genius* was exchanged between certain professors and their top students like gold stars, the way some students pinned the stars to their chests without a second of healthy self-awareness, Fred among them.

He shakes his head now though, his breath rushing jagged from his mouth. "I haven't told you everything." He meets her eyes. "I didn't just run out of funding in New York. I wasn't renewed. There were complaints. From the students."

She steps back. "Complaints. Why?" Her stomach constricts, but just then Willie appears, her little blond bed-fluff head and sleep-puffy eyes a bobbing manifestation of optimism.

"Today is my school day," she says, and her face might be a cloud break, light streaming from her grin. She bounds forward.

Bernadette touches Fred's shoulder. "You'll be fine," she whispers, and she leans to kiss his temple. She folds away her own news. *It will wait*, she thinks.

And by the time they've all eaten and are out the door, it's clear that she was right to say nothing. Fred seems to have tempered his worry, whatever he was about to tell her stuffed back into the past. She looks at him hard as they walk, but he's made himself opaque, cheerful even, her *genius* comment maybe enough, or perhaps it was Willie's excitement. He did have Willie stand still on the front walk of the apartment before they left so he could snap a photo of her—"First day of school!" he said, and Willie beamed at his pride.

Now, more subdued, he says, "This is good, isn't it?" He looks at her. He's not smiling—the edge of whatever came over him this morning is still there behind his eyes like a shadow, but he has returned to himself and is steady, his voice solid again, some kind of interior choice made.

He's holding Willie's hand and Willie is holding Bernadette's so that together they are a linked trio, Willie swinging in the center. "This is what brought me back to you," he says, nodding at Wills between them. "It's all going to be fine from here on out. You believe that, right, Bern?"

She could become the wind, turn into a bear, transform herself into a current of water and just run, run away from it all. Why won't he tell her what he's hiding? Still, she responds in the affirmative: "It is." This is good, yes, but the edges are already fraying, and then what? She nods at him, the cue to once again lift their arms in synchronicity and swing Willie high.

Willie's coat billows around her and she squeals with delight. "Again!" she cries. "Again!"

The day is cold, and there's a sparkle of thin frost on the sidewalk that makes Willie's feet skid when they return her to the ground. Every leaf and blade of grass in the neighborhood lawns glint in the low, gray light. "Will it be too cold to play outside at school?" Willie wonders aloud. "Will there be stories? Will there be paper for coloring? Will there be scissors to cut if I want to cut?" On and on she goes.

"You'll have to wait and see," Bernadette says after each. She feels Willie's anxiety like a current running wild from Willie's arm into hers where their hands are joined. Part of her wants to whisk Willie up and carry her home again, carry her away somewhere—anywhere—else, far from the messes and near-messes of the last months and whatever lies ahead. But she also feels a resistance to that. This is normal, isn't it? The first day of school worries and drama? This is just parenthood, wifehood, adulthood. Life is bumpy and uncertain, but mostly fine. She should focus her thoughts there—on mostly fine. She looks at Fred and at Willie, closes her eyes. And when she opens them again, like a gust of fresh air rushing in, she feels an anticipatory thrill at the idea that today is also the start of a freedom she hasn't known since before Willie was born. Each first day of school is closer to the day when Willie doesn't need her, which is the goal of motherhood, after all—successful severance. She can't let guilt or fear or second thoughts creep in and like rot begin to soften her certainty about this: her job is to give Willie freedom, and by doing so, to also free herself.

She squeezes Willie's hand. "I love you," she says. "You're going to have the best day."

Willie beams, shivers. "I know."

The nursery school is housed in the basement of a brick building on the far western edge of campus. They pass through the quad with its border of bare cherry trees and its muddy lawn, and when they reach the nursery school door, a young teacher is waiting for them with a clipboard under her arm. She introduces herself as Miss Lynn to Willie first—a good sign, Bernadette thinks, and then to Fred and to her. She can't be long out of her training. Her dark hair is wound into a bun at the nape of her neck, and she's dressed in denim pants and a sweater someone knit by hand. She says, "We start our day on the playground, Wilhelmina. Should I show you?"

"Willie," the girl says. "I'm Willie."

Miss Lynn nods, writes a note. "Thank you for telling me. I'll remember that."

She leads all three of them into a small cloakroom, where Willie is directed to a cubby on which her full name has already been written out in neat script on a piece of paper affixed to the wood. "I'll fix that," Miss Lynn says.

Willie sighs. "Good."

"Wills," Fred frowns. "That wasn't polite."

The teacher waves this off. "We like the children to express their ideas clearly. It's wonderful that she already knows herself well enough to correct me." She turns to Willie. "I wouldn't want to call you the wrong name all day, but how would I know unless you tell me what you prefer?"

Willie drops Fred's hand and reaches for Miss Lynn's. "I prefer the playground now."

Fred and Bernadette are free to go, Miss Lynn tells them. If there's any problem, she has the department phone number and will ask for Fred, as they've indicated on their paperwork.

"Great," Fred says.

"It's not that I'm unavailable," Bernadette finds herself rushing to add. "If she needs me, I'll be here. It's just that I don't have one place— you know, my own office. It's that I might be anywhere." Fred rests a hand on her arm, and she stops talking. The teacher grins, nods, doesn't care, Bernadette sees. She's blathering her mother guilt all over the poor young woman.

She and Fred watch Willie tug the teacher forward into the open nursery room and out the back door to the sound of other children playing outside. The place looks cozy, comforting, homey. There's a miniature wooden kitchen—*Montessori influence*, Bernadette thinks—set up in one corner, with miniature plates and cups and pans. In another corner, a table with a raised lip around all four sides, and inside it, a heap of fine, tan sand. There's a bookshelf crammed with books. Baskets of dolls and stuffed animals and blocks. She thinks of the room Nora Reach has made for Atalanta—this room, essentially, though smaller in scale, sized for one child—and it strikes her that the comfort of this place is the knowledge that there will be many children here, all playing with these toys together. The kitchen is a lesson only if it requires the cooperation and narrative building of collaborative play. The sandbox is good for children tinkering with concepts of space and quantity and dimension and cause and effect, but it is better if that tinkering can also happen in the context of conversation with another child, with conflict and resolution and agreement, observation and mirroring. How far can one child develop when that development must happen in complete isolation? Again, she comes back to the problem of keeping Atalanta alone at Elita—or alone, at least, as the only child among adults. At what point is her continued isolation itself the impediment to her progress? Would she not benefit from seeing other people her own size and developmental level?

"I'm heading the other way now," Fred says when they step out onto the sidewalk again. He kisses her.

"Fred," she says. She wants to spill everything—Atalanta and Brodaccio, Norquist and Starkey and all of it—but she stops herself. "Have a good first day, okay? The students will love you."

He grins. Slight puff of his chest. "Thank you."

Any other day, she might bristle at his confidence—years of golden boy charm coalescing around him at the precise moment he needs it. She might turn and watch him disappear into the building where, after years of work, all she has is a shared desk in a borrowed office. But she doesn't have time for resentment today—and, beyond that, if this is going to work between her and Fred, she has to find a way to let her happiness for him outshine her own feelings of displacement. She exhales a bloom of heavy breath into the cold air, shrugs her satchel up onto her shoulder, and reorients her thoughts to her own day ahead.

All the way back across campus, across the now-bustling quad, she considers this parallel: Willie's classroom and Atalanta's. They look the same until one steps back and reconsiders. Atalanta, of course, is looking at the shadows on the wall in Plato's cave, and Willie is skipping free outside in the sun. Until Atalanta is unchained from that den inside the cave, she'll never be able to truly grow. That's the truth, as much as Nora Reach would like to dismiss it. Brodaccio is right that the child would be better placed with other children, where she will at least have a chance of seeing the world for what it really is. And though a foster home might offer her a family, what family could possibly be equipped to care for her, this unusual child? No family with other children could accommodate the disruption Atalanta would be. It's not what Nora will want to hear, but the best chance for the girl might be an institution. Bernadette tucks the thought away for now. Like being Fred's cheerleader even at her own expense, she has more to gain by keeping on Nora's good side than by challenging her. She sighs. When did it all become so impossible to hold in balance? Why must she always step back to keep even the tiniest foothold on her own charted ground? She has no answers except to keep moving forward.

BY THE TIME SHE REACHES NORQUIST'S OFFICE, IT'S MID-morning. Norquist is in the hallway, smoking and pushing his hair back from his face and looking generally strained. "I'm not late?" she says—a question.

"No. Starkey was early." Norquist nods to the closed door of his office, lowers his voice. "He's nervous, and nervous men only go two ways when you push them—weepy or violent. I want weepy."

"What does that mean for me?"

"It means you do nothing until the moment is right, and then you work on his guilt complex."

"How do you know he has a guilt complex? He might be entirely innocent. Isn't it your job to believe that until you can prove otherwise?"

Norquist puts out his cigarette on the marble floor. "That's cute," he says. His shirt is wrinkled, stained at the armpits. Its tail pulls away from the back of his pants as he bends forward, and when he stands again, she has to look away as he readjusts himself and tucks his shirt back in. She's never met a man who is so lacking in self-consciousness. Academics are another animal—fastidious and hyperaware. Even the messy ones will change a tie they've dripped egg on at lunch, and they all smoke like they were trained to do it, paper roll between the fingers and an exhale that looks dainty next to Norquist's gusts. She imagines Fred and Norquist across a dinner table from one another and smiles to herself at the ridiculous picture.

"So I've come all the way here just to observe you at work?" she asks.

"That's not what I said. I said pay attention and get the timing right. I trust you. You're a teacher, so you're good at reading people."

She's surprised by the compliment—and the accuracy. So much of good teaching is exactly that—intuiting, observing, perceiving—but, if asked, even most of the professors she knows would say it's no more than the delivery of information from one mind to another. It frustrates her that her colleagues are so wrongheaded about the work sometimes. "I understand," she says.

"Remember, though—get your hanky out. I want mush, not snarl." He turns and opens the door.

Inside the office, the desk has been cleared, and there are two empty chairs on one side and Starkey seated on the other. Norquist's prompting and Signe's warnings and her own nerves have turned Bernadette into live wire. All her senses are at full volume. Right away, she's noting everything: the room's temperature is up, and Starkey's balding forehead is beaded with a line of pearled sweat; he's worn his uniform, and it's been pressed; he smells of pine-scented aftershave; he smiles at her the way he would at a bank teller or his high school principal's secretary—all tight-lipped reservation and good-impression eye contact.

"This is Bea. She's taking notes for me today and might ask a few questions." Norquist gestures to her, and Starkey nods.

*Bea?* she thinks. But it's a protection. She understands: he's made her invisible—just a woman, just his secretary. Charming little name. No threat.

It turns out to be a brilliant strategy.

Norquist makes Starkey shake. He asks question after question—all of them direct and brusquely voiced. Can Starkey repeat what he said in the first recorded interview? Can Starkey place himself in the prison both before and after the girl was found? Can Starkey say why he was in possession of rope and where on the girl's body he tied that rope? What time of day was it when he first saw her? Why did he believe he was seeing an animal and not a girl? What did the child look like when she came out of the grass? How long did it take to get her back to the prison? What had he just eaten for lunch that day? What had he drunk? How long had he lived on Adela and when had he moved away? What year did his work at the prison begin? Where was he during the years 1937 to 1945?

Across the desk, Len Starkey's coloring shifts from clotted cream to mottled pink. He runs a thumb under the top button of his shirt, then loosens his tie knot, then takes off his jacket and folds it over the arm of his chair. His voice shakes when he repeats the details of his war service. He was drafted in '42, ended up in the Pacific theater. He was injured in Okinawa in '45, and the war ended before he was released from the hospital.

"Describe your injury," Norquist says, no emotion.

Starkey's face blanches, and Bernadette interrupts, gentles her voice and her face. "I was a nurse. In Europe, though, not the Pacific. I saw too much. I'm sure you did too."

Starkey nods, won't meet Norquist's eyes. The room seems to sigh around them, and Bernadette lifts a hand—just slightly—to keep Norquist quiet. Starkey needs the pause, needs the way the moment is gathering on itself like fabric bunching close around a tugged stitch.

Finally, he speaks without lifting his face. "I was shot in the shoulder. Landed me in the hospital for a month." He meets her eyes, and she sees what she recognizes as the fear that never really dissipates but exists just under the skin, a kind of shrapnel one learns to tolerate. "Bastard missed my heart, but—you know—there for a little while, I thought I was over." A trembling smile.

"It's the kind of luck no one wishes for," she says. She's been waiting for her moment to swoop in.

Relief on his face. "Exactly. That's exactly it, ma'am. You said it."

"And they sent you home afterward?"

A frown, shake of his head. Now his face rumples, a worn rag, before he can smooth it out again. He draws in a breath. "Like I said, the war ended." When he meets her eyes, she can see that she's gotten to it—the bruise. It isn't the wound he's still nursing, but the guilt at never having made it back to his buddies. She wonders how Norquist characterized him so accurately. She needs to listen again to the first interview to catch the hook Norquist must have spotted then. Or maybe it's in Starkey's records—the details of his service. Whatever happened to his division.

To Starkey, she says, "I'm sorry for your losses, Mr. Starkey."

This breaks him. He puts his face in his hands.

Norquist looks to her and lifts an eyebrow. "I have a handkerchief if you need it, Len," he says, and Starkey shakes his head, sighs, looks up.

"I'm sorry. I don't usually get caught that way."

"No problem," Norquist tells him. "Take your time."

Bernadette looks at her notes, says, "Maybe we could actually step backward a bit? I think I missed something about what you were doing before the war. Would you mind helping me fill in those details?" Of course, they haven't really covered this at all—as soon as Norquist asked him about Adela earlier, he shut right up, answering with the husks of the facts Signe had already told her. Now, though, he's tired, and he trusts her. She's better at this than she expected herself to be.

"I was at Elita," he says. "I mean, before the war. Since I was eighteen. Soon as I finished high school, I got the job as a guard. They train you, you know. There's a few months of that before you really start on the job."

"That'd be a good position to get right out of high school," she says. "I'm guessing, anyway. Not a bad wage. I'm sure your parents were pleased with you doing so well right off the bat." She smiles at him.

This last bit puts him fully at his ease. He relaxes against the chair back. His legs fall open at the knees. He laces his hands together. He might be sitting on his grandmother's couch. He looks almost bashful as he answers her. "Oh, they were. My mom especially. They were happy about it. Not so happy I was leaving the garage—" He looks up. "My dad ran a garage out there on Adela. He wanted me to take it over someday, but it wasn't for me."

"He's retired now?"

"More or less."

"And you didn't want to be in the family business?" Bernadette asks.

Norquist interrupts: "No mechanical ability?"

Starkey frowns. "I could've run the place better than my dad, actually. It's not that."

"Of course you could have. It was about interest, right?" Bernadette says. "You had other ambitions."

Starkey nods. "That's it. Exactly. I just have no interest. Never did. I'd drive, but it's no life spending every day on your back, getting oil in your face and dirt in your scalp. That shit—excuse me, ma'am—that stuff never cleans up. I've no interest in that."

She nods, smiles, writes what he's said, though what's valuable is what he hasn't said—that he wanted off the family land, off the island. That he sees himself as an individual and is willing to do what he must—even disrupting the family vision—to define himself as independent of them. She notices again the clean press of his slacks and his shirt, the way he's combed and pomaded his hair with a single, clean part. What draws him about Elita, she guesses, has never been the pay, but the order, the authority implicit in his position there, the distinction of earning his own way rather than relying on an inheritance. Same as the military. She imagines his apartment is a study in good housekeeping. Sinks scrubbed to shining and the linoleum waxed, and it's just a step from there to the recognition that he wouldn't have been the one to toss cans and bottles out of the truck that day he and Ed Lind picked up Atalanta—that wouldn't do. Len Starkey is a man who respects order, who respects the island that has employed him since he was a boy. He wouldn't violate that internal sense of himself as a caretaker. She looks at him again, trying to take in every detail once more. His hands are large, and he holds them in his lap, fingers laced. He keeps himself fit—underneath his shirt, his arms are muscular, his chest broad. She mispegged him when she first listened to his voice on the tape. She remembers thinking there was something gentle about him, but now she thinks it wasn't nurture or curiosity or even intelligence she was hearing, but confidence in his own authority. He's a man who has intentionally constructed himself.

And what would Atalanta have meant to him? What would he have thought when he spotted her that day, a naked girl dashing through the grass? Norquist's notes from earlier suggest that the men believed they'd seen a deer or a dog. But that can't be true, can it? A deer or a dog would pose no harm, no threat, to the order of his world. A person—even a child—however, would.

She wants to know about the knots in those ropes around Atalanta's wrists and ankles. How were they tied? She wants to know more about Starkey's parents. These are questions she is in no position to directly ask, though, so on her notepad, she writes, *Follow me for a minute.* Turning to Norquist, she taps the pad until he catches what she's written and gives a nearly imperceptible nod. She says, "Detective, I have it in my notes that you intended to ask Mr. Starkey about his employment *before* he took the job at Elita." She feels her face flush. Her heart beats high in her chest. They haven't discussed this, and she's banking on Norquist stumbling so that she can reasonably ask her own questions.

"That's right," he says though, and then, as smooth as if it had indeed been the plan, he simply lets the question she's just posed hang between the three of them.

"Before Elita?" Starkey asks.

Bernadette looks at her notepad, and, as if she's reading from her own script, says, "What I have is this: Driver under the employ of Mrs. Haven Wright, 1932 until unknown date." She meets his eye. "Can you fill in the blanks for me there? Just so I have your history correct." A smile.

Beside her, she feels Norquist shift. He has no idea where she's leading them, clearly, but he doesn't interrupt, and Starkey seems to take this silence as pressure. He sits up, sets his hands on his thighs.

"Look, I was just a kid then, driving for Mrs. Wright. That was years ago. And I didn't know what she was doing. I wasn't privy to all that until later. Until, well—until I quit that job, to be honest with you. I was just driving and making a little cash, and that was it."

Norquist jumps in: "It seems unlikely that you could have known nothing."

Again, Bernadette is impressed with him. There's a level of theater in this that she wouldn't have guessed at before being on the stage with him, and it's artful how skilled Norquist is at catching the invisible currents of energy in the room and coasting in their wake. He sits forward now and puts his elbows on the desk, his eyes sharp on Starkey.

"Like I said, I was a kid."

"Tell me about Haven Wright," Norquist says.

Starkey sighs, shifts, lifts his hands as if to show how little he's holding back. "I know what anybody'd know about her. She was an old lady when I started driving for her."

"I have her birth written down as 1875," Bernadette says. "And you started in—?"

"Would've been '35, I guess? I was, what, fifteen, I think?"

"So, not that young," Norquist says. "You, not her. Fifteen's plenty old enough to catch on to most things."

"Well, what did I know? Like I said, I was just a kid. Maybe a dumb one, but I didn't know."

Norquist nods and waves him on.

"My job was to drive. I had a truck from my dad's garage."

"Drive whom?"

"Mrs. Wright, mostly, but sometimes other people."

"Other people?" Norquist sits back again, reaches into his pocket for his packet of cigarettes, taps one out for himself and another for Starkey. Bernadette watches Starkey hesitate but take the offered cigarette and lean in for the light. Smoke feathers out of both men's mouths, fills the little office with a cloud that rises and spreads. She'd love one herself, but Norquist puts the package back in his pocket.

Starkey pulls again on his cigarette before he says, "There were girls—women, sometimes. And sometimes babies. Mrs. Wright always came along if there was a baby."

"Where were you driving them?"

"Mrs. Wright would give me an address, and that was all I ever knew: go to this address, drop off the passenger, collect my pay for the night."

"It was always night?" Bernadette asks.

"Most often, yes."

"Always on Adela?"

"I took the barge off island usually. Usually to Steilacoom or Tacoma, or sometimes farther. Mrs. Wright arranged it. I just showed up."

"And you dropped women off at these locations—these addresses—Haven Wright gave you."

"Sometimes I'd get an address for pickup. I'd go somewhere, collect a girl—a woman, and bring her back to Adela. A few days later, I'd take her back to wherever I got her from."

Bernadette writes this down. It conflicts with what Signe has said—that Haven only helped the island girls.

They agree to return for the rest of the interview after an hour. Starkey stands on shaking legs, gathers his coat, thanks them, and closes the door behind himself on the way out.

As soon as the door is closed, Norquist says, "What the hell was that?"

"I didn't have time to tell you. He was here early, remember?"

Norquist stands and paces the five feet between his desk and the door. "There's nothing in any of the documents I have about Haven Wright running a child-trafficking operation."

"Not trafficking. Adoptions."

"Sounds like abortions too."

"I don't know about that. All I know is that she did deliveries, and when the mother opted to relinquish her guardianship of the child, Haven acted as sort of a conduit—a connection between babies and adoptive families."

"But there were no formal adoptions?"

"I believe this was all under the table."

"Goddamn it." Norquist slams his hand against his desk. "And this information is via—?"

"Signe Aalund."

"Of course." He shakes his head. "She skipped out on me, but you saw her."

"She invited my family for New Year's dinner."

"You didn't say."

"I would have."

"You didn't." He unbuttons his shirt sleeves and rolls his cuffs to his elbows, and for a moment a fear jolts through her—will he hit her? She steps back, toward the door. But after a moment he sighs, folds his arms over his chest. "Okay, then," he says. "Tell me what else she gave you."

Bernadette explains Signe's theory—Len Starkey driving for Haven for years, and then the accident and the baby missing. "And according to Signe, nothing was ever reported, and neither the child nor the truck was ever found."

Norquist has gone pale, and circles of sweat have blossomed on his shirt fabric under his arms. "Jesus," he says.

"Signe told me everyone out there knew, but no one said a thing."

"Those goddamn islanders."

"And—" she begins but hesitates.

"What?"

"She said they've seen the girl on Elita for years, picking around in the bushes along the shoreline, even swimming off the island. They made her into lore. A ghost. Apparently, there were stories about her protecting them from Japanese subs during the war."

"For shit's sake," Norquist says. "Not one of them said a thing when this all came out. Not one person from that goddamn place called in any information when the first stories came out in September. Not one." He continues pacing, and it's as if he's stirring the atoms in the room, churning them with his anger. A rush of his anxiety swims toward her on a current of air, but she refuses to absorb it herself, refuses to panic when she's been so successful today. She sets down the notepad.

"I think I can get him to confess," she says.

Norquist looks at her. "Confess to what?"

"I don't believe he crashed his truck into the Sound and managed to get out. He abandoned the child that night—for a reason he will, I think, eventually admit, though my guess is that he was the father—and then he took the truck to one of the island's bluffs and pushed it into the water." She's out of breath. "And I think I can get him to tell us. All of it. And I think he's been looking for her, too. Ever since the rumors about a ghost child on Elita started. I think Len Starkey knew who she was, and he hunted her."

Norquist's stare is searing, and in the stillness of it, everything goes soft and slow. The air in the room floats with dust motes. She thinks: *What am I promising?* Her pulse is loud in her ears.

"Why not just put the baby in the truck and send them both into the water?"

"Gutless," she says. "He's a kid, not a murderer. He just wants the baby out of sight. Have you heard of object permanence? A baby loses sight of his blanket and thinks the blanket is gone forever. If he can't see it, it doesn't exist. People grow out of that, of course, but it's possible to imagine a teenager capable of deluding himself in a similar way, isn't it? No baby in sight equals no baby." She's unreeling all her thoughts of the last several days now, unraveling all she's got.

"Well," he says. "That's a beautiful story, Bernadette." He shakes his head. "You think a stupid fifteen-year-old kid could construct that—and pull it off?" He laughs, one short, hard sputter. "This is messier than I thought, but the mess only makes it less likely Len Starkey was anything but gullible. Haven Wright is more likely, and she's dead, unless she too has been walking the island as a ghost. Can you get Signe Aalund to give you Haven's ghost next? I'd like to question her." He laughs, high and shaky and frazzled.

"Haven Wright wasn't a smuggler."

"Unless I'm missing something in your conveyance of Mrs. Aalund's story, she was a smuggler."

*Conveyance.* She could roll her eyes. "You think Haven meant to get rid of the child and Starkey helped her cover it up?"

"I think she coerced him into that, more or less, yes."

"He'd ruin his father's truck to help an old woman who was nothing but his employer?"

"For the right price."

"What would Haven Wright gain in abandoning a child? She was a midwife. Her work was delivering babies."

"Maybe that was her job. Do we have records of the births and deaths she attended?"

"You're jumping—no, leaping!—to conclusions for which you have no proof," Bernadette says. Her anger is a flame now. *Abortions*, she thinks. *That's what this is about.* That's what he's latched onto—why Haven is suddenly guilty, and Starkey is just a gullible kid. Signe was right. Once the accusation of abortion is present, it doesn't matter what a woman like Haven has or hasn't done. How many girls and women have narrowly sidestepped the catastrophe of an unwanted future. It doesn't matter. She's the witch, the crone, the villainess.

"We may never know why she did it," he says. "People aren't reasonable, and a lot more of them than you'd think are just selfish. You rarely get good answers to *why* in this line of work." He pauses. The frustration in the room is suffocating.

"So we find another source," she says. "We find Atalanta's mother, and we find the answer." She lets out a breath. Her chest is constricted now, as if she's strung herself in lacings and pulled them tight. She looks at her watch. It's been well over an hour since they broke for lunch, and she's neither eaten nor even stood up, but where is Starkey? "He's late," she says. "Weren't we starting up again after an hour?"

Norquist opens the door. She hears his shoes on the corridor floor, then the stairs, descending, getting quieter. From her purse, she pulls the bagged lunch she made what seems like a million years ago now and eats half her sandwich. It helps. The strings at her ribcage loosen, the wash of acid in her gut starts to still.

It's implausible to her that Haven Wright could be behind the missing infant. She thinks back to the photo on the wall of Adela's library. Haven in her white dress and headscarf, her face turned toward the camera, broad and open and bright-eyed. Not the sort of woman prone to secrets. Though, of course, her whole life became a secret in the years she was running her clinic out of her home, running babies between birth mothers and adoptive homes at night. What had Len said? When a baby was in the car, Haven always rode along. He drove them to Steilacoom, to Tacoma, even farther. Where? There must be records of these adoptions somewhere—at Haven's old farm or in the care of someone she'd trust. *Signe*. Bernadette thinks it and, like ice coalescing on the surface of a lake, she feels it harden in her, true and cold and obvious. Signe has Haven's documents. Or she knows where they are.

The other thing that occurs to her is that Len said he took the barge. To get off island, he took the barge. Whose barge? Who helped him? Also, those trips had to be paid for, and someone must have the barge operator's accounting books for all the years of its operation. What about the tug captain? He'd have seen Len and Haven and one baby after the next boarding a barge at the dock, wouldn't he? She writes it down so she won't forget it: *Barge records? Haven's documents?*

Of course, beyond all of this, what does not track, no matter who's responsible for abandoning Atalanta, is the girl's survival. How, Bernadette cannot answer for herself, could an infant survive in the cold, in the wet, in the darkness of Elita's wilderness? What's to say Atalanta is the same child who went missing that night all those years ago? What's to say she's the island's fabled ghost, materialized in the shape of a girl now? What's to say any of this, really, is connected?

Just as she is cutting open the hole of this question in her mind, Norquist appears again at the door.

"Starkey's gone," he says.

## 15

SHE'S NEVER BEEN IN A POLICE CRUISER, AND AS NORQUIST swifts them toward Steilacoom and the dock, she tries to memorize the details to tell Willie later. *It was like riding inside a steel orca*, she'll tell her, the car's swooped flanks and round nose unmistakably whale-ish. Willie, she imagines, is just finishing her after-lunch resting time. There are mats to roll out at the nursery school, and the children lie on them for a half-hour each day after coming in from their noon playground time. She wonders what Willie has thought of this first day. Has she found friends? Has she sat in the corner with the books and read? Has she made tea in the child-sized kitchen? It will be Fred who picks her up now, Fred who gets to hear all about Willie's day. She knew it was Willie she was sacrificing when she called the department from Norquist's office before leaving and had the secretary take a note for Fred: *Caught up in something. Home as soon as possible. Get W by four o'clock.* She didn't identify herself by name, and left no *love* or *xoxo*, but said only, "This is Fred Farrell's wife. May I leave him a message?" She'd worried for a moment that Mrs. Wahl would recognize her voice, but of course, that would never happen. Why would Mrs. Wahl expect that one of her professors was married to another? It wouldn't ever line up in her thoughts to attach the voice of a wife speaking over the phone to the odd female teacher, Bernadette. Wives do not have jobs. Still, Fred will be upset. He'll want to know what the hang-up was about. She'll have to tell him—or construct another lie. The whole thing—missing Willie's afternoon, leaving the message, getting into Norquist's cruiser—all of it is a risk, but how could she do anything else? She has to take the work as it comes.

Out the cruiser's window, the city smears into a slick of gray. It's one thirty in the afternoon and the light is already dusky under the heavy January cloud cover. They might have to take the boat all the way to

Elita, Norquist tells her, if Starkey isn't just at the dock, and she nods. It's not actually a chase, he says—it's not illegal to walk out on an interview, just stupid. But they'll surprise Starkey this way, catch him up when he thinks he's dodged having to answer more. And now they have more, don't they? They have what she's told him about Haven and the truck. They can leverage that information to their advantage, tell Starkey they'll go to Adela and talk to the locals, the boys he grew up with—now men, and probably his hunting buddies. Didn't he say he hunted with some of those men? The tug guy? Somebody else?

Norquist doesn't stop talking. Now and then she looks at him and nods, says a brief *mm-hmm* of agreement or consent, but he spins and spins like a dime on its side, driving too fast for the conditions—like all cops, she thinks—and smoking out the narrow crack in his window.

She can imagine him this way as a younger version of himself—wired, unable to sit still. She figures him for a kid who was often in trouble. She's met kids like that. They're bright, most of them. Too bright, somebody has usually told them. Too smart for their own goddamn good. Smart-assed. Smart-mouthed. Was this Norquist? She can see that about him. A kid who needed to move instead of sit, who needed to think in too many directions at once to do well with math tests and book reports. She despised that type of kid when she was a kid herself. Their derailments and irresponsibility. Their flighty inability to follow through. She couldn't understand it and so believed it was simply a personality fault. A failure. But there's something admirable in the energy now. She and Fred and all the good students were taught to move slowly, to be methodical, to drive forward toward visible, common, standardized goals. The rewards would go to those who stayed on course. And that molded them—not just their actions, but their thought patterns. Their hearts.

What does it mean, she wants to know, to live inside a life less corseted than her own has been? What would it look like to live without the laces and the bindings in place? What would her life have been if she'd attached herself to someone like Norquist instead of someone like Fred? There is a spectrum that includes Fred and her and Signe and Starkey and certainly Nora Reach on one side; and on the other, ranging further, one to the next, Norquist and Haven and, finally, way out on her own isolated pole of freedom and fear, Atalanta. Bernadette can see this line of lives unrolling, and she wants to know what it would take to step just a little closer toward free, just a little further from constrained. What would it take and what would it cost? She looks across the cruiser's front seat at Norquist, smoke tendrilling from his mouth like uncoiling vines. In her own seat, she holds her hands over her satchel in her lap, sits with her legs crossed at the ankles, just as she was trained to do. Nice girls, her mother reminded her often, are nicely behaved. What—or whom—could she love, Bernadette wonders, if she had been taught another lesson about herself instead?

Norquist pulls into the ferry's parking lot, walks around the car to open the door for her.

"You don't have to. I'm perfectly capable," she says.

"It's not chivalry. The lock only works from the outside." He grins.

"Of course. Cop car. Lock 'em in."

There's no line at the dock, and the boat is churning, ready to leave. "Just get on," Norquist waves her toward the boat and quick-steps up the ramp behind her.

"Don't we need tickets?"

"Unnecessary." He flashes the badge inside his coat flap and grins again.

"At some point, that crosses over from professional privilege to pomposity."

He laughs. "You're going to appreciate it in one minute when they let us on without questions."

They pass the guard and are whisked on board, where it takes no time at all to spot Starkey. He's seated near the front of the ferry, his coat on and his collar up. He's eating a sandwich from a waxed-paper wrapper that he folds neatly back over the bread and cheese when Norquist sits beside him.

"I'm sorry," he says first thing, no hesitation. Again, Bernadette sees that it's order he most respects.

"I don't like it when people waste my time," Norquist says.

"I'm sorry. I apologize, sir." Starkey sighs.

"*Detective* is good. *Norquist* is fine. Running out on me is neither."

"Detective Norquist, I'm sorry. I panicked. That's it. I should've thought."

"You should've thought." Norquist gestures to Bernadette to sit on Starkey's other side. She fishes her notebook out from her satchel and finds a pen.

"We're doing this here?" Starkey asks.

"I'd have preferred my office, but you ran out."

"I just—"

"Look, Mr. Starkey, it's here or I can follow you into the prison and talk to your superior about giving me the start of your shift."

Starkey nods. "Here, then." He looks over his shoulders at the others on board—a woman in a kitchen uniform, a man Bernadette would guess is janitorial staff, and two other guards in their own conversation near the back of the cabin.

"We can keep it quiet," Bernadette says.

"Let me get right to it." Norquist leans forward. "If I were to send out divers, on what side of Adela would I be most likely to find your truck?"

Starkey goes rigid in his seat. "I don't know what you're talking about, Detective."

"You don't? That's not what I've been led to believe."

"I don't have a truck."

"Maybe not now, but you did."

"You can check licensing. I never registered any truck."

"Mr. Starkey, my next move is to begin questioning other islanders. Your parents. Your hunting buddies. Your father's hunting buddies. You see where I'm going with this. You can talk to me, or I can talk to them."

Starkey nods. Something in him has hardened. "You go ahead with that, then. I can give your girl here their addresses."

Bernadette waits, but he says no more, and so she folds the cover over her notebook and tucks it away. "Can I ask something myself?" Her voice is a controlled pour of syrup. It catches Norquist off guard, she spots, because he frowns at her, waves her on. "Mr. Starkey, I can't help but ask about something that came up in the notes. Do you know someone named Marley or Marlowe? Anyone with a name like that?"

She's watching him when he answers—watching him close, as if she's peeled the scales off the air between them and can see with fine clarity his every facial twitch and tightening. But she sees nothing. Nothing.

He says: "There was maybe a family by that name on the island when I was a kid, but I couldn't say for sure." When he looks up, he meets her eyes dead on. "I don't really recognize it, no." He's not lying.

She sighs. "I must have it wrong."

Starkey shrugs and gives her a weak smile. He's off Norquist completely, but she's managed some rapport with him—just as Norquist said she would. To what degree that's just the consequence of her sex—the benefit of invisibility—and to what degree it's indicative of any real persuasive ability on her part, she couldn't say, and that, she knows, will be a thorn in her thumb all day. If she has any true power, she'd like to be in possession of it.

They sit in silence for the rest of the ride, Norquist waiting Starkey out and Starkey refusing to acknowledge Norquist's presence. At the prison dock, Norquist hands Starkey Bernadette's notepad and tells him to write down his parents' address and those of three other islanders he says know him well and will account for his good record, then they all disembark without speaking. Norquist and Bernadette are stopped at the first checkpoint while Starkey sails on through, free for now.

Bernadette watches him disappear into the prison. "What are we doing here?" she asks. "Are we following him in and talking to his boss?"

"Not yet. I want to track down these addresses before I try cracking anybody at Elita. These boys stick together. Nobody'll say anything against Starkey until I have more on him." He rubs his eyes, looks back at the stretch of water between Elita and the mainland. "But you might as well see your patient, seeing as we're already here, no?"

They aren't denied entrance until they reach the guard outside the hospital wing. No one gets into that room, he tells them, unless Brodaccio has given his permission. It's the same guard who was on duty the last time Bernadette visited—tall, broad shouldered, face like a root vegetable.

"You've met me," she says. "I'm Professor Baston. I'm working with the child."

"Not today, you're not."

Norquist steps forward, offers his badge again. "Look, she's with me, and I say she's fine."

A small smirk at the corner of the guard's mouth. "Like I said, Detective, no permission, no access."

Norquist taps his badge.

"You want to show me your local badge or your Scouts badge, that's fine, but neither gets you in here without the doctor's permission. That's my orders."

Norquist turns, but just as he does, Nora Reach appears inside the swinging door. Some internal weather system Bernadette can't quite read crosses her face before she can control it, but in an instant she's all broad smile and outstretched hand. Bernadette thinks of the camouflage certain animals put on in moments of threat—the chameleon, the octopus. Creatures that swiftly become tree or rock or pocked lump of coral on the seafloor to avoid being spotted for the soft bellies they truly are. She marvels at it in nature, but on Nora, it's off-putting. It's not camouflage, really, but the opposite—a mark of trickery or at least omission. Where is her face under that smile? What is she hiding there?

"What a surprise!" Nora says. To the guard, she frowns. "Why have you stopped Professor Baston and Detective Norquist?"

"But Dr. Brodaccio—" the guard begins.

"I authorize their entry." Nora pushes past him and ushers them into the room.

"That was impressive," Bernadette says.

Nora arches one of her perfect brows. "Really, who has time for these silly power games Brodaccio wants to play?"

Once again, the light and the softness of the room hit Bernadette, but there is also a smell this time—nauseating and bodily. It's feces, Bernadette recognizes. And just as she does, she spots Atalanta, once more wet headed and gowned, this time with her arms bound behind her in a white restraint jacket. She is in the crib, though it seems bigger than the one here the last time Bernadette visited, and perhaps this is true, because the child is also visibly bigger. Her cheeks have fleshed out. Her knees, which stick up bare from under the hem of her gown, are not so knobby.

"This looks harsh, I realize," Nora says. She smiles, tight. "It's a consequence, though. Just a consequence. We're working on training for appropriate social behaviors."

"What's she done?" Norquist asks.

Nora holds her stiff grin. "This is atypical, of course. You'd train a child without her specific needs differently. It would do her no good to allow her to continue acting instinctually rather than intellectually, though. She must survive in the social world, or we haven't served her."

"What'd she do?" Norquist asks again. He must smell the warm, awful odor—his expression is puckered—but he doesn't speak the obvious aloud.

"This looks draconian," Nora interrupts. "I know. But this is Brodaccio's hospital." She gives Bernadette a pointed look. "Atalanta can be violent. When she's reprimanded in gentler ways, she hits or spits. If we confine her to a corner, she soils herself and makes a mess of the waste."

The smell, Bernadette thinks. This is why she's wet headed. She's had to be bathed. Now, underneath the odor of feces, Bernadette smells also the high, acrid smell of bleach and notices that the rug from the corner with the books and bin of blocks is missing.

"This is why I'm recommending an institution." A big voice—Brodaccio at the door. Across the room, the girl rises on her knees and growls. She pushes her face against the crib bars. Her snarl is a rolling, open-throat rumble of warning.

"Jesus," Norquist says.

"You see," Brodaccio says. "We can't make progress with that. She's like an animal."

Nora crosses the room and stands beside Atalanta's crib. She raises both her hands, palms open. "I'm going to touch your back," she says, and Bernadette watches as Nora waits for a signal of consent from the child. When the girl averts her eyes, Nora reaches over the crib rungs and rubs a wide circle on the child's back. "See," Nora says. "You're safe." It's a hush taking the shape of words. A whisper. "Lie down," she says, soothing, calm. "Lie down and rest." Nora has made her voice like warm water. Like breeze in a tree's leaves. *Hush, honey. Hush.*

Atalanta rocks back and forth for another moment before she relaxes. She sinks under Nora's hand and rests her cheek on her pillow. Tears roll from her face down her nose, and Nora says, "Poor sweetheart. You don't need to cry. I'm going to touch your face," she says before she wipes the tear tracks from Atalanta's cheeks. The girl lets herself be touched. She closes her eyes.

Nora's voice in the room is a spell cast, a litany. "You're safe," she says. "You're safe. You're warm. You're fed. You're safe. You're warm. You're fed." The atmosphere stills.

"This—this is not medicine." Brodaccio bites out the words. "This is mothering." He shoves the doors open and storms out.

Nora doesn't turn her face from the girl or stop her lullaby. It takes a moment, but without Brodaccio's anger, the room eases. At the crib's edge, Nora croons and hushes. The light on the walls reflects the light of the sea outside, spangling in the rhythm of the waves. The room is as calm as an infant's nursery, and for an instant Bernadette could almost believe that Nora is the right mother for this girl—that she truly loves her.

But then—no. Bernadette draws a breath, tells herself, *No*. She reminds herself that Nora has masterminded the child's need in this moment with her consent to whatever has come before it. In better circumstances, the girl would be learning, thriving even maybe. What she's just seen— the child's fear and punishment—it can't stand, even against this lull of peace. No matter how strong Nora's will and maternal theater, this is not a child's nursery in a perch above a seaside cliff; it is a prison. And it is a prison for men, not girls. Just down the hall right now, hundreds of incarcerated men have just finished their lunch and recreation hour and are returning to their afternoon labor. Many of these men will never leave this place. And whatever has brought them to this place was not petty crime—it was violence. Violence against bodies. Being bound here is their consequence. It's isolation as punishment. But their isolation isn't truly isolated. The men here live and sleep and eat and cry and laugh and shit together. There's not one thing a man does here that twenty other men don't witness. The punishment of life at Elita is the penalty not of isolation but of a forced pack. It's a stripping of each man's human identity until he is simply part of the animal whole. A body and little more. And that's not what any man deserves, but it is certainly not a just sentence for Atalanta. What would this pack do to such a girl? What have they already done? That growling when Brodaccio walked in the room? It sent a trip of chills down Bernadette's neck and spine. Dogs growl like that at men that kick them—not at men who feed them. Girls learn to growl like that at men who—*God*, she thinks. *No.* She can't stomach it. She feels sick and weak.

Bernadette sees in her mind a terrible image, associatively conjured and unbidden. It's an animal hung and skinned. This is a memory, she realizes quickly—she's seen this in real life, when she was child. Her father hunted now and then, and one cold autumn day he brought back a deer and hung it from its back legs by a rope in the same tree by the lake where her own swing hung. Pink froth bubbled at the animal's nose and mouth and ran in a stream off its chin to the ground. Her father had Bernadette stand by with a bucket for the heart and the liver while he skinned it. She hasn't thought of this in years, but the memory drops like a glass slide into place behind her eyes, whole and unbroken, the picture of it awful—and behind it, like a shadow of the first image, a second also drops. This one is warped, though, and not as clear as real memory. This one is created from story, and it is a moving image, a film. In it, she sees a deer running in tall grass, a rock thrown, a leap. When the body lands in the road, it's a girl, not a deer. This is a fairy tale, a myth. This is another world, where girls and animals are not so far apart, where the shape of a girl's body can also be the shape of a deer's body. Where a truck can slip into the sea and vanish. Where a baby becomes either a wave or a pile of ashes or a girl without any words. Where the landscape and the creatures within it are bound to one another by more than the weight of a foot or a hoof on the earth.

"I need to sit down," Bernadette says aloud. "I feel—" Her head swims, and her vision goes black.

WHEN SHE SITS UP, SHE'S ON A GURNEY IN ANOTHER HOS-pital room. There's a guard—a different guard—at her side, and also Nora, and also Norquist. This room is wide and white and lined in beds, some of which hold men. She swings her legs over the side of the bed.

"Nope," Norquist says. "Too soon. You lie down." He touches her shoulder, and she lies back.

"What—?" she starts.

"You fainted." Nora's face is tight, and there's irritation in her tone.

"I don't do that," Bernadette says, but in the back of her pounding skull, she knows that's not true. She fainted more than once when she was expecting Willie. *Oh, no*, she thinks. She cannot be pregnant. She touches her forehead and pushes that thought out of her mind, says only, "Did I hit my head?"

"You went down on all fours," Norquist says. "It was impressive, honestly."

Bernadette sits up and ice bags slide off her knees. "I'm sure it's just bruises."

"You went down pretty hard," Norquist says.

"I'm fine." Again, she swivels, and now Norquist braces her elbow, helps her balance as she fumbles for her shoes. When she stands, he stays at her side. He smells of sweat and smoke and old coffee, and for a moment a wave of nausea passes through her, but she lets it roll like a wave, through her and away. She's fine. She's got to be fine.

"What time is it?"

"Four."

"Oh, shit. Four!"

Nora's expression hardens again at the curse, but she says, "There would have been nothing for you to do today anyhow. The child's still sleeping. It's been a waste of an afternoon."

"Nora," Bernadette stops her. "I need to meet with you. Not here. Privately."

"Meet with me about what?"

"Nora, you can't let this go on. Can't you see how she's struggling?"

"What are you saying?" Nora frowns.

"What I saw today—I can't condone it. I agree with him. With Brodaccio. She needs other children. She needs an institution. It's the best way." Bernadette's head throbs, and she puts her hand to the back of her neck.

"You don't have to talk about this now," Norquist says. "Come on. I'll get you home."

"You agree with him?" Nora's face is waxed. She is the color of scalded milk.

"She needs more than you can give her here alone, and she's terrified of him. I'm afraid of what's going on when you're not here. Did you see the fear on her? You have to see that." Bernadette wouldn't be saying all of this aloud, in front of Norquist and the men in the other beds, but her

160

head is a pulse, and her vision is throwing halos around every lightbulb dangling from the high ceiling, and there's simply no more time to wait. That image of the girl-turned-deer-turned-carcass is still fizzing like acid at the back of her brain. She could vomit thinking of it, so she pushes it under the next wave of nausea and wills it away. "There's no time to deliberate about this," she says to Nora. "The girl is suffering. It can't go on. You know that. You love her, don't you? You love the girl. You have to help her."

"Come on," Norquist nudges Bernadette forward. "You need to go home."

Nora's face is a blade. "I can't believe you think I'm not protecting her."

"That's not what I'm saying."

"I'm protecting her."

"I'm not saying you aren't trying. I'm saying you can't. Not really. Not here."

"Come on," Norquist says. "Let me help you. We need to leave."

Nora grabs her arm, squeezes. "What will you do? Are you thinking of reporting this? Putting this into your—" she sputters. Her voice is mottled with barely suppressed rage. "Into your pseudoresearch? I chose you, you know. I chose you as my partner because I thought another woman would understand. She's not just any girl."

"What?"

"Nora," Norquist says. "Please. Take your hands off her. You can meet another time. You can use my office if you want. Both of you come there and meet. That's fine."

"She's a child," Bernadette says. "Just like any other child."

"No! She's exceptional."

"Nora," Norquist says again. "Let go."

Nora looks at him. Her voice is the raw edge of a saw. She lifts her hand from Bernadette's arm. "You're removed from this case, Mrs. Baston. From this moment, removed. Your work has resulted in no positive linguistic development, and I am retracting our agreement with you as a consultant. Any mention of Atalanta, Elita Island Federal Penitentiary, or myself in your academic or personal published work will be cause for legal action. Do you understand?"

"Nora," Norquist says again, forceful now.

Bernadette's head swims. The circles of green and yellow and silver light that round each bulb overhead expand and contract. "I understand," she says. She turns to Norquist. "I need to get home."

He nods, and she lets herself be escorted out of the prison and down the ramp again into the wind and the sea air. She allows herself, for once, to escape.

NORQUIST INSISTS ON DRIVING HER HOME, BUT SHE HAS him let her out four blocks from the apartment. "Can't be arriving in a cop car or the neighbors will talk," she smiles.

"You're sure?"

"Just leave me here. I'm fine."

He lets her out, but she feels him following at a distance, his headlights low and tires just rolling softly forward over the wet street. She doesn't turn back and doesn't change her mind about walking. She needs the space and the brace of the cold night air and the darkness to braid herself back together before she has to face Fred. She's certain he'll be worried or angry or both—what about her work could possibly take all day, after all? But in the end, without really calculating how it will affect anything between them, she opens the front door with a gust of wind and bursts out a half-truth: "I've been in the hospital all afternoon. I fainted."

"God, Bern," he says, a rush of relief in his voice. He crosses the room and wraps his arms around her, ushers her to the couch and has her lie back with her feet up, brings her hot tea and toast. Whatever suspicions or anger he might have had about her absence all evening have fizzled, and he is only concerned.

"I'm fine," she assures him. "It was nothing."

"You're sure?"

"Of course. Nothing. Where's Willie?"

"Sleeping. Don't worry about her. She's fine. She had a great day."

He sits beside her and strokes the hair from her forehead and kisses her there as if she is a child, tucks a blanket around her as if she is bird with a broken wing. He eyes her with worry that says, *My poor fragile darling.* And she sighs and closes her eyes and lets him comfort her because maybe that's actually all she is.

# 16

FOR DAYS, THERE'S NOTHING BUT SILENCE. ONE WEEK passes, then a second. She ignores the continued nausea she feels, the worry about its cause. She's not ready to consider the possibility of another child and what that would mean. What she wants to focus on is Atalanta, but no one from Norquist's office or Elita contacts her, and finally she understands that Nora has really gone through with it and removed her from the case. The job is over, unfinished, and she—a failure—is out. She's losing everything she worked for.

Silence.

Every morning, she takes Willie to the nursery school. She walks beside Fred, holding his hand. They are in the soft, gray center of winter, all the trees bare as wrought iron and the sky and ground both swollen with rain. Twice a week, after dropping Willie, she and Fred part ways just outside the department doors, entering separately. He goes to his office on the second floor, and she takes the east hallway to the reading room, where she's been assigned a carrel this term. The space is small, but she doesn't dislike the quiet of the reading room, doesn't dislike being walled in by floor-to-ceiling books. Students come and go, occupying the other carrels, but rarely does anyone disturb her, and most days she is entirely alone. The windows look out on the east side of the campus—away from the western horizon and toward the gray-brown sprawl of the city's roofs. She can sit in the cushioned window seat for hours looking out at the students passing between buildings below or the pigeons perching on the metalwork fences that line campus. There's a sacred atmosphere in the reading room, and in it she feels the silence stilling and entering her rather than pulsing outside of her, as if she herself has become part of it.

After classes, she rejoins Fred and they collect Willie from the nursery school, and the entire day unspools until they end up exactly where they began, in the kitchen of the apartment, as if no hours have passed, or maybe as if all the hours are the same one running in a simple loop. Bernadette makes dinner and washes up while Fred prepares for his classes. She helps Willie with a bath, and then Fred reads to her. They both tuck Willie into the little bed Fred found secondhand and set up in the corner of the front room just after the holidays—a folding screen standing in for a wall. *Good night, good night. Kisses and hugs. Mama loves you, barnacle baby, wild girl, beloved one.* And then it is morning again, and the reel runs forward once more.

One empty morning, when Fred and Willie are on campus and she's home alone, she can't stop her thoughts from rolling over her like a storm coming in, and so she walks alone to the public library and checks out a novel and distracts herself by reading the entire book inside the day. Another morning, she can't bear the evidence of her failures, and so she retrieves her case notebook from her satchel and tucks it under a heap of sweaters in the bottom drawer of her dresser, then walks to the drugstore and buys a fresh blank notebook. Inside it, she tries to write, but finds herself devoid of words. *Thinking about language's limitations—,* she scrawls, the dash dropping off like a cliff into the sea of blank page. On another sheet, she notes five of Willie's new words: *arbor, kinship, hibernation, vibrant,* and *ardor. What to make of that rhyme?* she writes to herself. *Arbor and ardor. Curious! Words develop in patterns . . . Maybe next "harbor"? "Barber"? Will keep track and document.* This line of thought approximates real work, and for an afternoon, she is happy with it. But when she looks at these jottings the next day, she's disgusted with herself. The simplicity! The stupidity! She rips the page from the notebook, crumples it, and throws it away. It's a bunch of garble. A bunch of nothing. She's empty, and that's the truth. She writes: *YOU ARE EMPTY.* She puts the notebook in her satchel and leaves it alone.

Maybe boredom, she thinks, can be learned. Maybe stimulation is a drug she needs to wean herself from. Maybe she could learn to just live with what she has and be grateful for it—her healthy child, and maybe a second one on the way; her husband returned to her like a wish she stuffed in a bottle and threw into the ocean. This could be a whole life, she thinks. Just this and nothing more. A simple rhythm. Isn't it what she had before Nora Reach first found her? Isn't it what most women have and endure and learn to call a whole life? And what's wrong with it? Everyone else seems happy enough. Why should she be unsatisfied, really? What privilege is it to have all this and still find her life lacking? The questions circle and circle in her mind like the seagulls she watches from her reading room perch as they round the sky on gray mornings. *Why not find a way to be happy?* she writes into the notebook. *Why can I not just be happy?*

Beneath every day, though, the scene at Elita rests like stagnant water. When she closes her eyes and begins to drift at night, she sees it there again, just behind the curtain of her consciousness. Here she is in Atalanta's room at Elita, standing beside Norquist, watching the light flecks play on the wall. But from there, the memory splits all its seams and the guts of it spill out. The high sweet stink of the child's shit. The slosh of the sea rising beyond the prison windows while, in her head, the image of the skinned deer hangs bloody and dangling. She sees Atalanta in her white restraint jacket, and then a twinned image opens beside it: Atalanta lying on her belly in the road, rope around her wrists and Starkey standing over her. And then—what? The slide and the fall. Bernadette's own knees hitting the ground, and the burn of bruises after she fainted. The pulse in her ears and the back of her head. She wakes up from this recurring dream shaking.

It's her fault, she decides in those night hours. It's all her fault. She let Fred back into her life and her bed. She let herself be drawn into a case for which she was entirely unprepared. And why was she drawn into this case in the first place? What gave her the impression that she was qualified to get involved at all? She's allowed Norquist to use her. She has lied for him. She's let Nora bully her into silence when she should have spoken up right away in favor of Brodaccio's plan to institutionalize the girl, to socialize her with other children. She's failed Atalanta. How desperate for recognition must she be? How desperate for love? Every time she lets anyone in just a little bit, she's punished for it, she loses, and yet she keeps making the same mistake.

Shame floods her. She sweats with it.

For his part, Fred still knows nothing of the case, and he seems pleased with her new availability at home. "This is nice," he says one evening near the end of the month. He's sitting at the kitchen table, sifting through the photographs he took over the holidays and had developed. Now and then, he lifts one for her to see: Willie with a Christmas ornament in her hand, Willie on Signe's horse, all of them tucked in cozy together between the pillows on Signe's big couch.

"What's nice?" She's standing at the sink, her hands in the gray dishwater. She had been thinking about how a truck hitting the surface of the sea would create a splash any passing boat would absolutely hear, even if darkness made sight of it impossible. She was wondering how long it would take for that truck to bob and slowly fill before sinking. Hours maybe? Or just minutes? And where could a person find out?

"I mean us together, here," Fred says. "You're just present. It's nice."

"Where else would I be?"

"You know what I mean. I'm appreciating you."

She lets out her breath, smiles over her shoulder at him. Willie has been given a stack of books and tucked into bed to "read," but Bernadette is aware of her daughter's attention, which is always trained like a radio antenna to the adult conversation. Behind the screen that serves as Willie's wall, Bernadette feels the child look up from her book and cock her head toward her parents' voices. "Thank you," she says. It's a modulation.

"I want you to come with me to the faculty dinner," Fred says.

The invitation is a bullet piercing the space between them. It hits Bernadette in the chest. *The faculty dinner.* "You know why that's a bad idea," she says.

"It's a good idea. Didn't we just agree on how well this arrangement is working? Me at the school, you here, more or less?"

She dunks another plate under the water, watches the bubbles form on its surface, rise, and pop. "Fred, I can't go to the dinner."

"I need you. The wives will all be there."

"Some men go alone. I know this. Bill Watts—he's single. So's Richard Holland. So's Olin Lundgren. Single."

"They'll have dates, no?"

She laughs. "You think those men can just find dates?"

"Fair point, but you won't have me in their class, will you? Come on, Bern!"

"Mama," Willie says from behind the screen. "Mrs. Iversen can watch me."

Fred grins, gestures toward Willie. "See? She agrees with me. Thank you, Wills."

Bernadette says, "Wilhelmina, you go to bed now, do you hear me?" To Fred, she says, "I'll think about it." She turns her back, and behind her she senses him returning to his students' papers, satisfied. He's got his way. In her hands, the plates wobble as she dries them. They clatter, one against the next, as she sets them into the cupboard. *Careful*, she thinks. *Just slow down*, she thinks. But in the back of her brain, circling, circling, circling again, the word *fragile* flaps like a single wing against the quiet.

IN THE END, THOUGH, SHE GIVES IN. THE FACULTY DIN-ner is set for the last Saturday in January. Fred gives her money, and she goes to a boutique downtown to shop for a dress but comes home with a navy-blue skirt she finds at a secondhand shop and five dollars still in her pocket. She may need it, she thinks, and Fred doesn't have to know.

The evening of the dinner, Mrs. Iversen does come to stay with Willie, and Fred gets them a cab to the restaurant rather than walking to a bus stop in the damp and then sitting through a long, slow ride. "Wouldn't want to spoil your hair," he says, as if she's fretted about it, and when she says she'd be perfectly happy with an umbrella and the bus, he tells her to enjoy the luxury every now and then.

The dinner is across town at a seafood place on the waterfront. It has a round, glassed prow of a dining room that sits over the water, propped up on stilts. Below it, the black water laps and laps at the legs of the stilts, and the surface is dotted with the reflected lights of the dining room. From the sidewalk where Bernadette and Fred pause to look out, the restau-rant appears to float, a ferry just bobbing at the edge of the sea. "I guess the department goes all out for this dinner," Fred says. His face glows. It's the incandescence of being an insider, Bernadette thinks, and she bristles against his happiness despite wanting to share it. There's this conflict in herself—always this conflict in herself—souring every moment she could instead enjoy. And why? And for what? It's fruitless, this friction she cre-ates in her life. She wishes she were an easier sort of person.

Once they've deposited their coats at the coat check counter, they make their way to the table where the others are already seated, and Bernadette's heart chokes her throat when she sees the faces of her col-leagues recognizing her on Fred's arm. Handshakes all around. "Well look at this! Aren't you two the sly dogs, keeping it under wraps?" one of the men asks with a wink at Fred, who flushes and says, actually, they've been married for years. "Bern and I met after the war. I moved out here for her," he says, kissing her cheek, and Bernadette fights an urge to slip her hand from his and leave, to turn her back on it all.

The department chair, McIntosh, frowns and says nothing, but nods to the two empty seats on his left. "Professor Farrell, Mrs. Farrell," he says, and she thinks, *Yes—there it is—that alternate identity. Name that belongs to no one, really. I'm her now.* Mrs. Farrell in the blue crepe skirt and ivory silk blouse. Mrs. Farrell who turns her head away from the conversation McIntosh and Fred begin to instead meet Mrs. McIntosh's eyes and say, "Yes, our Wilhelmina is loving her new school, thank you for asking." Mrs. Farrell who, when the waiter asks what she's drinking is cut off and told the women are drinking sidecars—*Sidecars! Of course!* What the hell. She's Mrs. Fucking Farrell, and she might as well accept it. She downs the drink in two swallows and orders another.

Across the table, Mrs. Robert Nelson, first name Ingrid, recommends a salon she's just begun patronizing near the grocery on Campus Way. Does Bernadette know it? What clubs does she belong to? Mrs. McIntosh wants to know. Has Fred taken her out to that new restaurant—Lanna— yet? The waitresses wear real kimonos! Mrs. Peter Ives, mother of Sylvia and Barbara, who attend Seattle Day School, recommends the children's ballet classes offered at Fisher's School of Dance. Does Bernadette know of it? Wilhelmina would love ballet, and she'd get to wear the most scrumptious little tights and leotard! *Oh god*, Bernadette thinks. The tedium of this kind of conversation will kill her. She thinks, *This is why I can't have women friends.* Aloud though, she says, "These are such good recommendations." She smiles, thanks them, says it's just that her Willie is too young for anything that structured. "She prefers to play outdoors. You know, some theorists of human development suggest that play is the work of childhood. I've found that to be true in observing Willie myself. I have no need to prescribe her movement at this point when she's still just developing it intrinsically and intuitively through her contact with the world—trees and puddles and sand at the beach and—" Bernadette pauses. The eyes of the table have landed on her, the women and men alike silent, staring. She nods. "I just let her play for now," she says, and sips the sidecar, its acidic burn scorching all the way down her throat. Under the table, Fred's hand rests on her knee, squeezes.

They're just being served the hors d'oeuvres, dishes of oysters with onion ice, when, from down the table, Dr. Peresson says, "Isn't that your case study, Bernadette? The one in the news this morning?"

She turns. "My case study?"

Fred's hand on her knee is a weight. She shifts, and he withdraws it.

"The feral girl. She's yours, yes? Your subject? She was in *The Post* this morning. Front page."

The table constricts and lengthens. Bernadette's hearing goes underwater.

In her ear, Fred says, "You have a case study?"

Bernadette says, "I'm sure this is a different child." She does not look at Fred. She lifts her drink, sips.

"I'm sure she's yours," Peresson says. "Couldn't be two wild girls out there."

"We didn't see the paper today, I guess, did we, Bern?" Fred says. She can hear the tension of his smile around the words.

"I saw that too." This from Dr. Blethen. To Bernadette he says, "There's a mother, apparently, but you must already know this." He shakes his head. To the table he says, "Terrible story. The woman claims the child was kidnapped, but where's she been?" He turns to Bernadette again. "Do you know? There's no record of a parental claim, is there? The paper says not, but I assume you'd have found it if there had been one at some point. The girl's fourteen, the mother's saying."

"She's mute, though, isn't that right, Bernadette? So the age could be inaccurate." This is Peresson again.

"Not *mute*," Bernadette corrects, but the table isn't listening to her.

Blethen repeats himself, says, "The mother claims she's fourteen."

Beside Bernadette, McIntosh waves over the waiter. "I think we're ready for the main."

A raft of waiters appears as if McIntosh has manifested them in order to divert this conversation, and in choreographed perfection they reach around the diners and lift plates stacked in empty oyster shells, lay down new cutlery, refill water glasses.

Fred's face is frozen in that same, artificial smile he carved out of his mouth when Peresson first spoke. She'd like to pin the tines of her fork in Peresson's big fat tongue, but instead she leans into Fred's shoulder, whispers, "Later. I'll explain later." Her mouth is grossly salty with the brine of the single oyster she managed. She feels its slick tracks still lining her throat.

The waiters return with wide silver platters on which main course dishes are balanced. They freshen drinks. They offer pepper from grinders the size of summer garden squash. They dole out dollops of hot pink cocktail sauce and brown gravy-like sauce and viscous yellow hollandaise from which Bernadette must avert her eyes. *No, thank you*, she says. *Yes, another sidecar. No, this is perfect.* Her voice is a glazed version of itself, a sweetened other. She is Mrs. Fred Farrell. She is Bernadette Farrell. Mother of Wilhelmina who might—should!—soon take up ballet. She is a blue-skirted figurehead at the bow of this unearthly boat, floating, floating out into the dark.

People pick up their forks and knives. Clinking of cutlery. Ice against glasses. She listens to the scraps of other people's conversations for more about Atalanta, but they've moved on, and she has nothing but what they've already offered—a mother, a kidnapping, a solid age. She wants to leave the table, to move, to run out into the street and find a newsstand with racks of this morning's *Post* edition still stacked in gray piles. She'd like one of Norquist's cigarettes. But she sits, her muscles tight with not moving. She downs another sidecar. Fred doesn't lay his hand on her knee again, but she feels the bump of his shoulder against hers when he turns away from her.

Several bites into her salmon mousse, she excuses herself and crosses the dining room as if on wheels, her legs beneath her vanished somehow and only the skirt left swishing. She's disappeared inside the fabric, she thinks. She is nothing but air! She blows like a current between the tables of other diners, under the soft glow of the chandelier globes and the flickering of centerpiece candles, down the dark paneled hallway and into the bright light of the bathroom, where an attendant meets her eyes and immediately looks away. How many sidecars did she drink? Three? Four? One too many. She can't handle this many drinks even when she's not hormonal. She's lightheaded, her skull an aquarium and she the little silver minnow darting about inside it, looking desperately out.

She glides into a stall and lifts the hem of the skirt. Every time she's on the toilet now she wishes for blood, but again, there's none. Instead, another wave of nausea.

The skirt smells, still, of the secondhand store. She should have had it cleaned, but there wasn't time, and also she didn't care. Mothballs. A cedar chest. It's a little out of date in style and cut. Probably someone's prewar skirt. Someone else's happy day, long past now. Some widow somewhere, probably. Some woman who survived her own war years and put away her past and never wanted to look at it again. *Oh god, the nausea.* Bernadette leans forward, her head between her knees. When the lilt of alcohol-oiled vertigo sways her, she breathes.

"Are you okay in there, ma'am?" the attendant asks.

"I'm fine," she says. "I'll be fine."

"Should I find someone for you? Are you unwell?"

"I'm fine," Bernadette says. "The food is a little rich, isn't it?"

"Maybe so, ma'am. I wouldn't know, ma'am."

*I'm sorry*, Bernadette thinks, but does not say aloud. Now she's offended this stranger—this woman who can't even eat in this place where she spends all her nights handing out warm towels in the toilet.

Her mind reels. *Little fish, little fish*, she sings—a song Willie's brought home from nursery school.

Who could have found Atalanta's mother? Or did she just appear? The only story that's been publicly released about the girl came out in September, when she was first found—months ago. So why would a mother wait so long? And what's to say this woman actually is Atalanta's mother? Is she an Adela girl, all grown up and come back to claim her losses? Marley-Marlowe, in the flesh, after all these years?

Bernadette sweats and waits for the nausea to rinse through her. She'll never eat another oyster.

When she returns to the table, her mousse is gone, and it's just as well. There's dessert, and more drinks, coffee served in tiny cups the way she hasn't had it since Europe—hot and strong. This she drinks, thinking it will brace her and counter the alcohol. Dishes are cleared, goodbyes said. McIntosh and his wife leave first, and then the table relaxes. "We should go," Fred whispers to her, and she stands.

They say nothing in the cab on the way home. Fred has the driver let them out at the park. "I want to walk," he tells her when she looks at him. The sky is dark and high and blue-black, tufted with veined clouds made visible because of a nearly full moon.

"You've lied to me," he says as soon as the cab disappears down the road. "You've been lying and lying to me."

She walks ahead of him. "I told you I was doing some consulting work on the side. I told you about Nora Reach. You've met Signe. I didn't lie."

"You never said anything about this case study—the feral girl."

"You didn't need to know all the details, did you? You know there can be confidentiality agreements between researchers and subjects. I was bound."

"I'm your husband, Bernadette. Confidentiality stops at the door of our house."

She swings back to face him. "Our house? Our house that you suddenly appeared out of nowhere to claim? After years of nothing? Our house?"

"Bernadette—"

She stalks forward down the street ahead of him. The coffee and the cold air and the ire have shocked her back into her body. She is all nerve, all rage. Under her feet, the heels of her pumps hit the pavement in hard beats that rip back up her calves and into her back, an ache. He can follow her if he wants, or he can turn and leave. Again. She and Willie were fine without him for years, and they would be fine again on their own. She doesn't have to work for the university here. There are other schools, other cities. She could cross the border. Her French is impeccable. *Je n'ai pas besoin de toi.* She could teach at an international school, raise Willie bilingually, disappear. Or nursing! She was a nurse. She could take up again at some hospital or clinic somewhere. She has options. *I could disappear,* she thinks, and the thought is a nebula in her brain suddenly, opening out into a firing sputter of possibilities. There is freedom in vanishing. What has Atalanta taught her if not this? She clips down the street ahead of him, his shadow just there at her back.

At the apartment, she scares Mrs. Iversen by bursting inside so quickly that the door hits the wall. "I'm so sorry," she apologizes.

The old woman is flustered, half-asleep, just as Bernadette expected. "Are you okay, love?" Mrs. Iversen asks, but even as she says it, Bernadette sees her gathering her sweater, her bag, her book. She's in a hurry now—doesn't want to know too much, doesn't want to pry. There's a husband in this house now, and it's his place to take charge or sort it out, whatever it might be. Bernadette sees this all crossing through Mrs. Iversen's mind and waves her off just as Fred, coming up the step, that stupid smile quick-pasted back onto his face, proves it all by saying, "Thank you, Mrs. I! Great night for walking, isn't it? Bernadette's so tired, we're headed straight to sleep. She'll have to drop by and catch up with you tomorrow."

The door shuts at his back. He shrugs his coat off into a heap on the floor, toes off his shoes.

Bernadette remembers from her midwestern childhood the way the air before a tornado turns static, pulls tight at the edges of buildings and blades of grass and one's own drawn breath. She remembers the greening of the sky before the wind began. The sick turning of the clouds to soft smudges of olive green over the tousled crowns of the trees. *Après moi, le déluge*, she thinks. But no—she's not the cause of this. She's the eye, not the storm. This isn't her fault, whatever else may be.

She turns to Fred, "You have to just say it."

"Fine. You embarrassed me," he says. He sits, crumpling onto the couch.

This isn't what she expected, and it knocks the wind out of her. She sighs. "I didn't mean to embarrass you. I didn't know about the article." A sob chokes from her mouth before she can stop it.

Fred shushes her. "Don't wake Willie."

She hasn't realized the volume of her own voice. She peers around the screen at Willie, but the child is sleeping, her mouth open and her curls splayed on her pillow. The world slows again, the room releases, relaxes. Bernadette sits beside Fred. "Okay," she says. "Here's all of it." She gives him the summary version, and of course, he's heard of the case. Atalanta, the feral girl, is famous. He remembers reading about her in New York in the fall—the child found alone on a prison island. The child made savage with neglect.

"She's not savage," Bernadette says. "I hate that word. That's an exaggeration."

"You've met her then?"

"She's like Victor of Aveyron."

"Who?"

"It doesn't matter." She sighs. "I thought about telling you all of this sooner, but it seemed unnecessary. The details are mostly meant to be confidential."

"From your husband?"

"Would you tell me about your patients if you were a clinician instead of a professor? Of course not. Professional confidentiality is expected in our work. You understand that."

"This isn't a patient, Bernadette, and you're not a psychotherapist. This is just some tabloid freak you've attached yourself to."

*Freak*, she repeats to herself. "I'm not attached," she says, but she knows he can hear the lie.

"And professional?" he says. "It sounds a little disingenuous to me. This isn't exactly in the sphere of your previous study. And now you've drawn Willie into it too." His face shifts at the mention of Willie, that pulling of his skin against his jaw: anger. "Did you even think about the consequences for her? Who is Signe Aalund, really, to be introducing her to our daughter? What are you doing? You're in over your head. You're in way over your head."

Again, that heat, that rush of rage like a storm returned—sudden green sky sickness in her gut, her skull. She floods as easily as groundwater rising through the mud these days, and why? Why can't she control herself anymore?

She sits up against the couch cushions, tucks her hands between her knees so that she will not be tempted to reach out and strike him. "Did you think of her when you left us in Chicago? When you went to New York, were you thinking about Willie? Or were you thinking about yourself?"

A long silence, hard as glass. She could submerge him in a wave of grievances from that time when she had no money, nowhere to go, and Willie was entirely her responsibility, but she lets him sit in the vacancy and says nothing.

He says, "That was a mistake. I should have taken you with me. I regret that I didn't." He meets her eyes. "My research was going to be so demanding, and I—" He stops. "I've been a terrible father. I know that." He puts his face in his hands. He's crying.

*Terrible father*. She has never seen him cry, and it's alarming, somehow, but she doesn't move to comfort him. He should have said this when he first stepped through her door. He should have written it in a letter before that. He should have turned around halfway to New York and come back for her—for her, not just for Willie. She lets him sit in his shame. *It's not enough*, she thinks. *Shame is not the same as remorse.*

She gets up. Leaves him. In the kitchen, she puts on coffee. It's ten o'clock. She stands at the sink waiting for the water to boil. Her hands filling the pot with grounds are not her own. Her hands lifting the kettle and pouring are not her own. She says, "What haven't you told me about why you came back to us?"

She watches steam escape around the lid as she settles the coffee press. When she turns back, he's standing in the open space between the kitchen and the front room.

"It was—" He sucks in a long, audible breath. "There were some setbacks—in my research. It wasn't going well. Then a subject misunderstood my intentions, and she left the study."

Bernadette hears this from a distance, as if she's been pushed from a dock and has plunged beneath water. The notes of Fred's voice sift down to her. She has to swallow, has to gasp, before she can say, "Misunderstood your intentions?"

"It was a misunderstanding," he repeats.

"You and a subject? You—you—" Again, there's that image behind her eyes of the deer-become-girl. Of a girl running with a man at her back. A girl in the grass becoming a deer in the road becoming a girl on the ground, blood on her mouth and her legs. Bernadette swivels toward the sink, gasps, wretches, gasps. Nothing comes up. She wipes saliva from the corners of her mouth.

"Fred," she says when she can look at him again. "Did you—?"

He gapes at her for a moment, the truth surfacing and breaking open between them so that she can see it clearly—can see exactly what he's done. But then, just as quickly, like a cloud passing over the sun, his face closes again, and whatever is below is concealed once more, Fred's expression smooth. He shakes his head, says, "No, no. Nothing like that. But when she—I just, I sort of unraveled for a little while. I missed a couple of classes. I wasn't sleeping. A student happened to see me in a bar on what turned out not to be my best night. Just—" He lifts his eyes to hers, and in them she sees his fear, his shame, and also his pride. "Bern," he says. "Believe me."

She's sinking.

She thinks of Willie. She thinks, *Willie needs more than this.* She thinks, *Willie and I both need more than this.*

She says, "Did you come back to me because you wanted me, or because someone else no longer wanted you?"

"Bernadette, you know how much I love you." His voice is measured, even. She realizes he's thought about this question and has prepared an answer to it. Or, rather, he's prepared a not-answer to it. She realizes he's constructed exactly this moment, and this construction is all she's ever going to get from him. This enrages her. She is rage. She puts her hand on the coffee press's plunger and slams it down, but the force is more than she intends. The pot slips, opens. Scalding coffee explodes from between pot and lid.

Everything happens quickly.

The pot clatters to the floor, along with a mug, which shatters.

There's a sudden, curdling wail from behind the screen. "Mama!"

"What are you doing?" Fred's voice is disconnected from his mouth. "What the hell do you think you're doing?"

"Mama!" Willie is sobbing.

At the ends of her arms, Bernadette's hands are numb. No—not numb, burned. She's spilled coffee all over herself. She holds her hands out in front of herself like foreign objects and stares. The skin is shocking pink.

"Oh my god. Bernadette. What have you done?" Alarm on Fred's face, and then he's gripping her wrists, shoving her hands under the stream of the kitchen faucet, which is running cold and hard, and she can't feel a thing.

The kitchen fills, overflows, and she is under the crest of the wave. *Mrs. Farrell, your hands are burned.* Red streaks run up the backs of both her hands and her wrists. The kitchen sink is filling, filling with cold water, and Fred is holding her shaking hands beneath the faucet's flow.

"Mama!"

She hears the apartment door open.

"Willie?" she calls, but there's no answer. "Where's Willie?" she asks. She tears her wrists from Fred. "Where's Willie? Why's the door open?"

Willie's screen is folded at an odd angle, her bed behind it empty.

They run outside together. In the cold air, the burns on her wrists sting. "Willie!" she yells. She hears Fred's voice, already down the street, calling too. "Wilhelmina!"

It's almost eleven o'clock.

The streetlamps cast greening-yellowed cones onto the wet pavement. A car passes and stops. "Ma'am?" The driver inside is a young man, hair slicked back, cigarette hanging from his lower lip. "Can I get you some help?"

She realizes what she must look like—barefoot, the sleeves of her blouse rolled up to the elbow and coffee stains all over the fabric. "My little girl," she says. "My little girl got out of the house, and I can't find her."

"Get in," the man says, and without thinking, she does.

She leaves the passenger window down, sticks her face out into the roll of the night air. "Willie!" she calls. "Willie!" They drive the length of the block, and she directs him to the park, where she gets out at the curb and runs up the hillside to the playground.

"Should I wait for you?" the man hollers, but she doesn't turn back.

The playground is skeletal in the dark, the swings slack on the chains. "Willie!" she calls. She remembers that day at Adela—the panic. But there's no cliffside for Willie to tumble down here. No sea waiting to swallow her. Just the city. Blocks and blocks of houses all the same. So many fences to look behind. So many dark streets. Willie is not Atalanta. She isn't strong. She isn't ready for survival.

Bernadette crosses into one neighborhood and then the next. At the edge of campus, it occurs to her that maybe Willie has run to the nursery school, and so she races across the university lawn. She falls once and skins both her knees. At the nursery school gate, she rattles the latch and finds it locked. Shouts again, "Willie!" A light goes on in one of the dorm windows and the silhouette of a person appears in the yellow square. She runs.

Around the perimeter of the building and down another side street, through another neighborhood, back across the other side of the park, and then there, at the edge of the park closest to home, Fred with Willie in his arms, and also, an officer. Bernadette is nothing but a wave gone to froth. She pulls Willie into her chest, kisses her face, drinks in Willie's smell. "You never—" she says, and Willie nods against her neck. "Mama and you—" she says, and Willie reaches up and puts her hands on Bernadette's face. "We two—" Bernadette says, and she has no words to finish the sentence. All the words she knows have been ground to sand in her dry mouth.

"It's okay, Mama," Willie says. "It's okay."

## 17

WHEN SHE WAS YOUNG, HER MOTHER USED TO COMFORT her through rough nights by telling her that everything would be new again in the morning. But this morning, when she wakes up, Bernadette's head thrums and her body aches, and she's alone in the bed. She has little memory of falling asleep—everything after Willie was in her arms, a blur. In the bedroom, the light is frail and blue coming through the opened curtains. It's Sunday. Fred usually makes pancakes on Sunday mornings, and then they walk to the park and let Willie play. Maybe things can be mended enough for that walk, even today. Bernadette sits up in the bed, waits for the spinning in her head to slow, and stands to put on her robe and try.

In the other room, Fred and Willie are at the table, but with them is Nora Reach.

"Nora," Bernadette says. Her stomach seizes.

"Mama's awake!" Willie says. She's coloring a picture of a mermaid, the green fish tail long and curved around the bottom of the page.

"Wills," Fred says. "Park time. Get dressed, please." He clears away the drawing and the spill of crayons.

"Did she eat?" Bernadette asks. "If you're taking her out, you should pack her raincoat."

Fred says nothing, but he sets a full coffee cup in front of her. "Watch your hands," he tells her, and she remembers then the whole of the night before and is washed in shame.

He and Willie leave without a goodbye, and with them goes all the air in the apartment. Bernadette looks across the table to Nora. She gulps a swallow of her coffee, which is burned and too strong.

"Fun night out?" Nora asks.

"Fred lets me sleep in on Sundays."

Nora nods, but her mouth tightens into a single line, and it's clear that Fred's told her something, if not everything.

"You've met my family," Bernadette says.

"We had breakfast together. I brought rolls."

Bernadette sees a box on the counter and gets up. The floor tilts, and the countertop rocks, but she steadies herself with another deep breath.

The box is full of pastries from the expensive bakery downtown at the public market. A cherry Danish and an almond twist and a soft roll with half an apricot upturned like a thick yolk in its center. The slickness of glaze alone is enough to make her nauseous, but she takes the apricot roll and settles it onto a plate for herself.

"This was generous," she says. "Thank you. You didn't have to feed us."

"It's Sunday, and I wasn't invited." Nora shifts slightly in her seat and her tone constricts. "In fact, I've never been invited."

This catches Bernadette by surprise—the thought of Nora wanting to be invited here, to the tiny apartment she shares with Fred and Willie. She remembers that first lunch they had and the disappointment on Nora's face when Willie came up, as if motherhood were Bernadette's professional failure. She says, "I'd have invited you sooner if I'd known you were free for social engagements. But I am surprised to see you now, after the way we left things at Elita."

Nora says nothing to this. "Did you see the article?" she asks instead.

"I heard about it."

Nora bends, withdraws a rolled newspaper from her bag, and lays it on the table for Bernadette to read as she eats. "As far as I can tell, this woman is a complete sham. A hoax."

"You're sure?"

"Of course. This woman is a nothing. Just some fame seeker looking for her moment." Nora's tone is acid. She's nearly spitting.

Bernadette opens the paper to a full two-page spread. The article claims as its source an informant close to the prison. "Brodaccio?" she asks.

"He says not."

Bernadette reads aloud: "'The source says the child, whom he identifies as a girl between the ages of eleven and fifteen, is prone to violence and must often be restrained. He describes the child as fair-haired and muscular, for a girl. *Folk could easily mistake that bark she's got for a dog's,* the source claims.'" She looks up. "It's Starkey. That's the source. Len Starkey."

Nora's face goes tight. "How can you tell?"

"Norquist has seen this, yes?"

"Everyone in the greater Seattle area saw this. Except you."

"Except me."

Nora sighs. "I understand you hadn't told your husband about your involvement in this case."

"What else did he share with you?"

"He didn't have to say much. Officer Donnelson might have a few things to say, though, from what I've heard."

"Officer Donnelson—?"

"Your daughter's rescuer."

"You heard this from Fred?"

"I get all the reports involving children."

"I'm not your county, and it's Sunday. You get reports on Sundays?"

Nora smiles, slow and controlled. "I do when they're about you."

"Children run off."

"That's true. It's natural for a child to want to escape a domestic disturbance. It's unsettling for them to see their parents out of control."

The room shifts again under Bernadette's weight. She shakes her head. "That's not an accurate story."

Nora lifts an eyebrow. "I'm quoting the incident report. For now, Wilhelmina is home, safe, and the report is in a closed file. But if your name comes up again, they'll open the file. You don't want that, Bernadette. You don't want a social worker arriving at your home on a Sunday morning at ten o'clock to find you still sleeping off your evening's drink while your child sits alone at the kitchen table. That sort of detail can reopen the file."

"You should leave."

Nora sighs. "I'm telling you this as your friend."

"Whatever story you've heard is simply that—a story. Willie ran off. We'll add a lock to the door out of her reach. Children don't always behave."

The line of Nora's mouth purses. "Nor do adults."

Bernadette closes her eyes. The aquarium in her head sloshes left, then right. What's she doing, arguing with Nora Reach? She will lose. It doesn't matter what has happened or will happen, Bernadette will lose. "Who is this woman claiming to be Atalanta's mother?" she asks.

"I told you: she's no one." Nora laughs a clipped, hard gust of breath. "Some Tacoma woman with a record for petty theft and prostitution."

"Recent record?"

"Not recent. She's been gone for the last decade. She says she went to Alaska and only came back when a friend from here sent her the September news story. It took her this long to get the money for the trip, she says. It's in the article."

"Name?"

"Valeria Ricks. Nothing like Marley or Marlowe. That was a false lead, maybe."

Bernadette thinks back to that day on the Adela tug, the way the captain eyed her as he turned *Marley* into *Marlowe*. Of course it was a false lead. "It doesn't matter," she says now.

Nora reaches across the table and taps the paper. "What matters is that this woman is entitled to prove her claim on the child. It matters that this will slow everything down."

"But I thought you didn't want her moved? This will pause that, won't it? She'll have to stay at Elita."

"She's going to an institution. There's too much attention on the prison now." Nora leans forward, turns the newspaper page to a second article, this one titled "Elita Island: The Children's Prison?" She says, "You can read this too, but the gist is that politicians are calling for cuts to the prison's funding if the child isn't removed. They can't have her there. A little girl with all those violent men? It looks bad. Primitive. There's no choice but to move her, and then this woman—Ricks—will be given visitation. I have to prove she's not the mother."

"How will you do that?"

"I don't know. She says Atalanta's fourteen. Her idea of verification is a grainy picture of her holding a baby that could be any kid. She says the girl's given name is Ginny. Brodaccio thinks the child—in his words—'shows more life' when she hears the name." Nora rolls her eyes and slips the paper from Bernadette's hands, folds it into a tight tube again, and shoves it back in her bag. "He's delighted. Of course he's delighted. He can be rid of the girl, get his hospital back, *and* his name is in the paper. He'll be interviewed everywhere that will have him, and with no repercussions. He's a goddamn savior. The expert on the feral child sideshow. Horrible. All of it's horrible. I've looked for a way to stop this, but there's nothing." She sighs, and in her sigh Bernadette hears real desperation, real grief. "She doesn't deserve this, Bernadette. Atalanta doesn't deserve this."

Bernadette can't take her eyes off Nora's face. It's there—that same fear Bernadette feels in her own center: she could lose her girl. An institution has its own social workers, its own psychotherapist and physician and caretakers. There will be no need for her anymore. No professional reason for Nora to be in Atalanta's life. There are half-moon shadows under Nora's eyes, and her hair is oily. Only now does Bernadette notice the wrinkles in her blouse, the lipstick-bare mouth: she hasn't been to bed. She's been at the station, most likely, with Norquist, tracking down this woman's police record and searching for more—a birth certificate for the child, now that her mother has a name; anything on the father. Bernadette pauses. *The father.* "Is there a father?" she asks. "Is Len Starkey the father?"

Again, Nora laughs, resentfully. "That'd be something. But no. I don't think so. The woman claims the father worked at Elita. He went to the Pacific. He's dead."

The story lines up with what Bernadette has heard. "Tor," Bernadette says. "Tor someone, the cook who went to California, then died in the Pacific during the war. I've heard that. I'll have to look at my notes."

Nora frowns. "I'd remember a name like Tor. Viking god and all that. No, no. This was a simple name. Ben. Benjamin, maybe. She called him Benji. She didn't give a last name."

The room tips, and Bernadette's stomach burns. "Aalund? Benji Aalund?"

"Your woman with the farm out there is Aalund, yes?"

Bernadette nods. "Her son. That's her son."

Nora's face hardens, and she narrows her gaze at Bernadette. "Did you know this? You're close with her. Norquist said you've been to her farm as a guest. She never said?"

Bernadette feels the heat in her chest again. It can't be right. Something in the line of information given has been tangled, misunderstood. "It has to be another man," she says. "Another Benjamin. It's not an uncommon name." She looks at Nora. "I'm not hiding anything."

Nora chuffs. Tight grin. "We could ask your husband about that, your honesty. I'm sure he'd have another view."

"That's not fair. You know I've been honest with Norquist. I've been honest with you. You don't understand what it is to be married."

Nora turns her face away, and when she looks again at Bernadette, the skin at her cheeks is pulled smooth and her teeth are nearly bared as she says, "You know, I thought I knew you, but what do we really have in common, the two of us? Nothing except that we're always the only two women in the room."

"Nora—" Bernadette's head has begun to throb again. She tucks her hair behind her ears. Her eyes could be lined in sand. "I've told you what I know. All along. I've told you everything." Her stomach burns. "Maybe this woman is her mother—Atalanta's. And isn't that a happy ending? Why are you not happy with this?" Her head aches. She can't stop herself. "That's what I don't understand. What's this girl's hold on you? You must have others—other children who need you, other parents getting in the way. Yet, you clearly have an attachment to Atalanta. An unprofessional attachment. And I don't understand why this girl is the one."

Nora sits up. "You amaze me, you know? You can't understand? Truly?" She draws a hard breath. "Have you ever lived just as you wanted to? Even for one single day of your life? Just a single day? Me either. But she did. She did it. And don't you want to understand that? Don't you think there's something there to learn? The second this woman locks her claim into place, we lose any chance to know more about the girl."

"But she's the girl's mother."

"What's a mother? Just someone who got knocked up? This woman— she has nothing. No resources. No education. Nothing. You think she'll make the girl's life better than it is now? She can't take care of her like I can." It's nearly a growl. Nora's gaze has gone fierce, lit from inside with an anger Bernadette does understand.

"Nora—if Atalanta's her daughter . . . I just mean, the girl can't be your case all her life. She's a child. She needs to have a life of her own."

Nora shoves back from the table. "I thought you were one of us—a scholar, a thinker. But I was wrong."

"Not wrong. I do understand."

Nora's voice is hard and gruff when she speaks. "The girl survived," she says. "She's special. Not every girl survives, you know. Can you imagine how many cases I've worked where, after the system lets her go, the girl just vanishes? Prostitution or pregnancy or something worse? This one lived. She can't be allowed to just disappear."

"You can't keep a girl like a book on your shelf."

"And you can't let one run down the city streets after dark."

This is the line, then. Some part of Bernadette thought that what Nora wanted was an ally. That she was drawn to the idea of a sisterhood, and that what she felt for the child was more maternal than anything else. She thought Nora's fear of losing her grip on the case was the fear of a daughter lost. But their worries are not parallel, and this can never be an equal relationship so long as Nora can unravel Bernadette's life any time they disagree.

"Why did you come here? What is it you're asking me to do?" Bernadette says.

Nora meets her eyes. "You perhaps jumped to a hasty conclusion at Elita, siding with the doctor. Now you see what I'm up against. The child will lose everything if she is relinquished to this—," she taps the newspaper, "this person."

"What if this woman truly is Atalanta's mother?"

"You meet her, Bernadette. Meet Valeria Ricks yourself, and then you assess what you think of her, and you share it with Norquist. Officially."

"I'm not a psychologist."

"You keep telling me what can't be done." Nora chuffs. "You forget that I'm the one who found you. I know what you can do." She stands, gathers her bag, and buttons her coat. At the door, she says, "As women, we have a unique influence, Bernadette. Even you must see that. It can be used to build a family or to dismantle one. I believe you and I both want to use our influence constructively, if given the opportunity." She closes the door at her back.

It takes Bernadette several minutes of silence before she's able to get up. She feels something akin to vertigo, but not inside her body. Everything she thought she understood has come loose and without the root of any certainty, she is floating, unanchored, not sure how to right herself again.

In the empty apartment, she tidies the kitchen, dumps the rest of the coffee down the drain. She wishes Nora had left the paper so she could read it again more slowly. There might be something of use there. She tries to pull her mind back to the visual of the page on which the article was printed, to see again the words, but nothing will assemble behind her eyes. Everything is mud this morning, and it's not her case anymore anyhow. She was invited to meet Atalanta for a particular purpose, and that purpose has dissolved, no matter what now. And what about Signe? God. What about Signe?

Bernadette gets dressed and walks alone to the park. The sky is white and high and as brittle as an eggshell. Her breath is visible, and she keeps her burned hands in her pockets to avoid the cold on her raw skin.

At the park, Fred and Willie are on the swings—both of them, Fred swinging high, his long legs straight out in front of him on the up, tucked close on the fall. Willie, on her swing beside him, is watching with that same adoration Bernadette has seen on her face since the moment Fred walked through their front door. *Dad. Daddy. Dad-Dad-Dad-Pops.* It would break her to be without him again, Bernadette knows. *But still,* she thinks, *a father's absence can be weathered.* It can be forgiven as a mother's absence never can be. A mother's absence is fodder for fairy tales, for nightmares. It's a wound that doesn't close. A broken wing, never healed. A heart with an irregular beat.

It's also not even really an option, she realizes, leaving Fred and keeping Willie. He'll take Wills. He'll claim that Bernadette has been erratic, is untrustworthy, loves her job too much to be a good mother. And he'll have evidence—her job at the university, her work with Atalanta. All the hours she's hired out help since he came back and she no longer needed to work for the money but did it anyway, for her own satisfaction. He'll have that file—whatever it was that Nora referenced—on his side, as proof that she's unfit. She'll lose her daughter.

*Or,* she thinks. Say she fights, and maybe she wins, or Fred retreats—leaves her and Willie to start over with someone easier. What then? She has no money. No bank will loan her any. No place will hire her once she's actually divorced. She's in a cage. She feels frantic, a fluttering panic like a frenzy of wings beating discordantly in her chest.

On the swings, Fred and Willie are sailing in opposition to one another, Fred up while Willie is down, and vice versa. "Mama!" Willie spots her and calls, and Fred turns. Like a boy, he leaps from the height of his swing's arc, lands on his feet. Willie squeals. "Dad! Dad is a circus man!" Fred play-bows, taking an invisible top hat from his head for her and replacing it, winking. Willie trills a bubbling spill of giggles.

"Your friend gone?" he asks Bernadette.

"Not my friend, it turns out," Bernadette says.

"Well, people disappoint you too easily, Bernadette."

It stings, but she nods.

Fred's face is pinked and impossible to read. He squints at her against the glare of the white sky. "I thought this was going to work this time. I really did. I tried."

"Last night was one night."

"You've been lying to me since I got here."

"Not lying. And what about you, Fred? How can I ever trust you to stay this time?" Behind him, Willie on the swing is a metronome. *Tick. Tick. Tick. Tick.* Bernadette is inside herself and outside of herself. She can't give in to the vertigo.

"Mama! Watch!" Willie calls. "Watch, Mama! I'm going to leap like Dads!"

"Not lying, Fred," Bernadette says again. "This was my work. Can't you understand that?"

"Work, to go out there and play pretend doctor at the prison? What did you think would happen, Bernadette?" He steps close to her. She can smell the coffee on his breath. There's a brown slosh in her head and gut. She remembers the oyster from last night's plate—little brown slug of meat on its beautiful opal shell. The grotesque is always nestled inside the beautiful. Everywhere, everywhere that's true.

"Mama! Watch me!"

"And where were you, Fred? Where were you all those months? All those years! Where were you?"

She feels herself splitting. She slips out of her skin and drifts up above them all. There she is, a mad dog of a woman, all hackle and lunge. Her hair is a mess. She never combed it. She watches herself lurch at Fred, her finger pointing at his chest. She watches Fred, face contorted into a misery she can't touch, grab her by the elbows and shake her once. And behind them—oh! behind them!—Willie like a falling star. Willie with her blond hair for one wild moment sprawled around her head in a crown of curls. Willie with both her arms and legs out wide. A sea star, a bit of tufted dandelion seed, an explosion of sound flung off the swing's apex and soaring, soaring.

When Bernadette gets to her, Willie is down, wailing. There's dirt in her mouth. Her lip is bleeding. *Mama-mama-mama-mama*, she cries. Her cries are raspberries of wet sound. There's snot and saliva on her face, on the front of her dress, and in her hair. And blood. Where's the blood coming from?

"She's bleeding. Fred, she's bleeding. She's bleeding," Bernadette's own voice is saying, but Fred is gone, down the slope of the grassy hill, gone for help.

And then, for the second time in twenty-four hours, a police cruiser. A towel on the back seat and Willie spread out on it, wailing. The siren overhead, so that Bernadette's ears throb in a round pulse.

At the hospital, Bernadette isn't allowed to follow the gurney. She stands in the waiting room, Fred's arms around her. "It's okay," he says. She hears him say it close to her throbbing ear. His breath is hot and brown and stale. "It's going to be okay. She broke her arm. That's all. She broke her arm." But Bernadette cannot stop her whole body from shaking.

LATER, ONCE THEY'RE HOME AGAIN, WILLIE ASLEEP WITH her casted arm crossed over her body and her hair washed and wet on her pillow, he comes to her and says that this day was too much, it was all he can handle. She thinks—*Yes! It was too much! We're coming undone. Can't you see that?* She thinks he's going to tell her he's leaving again, and there's relief in that for her. *Goodbye!* she thinks. *We don't need you!*

But he doesn't say that. He doesn't say that at all. Instead, she watches him pack Willie's clothes into a suitcase beside his own. He packs her Christmas doll, and the books Bernadette bought her, and he says, "I'm taking her. For now, at least, I'm taking her with me. In the morning, when I take her to school, you don't come along. You're not well, Bernadette. You're not well. You're making irrational choices."

Bernadette closes herself into the bathroom and vomits. The world has been spinning too fast for its axis for two days now, and this is it—it's finally flung her off. She's lost the ground and is elsewhere. Outside of herself. Outside of the life she's worked so hard to construct for herself and for Willie. She vomits again and again.

187

All night, she stays in the bathroom. At some point, she falls asleep on the floor, her face on the bathmat. And when she wakes up and leaves the room, the apartment is empty. It's early and still dark outside. She opens the curtains and looks out. The street is dark and slick with rain. The clock on the wall in the kitchen says six thirty. She's alone.

# PART
# 3

## 18

IT TAKES A WEEK BEFORE SHE LEAVES THE APARTMENT. She considers every possibility, even writing to Fred's department in New York for the details of his termination. Maybe she could find the name of the subject who made the claim against him or speak to a colleague who was unhappy with his performance. She goes so far as to call the university and ask for the address of Fred's old department chair, but in the end, she does nothing with it. No one will give a wife information, and no university will get into the mud for a professor they've already let go—it would be unseemly, and he's someone else's problem now. She's lost. If she pushes Fred—if she tries to take Willie without his consent—he could punish her endlessly. In court, she'd surely be seen as an unfit mother. It wouldn't be difficult for him to paint their separation as her choice rather than his. And beyond that, he is a professor again, and at the state university. What is she? A woman desperately clinging to a tabloid case, spending her time with a divorced detective, parading herself through a penitentiary to visit a freak child, and letting her daughter run out into the night unprotected. Not a good mother. Not a solid guardian for a young girl. No, she can't be impatient. If she pushes Fred, she will lose for good.

The best chance she has to get Willie back is to give her up—to give everything up, at least for now—and to disappear until both Fred's anger and the public interest in Atalanta have blown over.

She sends the department her letter of resignation. It nearly kills her to write it. *My family requires my full attention at this time*, she types. She knows Fred will see it, that he will be called into McIntosh's office and asked about his wife. This wording is for Fred alone—a bet on his desires that she hopes will pay off in Willie's return to her.

She packs herself a suitcase of clothes and her satchel of work. On her way out of the apartment, she spots the stack of photos Fred took of

Willie, still lying on the table, and she tucks them, too, into her bag. Then she gets the bus to Steilacoom and the boat to Adela. She needs to talk to Signe. Whatever she may or may not be hiding about her son, Signe will take her in.

And Signe does. She seems surprised but says nothing unkind when Bernadette knocks on her door. She gives her a room at the back of the house and puts her to bed. "You need sleep," Signe says. "We can talk about whatever this is when you wake up."

Bernadette lets herself be directed. When Signe pulls back the quilt, Bernadette gets into the bed without changing her clothes or putting up an argument. Her fatigue is a tsunami. She's more tired than she has ever been. She hasn't slept since Fred and Willie left, the apartment around her at night like a hole that she's fallen into. Signe's bed, however, is soft and pillowed and smells of the soap that washed the sheets and the wind that dried them. Bernadette lets Signe pull the quilt up over her shoulders. She rolls onto her side and lets Signe rub her back. She closes her eyes, and she sleeps, finally and fully. Sleep without dreams. And when she wakes up, she is thirsty, and Signe is there at the bedside with water and tea and a bowl of potatoes soaked in butter and salt.

"You need to eat. You look pale." Signe spoons a lump of potato into Bernadette's mouth. The butter is light and salty and comforting, and Bernadette sits up, takes the spoon, and devours the rest.

"What time is it?" she asks.

"Three o'clock."

"What day is it?"

"Monday."

Signe's hair is down around her shoulders rather than braided. Bernadette has never seen her with her hair down, and it changes her. She is older with her long gray-white hair loose. Her face is sharp and craggy in the light of the old-style kerosene lantern on the bedside table. In its halo, Signe could be a woman from a fairy tale, her knitting clasped between her gnarled fingers. She's making socks, she tells Bernadette. Four slim needles hold the just-developing toe in the round. The wool is also hers, from the sheep out in the pasture. She nods to the window, and Bernadette looks at the field, where the grass has the yellowed, damp look of winter and three sheep stand chewing, their legs coated in mud.

Signe goes silent, but for the clicking of her needles. Bernadette watches the loop and tug, loop and tug of the knitting while she sips her tea. Her mind is quieting out here, just as she hoped it would. She feels like a dog that has turned and turned and turned on top of its bed and can finally lie down.

"So, are you going to tell me where that girl of yours is, or do I have to guess?" Signe smiles, sad.

"You know where she is, I think."

"I probably do. And how about you? Where are you?"

Bernadette begins to cry.

"Oh, honey." Signe sets down her knitting and takes Bernadette's hands in her own. *Grandmother hands*, Bernadette thinks, though she never knew her own grandmother, and her mother never held her hands this way when she needed to be held. Still, she misses her mother. She misses her mother more than she ever has.

"I'm sorry," Bernadette says.

"No need for apologies."

"I'm a mess, though."

"I've seen worse messes. And you'll clean yourself up. I'm sure of that."

The reassurance brings another wave of tears, and Bernadette turns her face away from Signe's and looks toward the window. Outside, the light on the pasture is bluing toward early dusk, inky, sooted, deep. The sky is turbulent, churning with big-bellied dark clouds.

She's always liked the idea that language is the house in which one dwells, and the windows of that house are the glass through which one sees the outside world. Now she sees that motherhood, too, is a kind of language. And she has lost hers. How is she supposed to sit inside her own body now, without Willie? How is she supposed to look out the windows of her own eyes and not find the world without Willie in it to be illegible, untranslatable, unspeakable? She has lost her mouth, her tongue, her words. She has lost everything in losing Willie.

"Signe," she says.

"You don't have to say anything, you know. We can just sit here together."

"Your son was killed."

"In the war, yes."

"And then what?"

Signe squeezes Bernadette's hands. There's an ache present when she says, "And then nothing."

"You mean 'carry on'?"

"I mean nothing. The bottom falls out. There's nothing. Someone dies, and you see how it's all always been nothing."

In the low light, Signe's hair around her face becomes a hood. Her face is furrowed. Again, Bernadette sees Elli—the crone of Norse mythology. Wise and ruined. Terrifying. *Crone* is from the same root as *carrion* and *carcass*. What's left when life has picked away all the pink, all the soft flesh and the tenderness? Bones and hair still walking upright, still speaking, unnaturally, from the black hole of absence that is an afterlife. A kind of afterlife, anyway.

"But you must still grieve. You must still hold on to him."

"It changes you," Signe says, her voice graveled. "I'm not the same as I was before. That's different from grief."

"But—"

"There's nothing else I want to say about it." Silence falls between them until Signe stands. "I need to help Martin with the animals. But you're fine here. Just rest. Sleep more. If you want supper, I'll be making soup and biscuits. I'll have Martin knock."

Bernadette nods. She'd resist this care if she were in a better state—would offer to help, would put on her coat and walk out to the barn to be of some use—but she doesn't have the reserves for manners. She lies back on the pillow, closes her eyes again, and slides once more into sleep.

## 19

IT'S MIDMORNING WHEN SHE WAKES, AND SHE'S DISORIented. She's slept sixteen hours. When she sets her bare feet on the cold wood planks of Signe's floor, she sways with vertigo. How did she sleep so long? Why is the house so quiet around her? It's as if she's stepped into a pause—the eye of a massive storm—and cannot see the other side yet. She waits for her vision to still before leaving the bedroom in search of her hosts.

But Signe and Martin are not in the house, and there's only a note on the kitchen table and a bowl of oatmeal in the oven for her, keeping warm. She finds butter, sugar, and milk and drowns the porridge before eating it. She's starving, and the oatmeal goes down soft and comforting, but then it just sits in her belly like a stone. She keeps waiting for life to stir in her, but there's nothing.

In the bathroom, she brushes the moss from her teeth, fills the bathtub and climbs into it. She smells animal. Her hair is oily. When she runs her hands over her shins, she finds herself with a downy-soft layer of fur—not even bristles—and wonders how long it's been since she shaved. When she towels off, she stands for a moment looking at herself in the warp and patina of Signe's old mirror. She's pale. There's a narrowed, shining ferocity in her eyes. Her breasts are small and zippered with the silver stretch marks left behind from when she weaned Willie. Her belly is pouchy and just rounded. She looks hungry and afraid. A frightened animal.

What has it taken to make that transformation? In fairy tales and myths, humans are always becoming beasts because of terror, because of sorrow. The princes become swans, Jorinde is made nightingale, and Daphne a laurel. Selkies leave their skins on the rocks and are trapped inside the human form. All those creatures in the book Signe gave to Willie were turned to stone. It takes so little, really, to metamorphose—loss and isolation, fear and love and longing. A moment of impulsive oversight. A second of heartbreak. It can make a gentle woman cruel. A smart woman mute with numbness.

Here she is in the mirror—woman gone mother gone carrion. She has seen a monarch butterfly be picked out of the sky in midflight by a passing bird and mangled, wing from body. She has seen a crow tear a kink of gut from the belly of a wounded, still-breathing rabbit. She's seen humans, too, of course, made nothing but bones and leather pelt, eye sockets and wild empty vision. Humans turned mouth and asshole. Hunger and survival. Claw and rage. She's seen a man carrying his dead son's body over his shoulders like the carcass of a deer, the eyes on both faces wide and no longer truly among the living.

Signe's note on the kitchen table said this: *Remember that your daughter is still alive and needs you.*

195

Bernadette wraps a towel around herself and moves through the house with the chill of the air on her skin. She shivers. In the bedroom, she dresses, borrowing a heavy sweater of Signe's that she finds in the bureau. She makes the bed.

What she needs to get out of this are answers. She needs to prove that her time on the islands hasn't been wasted, that her work with Atalanta hasn't been a bid for fame, and her hours in Norquist's office haven't been unnecessary. She needs to prove or disprove the identity of Marley/Marlowe. She needs whatever Signe's concealing about her son. She needs Len Starkey's truck and Haven Wright's medical records. Her mind sparks: *the medical records.*

For weeks she's believed that they must be somewhere in Signe's house, but she doesn't love the idea of digging around in Signe's things after all the care she's received here. Even despite the possibility that Signe's hiding something from her, she'd much rather give her friend time to come forward with it than to trespass in finding it herself. She could wait for Signe to come home from wherever it is that she and Martin have gone—probably only the barn—and simply ask about the records, but it seems unlikely that Signe will offer now what she hasn't already been inclined to turn over. There have been opportunities, after all—the first invitation to Norquist's office, the New Year's visit. Thinking about it, Bernadette realizes that Signe never followed up on the canceled interview with Norquist, or at least not so far as she herself knows, and Norquist would have mentioned it. Why not attend the interview? Or, at the very least, reschedule it? And, on the other hand, why dodge an interview with Norquist but open her home to Bernadette? It might be simply the comfort Norquist has pointed out—Bernadette's way with the islanders. But that's nonsense, really. She doesn't have a way with the islanders. Len Starkey walked out on her just as much as he walked out on Norquist. The tug captain is a vault. And even Signe, underneath her hospitality, has revealed very little of herself. What does Bernadette actually know about her, beyond that she wasn't born on Adela and lost a son in the war? She has seemed open, yes, but that perception is misleading. Under the warm meals and the maternal reassurances, what has Signe Aalund offered of herself as a woman, an islander?

Bernadette moves through the house in stocking feet, giving a small knock before opening each door. She pauses at the threshold to every room before entering, parts the curtains at the window to look out for Signe or Martin crossing the field from the barn, but the field is empty, muted by fog that has rolled in from the sea and hangs in a low cloud. She opens dresser drawers, lifts stacks of folded linens, afghans, dozens of hand-knit sweaters and caps and mittens she's sure are Signe's work, light summer quilts folded and tucked away. In a bedroom closet, she finds a chestful of newspaper-wrapped dishes—Signe's china, or perhaps her mother's or mother-in-law's; and in another closet she comes across a small, knitted blanket of blue yarn flecked in white *V*s that might be stars or snowflakes. Stitched into its corner are the initials *SA*. She looks on the bookshelf in the front room, the hutch in the dining room, the pantry. Nothing. It could be in the barn, but there's no way for her to cross the field now, in daylight. And maybe she's been wrong, after all. Maybe Signe isn't hiding anything. Maybe there's nothing at all to hide. It could turn out that Haven burned everything in her last months, or that—like Len Starkey—she sent any evidence of her own illegal doings over the side of the sea cliff.

When she's covered what she can reasonably search without turning Signe's house inside out, Bernadette gathers her coat, pulls her satchel strap across her chest, and steps outside. There is still Haven Wright's place, now the Mayer farm.

The Mayer property is a mile from Signe's, and Bernadette is glad for the walk. With each step, her legs feel more certain beneath her. She reminds herself that she's made her way out of unthinkable grief before. The year she graduated from high school, she nursed her mother through dying. Her mother had been sick for a long time—longer than Bernadette had known—but she'd hidden it well, and the sickness grew in her quietly, a kind of rot in the pit of her that made her back ache and her belly swell. And then one day Bernadette really looked at her and found her mother nearly unrecognizable. The decline felt sudden, vicious. Bernadette's father dragged a single bed into the front room so that her mother could lie there all day and look out at the lake. Some afternoons that fall, when the weather was golden and warm and sweet with the scent of the maple leaves from the two big trees in front of the house, Bernadette opened the windows and let in the breeze. The lake could be silent, invisible behind the trees all summer long, but in the autumn, as the leaves fell, the water appeared, just a shine at first, and then, as the tree branches went naked, a bright and constant movement of light on water, as if the atmosphere between the house and the lake was always trembling. By November, the lake light was flat and steel gray and cold, and the air hung with the mineral fishiness of the water and the acrid far-off burning of backyard bonfires.

Bernadette and her mother never talked about death, just about dying. Her mother was weak and tired. She bled sometimes, a thick, brownish blood that soaked the cloth pads Bernadette washed and folded and tucked under her in the bed. The smell of the blood in the room was heavy and undeniably the odor of sickness, and eventually Bernadette's father avoided the room where her mother lay on those bad days. In the evenings, though, he and Bernadette sat at the kitchen table together, just the two of them, eating whatever supper she'd prepared for them— beef soup or trout and potatoes or pot pie with chicken he bought and had butchered at the nearest neighbor's farm. And then he disappeared into the bedroom he and her mother had shared for years, and she often saw his light on beneath the crack in the door late into the night.

The week after her mother's burial, her father rowed himself into the center of the lake, stepped over the side of his boat, and let himself drown. Bernadette was shocked but not surprised. He'd had the look of someone already gone for weeks. At his funeral, someone said it was something, really, to love your wife so much you couldn't bear to live without her, and Bernadette went back to the house sliding that thought on and off, like a too-loose ring on every finger, until she was certain it wasn't love that carried her father into the lake. Maybe it was fear or loneliness or anger or even relief, but not love. He'd loved her mother—she was sure of that—but love is never an unbearable load to hold, even when the subject of your love is gone.

What was left to her, then, was the house and everything in it. She spent the spring cleaning it and sold it by June, and before the summer was out, she was gone to college in Ann Arbor, to carry on, all her life unrolling before her without the strings or the security of family. She was an orphan in the world, entirely on her own. Later, the war reinforced that feeling. Loneliness became like a walled garden—part of her life's landscape that she acknowledged but could close a door on.

Until Willie was born. That winter of her pregnancy, while she lumbered up and down the halls of the university, she thought of her own motherhood and she thought of her parents. She thought of what was growing in her and also of what was buried behind her and gone. The lake in Chicago was nothing like the lake at home, and most months of the year, she could think it was a sea, but the winter of her pregnancy, the lake was silver and frozen, its raw edge at the beach jagged with ice, and she could only think of her parents when she looked at it. She could think only that, like them, she would eventually vanish from her child's life and leave the child orphaned, and the thought took her breath away.

But spring came, finally, and Willie was born. The lake water softened, melted, returned to its lapping. Grief, she thought, is tidal too. It retreats and returns. And when it comes back, it is changed—never exactly the same wave rolling in as rolling out. And beneath it, the shore is changed too, constantly. Someday, she herself would die and leave Willie behind (if they were lucky that was how their future would unfold)—a new shore for the endless lapping of light and shadow and warmth and ice to shape. And so it would go and go and go, always wild, and also always the same. She understood as she hadn't before that the work of parenting is letting your child sit at the edge of the water, in both the warm season and the cold.

She remembers this as she rounds a bend in the road and the Mayer house comes into view—a little yellow clapboard structure in the center of a big garden—and she is flooded with a sense of calm about Willie that she hasn't felt since they were separated. *Willie is at school today,* she tells herself. *She misses me, but she is fine. The tide will shift, and we'll be together again soon.* She repeats this, a prayer, over and over until she is at the gate.

"Finally we meet, Bernadette Baston," a male voice booms, surprising her, from the other side of the gate just as she reaches to open it.

*This goddamn island,* she thinks, but she says, "Hello! What a welcome."

The gate opens, and the man on the other side offers his hand to shake. He's younger than she expects—under fifty, certainly, with a dark braid over his shoulder and a blue knitted cap pulled to his eyebrows. He introduces himself as Mayer Nakamura. She smiles—the farm is not the Mayer farm, but Mayer's farm. She's misunderstood.

"I thought you'd show up earlier than this. I heard you were looking for Haven back before New Year. Should I be offended it's taken you so long?"

She stiffens, but he laughs. "It seems everyone here is aware of my plans before I am."

"That's the island for you."

He invites her inside for coffee and takes her around the side of the house by a path of flat stones settled into the dirt. The late-winter garden is all spine and brown stem, but she can see that it must be glorious in the spring. The plot is wide and sectioned, and he's covered the dirt in hay here and there around the bases of what look to be rosebushes and lavender.

"Your garden is beautiful."

"It was Haven's. I've just kept it up. Herbs and medicinal plants there—" he points to the eastern corner, "and her favorite flowers on the other side. Peonies and sea thistles and several rose varieties. That tree is a cherry. It looks like a cloud in April. You'll have to come back."

A spotted dog greets them at the kitchen door, jumping up at Bernadette's knees. "Down!" Mayer says, but even his command is gentle. He takes a cube of cheese from his pocket and hands it to the dog, who wags and sniffles and settles under the wide trestle table with the treat. "Excuse Etsu," he says. "She's a mutt. Part herder, part birder. Not the better part of either." A grin.

The coffee is already hot in the pot, and so he hands her a cup, fills it, and nudges a canister of sugar and a jug of cream her way. There's bread cooling on the stovetop, and he slices her a thick piece, which he slabs in butter.

As she eats and he fixes his own plate, she tries to picture the Haven Wright of the library photo in this room—Haven with a pot of soup on the stove, bundles of her garden herbs hanging to dry from the rafters. There's a bank of paned windows looking out over the backyard garden, its sill lined with ferns and philodendrons and geraniums. The house is warm and close and homey. It smells of the coffee and the fresh bread, but also of the fire in the other room, which she thinks is burning a little sage with whatever wood Mayer has pushed into the stove's belly. It isn't hard to imagine that the mothers who arrived at this door felt safe in Haven's care.

When he sits, Mayer holds his mug between both hands and smiles. "So, you want to know about Haven."

"Did you know her?"

Mayer beams. "Of course. Like an aunt." He gestures widely. "I've lived here my whole life. My parents were her tenants. There's a house at the western corner of the farm, and we lived there. I only moved in here after Haven began to need help."

"With deliveries?"

Again, a smile, though this one is sad. "With her health. She had trouble getting around in the last years. She forgot things. I moved in to make it easier."

This surprises Bernadette—a man as her nurse. She says, "You must have been more like a son, then."

"We were close. She trusted me." He lifts his mug and moves it in circles, stirring his coffee. "I was a medic. During the war. When I came back—well, let's just say I needed some time to readjust. Haven and I got to know each other better then."

Bernadette nods. "Me too," she says. "A nurse, I mean."

"Italy," he says. "For most of it."

"France."

"Avez-vous appris la langue?"

"Oui. Avant la guerre. Je suis allé le savoir."

"Sei stata fortunata."

"Impressive, but you lose me as soon as you cross the border." She lifts her mug and sips.

He winks. "Ah, well, I never get to practice out here on the island, so I had to try. Anyhow, I was grateful to return the favor when Haven got sick. She kept me alive when she took me in."

"And your parents? They didn't mind?"

"Only my mother was living by then, and my sister needed her attention. That was enough."

"She'd been overseas too?"

"Not overseas. Idaho. The Minidoka War Relocation Center. The whole family went, other than me. My father had a stroke there and never came home, but Haven held the house for my mother. She didn't rent it, kept my parents' furniture just as they'd left it." He looks drawn for an instant, the memory still close, but when he meets her gaze again, the shadow has passed.

"And now it's yours."

A nod and a nearly imperceptible straightening of his shoulders. "And now it's mine. Not a gift. I bought it. You probably heard otherwise."

"I've heard nothing."

He shrugs. "I assume the worst sometimes. Can't help it, you know? It stays with you, you understand, what people say about you when your back is turned. The meanness stays with you."

Bernadette watches him raise his mug. He hasn't shaved this morning, and the stubble on his chin and throat shadow the movement of his muscles as he swallows. He could be just under fifty, as she first thought, or he could be thirty—his face is youthful but also weathered by what she assumes must be the hours working the garden. There's dirt under his nails and on the cuffs of his denim shirt. When he looks at her, she sees a mirror of the sadness she knows she herself carries—grief, deep and accepted.

"Did you always know, then? About what Haven was doing here?"

"Midwifery?" he says. And when she waits to see what he'll add if she doesn't fill the silence, he shrugs. "You mean the adoptions? Everyone knew. It was a kindness. That's all. Everyone knew."

"Illegal kindness."

"You'll forgive me if I don't always put much stock in following the law as a measure of virtue. In my experience, it's very rarely been anything but a knife in the back."

"Of course. I'm sorry." She sighs, leans back against her chair. Sitting here, in Haven's house, it's impossible to imagine her as anything but warm and comforting, a kind of mother of the island, who—as both Signe and Mayer have now said—only wanted to be of service to this place and its people. "Could I see her delivery room anyway? Just out of curiosity? Or do you maybe still have her records?"

"What are you looking for?"

Bernadette searches for the best way to answer this, and decides honesty is best just now. "I wish I could say. I'm looking for anything you might give me on Len Starkey or on a woman—possibly named Marley or Marlowe—who delivered a baby that never made it to the adoptive parents."

Mayer's face warms, and—again—for an instant she sees that same sheet of sadness drop over his expression. "Not Marlowe. Harlow. My sister."

"Harlow?"

"Our mother liked Hollywood. Mayer and Harlow?"

Bernadette smiles. "Of course."

He pushes back in his chair and stands. Beneath the table there's a scrabbling of dog nails on the wood floor. "Let's walk," he says.

The dog lollops a few paces ahead, used to Mayer's constant roving over the property, it seems. They follow the garden path out to a wide field of grass gone ashy and flaxen. The path is saturated in places and full of puddles in others, which Bernadette has to step around and over to avoid soaking her feet to the ankles. She can imagine that in the summer, when the grass is tall, the dog disappears here, just a tail tip bobbing above the points of the yellow-green blades. She can smell the sea—salty and fresh. They're not far, really, from the cliffs that drop into the water. The wind must rush up and over those stark hillsides and cross the island in one flat whoosh.

After what must be two football fields of distance, the grass stops abruptly before a circle of lavender plants, all of them sage green and woody and damp. There are something like fifty of them, and they make a living wreath on the ground, at the center of which lie three big stones.

"It must smell beautiful here in the summer."

Mayer nods. "There are always bees. The place hums. I love that about it. It feels like there's a lot of life here, which I think is what Haven wanted." He walks to the center stone and gets down on his knees, touches it. "This one is where Harlow's boy is buried. Three days old when he died. She didn't name him, so forever we thought of him as Sweetpea." Mayer's shoulders rise and fall. Bernadette can't tell if he is crying or praying or what. She isn't sure if she, too, should get on her knees here—if he would receive that as sympathy or show—and so she doesn't move.

He explains to her that he was there in the room with his sister the night she delivered Sweetpea. "Birth wasn't shocking to me. It wasn't uncommon for Haven to call on my mother for extra help during a delivery, and I was her tagalong. For a few years before the war, I actually thought I'd train to be a doctor, but it wasn't in the cards."

"It didn't bother you? A young man?"

"City hospitals have made birth shameful. Like it's a big, dirty secret. But like I said, I'd seen births since I was just a kid. No different to me than watching a cow or a sheep deliver in the barn."

"But the mothers—they didn't mind you in the room with them?"

A wry look. "I think a boy like me was mostly invisible to white women."

Bernadette looks at the stone where his hand is still resting. It's oblong and rough textured, the size of a small radiator even with some amount of its base buried in the dirt. Mayer's palm on it is open and flat.

"Was your nephew ill? Forgive me if that's not a question you want to answer."

"It's fine. I don't think death should be a secret either." He pauses, as if tugging the seam of the memory to draw it close. "We were all there—my father and mother and Haven and I—just saying goodbye." He turns his face to look at her over his shoulder. "We were happy there'd be an adoption. My sister was young. The father was white, and older. He already had a family. It was a mistake, Harlow with him, and our parents were ashamed. Some people here think Haven did witchcraft, which is just ridiculous. She was a diplomat. That's how I think of her. Without her, my parents would have sent my sister away for good too." Mayer pats the stone—gentle, like patting a child's back. "The family Haven found was Japanese. She understood that was important to my parents, and she found them for us."

"And your sister was ready to let him go?"

"My sister was fifteen." His face shifts, the grief a flare that goes off behind his eyes suddenly. "But then, he just went. Suddenly." He recounts it for her: the baby was fine one moment, and the next moment blue and gasping. No reason. Haven did what she could, but he was gone in seconds. And that was it. "We think a heart problem. Something wrong from the beginning that we just couldn't see. He looked perfect, though. Just perfect."

Bernadette gets on her knees beside him. The ground is cold and damp through the fabric of her pants. "I'm sorry," she says.

"The rest of what you mentioned back there at the house? That's nothing," he says. "Gossip. I've heard it all. Len and the truck and the father on Haven's doorstep? Gossip."

"Yes. That's what I've heard."

"Islanders. They won't come right out and ask you your private details, but when they don't get the whole story, they'll write it themselves." Mayer stands and brushes the caked mud from his pants.

Bernadette follows him. There are two dark spots on her knees as well. She feels the cold all the way through to her skin. "And those?" She points to the other two stones.

"Haven was an excellent midwife, but not every baby enters the world living. You said you were a nurse, so you know this."

"Did she record them? The deaths?"

"I have no idea about that. Sweetpea's death is recorded in my memory. July nineteenth, 1938. I don't need that on a stone to know it." He touches his chest, taps where his heart is, below bone and skin. "One of the mothers comes here every year on the anniversary and puts out flowers. That's the only documentation that really matters." He turns, snaps the dog to attention, and they take the same path back to the house, the dog's tail loping side to side and Mayer's braid swaying against his broad back.

In the house again, he shows her the delivery room—unchanged much from Haven's days in practice. There's a single bed against one wall, the footboard removed. A glass-fronted cabinet full of stacked emesis basins, folded towels, a tray of metal instruments. In the corner, Bernadette recognizes an old-fashioned birthing stool. It's homey enough but also clearly more than just a bedroom.

"No one uses this now?"

Mayer shakes his head. "I've thought about cleaning it out, but I'm not done living with her ghost." He turns and leads Bernadette out.

In the kitchen, the light has shifted. It's afternoon. The sun has broken open over the water to the west, daffodil-tender and fragile.

"And her files?" she asks.

He opens a high cabinet over the stove, pulls out two latched metal boxes, and sets them on the table. Inside, there are files, each labeled with a name—Alma, Astrid, Brigid, Dagne. All written in what must be Haven's tidy hand, all alphabetized. "You can take these, if you want. I don't think you'll find what you're hoping for, but they're yours if you want them."

She walks her fingers through the files for a moment, then slides one from the box and opens its to a single sheet of longhand notes, detailing a morning birth after seven hours of labor. *Five stitches to the mother. Baby presenting typical with a clear wail and no indication of jaundice.* It's all very clinical. Bernadette closes the file and returns it to the box. "I don't need these, but thank you." She gathers her coat and her bag. "I should leave you to your day."

"I'm happy to clear Haven, if that's what this was."

She smiles. "Not clearing so much as confirming."

"Good."

She turns. "Is your sister still living here, then, and your mother?"

He draws a breath, and she sees again that bruise behind his eyes. "Mom is buried in the Japanese corner of St. Eulalia's graveyard."

"I'm so sorry. How long?"

"Mom went three years ago. Harlow took her own life in August of '47. They wouldn't have her in the cemetery. She's here, on the farm. With her son, as it should have been."

Bernadette pauses. She could offer her own story—her mother and father, her grief—but she doesn't. No one knows that history—not even Fred—and where Mayer has chosen to stay and live with his ghosts, she chose to tuck hers away inside herself. It's the only way she can hold on to them. She nods, says, "I'm so sorry." But then, before she can filter herself, she adds, "Mr. Nakamura, do you believe in heaven? Or an afterlife?"

"You've seen Haven's gardens," he says. She smiles at this, but then he shakes his head, serious. "Honestly, though, no. The dead are dead."

"The war did that to a lot of people's heaven," she says.

"It did, but not mine. I've never—" He stops, starts again. "It's just, my vision of a good eternity is so much like this place that I think we all might be looking for heaven on the wrong side of death." A smile. "Don't tell anybody though. I don't need to give them another reason to wonder about me."

She'll keep it to herself, Bernadette tells him. She thanks him for the warm welcome and lets him show her out, passing again through Haven's winter garden, which she can picture as absolutely heavenly at its blooming apex in late spring—all wild racket of briar roses and leggy aquatic-looking rosemary, the lavender pulsing with bees. She'd love to see it like that—the best version of itself. The wild, overrun, full-budded version of itself. It must really be something.

She walks back to town with the sun warming the top of her head and her mind clearer than it's been in days. *Not everyone is hiding*, she thinks. Not everyone is guarding decay. Sometimes, the mystery is not the shadow, but the persistence of the light.


## 20


BERNADETTE HOLDS ON TO THE VISIT TO MAYER'S FARM for several days without knowing how to unfold what he's given her. In Mayer's version of the past, Haven is the heroine of Adela Island. In Starkey's version, there's room to see her as suspicious. The truth, of course, is probably somewhere between these two stories. Haven was an ordinary woman, who did some real good for the women who came to her. And even if the good she did was occasionally at the expense of legality or honesty, those stones in Mayer's back field make it impossible for Bernadette to imagine Haven as a woman who could rest—let alone cover it up—if she believed Len Starkey had sent his truck with an infant inside its cab sailing over the seaside cliffs and into the water. Haven's entire life, it seems, was poised on a belief that women and children deserved better treatment and more opportunities to thrive. She wouldn't have sanctioned violence against one of her own charges. Bernadette doesn't think so, anyhow.

But people don't always stay on the paths they've carved for themselves. When up against fear or danger or personal threat, a person can transform and become the very wolf from which they've been running. Bernadette has seen this, too. Haven was a woman alone, working despite the blockades stacked against her, an outsider in every community she entered. The isolation must have been palpable sometimes in that house, the farm spread out wide and empty around her, and beyond it nothing between her and the horizon but the lonely hushing of the sea. That's freedom, yes, and also terror. Bernadette knows the exact double tension of that life. There's no room for error or slip. No room for the dip of a toe into the swim of nothingness below you. No room for wavering. *Freaks*, she thinks, *we women who walk that line.*

When she was big with the last days of her pregnancy and tired of waiting for Willie's delivery, she believed that the most wild, radical transformation she'd undergo as a mother had already passed. She had no idea then that a woman could become a boat, could become a net, could become a whole sea. She thought of Willie growing inside her like a fat little caterpillar, a chick in an egg. Willie, the little winged hatchling. But she overlooked her own transformation, saw herself—the mother—as beside the point. What a failure of understanding that was. She did not become unnecessary to Willie as soon as the work of birth was behind them. How could she have so misjudged things? A mother is less cocoon than full sky. And now—like her own mother did before her—she's left her girl earthbound, trapped, halfway through the transformation with nowhere to become. The thought sucks Bernadette's breath from her.

Eight days into her stay with Signe, she can't bear it anymore—their separation. It's night, and she puts on her coat, leaves the house as quietly as she can, and walks out into the field. There's no visible moon, but the low clouds lighten the sky and color the field's mud silver-blue. It has rained all day, and she can smell the weep of the groundwater welling up, manure sweet and brined in sea salt like everything on the island. She's been conscious of her own noise in the house—afraid to cry unless she can do it silently—but here, in the open, there's no one to hear her, and so she wails, open mouthed and snotty. She puts her hands over her face and lets herself shake.

She's halfway to the barn when she hears Signe calling her and turns.

"Oh, my dear," Signe says as she strides forward. She has a shawl in her arms and wraps it around Bernadette's shoulders. It still smells of sheep's wool next to Bernadette's face—like lanolin and grass. "Oh, sweetheart. Oh," Signe croons.

Bernadette lets herself be held. She couldn't stop crying now if she wanted to, and she doesn't. She's come apart, all the seams opened. She could shake herself to nothing. She almost hopes this is the moment when she finally fails to keep herself inside the boundaries of her own body, when she shakes so hard that she vibrates herself into particles, vanishes into the mud or the wind.

"How did you know I was out here?" she asks between sobs.

"I'm a poor sleeper. And you weren't entirely quiet, you know." A smile.

"I'm so sorry. I just—"

"Oh, honey. Hush now. You'll be sick," Signe says. She rubs circles on Bernadette's back. It's motherly, and Bernadette can only shake harder under the comfort of a kind hand. "You have to calm down now." Signe shushes her, rocks with her back and forth, foot to foot.

It's several minutes before Bernadette can breathe normally again, can stop shuddering with each draw of cold air into her lungs. "I'm sorry," she says. "I left so no one would hear." Even in the darkness, she can see the worry on Signe's face.

"Come with me," Signe says, and she takes Bernadette's hand.

They cross the field again, and Signe pulls the car around from where it's parked at the back of the house, then helps Bernadette into the passenger seat.

"It's the middle of the night," Bernadette says.

"No one on this island cares what an old lady does with her nights."

They wind the curves into town and keep going—past the school and the graveyard and farther, all the way to the island's northwestern point. There's nothing there, where Signe pulls over. Just trees. But Signe takes Bernadette's arm. She's brought a flashlight, and when she turns it on, the beam illuminates a path. The air smells wet and sweet with cedar. As they walk, the only sounds are their own feet on the ground and the dripping of raindrops from needle to needle overhead.

Then—surprising—the darkness drops away like a drape has fallen, and the sky opens up over the width of the sea.

"Careful now," Signe says. She goes first down the path, though she's less stable on her feet, and Bernadette watches her wobble once, catch herself another time. The path is steep in spots, made of dirt that's gone slick with the days of rain. Signe throws her arms out wide like wings when she steps down. "Careful," she says again, as if she's the one best equipped for this night walk.

Bernadette's breath billows out in front of her. Her face is tight with the effects of crying and of sleeplessness. She can feel the salty lick of the sea air pressing on her as they get closer to the beach.

When they reach a rack of driftwood, Signe sits. She's out of breath. She swings the beam of her flashlight once, twice, a third time over the beach—looking for anyone else out there, Bernadette assumes, but they are totally alone.

The tide is neither low nor high, and a wrack line of detritus—driftwood and bark and seaweed—clutters the space between them and the water.

"Just sit. There's no way to walk here," Signe says, as if she's read Bernadette's mind.

Bernadette narrows her eyes until the wavering darkness focuses and a hump of land comes into view. "That's Elita," she says, identifying the island across the channel.

"Why are we here?"

"Hush and listen."

They sit. Bernadette pulls Signe's shawl up around her shoulders. She's still shaking, but less violently now. She feels hollowed out by this night, her stomach cramping around its own emptiness.

It's not right away that she hears a caroling, but when she does, she can't hear anything else. It's dogs, she registers. The pack. She can't believe it's real.

The tide's rhythm falls away, and so does her own rattled breathing and the chaos inside her head. Everything but the dogs' voices goes silent. The dogs send their howls in chorus across the water, a threaded, keening sound.

She looks across the dark stretch. Elita is nothing but a shadowed bulk, the dogs, wherever they are, invisible. Still, their voices are strong, a full pack. An instinctive wire of fear rips up her spine at their sound. "There must be twenty or thirty of them," she whispers.

"Fewer. More like ten. People have tracked them."

Bernadette listens. They might be coyotes, not dogs. They might be wolves. She pictures Atalanta curled into her night spot—a pyramid of driftwood on the beach, maybe, or a den bedded down with leaves—listening to their howls. It's not difficult to believe there's language in the dogs' carol. There's a hymnal quality to their voices wound as one, and maybe the girl came to understand the lament or the joy or the question of the dogs' song. Maybe it vibrated in her chest as she lay waiting for her own sleep and she was comforted by it, the way a child is comforted by a mother's bedtime lullabies.

Bernadette says, "One of the men who found her, he mentioned the dogs."

"Lenny, right?" Signe nods to herself. "He knows about them. I wouldn't be surprised if he'd tried to hunt them. Some do."

"Hunt dogs?"

"Not for meat. For sport. The dogs are wild. They've become island legend. It'd be a feat to kill one. Len's the sort would want a trophy."

Bernadette remembers the transcript in Norquist's files—the note about Starkey and Lind believing the rustling movement they saw in the grass was the pack. She recalls Starkey on the first interview tape saying that Atalanta came at them "like a mad dog." He would have wanted her—the trophy Signe's talking about. He threw the rock at her back because he didn't have his gun.

"I didn't believe him. Not really," she says.

"Lenny?"

"When he said he thought the girl was a dog. I didn't believe him. How could you mistake a child for a dog?"

Signe sighs a deep cloud of breath. It rises and dissolves. "You know, this whole business of you coming out here to rest, it's not working. You've been out to Mayer's." She catches Bernadette's eye before Bernadette can protest, says, "I knew you'd go. And I also knew you'd look around my house."

Between them, Bernadette feels the air pull tight. She doesn't want to admit to looking through Signe's drawers and cupboards, but she won't deny it either, and so she says only, "There are answers somewhere."

"Maybe," Signe says. "Though there aren't always answers, you know. And even if there are, and you find them, what does that do for the girl? For you? That girl, is she ever going to live a normal life? Poor thing. She's never been normal."

The question is odd. It raises a tendril of discomfort in Bernadette. "What is normal?" she asks. "And anyhow, that shouldn't matter. She's living. That's enough. I want—" She pauses, not sure how to end the sentence.

"What? What do you want?" There's an edge of exhaustion in Signe's voice.

"I want something better for her than most girls who don't fit ever get. I want justice for her. I want resolution."

"Resolution," Signe says with bitterness. "You're looking in the wrong places if that's what you want. Resolution is ahead, not behind. Always. I know that for sure. You think knowing the details of my son's death brought me resolution?"

"I'm not saying peace. I know there's no peace."

"You're simplifying everything to make it bearable, and none of this—" Signe gestures at the breadth of darkness around them, "is bearable. It's not."

"Why would you tell me that?" Anger blooms in Bernadette's throat, hot, a held yell. The muscles of her neck ache at the withholding.

"I'm telling you that you have a perfect, beautiful, living daughter whose future is entirely unresolved, and that is where you should be looking right now." She lays her hand on Bernadette's knee, warm and firm—the press of a command. It's maternal.

"Signe. She's with her father. I have no recourse. You know that."

"A solution will present itself. You just can't see it yet."

The water catches the loping of Signe's beam crossing back and forth over the waves, and Bernadette can see a strip of blue-green, a snag of wave tip and then the sink of the dip as the water pulls back again.

"Listen to those dogs," Signe says. "I like to think about them over there, the only free creatures on that island where everybody else is caged."

Across the water, a long, low, reedy note follows a high, vibrating one.

"I read somewhere that deer sometimes swim between the islands. Have you seen that? Why don't the dogs swim? What is it? A mile? They could swim it if a deer can. There's food here."

Signe shakes her head. "The deer swim, yes. But the dogs? No. And better they stay over there. They'd be shot here. For certain, they'd be shot. No one wants feral dogs running loose over here. It's one thing to leave the wild to the wild, and another to have it in your home." There's bitterness in her voice now.

The dogs howl one more echoing, chorded thread of song across the water and go silent. Bernadette waits, her ears tuned for more, but that's it. It was a last call, a good night. The dogs have retreated from their beach, and only the even hushing of the tide against the rocks on shore is left.

Signe stands, brushes off the seat of her pants. "Well, shall we? Time to go home?"

The hike up the hill again is stiff and slow. Bernadette follows, ready to catch Signe if she slips, but the older woman is sure-footed. When they get to the top, the car is there, a hulking shadow. They get in, and Signe runs the heater until the windows clear, and they follow the road back to the farm.

At the farm, Bernadette thanks her without really knowing what she's grateful for. She lets herself inside ahead of Signe, gets in her bed, and sleeps heavily through the rest of the night. And when she wakes up, she hears Signe's words from the night before ringing like a bell in her head. *It's time to go home.*

She strips the bed and packs her bag. She hasn't gotten to any of her work—but she's clearer headed, and that's ultimately why she came out to Signe's. On a piece of paper, she writes, *Thank you for everything. I'll be in touch when I can.* She leaves by the front door before Signe and Martin are back from the barn.

By the time she gets home, she is bleeding—at first just spotting, and soon a heavy rush that carries her to the toilet, bent over with cramps. She cries, but it's only relief that she feels. Nothing else. She should feel ashamed of that, maybe, she thinks, but she can't. She can't. She hasn't been willing to really entertain the idea that all of it—the fainting and the vertigo, could be another pregnancy, but the possibility has been there—lodged like a bit of barbed wire in her gut all along. She and Fred have not always been careful, though they should have been. They invited disaster. She imagines herself with a second baby, fully trapped this time in a life she knows she doesn't want. But no, that's not her future now. Thank goodness, that's not her future. She's just herself again, and all the cage doors are open.

## 21

THE NEXT MORNING, SHE'S AT THE GATE OF THE NURS-
ery school when Fred and Willie arrive. It's a risk, this surprise, but her
choice is either to meet Fred here or in the department, in front of his
colleagues, and she figures her chances of restoring his trust in her are
better without a public scene.

Willie spots her from a distance—Bernadette watches the light of
recognition fill her daughter's face—and she comes running, all gangly
legs and wild gallop. "Mama! Mama! Mama! Mama!" Half joy, half cry.
Bernadette goes to her knees in the grass, lets Willie collapse into her.

"I've missed you," she breathes into Willie's hair. "I've missed you so
much, Wills." She feels the gush of air from both their chests as they press
against one another. She feels Willie's heart pounding under her cotton
dress. Willie smells of new shampoo, of someone else's home, but also—
under that—of her sweet self. Bernadette notices that she's still holding her
casted arm at an odd angle. "Does it hurt?" she asks, but Willie shakes her
head and touches her free hand to Bernadette's face. Her hand is clammy,
sticky with whatever she's eaten for breakfast. She pats and pats Bernadette's cheeks, bends forward and puts her own cheek against Bernadette's.

"Mama, mama, mama," she says. A litany. A sorrow. Bernadette hears
the questions under Willie's repetition. *Where have you been? How could
you leave me? How can I ever trust you again?*

"I'm home," she says. "I'm not leaving again. Not ever without you
again."

Willie draws back and for a long second she steels her eyes on Bernadette's, trying in that child way she has to read a text she entered the
world intuitively knowing but still cannot comprehend: her mother.
Finally, squinting, she says, "I hate you."

Bernadette nods. "I know, but we'll be all right now."

"She has to get inside, Bernadette." Fred has given them space, but
now he steps closer, hands Willie her lunch. It's a cafeteria lunch sack.
Bernadette recognizes the neat fold-and-staple, the printed last name
across the top. He's living on campus with Willie, then. Taking her to
eat at the cafeteria. Probably paying a coed to babysit while he works.
Of course. It makes sense that he'd never know where to begin in an

off-campus apartment with Willie alone. The realization hits and Bernadette turns her face to him and smiles. There's hope in his overwhelm. He needs her. Or, at least, his life is easier with her in it. Whatever punishment he's meant to impose on her could be finished right now if she can handle the next few minutes well.

She stands and sweeps her hands along her pant legs. "I've left the case. I'm home. I'm hoping Willie—and you—will come back. Whenever you're ready, that is."

Fred's face is tight. He keeps his hands stuffed into his pockets, the flaps of his blazer sticking out like duck wings. He's a ridiculous man, unable to simply say what she can see written just under his frown. She knows he wants to admit how hard it's been without her. He wants to tell her he'll be home for dinner at six. He wants to ask if she can pick up Willie after nursery school. He wants to say he's missed her. He regrets it. He doesn't want to be this proud.

He looks at his feet. "Wills," he says, "we better get you inside, or you'll be late."

"But Mama—"

"I'll talk to your mother. Don't you worry about it." He hands Willie the lunch sack, and she takes it, looking over her shoulder at Bernadette. The softness of her face is thinning already, and there's a new blade of doubt in her, like a weed, sprouted now and forever impossible to rout out. Bernadette can see it. She planted it there, she knows, and now there's nothing she can do to uproot it. God, the guilt of that! But it was unavoidable. She thinks of her own mother holding back her dying until the inevitability of it crashed over both of them. A mother always fails in the end, doesn't she? The whole arrangement of motherhood is one of designed decay. Take my body. Take my heart. Take the best of my love and my energy and my thoughts and unmake me so that you can become. That's the bargain. Let me fail you, daughter, so that you can separate from me and become your own. Bernadette sighs, feels the shudder of it run all through her.

She reaches out and takes Willie's free hand. "I'm here. I'm not leaving again."

Willie scowls but nods, pushes inside the gate, and disappears into the nursery school.

"Her arm," Bernadette says. "How's her arm, really?"

"Walk with me." Fred's tone is stoic. He turns and stands with his back to her, waiting until she's beside him to start talking. "You left. You left with no word."

She's caught off guard by this—the sting in his voice. Did he think he could take Willie, and she'd just close the curtains and stare at the wall until he came back? "I was at Signe's."

"I know that. She called the department."

It's a punch. Bernadette swivels to look at him. "When?"

"You went through her things, Bernadette. You could barely take care of yourself. What did you expect she'd do?"

"She called you? But she never said—"

"Because I told her we weren't coming for you, Willie and me. I told her you could sort yourself out." He pauses, stops walking, and grips her wrists in his hands. "You're not well. Signe says you're not well at all. She says you need a doctor."

She laughs, shakes her head. "That's nonsense. I'm not unwell. And this is all just so rich coming from you—the man who took off and didn't return for years." Again, a laugh, but it comes out shaky with fury. Her voice splits. "I was gone days. Days, Fred. And now I'm unhinged?"

"Bernadette, you're seeing a doctor before you see Willie. That's my final decision."

She jerks her wrists from his hold and raises her voice. "Don't you touch me."

Across the university lawn, a group of students has stopped to watch the argument. Bernadette raises her eyes to these young people—a couple of girls and three male students dressed just like Fred, in shirts and ties and blazers. They tip their heads toward one another and whisper, not lifting their gaze from Bernadette, and she is moved by something intuitive and deep. Without thinking, she opens her mouth and screams. The scream is disembodied, a howl of pain and rage not just her own, but also of something bigger than her, of something outside of her. She hears it unspooling around her like a ribbon of water let loose from a hose, and when it stops, she is raw throated and shaking, and the young people gape and turn their backs and scatter, afraid. She's a madwoman to them. A danger.

Fred, blanched and stiff, reaches forward and slaps her across the face. "Look at yourself," he hisses, low. He takes her wrist in the big circle of his grip. She feels the eyes of the university on her. She wants to vanish. *Can shame swallow a woman?* she thinks. The question is a sinkhole, sucking her under already.

She bows her head and follows Fred where he leads her, dog on a leash, without speaking, numb everywhere except the needles of her cheek where his handprint must still be on her skin. They cross the campus, cross a street of narrow brick apartment buildings. She trips on the curb and nearly falls, but he tugs her to her feet again. A woman on a bike passes and looks back, embarrassment on her face. Bernadette refuses to look away. No one wants to know what's happening here.

At the corner, a cop car pulls up while Fred waits for the lights to turn. "You need help, mister?" the officer asks through his open window.

Fred bundles Bernadette into the cruiser's back seat, tells the officer they need the hospital, it's an emergency.

Bernadette is a fish in a tank. This cruiser looks just like Norquist's. Part of her wishes it was Norquist's. He wouldn't allow this. He'd take her home, tell Fred to back off. She presses her hot cheek to the cool of the window. Something has drained from of her. She's limp. Her heart is hooked and bleeding out. There's no point in fighting.

At the hospital, the officer comes around the car, and she takes his arm and allows herself to be led into the ER. He sits beside her while Fred speaks to the registrar.

"You'll be okay, ma'am," he says.

"You think I'm crazy," she tells him.

"You'll be okay." He has doe eyes and the pouchy, drawn face of an old pet. When he takes off his cap and lays it in his lap, she can see that his hair is the color of a new carrot, clipped short and bristling like a neat nailbrush on the top of his skull. She thinks of the doctor in France—the young one she kissed to keep him from crying in the middle of the night. He looked nothing like this officer, but there is a parallel kindness in this man now, and she's grateful for that.

Fred goes for coffee and brings back two cups—one for the officer and one for himself. She watches them drink. They stand like sentries, one on each side of her, neither speaking. When he's finished his cup, the officer returns his cap to his head, lays his hand on Bernadette's shoulder for a moment. "Your husband's got things from here," he says, and he leaves.

Bernadette's gaze follows him out the door. "I want to go," she says.

"It'll be just another minute," Fred tells her.

She has water in her ears. She remembers her mother saying that at the end of her life, in the last days—that she couldn't hear anything. That there was cotton in her ears. It was the morphine, Bernadette thought at the time, but now she wonders if this is what happens when the unraveling begins—a shutting down of perception. It would be self-preservation, if true. First the world might go silent, then dark. The altar stripped. The black cloth dropped. All the beauty bleeding away like ink diffusing in saltwater—the body's way of making it less difficult for the dying person to leave earth.

A nurse arrives with a wheelchair, and Bernadette gets in it.

"You're not coming?" she asks when Fred doesn't move. "You're not coming?"

He puts his face in his hands. He could be a stranger. A tall man at the door of the hospital with his face in his hands.

She's wheeled away.

22

SHE GOES BACK TO THE BEGINNING.

The first sound a baby makes is a cry. There are different cries, as any mother knows. There is the cry of hunger, and the cry of fatigue. The cry of fear, and the cry of discomfort—gas in the belly, a tooth rubbing its way through a gum. There's a boredom wail. Willie cried this cry often. She was born wanting to see and to know, and sometimes the world was too still for her.

That's where words come in. *Mama* and *Dada*. *Apple, tree, dog. Ball, you, bath. Mine, no, please. I, love, we.* Words formed like bubbles, just a caul between the parted lips at first, slick and viscous. Drool. Then, a curvature. A sound. A syllable. A string of syllables like glossy opals all in a row. Beautiful diphthongs and the plucked thread of a fricative. Tongue twisters. *A big black bug bit a big black bear.*

The baby looks around the world and sees, and her mother names everything for her. *Flower, ant, car, bus. Street, tree, house, me.* The baby looks around, and the mother makes meaning with story. *We two are in our house together, a family. Before you were born, I was one. Solo. Like a single star in the wide night sky. And I didn't know I was waiting for you. But then, you arrived, and I knew you were mine and also your own. Barnacle daughter, my blood and my work, my heart and my fear. Little one, you.*

ALL DAY, BERNADETTE WAITS IN A HOSPITAL BED FOR something to happen. They've given her a sedative. Seconal, she thinks. She falls into and climbs out of sleep. The room swims, and once she vomits and is given a second pill and a glass of water. She wonders where her clothes have been taken. She had her satchel when she left the apartment, and she's lost track of it. Maybe it's still sitting on the university lawn, a bag in the grass. She dreams of balloons—white balloons—that become a kaleidoscope of fluttering moths rising into a cloud-banked sky. She dreams of her childhood house, the rooms all rearranged from their reality, skewed just slightly, but still familiar.

Now and then, a nurse appears to take her temperature and listen to her heart again. She's still bleeding, the blood wet and warm on the sanitary napkin. She's vaguely aware of the smell of it on her—like copper and dirt. It makes her think of her mother's death. It makes her think of her daughter's birth. The body is such an inevitable boundary.

At dinner time, a tray is delivered to her, though she doesn't eat. She sleeps and she wakes. Sleeps and wakes. Hours pass. It goes dark outside the window.

IN THE MORNING WHEN SHE WAKES UP, THERE'S A MAN sitting beside her bed. Fred, she thinks, but when she rights herself and focuses her eyes, she sees that it's Norquist.

He smiles. "Rough patch, eh?"

She hears him through the water in her head and nods.

She wishes he weren't here, but she's also grateful—immensely grateful—that he's come. He shouldn't see her a mess. She stinks and her face must be swollen, her makeup smudged. Her breasts are loose under the hospital gown, and every time she moves, she gets a draft of her own sweat. She crosses her arms over her chest. She wants to apologize for herself, but if she does, he'll feel he should leave, and she doesn't want him to leave. At least with him in the room she's not alone.

"What did you hear?" she asks.

"Fight on campus, you screaming your head off, a ride with an officer, and here you are."

She closes her eyes. "That's what I thought happened. I was hoping I had misremembered."

"No one ever misremembers. It's always exactly as bad as you think it is." Another kind smile. He offers his open palm, and she slides her hand into it. His hand is warm and dry and friendly. That's all, and that's what she needs at the moment. She closes her fingers around his.

"It's all falling apart, and I don't know what I'm going to do."

"You'll figure it out. You're a sharp lady."

She sighs. "Thank you."

Out the open window, there's actually sun. The day is pale blue and the sky is spotted with fat clouds. A band of light lies in a strip across the floor. It might be ten in the morning, or it might be two in the afternoon. She's lost all sense of her orientation to the world.

"They think I'm crazy, you know."

"Well, the screaming didn't help your case."

She smiles. "I don't know where that came from."

"Sure you do. Once, when my ex-wife was not yet my ex-wife, I punched my fist through the wall of our bedroom. Tore out the plaster, busted a knuckle. And then the hole was just there for me to look at. I didn't know how to patch it. I'm not very handy." He grins.

"I appreciate the commiseration. But no one locked you up and drugged you silent."

"You'll get back on track."

"Will I? Every time I think that, the gates come slamming back down on me."

He squeezes her hand.

"I'm sorry," she says. "I'm a mess."

"I didn't expect you to be dressed for a cocktail party here."

A new nurse arrives with a breakfast tray. She's cheerful and high-pitched and young. Bernadette goes flat.

"Thanks," Norquist says. He takes the tray.

"Her pill," she says. "You'll need to move aside while I give it to her."

"I'm awake. I can take it myself."

The nurse looks blankly at Bernadette, then at Norquist. "I better do it," she says.

"She's trustworthy, I assure you." Norquist beams at the woman. He's charming when he wants to be—clean shaven today, and a fresh shirt on. He smells of aftershave, Bernadette notes, rather than his usual sleep and smoke. He assures the young woman that he'll keep an eye on the patient—he's a cop, so nobody gets away with anything in his presence. The nurse laughs but hesitates. "Look at her," Norquist points to Bernadette. "Don't you trust her? She's a mom, you know. Kid at home. She's just overtired. You know how exhausted moms are. She'll take your sleep in a capsule, happily. It's like a vacation."

"Happily," Bernadette says.

Norquist makes a show of lifting the silver domes off each plate and bowl on the tray, exclaiming over the food—which is just toast and jam, a single fried egg, and a cup of applesauce—as if Bernadette is a child in need of encouragement, and finally, apparently convinced, the nurse goes.

"That was some brilliant acting there," she says.

He offers a minor bow. "You in need of more rest?" he asks, and when she shakes her head, he drops the pill from its paper cup into his own palm and pockets it. "Insomnia. Thank you for your contribution."

"No, thank *you*. They're worried I'll choke myself or turn the spoon into a shiv if I'm allowed full consciousness for long, but I hate the drugs."

"Most of us think about the spoon shiv sometimes, but, honest to god, there are better ways." He leans forward and opens his jacket. The butt of his service revolver sticks out just under his arm. "Much faster."

She laughs. "Dark humor. I appreciate it."

"Not humor. Truth." He tips his head to her tray. "You hungry? You must be."

"Just hand me the coffee if there is some."

"Good. I missed breakfast."

She watches him settle the egg between the toast slices just so, then salt it from the little plastic shaker, fastidious before the first bite.

Outside the window, a breeze has billowed in off the sea and blown the clouds to nothing but brushed wool. The coffee hits Bernadette's empty stomach and scorches. At least it fills the empty bowl of her gut, tastes like something other than the acid in her mouth. She sips and breathes and is glad for Norquist's quiet chewing beside her.

"Listen," he says when he's done. He wipes his mouth with her napkin and wads the cloth in a ball under one of the domes on her tray. "I came for two reasons. One was to check up on you, which I've done. The other was to tell you about your girl."

"Willie? What's happened?"

"Calm down. The other girl. Atalanta." He sets one saucer on top of another, lifts the lid on the applesauce, sniffs it, and replaces the lid. "They've moved her."

"Moved her?" Bernadette sits back against her pillows.

"Rose Hill. It's a facility for children. Nora arranged it. It's a nice place. I assumed she told you that was the plan."

Bernadette is sluggish under the quilt of the drugs, but her nerves stir at this. In her chest, her heart ticks like a hummingbird's. "She did tell me, but I thought she was against a facility. I wasn't sure it would really happen." She raises her eyebrows. "I believe she said she would use her 'influence' to stop it."

"Well, formidable as Nora's influence may be, no dice. After the woman came forward claiming to be her mother—"

"Valeria. Nora told me."

He sucks his teeth, slides a cigarette from the pack in his breast pocket, and lights it. Whiskers of smoke tendril from his nostrils. "Valeria," he says. Tone of dislike.

"What? You don't really believe she's the mother either?"

Norquist shrugs. "Maybe. She's a piece of work, though. After she came forward, Nora got the girl moved to Rose Hill. It's private. They're taking the girl on a provisional basis."

"Provisional?"

"Again, Nora's work. It's much nicer than the state-run sites. It's in Steilacoom. For kids with difficulties. Physical, mental, the whole gamut. There's about sixty kids. The families come on Sundays. They play games and have cake and what have you. Posh, nearly." He describes it—a big dining hall, like at a school. A playroom and a library. Dormitory-style beds in a girls' wing and a boys' wing.

He says, "The arrangement is that the mother can visit. Nora doesn't like it, but that's the way it is, so—." He shrugs and ashes his cigarette into her empty coffee cup. "The court could eventually step in and grant her full custody—Valeria. And then Nora will be out, and the mother will have to decide whether she wants to take the kid home with her or find a way to pay for the place, which I doubt she can afford."

"What's she do? For a living? Valeria?"

"There's a record of some illegal—let's call it employment—in the past, but she seems to be entirely unemployed now."

Bernadette's head is cotton, but she can't put the pieces together. "I don't understand."

"What? It's pretty straightforward from here."

"Everyone's just going along with her story about being Atalanta's mother? No one's following up on her ridiculous claim about the father? Isn't that a giveaway that she's a liar? I know I told Nora that Valeria's Benji could be Benji Aalund, but it's got to be another man, the father. Benjamin's a common enough name. I just can't quite believe it's him. I was out there with Signe, and she never said a thing." Bernadette sits back against her pillows and closes her eyes. If her thoughts would just clear for a second, she could find the throughline here. "Do you have another cigarette?"

He's frowning, but he offers her the package, and she leans forward for a light. She hasn't smoked since before Willie. She used to do it for the relaxation, but now it cuts through the fog and wakes her up.

Norquist says, "I don't know what you're talking about. Who's Benji Aalund?"

"Nora didn't tell you this?"

Norquist sits forward. "Just give me what you know."

Bernadette recounts the conversation with Nora. "I can't say how true any of this is," she tells him as she finishes. "Signe's Benji may have had a child. I don't know. It's possible, though no one's ever said as much. Not to me. What I do know for sure is that he did die in the Pacific. And he was childhood playmates with Len Starkey."

"And what's she say about Len? Signe."

Bernadette grins. "I believe she called him a little shit."

"I can see that," Norquist says. "Why wouldn't Nora mention this?"

Bernadette shrugs. "I made the connection, I suppose, and everything I do is up for question, as far as Nora's concerned. Gossip, nonsense. Who knows. She's not on my side anymore, Nora."

"Honestly, Baston, she never was, but I'd put money on it not being about you." He shoots her a look. "Nora's a competitor, she likes to win. And she's never been eager to prove the girl's got parents out there."

Bernadette nods, though she hates that he's likely right. She sighs and says, "When I was staying on Signe's farm, I searched her house." She raises her hand before he can interrupt and tell her he already knows this and chastise her for it. "Don't tell me off," she says. "I know I shouldn't have done it."

He looks at her with clear approval. "Who am I to tell you off? You have guts, Professor."

"Well, I didn't find anything."

"Still."

For a moment they sit in silence. Norquist smokes and squints at the wall. Finally, he exhales a cloud that rises, as if his thoughts are taking physical shape over his head. "Okay, play this out with me. Signe's son gets this girl in trouble. He and Len Starkey go way back—high school buddies who just carry that adolescent boy shit into manhood like nothing ever changed. We've all met them. Say he tells Len about his problem. Len's working for Haven Wright on the side. He makes an arrangement so it looks above board, but then when the kid is born, instead of delivering her to her new parents, he and Benji row over to Elita one night, leave the kid in the woods to die, and dump the truck to make the whole thing look like a bad accident." He frowns.

Bernadette shakes her head. "It's too complicated."

Norquist taps his cigarette against the rim of her cup again. "Not that complicated to drop a baby in the woods and get rid of a truck."

"If the baby actually dies, it's not too complicated. But Atalanta is alive. And this would have been years ago. Hasn't it always bothered you that the working assumption is that she survived alone on the island all this time?"

"You wouldn't be involved in this case at all if she'd lived with people long enough to learn to speak." He rubs his eyes. "But okay. So, say she got to the woods later. Where's she been all this time? You saying Starkey kept her in a cage somewhere until last September? And no one knew? What about the war? Where was she during those years? There's too many holes."

"There are too many holes," Bernadette agrees. She pulls up her blanket. The room has chilled—or she has. The drugs are wearing off. It won't be long before she starts shaking—the come down. Shaking and nausea. She wants to stave it off, but already she can feel the wires of her nerves waking up under the skin again. She changes the subject, says, "Brodaccio was glad to be free of her, I heard."

The frustration on Norquist's face breaks. "He practically did a jig the day we came to get her."

"Did you see the way Atalanta looked at him that day we were there? She was terrified."

"He was punishing her. Spankings and restraints. Nora knew."

"And she did nothing?"

"Don't be naive, Bernadette." He gives her a glance that tells her he knew too and looked the other way. "Brodaccio was the physician. De facto guardian. He knew the legal line, and he stayed just inside it. There wasn't much Nora could do without making a nuisance of herself. One word from him, and the case could be reassigned to another social worker who'd simply comply."

Bernadette's anger flares. "That's no excuse. She put herself before the child? There's no excuse."

"You've never fudged your own integrity to keep a job?" He shakes his head. "Then you're the only one."

She turns her face from him. He's right. Of course Nora was in the same position she herself was in. Of course she was. But still, she wants to rage at everyone who would hurt the child—would let the child be hurt. She breathes, settles herself. Anger will get her nowhere, and Norquist isn't the right target for her anger anyhow. His concern is legal—it has to be.

She says: "I told Nora I thought she was unprofessionally attached. To Atalanta. I told her that the morning she told me about Benji."

"I'm sure that went well."

"She threatened my custody of Willie."

"Shit. Bernadette. Is that why you went out to Signe's?"

"It was at first. I needed perspective." She feels the ache of her throat tightening against tears, puts her cigarette back to her mouth. It's nothing but a stub now. "I won't lose her," she says as she exhales.

"No. You won't."

The room has gone soft with the smoke. Bernadette has stopped shaking, and everything in her feels still, like a breath held. "Why would she leave her daughter?" she says. "Valeria. If she's the mother, how could she let herself be separated?" Even as she says it, she hears the bitter edge of it curling in her mouth. She drops her cigarette into the cup.

"It's not always so straightforward. As you know."

"Right. But what'd she tell you?"

"She has a story about the father. They weren't married, living in some dumpy studio over in Steilacoom. He drank, they fought, on and on. Says sometimes he hit her. Etcetera. Anyway, by her account, they had it out one night, she ran off, and when she came back, he and the baby were gone. Claims she tried to find him for months, but you know—she doesn't exactly strike me as forthcoming. She's got a citation for disorderly and another for prostitution from that same window of time, so you figure it out. Anyway, then the war. Eventually she went to Alaska—she says to start over."

Bernadette's eyes well again, and she digs the heels of her hands into them.

"Hey," Norquist says. "What?"

"She lost her girl. Whatever she did, I'm sure she missed her girl."

He leans forward, reaches for her wrists, gentle. "She's not you. You won't lose your kid. I promise."

She nods. "I know. It's just, I have to get out of here."

Norquist meets her eyes, serious and intent.

She searches his face, but he seems earnest. "I'm not crazy," she says. She needs him to believe this—to believe her.

"I know you're not." He stands and bends forward toward her. For a moment she thinks he will kiss her—she wants him to kiss her—and he does, but it's friendly more than anything else, his lips against her forehead. "Let me help you," he says, a whisper. "I want to help you."

What does that even mean? Bernadette could lean into him, could tip her face up for the other kiss—the one she's certain will confirm for him that what she wants is to be rescued from this place, to be taken home, to be taken care of. And then—? She doesn't know. Another set of expectations. Another person's needs to consider at every turn. She doesn't have it in her anymore. "You're a good man," she says. "I'm glad I know you."

He kisses her hair, and she feels the heat of his breath on her scalp.

When he pulls away, the moment hangs between them, silent but not uncomfortable, and Norquist sits back down, sorrow on his face.

Her voice catches in her throat as she says, "Signe took me to the beach one night while I was out on Adela. We listened to the dog pack across the water, on Elita. They're real, you know. They howled into the darkness. I haven't stopped thinking about it."

"Why?"

She thinks, and then the answer rises in her, clear, finally. "They're the offspring of pets, those wild dogs. Their parents were the animals the village left behind when it closed. Doesn't that strike you? One generation from pet to wolf."

He shakes his head. "Goddamn, Baston. That's too much metaphor for me."

A laugh. "Norquist," she says. She reaches out and touches his face, a gentle tug at his chin to turn him toward her. She needs him to see her. "I do need your help. I have to get out of here."

"You don't want to wait for him—for—" he stumbles, "Mr. Baston?"

"Fred?" she says. "No."

He nods. "You're sure?"

Her body feels as if she's swum miles and is waterlogged, nothing but jelly beneath the skin. But if she wants to leave—to prove that she's fine, capable, clearheaded—she'll have to stand. She'll have to walk out on her own two feet.

"There's never been anything wrong with me," she says, and she hears certainty in her own voice. She doesn't have to perform wellness; she is well. The recognition anchors her. "I'm going to be fine," she says again.

Norquist looks at her approvingly and nudges the applesauce toward her. "You better eat then. I should've left you the egg." He stands and buttons his jacket at the waist. "Give me about an hour to sort myself. I need to look into something. I'll be back, though." He stops. "And I almost forgot." He reaches into his pocket and withdraws a photograph. "It's what the mother brought us as proof. Claims it's her and the girl—Ginny, she says. It's nothing, but I thought you'd want to see it." He drops it onto her breakfast tray.

At the door, he pulls a long breath. "Baston," he says. "I told the nurse you're trustworthy."

She meets his eyes. "I am."

And then he's gone, down the hallway, already too far away to hear her second-guess herself.

## 23

SHE HAS NO CHOICE THEN BUT TO WAIT. THE NURSE returns for her tray, checks the empty pill cup. Under the blankets, Bernadette's legs tingle with the retreat of the drugs, but at least she can feel them again. She can feel her face more fully, and her tongue is less a slug in her mouth and more a dry square of sandpaper.

She waits to be alone again before easing herself out of the bed and testing her balance. Her legs are more fluid than solid beneath her, weak from the meds and the hours of stillness. She's reminded of the first time she had to walk on her own after Willie's birth—the strange sensation that she was floating, just a torso. She's never coped well with medication. The syrup her mother used to give her for a cough when she was a child always made her sick to her stomach. She'd rather have all her faculties intact—would rather feel pain than be made a swimmer inside her own skin.

At the window, she can see across the hill on which the hospital sits, over a neighborhood of shops and rooftops. The cherry trees have tiny buds. In another couple of weeks, they'll all open at once—a froth of pink and white, the whole city dressed like a bride.

When she married Fred, she believed that was what she wanted—the froth and the beauty of the domestic. The order and security of it. The promised mystery of marital transformation—from two to one, bone of my bone and flesh of my flesh. Family. Her father couldn't bear the parting when her mother died, and she never wanted that. But she did want transformation. How could she have known then that some transformations require erasure rather than evolution?

Now she sees that as long as she's in Seattle, disappearing into Fred's life will be her only option. As long as she's in Seattle, he will want what he wants from her, and she—girl gone woman gone mother gone undeniable self—she is no longer capable of disappearing.

She finds her clothes—they've been here in the room with her all along, tucked into a bag with FARRELL written across it—as well as her satchel. She can't get dressed until she's sure that whatever Norquist is doing will get her released, though, and so she sits on the edge of the bed to wait, picks up the photo he left her and looks at it for the first time. A woman stands against a fence rail, her wide face tipped skyward in a caught laugh. She's small in stature, but broad shouldered under her pale blouse. She's wearing her fair hair bobbed and curled. In her arms, a baby is bundled, its face just a spot of white, impossible to identify as any particular infant. Except—Bernadette holds the photograph close and narrows her gaze. The child is wrapped in a blanket that she recognizes. It's knitted, the repetition of simple stars and the flecked spots—*lice*, she believes they're called—so familiar. And there, at the corner, letters knitted into the pattern. *Isn't that—?* Bernadette strains to make out the lettering. *Yes*, she thinks. She can just pick out the same letters she saw on the blankets at Signe's—*SA*.

She could be sick. Under her, her knees have stopped feeling like jelly and instead have gone steely, locked. Certainty races through her, stiff and cold and terrible. She can't believe how much she's missed—overlooked. What if what she needed was right there all along? Sometimes you see, but you don't want to know.

IT'S JUST OVER AN HOUR BEFORE NORQUIST STEPS BACK into the room, he says, "We need to leave." There's urgency in his voice—a match to her own.

"Yes. Right now. We're going to Adela."

"I know," he says. "Wait." A look of confusion. "Adela? I haven't even told you."

"What?"

"I verified with Valeria Ricks, and it was Benji Aalund. You were right—he's the father. We need to talk to Signe." He pauses, eyes her bag and clothes laid out on the bed. "What's happening? You know something."

"I do, but am I free to go?"

"Sorry," he says. "Yes." Signed out. Free. Police privilege, he explains. "Now, what do you know?"

"Just let me get dressed. I'll explain on the way."

He steps outside to wait, and when she's dressed, she walks beside him down the corridor, down the stairs, and into the air, her steps sure and even. It's breezy, midday. The last of winter's leaves skitter from the corners of restaurant vestibules and whisk away down the sidewalk. There's the noise of cars, of bicycle bells, of chatter lifting up from the street and kiting out over the rooftops. Far off, a church bell rings heavy and brass—the beginning of noon Mass. Life happening. Carrying on.

"You need to eat?" he asks.

"No time," she says, but when he insists, worries she'll get faint again, she lets him buy her a grilled cheese sandwich at a diner rather than explain that fainting is no longer a concern. Finally, she settles into the passenger seat of his cruiser, the satchel between her feet on the floor. She doesn't think she's hungry, but she devours the sandwich as Norquist pulls onto Pacific Highway and heads south. She licks the grease from her thumbs. She could eat a second. She could down a milkshake. Her body is materializing around the core of her again, and it's a relief. The longer she's upright, eating, walking around, the less she feels the drag of the drugs at the edges of her mind, the undertow of the last few months. She knows who she is and where she's headed. She's been fooled, but she has clear eyes now.

"You going to tell me what you know?" Norquist asks. One hand is on the wheel, and in the other, another cigarette burning off a thread of smoke.

Bernadette retrieves the photograph, points to the blanket, and tells him what she saw in Signe's house.

"I don't know, Baston. Initials? That's it? Seems like a stretch. Maybe you—"

"I'm right. I know it." She sighs, frustrated, then—like a lock clicking into place—she remembers: Fred's photos are still in her bag. She stoops forward, rummages at her feet until she comes up with them. She knows she's seen the blanket in these photos. Here's the one of Willie at the Christmas windows downtown, Willie on Signe's horse, Willie sitting on Bernadette's own lap at home in their apartment. "Where is it?" she says aloud. "Hold on." And then—*yes*—there it is, just what she's recalled: the photo of the three of them on Signe's couch on New Year's. "Look!" she says. She points to the background and Norquist flicks his eyes from the road to the image. "See?" She holds it next to the photo of Valeria and her baby. "Same blanket. *SA*. Right there."

"I don't follow."

"This was taken at Signe's. That's her couch. I saw this same blanket later, tucked into a drawer, when I was staying with her. It's hers. She made it. The women—the islanders—they used to knit their initials into their patterns. I read it when I was researching, way back in the fall. It's traditional. And this, this is Signe's work. I'd bet on that. She made it."

Norquist's shoulders rise, harden. Bernadette sees a bloom of questions opening up inside his head, just as it has in hers.

He whips a look at Bernadette. "So, you think it confirms Benji as the father. So what? We already know that from Valeria."

"I think there's more, though. I think Signe knows more."

"You think Benji's still alive? You think she's hiding him somewhere? That he's had the girl all this time?"

She recalls the conversation with Signe about Benji's death, the way Signe's face hollowed into shadow when she said *And then nothing*. "No. No—he's gone."

"You searched her place. You're sure about that? She's not hiding him there?"

"I'm certain. But I might have overlooked something else. I don't know. I was looking for Haven's medical records. I was looking for proof that Signe was such a good friend, she'd cover up someone else's mistakes."

Norquist shakes his head, exhales a plume of smoke into the car's cabin.

In her head, Bernadette lines up the fragments of narrative she has, like stacking a row of dominoes: Benji's attachment to a woman Signe certainly wouldn't approve of, followed by a baby. Norquist said Valeria's account spoke of fighting, of Benji running off with the child and never coming back. Which would mean what? That he took the baby to Signe's, and she had the child there through the war? How could she hide an infant from everyone for that long? The island is small. Everyone knows everything about their neighbors. And where would she have kept the child?

As she asks the question, she remembers New Year's and Signe warning Martin to keep an eye on Willie at the barn. And then later, when she herself was staying on the island, it was only because Signe spotted her on the way to the barn that night that she came out to comfort her, to take her to the beach instead. A distraction, maybe. She'd been watching, Bernadette sees now—watching all the time that Bernadette was in her house. She'd been waiting, anxious not to be discovered.

She says: "Norquist, we need to search her barn. I think there's something in the barn."

THEY PULL OFF THE HIGHWAY, DRIVE THROUGH TOWN toward the water. Details she overlooked in the past begin rising to the surface of Bernadette's mind: it was also Signe who first suggested Len Starkey. Signe who offered up Haven. Signe was the one who told her about the ghost girl of Elita being island myth. Signe called Fred to tell him Bernadette was unwell. She sees Signe's face in the lamplight of the farm's bedroom—Elli, the crone. Like she'd been to the other side of death and had come back but no longer whole. What was it she'd said about losing Benji? *The bottom falls out, and you see that it's all always been nothing.* Where before Bernadette heard that as acceptance, now she hears it as desperation, as fearlessness. What wouldn't a person do if the worst had already happened? The recognition chills Bernadette to the pit of her gut.

At the dock, they park, wait for the tug. Norquist paces. He goes to the payphone, and she watches him place a call, his hat low over his forehead. "Everything okay?" she asks when he returns.

"Just lining up some help in case we need it."

She sees him touch the gun under his arm once, then again as they board the boat.

"Can't get enough of this place, eh?" the tug captain says to her. Bernadette considers that the whole of Adela Island might be together behind this secret. What if the tug captain can radio to Signe ahead of their arrival? In the cabin, once they're alone and motoring toward Adela's shore, she leans close to Norquist and says all of this. It's paranoid, he tells her. Maybe Starkey knows. Maybe a couple of others. But the whole island? "You can't start thinking everyone's twisted." He offers her a sad smile. "Hazard of the job, I know, but it'll rot you. And it's not true."

The tug docks at Adela. They walk to Signe's. Bernadette is glad she ate before arriving. She feels stronger. She feels more certain that this is the right path, the closer they get to the farm.

"It's beautiful out here," Norquist says as they walk. The afternoon light is honeyed, creamy. The trees are just leafing again, and the leaves are lime green. Signe's lane is muddy, but clear, and her land stretches like a swath of emerald velvet before them. Behind her house, a rill of smoke is rising, and there's the smell of a campfire on the air. It's impossible to believe ugliness could exist here.

"I thought I could live here." Bernadette smiles. "I had a vision of Willie and myself in a little cottage somewhere on the island, peaceful."

"Yeah, well, that's the trick mirror of the place, isn't it?"

They knock on the front door, and it's Signe who answers, the look on her face enough confirmation that the trip hasn't been a misstep. "Bernadette," she says. "I thought you were—"

"I'm fine," Bernadette says. "This is Detective Norquist." He touches the brim of his hat in greeting, steps past Signe into the house.

Signe's expression shifts, just a flicker. "Yes, yes. Come in," she says. "I'm just pulling a pie from the oven. You'll stay for coffee and pie?"

Inside, the house is as warm and comfortable as always, but Bernadette has the feeling that her nerve endings have all been cut and are jagged, sizzling. What should she look at? What should she have seen here before that she missed?

"Martin's out, I'm afraid. We've had some trouble with one of the mares. He's tending her."

A current of electricity passes between Bernadette and Norquist. "I'd like to talk to him, actually," Norquist says. "Barn's that way?" He doesn't wait for her response before he starts in the direction of the back door.

Signe is fluid calm as she stops him, touches his shoulder, smiles. She hands him a cup of coffee. "Oh, no hurry. He'll be back. We can wait in here. Not the best place to talk, the barn. Not when Martin's got his head on the animals." She laughs. "Forty-five years of marriage, and the man won't listen to a word I say when he's working."

Bernadette meets Norquist's eyes, a question. *Yes*, she reads in his returned glance. *Go ahead.*

"Signe," she says. "We've come to talk to you about Valeria Ricks." Her whole body is wound, a coil around a pin. She waits.

Signe turns her back, begins cutting the pie. She's giving herself time, assembling the pieces, Bernadette knows. Recalibrating. Bernadette pictures the gun under Norquist's arm, pictures the lap of the water against the shore at the beach where she sat with Signe not three days ago. What happened at that beach, really? Why did Signe take her *there?*

Bernadette says, "The girl was here, wasn't she, Signe?" Again, she catches Norquist's eye. *Should I keep going?* Small tip of his head. He takes off his hat, sets it on the table, but doesn't sit. "Ginny," Bernadette continues. "She's your granddaughter, isn't she? She's Benji's daughter."

Signe turns. There's blackberry on her fingertips, on the sticky blade of the knife. "My son never could see through that woman's lies." She smiles, quiet. "I hope you've been smarter than that, Detective."

Norquist steps forward and pulls from his pocket the two photos— Valeria's and the one Fred took on New Year's. He lays them side by side on the table.

Signe looks down at them. Small sigh. "Yes. That's Valeria."

"And the baby?" Norquist touches the blanket in one picture and then the other.

Bernadette feels the kitchen contracting around them like the eye of a microscope dialing in to focus. No one speaks.

"Signe," Bernadette says, note of pleading in her voice.

Signe shakes her head. "There was a baby, yes. How am I to know what that woman did with her child? I haven't seen either of them in years."

"Valeria claims it's the other way around," Norquist says. "That Benji left with the baby."

There's a flash of fury in Signe's eyes, though maybe only Bernadette sees it. She says, "My son is dead. There's a record of that, Detective."

The kitchen is overwarm now, and Bernadette is sweating beneath her clothes. They can't have come all this way for another frayed ending, another loose tether that results in no closure. She rattles the images she's accumulated in her mind, reordering them—desperate. Here's Atalanta with her hands roped behind her back. Atalanta curled into the crib on Elita. Here's Mayer's graveyard and his palm on his nephew's headstone, so tender. Here's Willie. Willie flying like a shooting star from the crest of the swing's high arc. Willie with her book open over her lap. Here's Willie feverish, Willie cold, Willie sleeping tucked into Bernadette's side. *Little pearl. Little barnacle.* Bernadette thinks: *What does a mother most want? What would she do to get it?* Willie's words come back to her like a tide rolling in: *A mother can be a mountain, but a man can't.*

"You wanted to protect her," Bernadette says without thinking. Norquist ticks her a frowned glance, but he doesn't stop her. "Benji died, and she was all you had of him. I understand that, Signe. You wanted to protect her."

Across the table, Signe's face goes waxen for a long moment, then it falls. She sinks into the chair opposite Bernadette's.

*There she is,* Bernadette thinks, *the crone.* That face of terror and wisdom she saw on Signe once before. Every wrinkle and crease has deepened around Signe's mouth. Her eyes are the eyes of a trapped animal. It's been a lifetime—a child's whole lifetime—of holding her secret, and now they've shown up at her door, and this is it. Enough.

"No need to go out to the barn," Signe says. "It's gone. All of it." She looks to Bernadette.

The smoke they saw in the distance as they walked up the road just now—Bernadette remembers and, like a lock opening, she understands. "Oh, god," she says. She turns to Norquist. "The fire," she starts, but he's caught it too and is already up and out the back door and into the field. Bernadette watches him run, a body racing across the field, the flaps of his jacket lifting at his thighs like dun-colored wings. He's taken the gun with him, but Signe's pie knife is resting on the edge of the table.

"He's too late," Signe says. "It's burned. All her things. The blankets and the toys. All her clothes." She moves her eyes to Bernadette's, slow and deliberate, and stares, unwavering.

"How long, Signe? How long was she here?"

Signe's gaze has gone flat and faraway. She's not looking at Bernadette when she speaks. "You went through my drawers, and I thought you knew. But then you went out to Mayer's, and I saw you weren't sure. You still weren't sure."

"I was looking for Haven's files. There's no birth record anywhere else. I thought it must be Haven who—"

"Oh, Haven delivered the child, yes, but here at the farm, and under the agreement that there would be no record. It would've been talk. They weren't married, Benji and that woman. That whore." She says the word low, like she's swallowed it and it's heavy and caught in her throat. "I couldn't have people knowing they had a bastard together."

"Signe—" Bernadette's voice breaks.

"But then they left, right away—out to the city. The three of them." She turns her eyes to the photo of Valeria and the baby. "That was the last day I saw her before they went. I told Benji he was dead to us if he chose that woman, and he did it anyway." She pauses. "I told Haven the baby died. And she should have. That baby should have died then, poor, miserable girl."

"Signe—" Bernadette says again.

"No. You don't know, Bernadette. That child was a miserable creature. Always. She had no life with that woman." Signe's face is a mask of itself, hard and fixed and fearsome.

Bernadette wants to look away, wants to run. She wants to get on the boat and go back to her own child, sweep Willie into her arms, and never look back at Adela. But she puts her feet flat on the floor. "She came back to you, though, the child. When did she come back to you?"

Signe hesitates and Bernadette sees the skeins unraveling in her head—everything she's worked to cover is coming undone, whether or not she speaks. She looks pained for a moment, then nods. "She's told it to you wrong," Signe says. "Always a liar, that woman. It wasn't Benji who left them—not by his choice, anyhow. I raised him to do right, and he would have. She can't be tarnishing him when he's not even got a voice to defend himself anymore."

"What's the truth, then, Signe? You want to spare Benji's memory, don't you?"

"Don't you patronize me." Again, her face goes stiff. "It was she that came bringing the child back after he died. Summer of '42, after he was gone, she came bringing that child back to me. Little child with no words, flinches when I look at her like a dog that's been kicked too many times. Bruises all over her. *Has she never had a bath?* I said. There was lice in her hair. She brings her to me and says she can't. Benji's never coming back, and she can't." Signe's eyes go dark and small. "So, what do I do? I take her in. She has Benji's feet and hands. Same as his when he was small. I can see she's ours, so I take her in, but she's already been fouled, that child. She's four when I take her, and she wets herself and spits in my face. She's like an animal. That never changed."

"Didn't you find help? Wouldn't Haven have helped you?"

Signe lets out a deep sigh. "I knew she'd never be well, Ginny. She was miserable. It would have been a mercy if my fib had been true—what I told Haven. A mercy if she'd died as a baby, that one."

Bernadette's head reels this story backward like a strip of film on a wheel. She sees the Valeria of the photograph standing on Signe's doorstep in the darkness, a little girl in her arms.

"I don't—" Bernadette says. The words won't solidify. "I don't—"

"No, you wouldn't understand. That's the natural thing, isn't it? You can't understand because you love your girl. Your girl is perfect. You come out here bawling that your life is a mess, and you have no idea. No idea what other people live." Signe makes a hard, dismissive sound. "And you a professor, thinking you know everything. Hoity-toity, like. But you don't. You have no idea, Bernadette."

Bernadette's face flushes. It's shame, she recognizes. "That's true. You're right. I don't know. I don't understand. You had her here all that time, Ginny, and you didn't love her?"

Signe meets Bernadette's eyes. Her voice is quiet but brittle. "We take her in, and she won't let Martin or me get near her. Won't let us hold her or bathe her or hug her like a normal child. Bites us. Spits like a camel." A bitterness twists the next words as they come out of her mouth. "This farm was to go to my Ben, you know," she says. "But that's not how it worked out. Instead, he leaves me that child, and there's nothing to be done with her. Nothing I can see to do. And I was a good mother before. Before her, I was."

"But how—" Bernadette pauses. "That doesn't explain how she ended up on Elita." The questions are knots of questions.

"How nothing," Signe says. "We kept her here, out of sight. A room we made up in the barn where she couldn't be heard. But eventually—she's stronger than you'd think." There's an edge of pride in her voice as she says this, and it sets Bernadette's teeth on edge to hear it.

"She ran away, then. Swam to Elita," Bernadette says.

"Heavens, no. That's fantastical nonsense. We rowed her out, me and Martin. One night last spring, we rowed her out. She'd just got too big. And violent. She hit Martin and blacked his eye. Knocked me over so I bruised my shoulder and was no use for a week. You've seen her growl, I imagine. She could climb, too. Out of the stall one day, even, and into the field. I'm looking out my window in the middle of the day, and there she is, thrown off all her clothes and streaking across the grass." Signe's shoulders rise and fall. "She was too big. Too strong. And she was old enough, she'd be bleeding soon, too, of course, I thought. Bleeding would be a whole other problem. We just couldn't have here anymore. She had to go." Now she turns her face to Bernadette's, and the shadow under her cheeks isn't terror anymore, just exhaustion. "They'd find her there, we thought. Prison and all, they'd have guards searching the grounds. That's what we thought. They'd find her and put her somewhere for folk like her that can't live with others. They'd not trace her to us."

A bolt of understanding. "On the beach," Bernadette says. She sees the constellation now, clear as if a line has been drawn between each point in the darkness she's been swimming in for months. "On the beach where you took me. You rowed her out from there."

The image is horrible: the two old people in the rowboat with the girl between them. It would have taken one of them to row and one of them to keep her still until they could get her to the other side, where she'd disappear forever. The girl surpassed their imaginations, though. She was stronger than they believed her to be. She hid and survived. She found a life outside of anyone's captivity.

Bernadette sits back. She feels the circle of the room's hold on her tightening. "And Len Starkey? When he found the girl, you thought he recognized her?"

"What I've told you there is mostly the truth."

"The truck?"

238

"Oh, he did wreck that, but just out on a drunk one night. No baby in the cab. He wrecked it all himself. Left it idling while he went off to piss in the brush, and the thing rolled right off the cliff all on its own. His father beat him that night, Len, and he came hobbling over here, bruised and with a fat lip, and stayed a couple of weeks until he and his dad patched it up again." She sets her chin at this—still angry, though Bernadette can't tell whether that's about Len or about Len's father. "Nothing to do with Benji's mess. Far as he knows, Benji died and left a widow and a child somewhere on the mainland. Lenny's stupid. Always has been."

Bernadette thinks back to the interview with Starkey, to his clear sense of order, his decision to offer up the names and addresses of his people on the island rather than say anything about the truck. Now she sees that wasn't a bluff—there was nothing to confess there. The reluctance she saw as suspicious was likely just shame. Norquist would talk to his father and dredge up an old story about a drunken mistake. That was all.

"And Harlow Nakamura?"

Signe chuffs. "I had nothing to do with the Nakamuras. Didn't know Harlow from Eve. They were Haven's to do. And I never understood that either."

This settles in Bernadette's gut like curdled milk—the meanness of it. The smallness. She remembers Mayer's words: *The meanness stays with you.*

Bernadette sits forward. "But you must have loved the child. Somewhere in yourself, you must have loved her." She taps the photo. "You gave Ginny your blanket."

Signe's mouth tightens, and in her face, just for an instant, Bernadette sees Atalanta. For the first time, the lineage is clear in the hooded stare, the fear, the pull of the old woman's lips against her teeth. Signe and Atalanta are two points of the same star. "It was Benji's," she says. "When he was a baby. I made it for my Ben."

Bernadette feels gutted, all her joints loose and her stomach empty. There's nothing more to say. She braces her hands against the table and pushes herself to standing. "I'm going to find Detective Norquist."

Across the table, Signe looks older than she did even a few moments ago, her hair fraying in that white corona from her braided crown and her eyes watering. "You could do nothing, you know," she says. "You could walk out of here and get on the boat and go home to your beautiful, living daughter, you. She wants you to come back to her, that sweet child. She needs you, doesn't she? You don't have do anything about my family's trouble." It's a last grasp at another story, Bernadette knows, though Signe's voice as she says it is dry and frail. It's enough. It's the end. She knows it.

"Signe, you left the girl to die. Your granddaughter. You tortured that child and left her to die."

Signe shakes her head. "You don't know. You don't know what we had to bear."

It's as if the air thickens, then furs. There's a horrible silence, suddenly, and a pain in Bernadette's chest like her breath has been caught and trapped there. Then nothing but the roar of it—ferocious and awful, as if the mouth of the world has opened up to swallow everything.

On the other side of the kitchen window, Bernadette sees a flash of movement. A man is running toward the house through the field, his shirt sleeves rolled up and his arms black with soot. He moves in wild, reaching strides. It's Norquist. It's Norquist, but his hair has been singed from his head, and the white fabric of his shirt is stained and dirtied.

"Oh," Bernadette says, her breath returned to her. "Oh, god." She's out the door, off the porch. The grass is tall and green, and she throws herself onto Norquist, knocks him down onto the damp earth. There are still embers on his back, spots of orange burning bright holes into his shirt, his pants. She blots them out with her hands, her coat.

"I'm okay," Norquist says. He's gasping. "I'm okay, Bernadette. Bernadette, I'm okay."

She hears him through the matted layers of too-heavy air, and only then does she sit back and look up and see that the whole of it is burning now—the barn and the garage and the fence around the horse pasture. All burning. The smell of it is the smell of the war. She remembers. It makes the bile rise up in the back of her throat. Fire on fabric, on wood, on bodies—the animals, she realizes. The sheep and the hens, the mare Willie rode. All the barn doors are closed. There's an awful keening sound lifting from the barn and no life in the field. "No!" she yells. "No!" But Signe and Martin are in their car, already at the end of the drive, and there's no one but Norquist to hear her.

## 24

THE FIRST THING SHE HEARS IS ALL THE BELLS RINGING in town, the sound peeling across the island, just like the end of the war. But these are fire bells—the island's volunteer fire department. They've set the alarm, and soon she sees the water wagon on the road, and not far behind it, trucks from which men spring out and run across the fields to the burning barn. The water wagon lumbers all the way up Signe and Martin's mudded drive, and from where she sits with Norquist on the grass, she watches the arcs of water shoot from hose to barn roof, beautiful and useless. There's nothing left to save. The barn is black bones, the fence is ash, the animals are carcasses. Nothing.

It's only another moment before Norquist's backup also appears at the end of the road, the whale flank of a cruiser unmistakable even at a distance, though also too late: Signe and Martin have long since disappeared. Norquist has told her already what he found when he first reached the barn: a pile of children's clothes and toys, a dirty mattress like the sort you'd give a dog to sleep on, a few broken up crates. They'd been keeping her in a stall, the child. All these years since her father's death, they'd been keeping her in a stall like an animal.

"These people," Norquist says now to his officers, disgust in his voice, his face in the grass and his breath coming short and hard with the pain of his burns, "they can't get away. Tell my guys to run down to the dock and stop anybody leaving."

Bernadette doesn't imagine this will do any good. Signe and Martin don't plan to get away. This is the end. They'll run their car off the cliff like Len Starkey's truck, or drive to the beach and row out to the center of the water before capsizing themselves. This is the end. To Norquist, however, she says only, "Don't worry. It's okay. Everyone's safe now. It's okay."

His burns aren't as bad as they first appeared. For the most part, his coat seems to have saved him. She touches his face, his neck, his head with a cold cloth she retrieves from Signe's kitchen. His skin will blister and peel where he took the worst of the heat—like a bad sunburn, she tells him. Thankfully, he ran from the barn before the explosion. He realized what Martin was about to do—the lit oil lantern in his hands and a burn pile stinking of gasoline. It flung heat and embers at Norquist as he fled.

Now, as his men climb out of the cruiser, he props himself up to sitting, winces. "New look," he says, gesturing at his bare head, the lobstered skin at the nape of his neck.

"Shit, Norquist," the first officer says. "You need a hospital."

"It's not so bad," Norquist says.

"At least your eyebrows will grow in again," Bernadette says. "I'm not entirely sure about your hair."

He smiles, half grimace. "Good thing I like hats."

She helps him stand, and the officer opens the cruiser's back door for them both.

"I'll write out everything Signe told me while you were in the barn," she says as they drive to the dock. "Or enough of it to get what you need."

"Baston, you'd make a good detective."

"So you've told me."

There's nothing more to say, and Norquist is, despite his bravado, exhausted and in pain. She watches him lean his head against the window and close his eyes. He doesn't open them until they get to the water, where a barge is waiting for them, and they drive right on.

As soon as they pull into the station lot in Steilacoom, an officer meets them with the news that Signe and Martin have been stopped by a citizen in a rowboat off the north side of the island. And Valeria has been taken into custody for more questioning as well. "Good," Norquist says. The burns are deepening, red-purple in spots and weeping where the skin has cracked across his scalp. An ambulance is ready for him, and he walks stiffly toward it, holding his arms away from his body as if his skin is a cast of itself.

"I'm so sorry," Bernadette says as he steps up into the ambulance. "This is all just—" She stops, uncertain what else to say.

"Couple days off, and I'll be fine. No spoon shivs in my future, I swear." He smiles, dips his head, and when he lifts his face, she sees concern, but also something softer. "What about you, though? What'll you do?" he asks.

It's the question she hasn't allowed herself. "I don't know yet."

He nods. "You will."

He means it to be encouraging, supportive—she knows that, but she thinks, *How can you be so sure?* She reaches forward and takes his hand.

She wants to thank him. She wants to say she'll come see him in the hospital, but it's a promise she won't keep. Instead, she says, "Can I tell you one thing? You might be the best man I know."

"What ringing praise." A wry grin, but he squeezes her hand in his.

An attendant in a white gown steps forward and indicates the gurney. "Ready, sir?"

"You're going to be just fine," Norquist says as she steps back. "You know how to take care of yourself, Baston."

It washes through her, what he's said: she knows how to take care of herself. She does. She knows he's right. She's already done it for so many years.

"Thank you," she says.

She watches him lower himself onto the gurney and waits for the ambulance doors to close before she turns and begins walking in the direction of home.

## 25

A DAY LATER, SHE TAKES THE FIRST BUS TO THE ROSE Hill Center for Children. It's just as she pictured it: a width of clipped green lawn and a big white manor house at the end of a long drive. The roses for which the place is named run the length of the front of the house, and though they're not yet blooming, Bernadette can imagine them flowering and full. In another couple of months, they'll be beautiful, the scent of roses floating inside to the children through the opened windows, the promise of another summer on the way. She climbs the step and rings the bell. There's the sound of young voices, and then a woman in a pale blue uniform appears and invites Bernadette inside.

The building smells clean, like lemon and furniture oil and Ivory soap. The woman leads Bernadette into a big room at the back. It's banked in paned windows that look out on the lawn and, beyond that, a navy-blue sea in the distance. This is the dining hall, and the children are all gathered for breakfast. Most of them are eating toast and eggs and drinking glasses of milk. A tray stacked in paper cups waits on the sideboard, each cup holding three neat apple slices. Here and there, nurses in the same blue uniform help feed those who need assistance. The room lifts and falls with the lilt of chatter and laughter.

Bernadette spots Atalanta right away at the end of the far table. A nurse is seated next to her. She looks up as Bernadette approaches and indicates an open chair. "I'm Margaret. You here to see Ginny?"

Of course. Ginny. That's her name.

There's a look of recognition in the girl's eyes.

"Do you remember me? I'm Bernadette. We've met before."

The girl looks well. There's light in her eyes—a look of attention and a spark that Bernadette hasn't seen in her before. She reminds herself that the child has always been drugged when she's seen her in the past. The child has always been afraid. Now, though, she looks at peace. Her hair is clean and done in two fawn-colored braids. She's wearing overalls and, under them, a button-front blouse—clothes made for play. She's eating an egg, but she's plucked the round yolk from the white and is rolling it around her plate like a ball before putting it into her mouth. This, Bernadette knows, would have been punished at the prison, but here the nurse simply looks on, placid.

Bernadette has thought for days about what to say. *You're safe now. Your grandparents won't hurt anyone anymore. You're free here.* But, of course, none of that is necessarily true—not from the girl's perspective. What does safe mean to this girl? What does free mean to a child who's known only a barn stall and the isolation of the woods?

Bernadette can see Signe in the girl—unmistakable lineage, now that she knows to look for it. It's the draw of her mouth as she eats. Straight nose and strong brow. Broad shoulders. She inherited all of this, despite her grandmother's wishes and denial—this, and also a ferocity of spirit, the trait that most certainly is what kept her alive all those months on Elita. *She's a miracle,* Bernadette thinks—but, no, that diminishes the girl. She knows how to take care of herself. That's more valuable than any magic.

A bell sounds, and all along the length of the two dining tables the children push back in their chairs and stand to clear away their dishes.

"Time for reading," the nurse at Atalanta's side says. Her voice is light, cheerful, not at all threatening, and yet, when she reaches for the plate, the child grips it.

Atalanta turns her face to the nurse and clear as morning says, "No."

"Oh my god," Bernadette says. It spills out before she can help herself. She turns to the nurse. "Did you hear that? Did she—?"

"She says it all the time, actually. Quite the back talker, this one." The nurse releases the plate. "Miss Sass, you are," she says as she winks at the girl.

"Are you certain?"

"Oh, sure as anything. She says *No* and *I*. Those are her words."

Bernadette reaches into her bag for her notebook but finds she hasn't brought it along. She repeats what the nurse has told her. "*I*?" she asks. "Can you tell me in what context she uses the pronoun?"

"You mean how she says it?"

"When. When would she use the word in a normal day, I mean."

The young woman pauses, thinking. "Well, so we're dressing her the other morning, and she pushes my hands away when I get to the button, and says *I, I*, then she does it up herself. That sort of thing."

"Assertion of independence," Bernadette says. She's gobsmacked. Could the girl speak all along? Did she speak for Signe, but go silent on Elita? Or was it a trauma response to the prison hospital? She wants her Dictaphone, wants to record this for—but there's no one to listen now. There's no purpose to gathering data. The girl is not a subject, she's simply a child growing up and healing. Bernadette's heart slows again, and she settles her hand near Atalanta's on the tabletop and looks at her. "You're doing so well, you know?" she says to the girl. She stops the next thought before she can speak it—it's maternal, unprofessional, pure praise. But then, what's to hold her back now? She should say what she means before the chance is lost. "I'm so proud of you," she says. "I feel proud of you, Ginny." The girl raises her eyes to Bernadette's and for a long moment they meet one another in the stare before the child looks away again, returns to chewing her egg.

A few moments later, walking back toward the road, Bernadette sees Rose Hill the way it must have looked to the girl after her months trapped inside at Elita, all this space. The child could certainly smell the wet scent of the cedars bordering the grounds, the salt lilt of the sea breeze rising off the cliff to the west. It's surely why Nora chose this place rather than any other, too—a final gift to the girl no one could claim.

245

What must the child have felt when the numbing sameness of her days at Elita lifted? When the grainy sleep sand of Brodaccio's tranquilizers cleared from her eyes, and her throat opened again and ached to howl? Bernadette can picture her running, her long legs stretching in wide, loping strides across the grass of this big lawn, the sky as blue as a butterfly wing and incomprehensibly wide overhead. It makes everything seem possible, and in the expanse of possibility, Bernadette realizes that, while her own break will be less clean, she, too, has a future to map out. Finally.

BACK AT HER APARTMENT, SHE PACKS: A SWEATER AND A pair of warm socks for herself and a knitted hat for Willie, a blanket, all the money she's saved from work and the bits left over after scrimping on groceries. It's her lineage—her inheritance—this frugality and the will to raise her child far away from the press of other people's expectations. She'll take Willie somewhere quieter, somewhere removed, where they can live as they wish and not as they're told. This is what her parents gave her—an entire childhood to solidify her sense of self, away from the crush of society, and it is what she will give Willie. She has the shaky outline of a plan: travel light, move quickly, leave everything behind. The fastest, surest route she's found is by train.

She shows up at Willie's nursery school in the middle of the day.

"Mrs. Farrell!" the young teacher exclaims. "I'm glad to see you're on the mend! But, you know, school doesn't end until—"

"Oh, yes! I'm fine. Thank you. Just here for my daughter. Something's come up. Professor Farrell should have called ahead? We have a family obligation and need to take Willie home early today."

"Oh—" the teacher hesitates, her hand on the school gate. "I don't think he—"

Bernadette feigns forgetfulness, apologizes. "That's right!" she says. "He said he *couldn't* call between classes. I have a note. Just hold on—" She makes a show of fumbling through her pockets, picture of the befuddled scatterbrain of a wife. *Funny sidecar, unreliable little bird of a woman.* She must make the story he's told about her true, at least for now. "Here it is!" She comes up with a folded piece of paper and watches the young teacher read it, scan the bottom where Bernadette has signed Fred's name—proof enough. A smile, a nod. His name is her bond.

"Just a second," the teacher says, and she disappears into the school and returns with Willie, who looks stunned to see her mother after all this time, flustered to have her day interrupted.

For a panicked moment, Bernadette is certain Willie will be the complication she hasn't predicted. "Come on, Wills," she says. Big smile. "Dad and I have a surprise." It's a lie, and she'll pay for it later, perhaps, but it works—Willie shrugs her coat over her shoulders like a cape and walks forward. She waves to the teacher, and they're off.

Only once they're halfway across the campus green does Willie slow, tugging on Bernadette's sleeve. "Something's wrong, Mama," Willie says. "What's wrong?"

Bernadette bends, kisses the crown of Willie's head, then pulls the knitted cap down to cover Willie's hair. "Nothing's wrong, love. But do walk as fast as you can. We have somewhere to be."

She pays a cab driver to take them from the edge of campus to the King Street Station. It's expensive, but a cab is faster than the bus, and she feels the press of time like a brick on her chest.

Beside her, Willie is silent, wide-eyed. She holds her still-casted arm—the fall from the swing both a lifetime ago and also not that far in the past, Bernadette thinks—like an object she's carrying, the elbow bent at a right angle and the forearm crossed stiffly over her body, little useless wing. Bernadette watches her daughter. Something in Willie is afraid. Something inside her is lying down, submissive now, but waiting.

It crosses Bernadette's mind that this day will mark Willie's life like a burn, like a hole cut into the center of a page. After this, some of the words will always be missing for her. She will be fatherless again. She will remember her mother's rush and her own silence, will wonder if she could have changed the course if only she'd resisted, spoken up. No matter how well the next few days, months, years go, Willie will wonder who she could have been. It guts Bernadette to know that this is the cost of her freedom.

At the station, there's a wait for tickets, then a wait for the restroom, then a wait for the train. The route takes just over four hours, and it's already early afternoon. Sunset will fall around six, and that feels too soon. Fred will discover that she's collected Willie the moment he shows up at the school. From there, he'll go to the apartment, where Mrs. Iversen's confusion will delay him at least a few moments. When he panics and uses his key to get into her place, he'll find the envelope she's left with the rest of the month's rent on the kitchen table—the thought of stiffing sweet Mrs. I or of leaving Fred to pay her bill was impossible, even under these circumstances, but when he finds the money, he'll know. The only mercy will be his ignorance. He'll try Signe first, and there find a dead end, no one home on the farm to answer his call. Norquist has hushed up the story for now, but it will be in the newspapers soon enough, and she has to be long gone by then. Once Fred realizes she's not at Adela, he'll try Norquist maybe. Or Nora. Neither of them know anything, but still the ball will be rolling then, unstoppable, a boulder rushing downhill toward her. It's not difficult to find a frightened woman. It's not difficult to catch her when she runs. The entire system of society is set up to stop her from freeing herself.

At the first whistle, they board the train. Bernadette finds a seat squarely in the middle of the car. They need to look at ease, just a pair traveling home to visit family in Canada. She leaves Willie's knitted cap on her head, tucking the blond curls under the ribbing so that they—her most defining trait—aren't visible. "It's still chilly," Bernadette says. She kisses Willie's face. "Got to keep your ears warm, yes?"

"Where's Daddy?"

"He has to work, doesn't he?"

Willie's eyes are pools, wide and deep.

The train lurches forward. The other passengers seem to collectively sigh, shift, and settle in. Bernadette turns her face to the window. Soon, the city will fall away, and the afternoon will become evening. The train will swim through darkness. Soon there will be water in sight—the vast, sparkling stretch of Puget Sound. It's easy to imagine the world unraveling at her back, but it's terrifying to imagine herself somewhere she has never been before, an explorer, a charter of new land—her life—truly all her own to name. What does she think she's doing? What is she going to do? But, no. She stops herself before the current of worry can ripple all the way through her. No. She's done it before, she reminds herself. She's done it before, and she's survived.

She pictures Atalanta, months ago and just a few miles down this same coastline, high-stepping in her deerlike way over driftwood, brushing her shoulders past the bobbing heads of tall grass. Whatever language she had for these familiar traits of the landscape she used to name them. She sank her feet into the sand like it belonged to her, lifted her face to the breeze, bared her teeth to the air. She discovered she was good at living. Good at staying alive.

A train attendant stops at Bernadette's seat and taps the backrest. "Everything all right here, miss?"

"We're fine," Bernadette says, a whisper because Willie has fallen asleep across her lap.

He smiles, nods, and moves on.

*We're fine*, she repeats to herself.

She and Willie will be over the border before midnight, and then what? She doesn't know. She touches Willie's warm cheek. *Cusp* and *corner*, *precipice* and *edge*. She doesn't know what comes next yet, but she will.

# AUTHOR'S NOTE

THIS BOOK IS A WORK OF FICTION, ITS CHARACTERS AND plot fully the inventions of imagination. That noted, in constructing the novel's setting, I drew heavily from the actual landscape of my home, the Puget Sound region. Elita Island and the prison at which Atalanta is held are fictionalized versions of the real McNeil Island and its penitentiary. McNeil is located in south Puget Sound, and from 1875 to 1976 it was the home of a federal penitentiary and, for a period of time, a civilian village. In aiming to understand McNeil's history, I looked to several resources, primary among them the Washington State Department of Corrections website, the McNeil Island Historical Society website, and the podcast *Forgotten Prison*, a special project of KNKX Public Radio and the Washington State History Museum.

Like Elita, Adela Island is also a fictionalized version of an actual place (Anderson Island), as is Dog Island (Fox Island). While I never set foot on these islands, I'm deeply familiar with the landscape and waterways of Puget Sound, where I have spent much of my life. Nevertheless, as I wrote this novel, I reminded myself of what I have taken for granted—the look of the sea and the light and the flora of this region—by exploring south Puget Sound via sailboat. Migael Scherer's *A Cruising Guide to Puget Sound and the San Juan Islands, Olympia to Port Angeles* (2nd ed.) was an incredibly helpful resource for this form of research.

In addition to the influence of place, this novel has been shaped by my interest in and study of education. I have been a teacher for over twenty years, and Bernadette shares with me all the knowledge I've acquired from various sources over the length of my professional career. However, I want to particularly credit here the many works of John Dewey, as well as the references to his lab school—a real place, the University of Chicago

Laboratory Schools—which Dewey founded in 1896. (I once told a fellow educator that I was "a dork for Dewey," and while the statement itself proved both dorkiness and my ability to embarrass myself publicly, I won't apologize, as Dewey's thinking about teaching and learning has been essential to me.) Also central to my educational philosophy, and so foundational to this novel, are the works of Jean Piaget, bell hooks, and Paulo Freire. Bernadette and Fred also reference Erik Erikson, B. F. Skinner, Sigmund Freud, and Carl Jung, and though my own scholarship in the field of education has incorporated a surface-level familiarity with this work, any misunderstandings of it represented in Bernadette's and Fred's thoughts and dialogue are my own.

Atalanta's presumed history as a child who survived in the wilderness drew on the reported story of an actual child, Victor of Aveyron, who was born in France in 1788 and found living "wild" just prior to adolescence. He was captured and observed by Jean Marc Gaspard Itard. Their story is covered in the 1976 book *The Wild Boy of Aveyron,* by Harlan Lane, which I found via a review of the book by Roger Shattuck published in *The New York Times* ("The Wild Boy of Aveyron"). I was later led by Andy Meyer to Adrienne Rich's long poem "Meditations for a Savage Child," which was published in her collection *Diving into the Wreck: Poems, 1971–1972* (W. W. Norton, 1973).

One final note of credit goes to my mother, a fiber artist, who suggested to me the history of the Gansey sweater and the tradition of knitters stitching initials into the patterns of their sweaters. Mythology (or, by some accounts, historical fact) states that it was by these initials that fishermen lost at sea (and disfigured beyond recognition by their time in the water) might be identified by their loved ones when their bodies washed ashore. I borrowed from this narrative in imagining Signe's knitting.

There is, of course, much more here that was influenced by my years of fascination with the post–World War II period, with World War II nursing, with medical history, with academic culture in the United States, and with feminist thought, but a lifetime of obsession cannot be boiled down to specific textual references, and so I will say that I carry in my mind an archive of information, and I'm grateful beyond words for the libraries, films, galleries, and discussions with other curious people that have richly fed my interests all my life.

# ACKNOWLEDGMENTS

THIS NOVEL IS ALREADY A LOVE LETTER OF SORTS, IN adoration of the place I am lucky to call home and with affection for the people who have defined my life there. But let me now offer some specific praise and gratitude.

First, thank you to Marisa Emily Siegel at Northwestern University Press for seeing value in this story and giving it an avenue to readers. I am so immensely grateful for Marisa's insights, expertise, and kindness as an editor. Thanks, too, go to the whole team at TriQuarterly/ Northwestern University Press. It's a privilege to work with people who love and steward literature as they do.

Thank you forever and always to my literary agent, Gail Hochman, whose early reading of this novel encouraged me and who has stuck by me for nearly two decades of work. My appreciation is endless.

Thank you to Pat Orrell, whose mentorship and knowledge as an educator has been a central influence on my own understanding and practice of teaching and learning, and in many ways a cornerstone of this novel. There have also never been better colleague-friends than Hannah Earhart and Norma Wainright and Tamara Scott, whose friendship and support saw me through the dark year in which I wrote this novel's first draft. I'm so grateful to know these educators (and truly excellent humans) and to have taught beside them.

Many other people encouraged me to persevere with this project. Thanks to Kira M., who gave me a lamp when I was trying to see the way through some of my toughest days. Thank you to Laura Maestrelli, Kristin Awsumb Liu, Jane Hodges, and Anca Szilágyi, as well as to my 2021 Tin House Summer Workshop group and our incredible leader, Laura van den Berg. Gratitude always, always to Pam Houston, for everything.

Thank you to Margot Kahn and Frances Cheong at Hugo House. Big, big thanks to Alix Ohlin and Melissa Febos, writers whose work has exploded my heart many times and whose kind words about my own mean the world to me.

And now here's where I weep with gratitude: Kristen Millares Young and Jean Ferruzola are the reason this book exists. Our workshops possessed a special alchemy, and it was their brilliance, their curiosity, and their creative companionship that conjured this book into being. Post-drafting, Kristen's generosity with her publishing wisdom, her invaluable editing support, and her boundless championing made all the difference. These two women are wonders, and I'm regularly awed by my good fortune in finding such literary sisterhood.

Finally, thanks to my family. This is a story about love, really, and so my family and their incredible love are everywhere in these pages. In both abstract and concrete ways, they supported the creation of this novel. I thought often of my grandmothers as I wrote Bernadette. For Marion and for Kay, both gone now, I am grateful. My parents made meals, provided childcare, talked me through half-formed ideas as I wrote, and then read drafts. They also, of course, gave me a model of parental love that runs like a throughline of truth beneath Bernadette's story. My gratitude for them is boundless. My sister provided weekly talk therapy via our Saturday morning walks as well as generously sharing her expertise as an educator—a great help as I wrote Bernadette. My husband literally and with his own two hands built me a room of my own so that I could keep writing through the intense domestic intimacy of the pandemic's "isolation." He also sailed me up and down Puget Sound as I researched. He is, ever and always, my favorite human. Last, but also always first, gratitude goes to my children—oh, my children! They gave this story its heart (as well as the myth of Atalanta). They are the best of me, my daily marvels. Thank you, Finn and Virginia, my own beloveds.

As I tell my students, all art is collaborative, and for my collaborators (those noted here and the many unnamed but still essential), I am so abundantly grateful.